Temple Grove

TEMPLE GROVE

A NOVEL

Scott Elliott

UNIVERSITY OF WASHINGTON PRESS
Seattle and London

Printed in the United States of America
Design and illustration by Thomas Eykemans
Composed in Chaparral, typeface designed by Carol Twombly
17 16 15 14 13   5 4 3 2 1

UNIVERSITY OF WASHINGTON PRESS
P.O. Box 50096, Seattle, WA 98145 U.S.A.
www.washington.edu/uwpress

LIBRARY OF CONGRESS CATALOGING-IN-PUBLICATION DATA
Elliott, Scott, 1970–
Temple Grove : a novel / Scott Elliott.
pages cm
Includes bibliographical references.
ISBN 978-0-295-99280-8 (cloth : alk. paper)
1. Loggers—Washington (State)—Fiction.
2. Logging—Washington (State)—Fiction.
3. Forest conservation—Fiction.
4. Ecoterrorism—Fiction.
5. Olympic National Park (Wash.)—Fiction.
6. Suspense fiction.
I. Title.
PS3605.L45T46 2013   813'.6—dc23   2012045431

The paper used in this publication is acid-free and meets the minimum requirements of American National Standard for Information Sciences—Permanence of Paper for Printed Library Materials, ANSI Z39.48–1984.∞

For My Family—
Elliott, Crist, adopted,
and the Walla Walla branch

The OLYMPIC PENINSULA

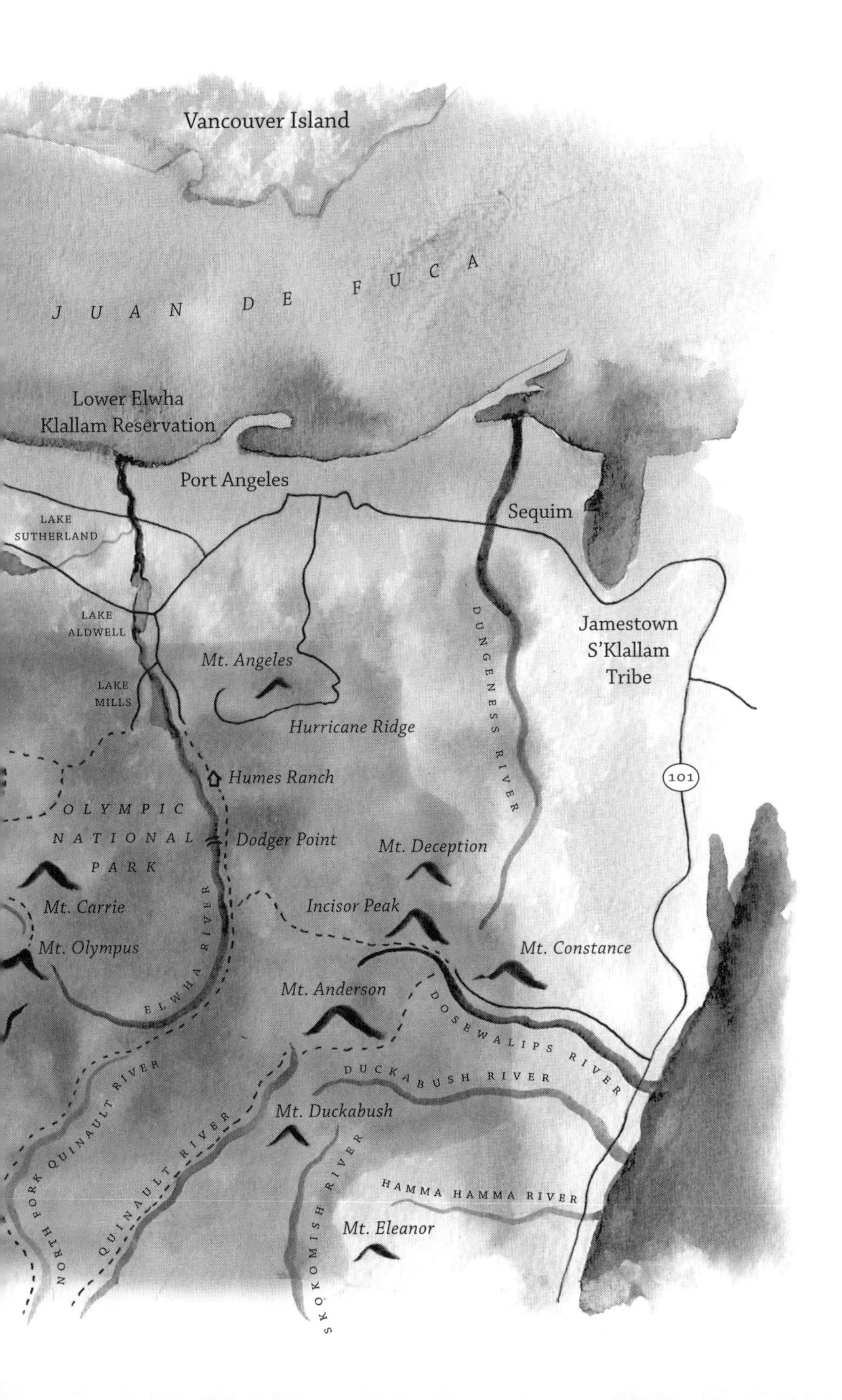
Vancouver Island
JUAN DE FUCA
Lower Elwha
Klallam Reservation
Port Angeles
Sequim
LAKE
SUTHERLAND
LAKE
ALDWELL
LAKE
MILLS
Jamestown
S'Klallam
Tribe
Mt. Angeles
Hurricane Ridge
DUNGENESS RIVER
Humes Ranch
101
OLYMPIC
NATIONAL
PARK
Dodger Point
Mt. Deception
Mt. Carrie
Incisor Peak
Mt. Olympus
Mt. Constance
ELWHA RIVER
Mt. Anderson
DOSEWALIPS RIVER
DUCKABUSH RIVER
NORTH FORK QUINAULT RIVER
QUINAULT RIVER
Mt. Duckabush
SKOKOMISH RIVER
HAMMA HAMMA RIVER
Mt. Eleanor

Temple Grove

1

Trace strapped her two-month-old son Paul into the rear-facing infant car seat of a blue '79 Dodge Omni and drove and hiked him from Neah Bay to the Olympic National Park near the place of his conception on the banks of the Elwha River.

They drove past a rusted '48 Studebaker with a western hemlock, two fledgling alders, and clutches of fireweed and Scotch broom growing out of its engine cage; and the skull of a gray whale beside a blue plastic slide in the front yard of a house whose roof was lost to moss; and the marina full of fishing boats where there had once been redcedar canoes famed for their perfection; and "the café" that had operated under five different names within Trace's memory; and the Makah Cultural and Research Center built to honor and keep alive the thousand-and-more-years' tenancy in this place of the Qwidicca'atł (kwih-deech-cha-ahkth), the People Who Live by the Rocks and Sea Gulls.

The people had come to be known as the Makah because the Klallam tribe, their enemies to the east, had told the newly arrived bubuthli-dithls (the House on the Water People) that "your belly would be full in this place." The word had sounded like "makaw," and the white namers had written it down and it'd stuck. Trace knew how to say the old name because her grandmother, mother, Uncle Jack, and other elders had recovered it from the U.S. Government's systematic cultural burial to teach it to her. Now, amid the noise and welter of mainstream American culture, 1989, and in her current troubles, it was difficult for her to understand what use this collection of sounds might ever serve.

She and Paul sped under the joined branches of alders, past a graveyard where she had seen too many of her friends and family interred to be just seventeen. Totem poles and images of Thunderbird grasping lightning serpents stood beside headstones, American flags, live and dead roses, crosses. Some of the elders, recounting stories from their grandparents, still told of canoe burials deep in the woods—bodies in canoes high in trees with their hands bound so they wouldn't return for their divvied-up things—but this practice had been abandoned and anyone who could tell you anything about it even secondhand was dead or dying.

They moved away from the reservation along the coast-hugging road, sometimes in one lane beside mudslides from the previous winter's storms. They wound up and down dragon curves that seemed to want to shake them over the guardrails into charred wreckage on the rocky beaches below, the Dodge's engine coughing, Trace's long black hair restive in the wind through the open windows, Paul's dimpled arms moving as he cooed at the colors, mostly greys, rushing by as the hairpin turns gently rocked him.

The land mass of Vancouver Island was electric blue across the Strait of Juan de Fuca. Sea otters, making a slow comeback since their near extinction during the days of the Hudson's Bay Company, heads indistinguishable from floating mounds of kelp till they moved, flipped onto their backs to smash open horse clams on their chests. Ships crawled toward ports in Vancouver and Seattle.

They wound around the shore of Lake Crescent, over 600 hundred feet deep and glimmering turquoise below timbered ridges—Pyramid Mountain and Storm King, the peak named for the ancient spiritual ruler of the area who was so angered at fighting between the Klallam and Quileute on the shores of a river below that he blocked the river's flow with a great boulder so the water would back up to erase all evidence of the battle. Trace remembered the story of murdered Port Angeles waitress Hallie Latham Lillingworth, "the lady of the lake," whose husband, Monty, killed her, tied her up, and threw her into the lake in December of 1937, never anticipating that three years later her body would float to the surface, preserved by the cold deep water, her flesh turned to soap you could scoop out like putty, to reveal what he'd done. In another tale about the lake, a young boy swam out after a beach ball. Whenever he got close to the ball, a small breeze sprang up to gently blow the ball just out of his reach until he was out too far. Divers found what looked like footprints at the bottom of the lake, hundreds of feet below the surface where he'd disappeared, never to be seen again. In Trace's grandmother's stories Lake Crescent was the place where a girl named Wiki-baquak lived in exile. She was all alone and didn't know how to take care of herself until she was adopted by beautiful swans near a waterfall made of tears. The swans taught her how to survive, and she brought what they taught her back to the people.

They passed Lake Sutherland, emerald through the trees and surrounded by vacation cabins, the distant whine of boat motors and jet-skis calling weakly, as if from another world. Trace remembered that Indians had named the lake Nahkeeta for a beautiful girl who'd gone into the mountains one fall with her mother and sisters to gather currants, roots, and tiger-lily bulbs. Nahkeeta had wandered deeper into the woods than coast Indians usually ventured, enjoying the pleasant hum of the forest with its gentle green and golden light, delicate ferns, and moss-covered logs and trees. As the soft light of the forest diminished into darkness, Nahkeeta realized she was lost. She called out for her mother and sisters but heard no answer. As true dark settled in, she ran blindly, entangling her legs in vines and ferns and stumbling among logs and branches. The next day her people went looking for her, calling "Nahkeeta! Nahkeeta!" They found her torn body in a bed of maidenhair fern amid signs that an animal had preyed on her the night before. The tribe buried her where they found her and for several days many of them moaned and wailed at her loss. A spirit heard the people's sorrow and, moved by it, made a lake spring up in the place where Nahkeeta was buried. In the fall, so the story goes, birds near the lake crying "Nahkeeta! Nahkeeta!" are answered by ripples in the water, wind in the alders and firs. If birds sang her name now, thought Trace, their cries would be drowned out by the sounds of these vacationers with their loud machines, contented in their generic relaxation and sport, most of them ignorant of Nahkeeta's story. Now the lake is named for

Canadian fur trapper John Sutherland, who happened to be the first white man to see it in 1865.

Trace turned off Route 101 and paralleled the Elwha. On the other side of the river and to the left of the road, meadows dotted with lavender foxglove and red fireweed rose to tree-filled ridges, which gave way, out of sight and deeper in the interior, to the snow-capped peaks of the Olympics, some as high as 8,000 feet—range upon range laid out in no discernible order, pushed up from the bottom of the ocean over millions of years by tension between the Juan de Fuca and continental plates beginning 50 million years ago, the highest peaks surrounded by glaciers whose advance and retreat had further carved the mountains and valleys.

Beside the old blue Dodge, the Elwha rushed toward the Strait, chalky-turquoise with glacial silt in the pools, clear in the shallows, milky-white between mossed-over rocks.

They took a left onto a gravel road called Whiskey Bend and wound away from the river, past stables where lazy veteran pack horses on the U.S. dole twitched off flies with hide and tail behind lodgepole fences. Displaced flies, run through with early evening light, zagged up to luminescent invisibility.

Steadily up, around blind corners, they moved through cavelike coolness and sunlight-dappled shadow, gravel crackling against the engine cage, the dust of their passage dispersing smokily in streaks of sunlight. Thick stands of western hemlock, redcedar, silver and Douglas fir, alder, vine maple, and the occasional big-leaf maple stood on the steep downward slope to the right and on the upward slope to the left. The trees seemed to stand witness to their progress, limbs leaning down toward richer shadow as if to embrace them or suggest they proceed no farther.

They passed the Glines Canyon Dam, Lake Mills glimmering turquoise behind it, and she thought of the Elwha Dam, Thomas Aldwell's prideful achievement and folly, below them, five miles from the Elwha's mouth at the Strait. People were always talking about tearing down the dams to restore the great lost runs of steelhead and salmon. The lower dam's sole purpose had been to power the pulp mill in Port Angeles, and when it was first built, they said you could walk across the backs of the uncomprehending salmon lined up behind it, mad to spawn upriver in the pools of their birth. Great Kings, some of them hundred-pound silver slabs of sea-sculpted muscle, leaped as high as they could, hit concrete, and fell back dazed, again and again. Above the lower dam the waters of Lake Aldwell were supposed to have covered an ancient site, sacred to the Klallam—two holes in the rock where the creator of the universe was supposed to have bathed before blessing the tribe.

A fawn loped across the road, collapsed its legs, and dropped to the ground at the shoulder, a trembling pile of dappled fur. Trace idled for a time to watch it, remembering having heard somewhere that early in their lives fawns are nearly scentless. Even with that defense, its fragility was pitiable. Trace shook her head and inhaled through o'd lips, imagining a mother bear or cougar finding, catching, and killing the fawn, discerping it to share with April-born cubs or kits. In the end, there would be nothing left of it but four tiny hooves in a pile of scat, transferred energy fueling two-month-old predators. She asked it softly, *Where is your mother*? and drove on, wondering, as the car jounced over the gravel, whether, if she absolutely had to do it—say to save her own life—she would have been able to turn the wheel and accelerate to crush the fawn under the tires.

Trace parked at the end of Whiskey Bend. The cars, trucks, and vans already at the trailhead made her pause after she'd stepped onto the gravel. The engine pinged. She looked around: a few California and Oregon plates, one Kentucky, one Missouri, one Florida, mostly Washington State.

She bound Paul to her in a carrier, hitched a pack onto her back, and hiked into the forest, its shadows and multiple shades—greens, yellows, browns, greys, silvers, and the fading blues and whites of the sky—swept together in the prism of her tears. After a few minutes of the gentle jostling, Paul slept in the carrier, warm against her chest. His weight seemed to want to pull her into a hunch; the packstraps dug into her shoulders. For a mile and a half she hiked and cried, conscious the entire way of the weight and warmth of him at her chest. He awakened and drifted back to sleep several times, moving his hands and gurgling as if to ask her questions.

When she stopped to rest, she felt her own heart beating in her chest, his heart beating against hers, so that together the beats formed an erratic concatenation, as if emanating from some organism too frenetic in its life to live for long.

All through her pregnancy and even after delivery, Trace had dragged herself around Neah Bay like one of the dogs that roamed the streets (dogs visitors imagined unclaimed, though if you lived there you knew whose they were). Her mother and a woman named Carol, who administered prenatal sessions to young mothers-to-be, and some other women on the reservation had taken to giving her (and one another) long concerned looks when she did not respond, did not even seem to hear their cheerful greetings and words of support. Some of them clucked their tongues at how joylessly she seemed to carry her burden and, once he was born, her new responsibility. In those days before Paul was born and in the days since, Trace had felt buried beneath the weight of the story that seemed permanently affixed to her in the small place where she lived. She struggled to think of Paul, with his full-throated cries and gentle coos and an alarming hunger for her milk and for the world, as anything but evidence of this burial. After he was born, she found herself thinking all the more about people from Neah Bay, even sometimes young people, who'd gone to live in Port Angeles, or Seattle, or to places in California where no one knew their stories well enough to level that double-edged claim: *I know you; this is who you are*. The idea of leaving came to seem like swimming up through the landslide that had covered her. Even going a short distance away came to seem like a way to breathe again. She knew a group of young people who were living together in town, in Port Angeles, where she'd been a handful of times to shop and to stay at a hotel, ride an elevator, swim in a pool. One of these young people even had a baby. Trace convinced her mother that this would be good for her as well, but she didn't tell her about a stop at the Elwha she was contemplating along the way.

At a place called Elk Overlook, Trace stopped to rest, imagining the white namer of the place years ago looking down at the island splitting the Elwha hundreds of yards below and seeing on the island, chest-deep in the stream, a milling herd of the elk named for Theodore Roosevelt by Clinton Hart Merriam, a biologist who first identified the species, though the Makah and other tribes had seen and named and hunted elk for thousands of years before Merriam. What name, Trace wondered, might the Klallam, ancient enemy of the Makah, have had for this place?

The sun had just begun to set. A line of shadow advanced down the tips of the trees a mile across the valley, on the western slope. She had stopped crying, traded sweat for tears. She stood for a time and breathed. A clean conifer scent sluiced her lungs, finding its way, it seemed, straight from nostrils to brain—invigorating, intoxicating, the smell suggestive of forest fires to come, a faint mineral tinge, the promise of renewal. How strange, she thought, that she had not felt so good in months and months, maybe even years.

She picked up her pace and passed the wall of rock near the river called Goblins Gate, where the faces of monsters looked to have been chiseled into the riverside rock; and a stand of silver firs with charred boughs, where a fire had raged in the 1970s; and Cougar Mike's Cabin, named for the man who'd helped his clients kill hundreds of the animal for which he had come to be named; and the former site of Geyser House, Doc Luden's cabin where the good doctor who was not a real doctor had lived on poached venison, elk, and honey, and played his fiddle and recited original poems for guests who happened by; and Krause Bottom, named for a plucky German couple, Ernst and Meta, who had carved an existence from a section of forest now under Lake Mills directly above the upper dam. She would learn all of this later from Tom. A palimpsest of human history even here in what seemed like wilderness, the white history recorded, the native history subsumed like the story of Nahkeeta, unrecorded, unofficial, secret, passed on by word in stories or else buried with the old ones, if it didn't linger in the place itself. She felt she could sense the old ones' presence. What ancestors of hers might have ventured this far on their own? Who might have traded or fought with the Elwha Klallams here? Killed the men, stolen their goods, brought home slaves? Wandered up into the green light of the glimmering forests far from the smoky cedar comfort and the roar and hiss of the waves in the longhouse by the sea?

Trace didn't want to confront her own unwritten personal history, which was sure to find her in the meadow where the sedge gave way to a copse of alders interspersed with a few moss-covered big-leaf maples bordering a small laughing branch of the Elwha. So she paused for a moment but did not take the trail leading down into the heaviness of the witnessing meadow.

In the day's gloaming, not far from the place where she had made the decision not to descend, she made camp near a brook trickling down the ridge in the damp coolness under the lowest limbs, in the shadows of the undergrowth—rhododendron, sword fern, salmonberry, spike moss, sorrel—its murmur approaching with growing fervor the distant roar of the Elwha, raucous with runoff in its long-carved valley. A tale the Klallam tribes told said that the Elwha and the Sol Duc, in its valley to the west, sprang from the tears of two dragons who had once risen from their respective valleys to battle each other. Both thought they'd lost and retreated to cry.

She opened a plastic bag, munched on some barbecue potato chips, bit into an apple, and watched the last of the sunlight fade from a grey, human-heart-shaped rock in a meadow a long way up the ridge. The human heart is the size of the human fist, she remembered, and she wondered how big Paul's heart might be and thought it was probably the size of the little fist he made when he gripped one of her fingers. It occurred to her, too, that the rock was the size of the Thunderbird's heart and also the size of one of its clutched talons when it went to the sea to battle whales in her mother's and grandmother's and Uncle Jack's stories. The Thunderbird had an aerie on Mount Olympus, the highest peak in the Olympics. Tom, who knew these things, would later tell her the peak had been named *El Cerro de la Santa Rosalia* by Spanish explorer Juan Perez in 1774; then, four years later, British explorer John Meares named it Olympus, for the dwelling place of the Greek gods. Trace wondered what the Makah had called the peak, if anything. In one of her mother's stories, Thunderbird swooped down from its aerie to carry away whales so the salmon would return and the people who'd been starving would have plenty to eat. Its flapping wings made thunder and a great wind, and lightning serpents flashed from its eyes.

That night she woke up to the faint glow of the dying campfire and could not go back to sleep. The brook seemed to teem with changeable voices. She heard in the stream the shrillness of Paul's first scraughy voicing, the echo of someone saying, *it's a big boy nine pounds*. She remembered the redness of his skin, his eyes slit like a baby sea otter's against the delivery room light and the uncomfortable chaos of his new world. She remembered looking up at the ridges on the plastic fluorescent light coverings and searching for but feeling no joy or relief. Her mother said in Makah—a language whose sounds made Trace think of the rubbery texture, the murky taste and smell, the sandy grit of clams and mussels, the secret lives of seals, sea lions, and whales—that she thought the child had a *hutsxuk chupaxkwixi,* a bold heart. Tongue in cheek, Uncle Jack used the Chinook Jargon to say the same thing but with slightly darker implications: "skookum tum-tum."

A long way up the valley, the wind began its sweep, its whisper through needles and leaves like the weary sigh a judge might draw before pronouncing sentence. When the wind finally reached the campsite, orange sparks scattered like wild insects into the darkness, spiraling up a distance to expire against the bluish silhouettes of the trees. The brook's voice continued down the ridge, both leaving and staying.

Paul rested on a mattress of soft moss and blinked up at the cold clean wash of stars shining between cedar limbs as if for him alone, winking back at him in a way that suggested they could see the entire arc of his life. So different from the amniotic burrow he had come from, the cold drafty rooflessness of the wide-skyed world with its filigree of stars. *We will see you here again, little friend,* they whispered down to him, through light years, in the icy-cryptic language of stars. Paul moved his right hand to trace the trajectory of sparks as they left the campfire to curl up a distance before dying. It appeared that something in their flight pleased then troubled him; he gurgled and cooed then frowned as if he thought he'd witnessed the sparks' aspiration and failure to become stars.

He began to fuss, so Trace lifted him up to nurse and watched his avid, closed-eyed attention, felt the press of his fingers on flesh and aureole, his hard gums at work. Her expression at first suggested maternal duty, gladly accepted, then shifted to tolerant disgust, before landing with a painful pleasant stab on the darkest feelings she had ever discovered in herself. When his desire—she had come to think it was an animal hunger with no regard for her presence, no hint of an awareness or gratitude that she was the source of its satisfaction—reminded her of his father, a rage fired in her chest, and she fought the temptation to tear Paul from her breast. When he stopped nursing, she set him down on the bed of moss, where he blinked and took in breath as if the cold night air with its chorus of sheltering stars might be another kind of mother's milk.

From the dirt at fire-edge she picked up the vertebrae of some former animal, turned it in her hands, and remembered nine months earlier fleeing the medicine-reek of the clinic in Port Angeles. A light rain had pattered the windshield on the silent ride home through the merciless Route 112 curves, the road's seeming indecision mirroring her own doubts. When her friend Jeanie dropped her off, Trace's mother met her on the front porch. The light spilling through the doorway and taken up by the raindrops percolating in puddles seemed insufficient against the pressing darkness. Seeing the diapers and wipes, the pacifiers and soft blanket in the Payless bags Trace had bought to convince herself there was no turning back, her mother understood the decision, though she didn't agree with it. She had thought Trace might be different from all the girls on the rez who started families young. She had convinced Trace, who seemed to want nothing so much as to curl up and let the storm pass, to press charges against the father. She stirred up the tribal council and gently urged Trace toward a visit to the clinic. With a heavy sigh and some unexpected relief, she gathered Trace into her arms and rocked her so that it seemed like they were two open shells winking down into deep water.

Trace put the bone in her pocket, took Paul up again, bit her lip, shook her head: "Oh, please help me," she said, imagining the Thunderbird's eyes flashing lightning serpents, the thunderclaps and wind caused by the flapping of its wings. She rocked him like her mother had rocked her that night and the dying fire threw their shadows against the cedar limbs.

Just after the sun's initial gleam appeared over the high eastern ridge, she hiked farther up the trail through silver fir. The trail's tamped needle-strewn length flirted with the river below, ran beside, then rose above it along the edge of a cliff. From the bottom of its valley the Elwha's hushed roar seemed to make predictions, cast doubt, offer unintelligible counsel.

She hiked down a series of switchbacks and stepped onto a suspension bridge spanning a canyon. Upstream, she saw the beginnings of the tight sheer walls of the Grand Canyon of the Elwha. With each of her steps, as she approached its center, the bridge wobbled and creaked. In the narrow canyon bottom the river ran in a tumultuous white ribbon punctured by rocks, each drop of the cascade part and parcel of the hungry roar that even from that distance filled her head and made it seem as if the river were struggling to express long-accumulated wisdom or rage, the unspoken regrets of the voiceless dead, the repressed laments of the shrinking glaciers far above.

She stopped midbridge and could not control her trembling as she pulled Paul's dimpled legs through the legholes of the carrier. Her arms continued to tremble as she held his body over the thin-aired vacancy answered, in vertiginous zoom, by river. Mist from the roaring water rose to cool the air. Her fingers and toes swarmed with tingles. She stood for a time, midbridge, holding him out over the rail in quivering arms. Then, shaking arms. She tried to make herself release him.

And could not.

Paul regarded his mother evenly. He fidgeted but did not cry. He wiggled his arms and legs, enjoying the increasing warmth of the sun, the coolness of the rising mist. He mouthed some whispery sounds and squinted up at the blue sky where a few clouds were adrift and evaporating at their outer edges. A plane trailed a white plume, its passengers oblivious in the pressurized fuselage, to the drama of mother and son thousands of feet below.

When she tried to reposition him, a sudden gust caught him. He slipped from her grasp and fell toward the river, feet first, at a slight angle, away from the bridge, his shadow bumping over depressions and irregularities in the western cliff face as the sun shone over the high eastern ridge to cast it there.

And then he was lost in white water.

The center of himself—he did not know to call it his heart—was attempting to exit through his mouth. Then, there was an enveloping coldness, breath-stealing, a primeval wetness. A burst of wild river, colder than anything he had known, rushed up to meet him and caught him before he could sink to hit one of the rocks. The experience was like a second birth in a life that might include several births and rebirths. Perhaps at the end of this cold wet birth he would return to the warm dark place with the loud steady beat.

Trace ran across the bridge and as fast as she could through thin trees before trying the unsteady, eroding soil at cliff-edge where scraggier trees gave way to rock. Frantically, she searched for a way down into the canyon. Seeing no clear path, heedless of the drop, she scrambled straight down, falling and catching at sliding moss, roots, and cracks in the crumbling cliff-face, unstable soil, rock, and grass staying her freefall at intervals. She slid down where she never would otherwise have slid, throwing caution to cliff-face, following a path she would, later, under ordinary circumstances, never believe she had taken.

She reached the bottom of the canyon and staggered upright, scraped and bruised, a line of blood trickling from knee to socktop, needles and twigs clinging to her hair. Immediately she started toward the river across a small rocky shoal at the edge of which the water evened as if resting from the rage it had vented upstream: the water through which he had had to pass. She made her way out, tripping over rocks for watching the river, searching the large pool the cliffs cupped there, for any sign of him.

The cold and the flow gave a feeling of pulling, as if there were a hundred angry mothers surrounding him, whisking him from one to the next with hands of ice. He was too rapt and dazed at the new sensations to cry. At first he spit against the water but then he saved his life by filling his lungs with air and closing his mouth to keep out the water and holding his breath as he was rushed downstream, narrowly missing rocks and limbs.

She saw him swirling in an eddy of the silty-turquoise pool, slow-spinning, face up, among yellow and brown hole-ridden alder leaves, below the white rapids that had carried him there. Several trout shadows lifted and held in the deep pool below him. A mossed-over log, seven feet in diameter, curled at the former root end like a shepherd's staff, ran from the bottom of the cliff into the depths. A little black bird she'd heard some elders call the gakatas landed on the end of the log, cocked its head, chirped as if to tell her something, flew off.

Trace stumbled across the rocks, spurred by the fear that he might be swept into the next series of rapids before she could reach him. But just as she was nearing the edge of the pool, a soft tendril of current carried him in a wider arc and, in one of its circles, wider still, released him to glide into shallow water, over sand, where he rested in gently lapping waves, fingers wiggling, face frowning up at the sun, presented cleansed and gift-like.

She bent down and lifted him up for examination. He did not appear to be hurt—not a bruise, not a scratch. It was some sort of miracle. Gold-starred sunlight glistened on his cold skin. Her hands and warmth and tears began to un-numb him. When he recognized her, he smiled. She exhaled: *What kind of a child are you?* She was suddenly overcome with the certainty that they must be in the presence of one or several of the *tumanuwos*, strong spirits of the sort she'd heard about in the elders' stories but in which she'd never believed. Until that moment she'd dismissed these stories as merely amusing, somewhat embarrassing if aired before nontribal members, but now she found herself searching for remnants—in the river and its roar and mist, in the rocks on which she stood, in the alder leaves tumbling in the depths and the caddisflies flitting above the glassy surface of the pool, and in the trees leaning over the canyon—of some kind of otherworldly intervention. She found none but the ordinary wonders beyond the miracle of Paul alive in her arms.

As she apologized and promised him her lifelong devotion, he gazed up at her with eyes that had changed from blue to rich brown, she noticed fully for the first time, to match his father's eyes. She interpreted his oddly beatific expression as containing no accusation, a hint of forgiveness, a knowledge beyond his age. There seemed to be a promise, too, in those eyes, of remembrance.

2

Remembrance of what, Trace sometimes wondered, had she seen in Paul's eyes that day? A muffled echo deeply buried, like the earliest rings in an old-growth trunk, of the coldness of the river; the way the wind whipped up the valley through a million conifers; a transmission, as if from outer space, of the feeling of Mommy's hands holding then not holding him as he dropped (which always makes her shudder); some pulsing scintilla of knowledge that repeats *don't count on anyone*; a sense growing in his marrow that you *could* count on a place?

Years later, in 2007, on what had to that point been an ordinary Tuesday, Trace saw Bill Newton standing in front of the meat bin at the end of the frozen-food aisle of the Port Angeles Albertsons. His broad shoulders bulged blue flannel, his black beard was flecked with grey, and his hair sprang out in curly riot above his bearish head. She drew in an astonished breath and dropped her shopping basket. Almost nineteen years since she'd felt that beard, coarse as dogfish skin, against her face, neck, and shoulders.

Bill heard the small clatter and turned from ground beef and flank steak to stare at the red plastic basket for a few seconds. When he looked up, he saw the Makah girl with the long black hair who appeared so regularly in his thoughts and dreams that it sometimes seemed like he'd never left her in that meadow on the banks of the Elwha.

Trace watched recognition leap into Bill's eyes, which were Paul's absent a good portion of enlivening wonder. Though he looked like he wanted nothing so much as to run, he took two wide steps toward her, fell to a knee with a grunt and the small squeak of stretched denim, and bowed his head as if in prayer.

On either side of them the freezers hummed. A woman pushing her cart past the aisle pretended nonchalance, though her eyes strained for the view that might help her fix the odd tableau with a meaning.

Trace waited to hear what Bill Newton had to say after all this time and finally heard him mumble something—a garbled prayer? a plea for forgiveness? a declaration of love? a proposal of marriage? a melodramatic commentary on the price of meat?—she couldn't tell. Then he stood, turned with a flutter of flannel, and walked away without his empty cart, boots clocking the speckled tiles.

She woke up in her bed at four a.m. the next morning to an unsettling feeling whose source—a dream about Paul in some kind of danger—receded like a plume worm disappearing into its chrysalis when a finger grazed its plume. She rolled over and reached out an arm to feel the coldness where her husband, Tom, would have been if he wasn't running an old ship aground at the Alang beach in India for hordes of shoeless shipbreakers to descend upon and cut apart with blue-flamed acetylene.

When he was away at sea, she imagined Tom as a pensive mechanical whiz (still and always the Chimacum valley kid with a passion for building model airplanes and destroyers), standing on the deck of one of the rusty, last-leg ships he captained to their doom on the beach at Alang, his eyes locked on a dim horizon, thinning hair blowing in the wind. Other times she saw him alone in a decaying ship's bridge, hunched over glowing switches, gages, throttles, lights—powerless slave to failing technology.

It seemed unfair to Trace that Tom and Paul—husband at work and runaway son—could create such a vacuum in her life without seeming to suffer from her absence from their lives—at least not that she ever saw or that they ever brought themselves to admit. She imagined them out in the world living their lives with no appreciable awareness of her—Tom on the deck or in the bridge of his doomed ship, the rusting old whale he was bound to beach; Paul who knew where?—out in the woods somewhere, up in his beloved Olympics?

Back in the house, her heart still racing from the Bill Newton sighting, Trace at first thought to call her mother at Neah Bay, but four digits into the call something checked her hand. If what Bill Newton had done was wrong, which it was, to the point of thinking the world would have been better off if he hadn't done it, then what did that make Paul and the man he was growing up to be?

A fresh memory of Bill Newton joined her thoughts of Tom and Paul—those thick shoulders under blue flannel, the bearish girth of him, the black and grey beard, Paul's eyes, absent of wonder in Bill's sad face, boots clocking the Albertsons floor over the thrumming freezers.

She shuddered the fresh memory back into hiding (though its prickly residue remained to gall her), got out of bed, pulled on her robe, walked into the kitchen, set some coffee brewing, and when it was ready and poured, carried the cup into the living room. Beyond the floor-to-ceiling windows, down beyond the bluff, the slate water of the Strait of Juan de Fuca melded on the horizon with a low-hanging bank of fog: the view Tom's job and her decision to settle for him (though many called it marrying up) afforded them. On clear days the windows filled with an expansive view of Victoria and the mountains of British Columbia seven miles across the glittering water. On the American side, almost directly below the bluff and to the east, a crooked plume of smoke rose from the paper mill. A few boats heading out to Ediz Hook trailed white wakes. In a few hours, she knew the sun would enfilade the fog with god light and burn away the clouds obscuring the foothills to reveal the snow-capped peaks of the Olympics rising to the south, above the Strait, in back of the house and behind the scattered, gradually inclining buildings and houses of Port Angeles.

She felt the warmth of the fragrant steam on her face. A wind shuttled up the bluff, worrying familiar trees with its old plaint, rattling the giant panes. Sometimes, more often when Tom and Paul weren't home, she thought it miraculous the wind didn't break the windows and scatter shards over the white carpet in which her bare feet now luxuriated—so strongly did it buffet the panes.

Far out in the Strait a black tanker inched across the water. It looked about the size of (it certainly could not have been as old and dangerous as) a tanker Tom was perhaps at that very moment running aground at Alang for the shipbreakers—who died one a day and who made about a dollar a day—to slice up with their torches. Tom didn't like the part he played in the business, but it was all he could find at sea after some higher-ups at his old company scapegoated him for a small oil spill in Prince William Sound three years before she'd met him. Two new-looking tankers rested out in the harbor. These were probably double-hulled to keep the oil from spilling, the bright blue and white, safe, closer-to-home ones Tom would be captaining if he had his wish.

As she sipped, she ran through the ways she could have better handled telling Paul the story she'd told him a month before he'd run away. The story—nothing less than the strange story of his conception—had tumbled out of her in an unguarded moment. She wondered if she should believe the message Paul had left on the machine, three days after he disappeared without telling her where he was going, a message she'd heard five times since he'd left it.

> Hi Mom. It's me. Paul. I'm okay so don't worry. Can't really tell you what I'm doing because of . . . Tom and his job and whose side it seems like he's on. And because . . . well . . . I just can't talk about it. I wanted to tell you I didn't leave because of what you told me. This is something else I'm doing. So don't worry. I l— . . . I'll call when I can, but it won't be for a while.

The message had left her with many questions. Why couldn't he talk about what he was doing? What followed the "l" he'd tripped over. *I l*-ost one of my good hiking boots? *I l*-eft a more detailed and satisfactory note for you under the cookie jar? *I l*-ove you? And if he felt the need to tell her he loved her, now, when it came so rarely—had he ever said it in the last ten years?—what did that suggest about the sorts of dangerous things he was doing out there in the wide world? What side was Tom on? What side was Paul on? Weren't all three of them on the same side?

Only two weeks before his high-school graduation, Paul had been suspended for punching a fellow senior named Brink Forger, a star defensive end for the Roosevelt High School Roughriders and son of Ernie Forger, city councilman and owner of the biggest truck dealership on the Olympic Peninsula. Ernie's ten-foot-tall photograph stared down from billboards all around town and along Route 101, beginning in Sequim ten miles to the east, under the slogan *Peninsula Tough!* That Saturday, a day after the incident, just an hour after Paul had left for a hike into the Olympics, Trace answered two calls in quick succession from the principal of Roosevelt High and Ernie Forger. This was her first inkling that Paul was in any kind of trouble, though she'd talked to him at dinner on Friday night and the next morning while she had her coffee and he prepared to go on his hike.

When Paul got back late Saturday afternoon, she said, "Well, you went and did it now, didn't you?"

She could tell he knew what she was talking about, though he didn't give any sign. He stood quietly in the doorway while she told him how disappointed she was and how angry that he would jeopardize getting his diploma this close to the end. She echoed the principal's and Ernie Forger's language in expressing her dismay at his violence. Possibly (there was some doubt about this) breaking this kid's nose!? Ernie Forger had asked her if she knew what it felt like to know your son's face would never look the same again. He'd told her they could expect a lawsuit and criminal charges. She marveled aloud at the fact that Paul hadn't told her one word of any of this before going off on his hike.

Paul listened in silence, never offering a word in his own defense.

Before she knew what she was doing, she gave in to the cathartic spill, surprised by how close the story was to the surface—one good tug and out it all came. In a single sustained gush, the story she'd carefully guarded for eighteen years tumbled out into the air between them like a living thing that might growl, snort, clamber up the walls. She heard herself saying "Bill Newton," a name she'd never said to him before—Bill Newton, his "real" father, whose fickle bad nature he seemed to have inherited, something for which she refused to bear responsibility any longer. She told this story, and toward its end she felt it flowing directly toward the story of his baptism in the Elwha, whose possible telling scared her so much she stopped talking midsentence in the hope that the urge to confess any further would subside.

Paul heard the impromptu version of the story of his conception with the same equanimity as her Brink Forger lecture. His calm silence for some reason made her so mad that, in spite of the guilt called up in her by the mere prospect of telling the second story, she leveled on him the worst punishment she could think of for this mysterious son who always seemed to ripple out of focus the moment she thought she had him fixed: he couldn't go up into the Olympics for a month, maybe longer than that—maybe never again.

The following week a different kind of call starting coming in to the house on the bluff. A veteran English teacher at the high school named Maude Foster called to say that Brink Forger had a good punch in the nose coming to him more than any kid she'd worked with in thirty-five years. A doctor named Charlie Klapp, the father of a witness to the event, called to say that Paul had acted in defense of a boy who'd suffered Brink Forger's bullying for months, and that Ernie Forger had strong-armed the principal to get him to suspend Paul. A girl named Stephanie Barefoot, one of Paul's classmates, called and asked to speak with Paul. When Trace told her he wasn't there (he was out trimming Scotch broom, that invasive species in the front yard, he liked reminding her), the girl said that she was in charge of a petition with a hundred signatures so far from students and teachers asking that Paul be reinstated. The girl's father, some kind of high-powered attorney, who someone later told her had helped the school get a grant for new computers, was the second name on the petition, after Stephanie's. It amazed Trace how quickly things turned around. By the beginning of the next week, in time for graduation, Paul was back at Roosevelt High in good standing. She had watched him graduate, and since then had been mentally preparing herself for his fall departure for Oregon State University, where he planned to study forestry.

Looking down the bluff and out at the lifting fog, Trace reminded herself she had to believe what Paul had said in the message on the machine—that the story she'd told hadn't driven him away and that he'd be back soon from whatever mysterious, dangerous things he was doing. She also had to believe he would have finished "*I l-*" in the best possible way—in spite of the story and everything else. Even so, she was worried for him, and a stinging sorrow, not only for the way he'd heard the story but also for her lapse of faith in him, clunked through her like his hiking boots tumbling in the dryer (a sound she hoped to hear again soon). She also felt the presence of the second story, the story she'd thought she'd never tell him, intensified by Bill Newton's sudden reappearance and aching to emerge so that she might come clean and be forgiven.

3

An olive-drab truck with National Park Service insignia jounced up a defunct logging road, its front bumper whispering strands of beargrass, buckwheat, saxifrage, showy sedge, and Parry's silence under the front bumper, its headlights cutting the four a.m. darkness to flash on tire ruts, insects, the thin lower branches of alder, hemlock, and silver fir.

The driver wore the uniform of a National Park ranger and spoke steadily out of the right side of his mouth in a way that made it seem as if he was speaking for his own benefit or to try to mask his nervousness as much as to provide important information to the younger man seated beside him. The left side of the older man's face, from below his undamaged left eye down through his chin, had been raked in a single blow, fifty-two years ago when he was ten years old, by the claws of a sow grizzly protecting her cub in Glacier National Park.

He offered a steady stream of advice: "Make camp just inside the Park boundary, as we discussed. They're working the next ridge over, near the bottom of that valley, not even in the buffer between Park and Forest land, but right smack dab in the Temple Grove. Brazenly in National Park land. I marked it on your topo. It's a clear encroachment into one of the most impressive remaining stands of old-growth Douglas fir in the entire world. Make yourself a nuisance. Use the spikes. Mix up grit to put in their engines if they come in with big machinery. Do what you can to sabotage their saws. Slow them down. Stop them if you can. If they won't let us have an appeals process legally, we'll make sure they by god hear our de facto appeal."

The young man gazed fixedly into the darkness beyond the headlights, listening and nodding as if mishearing any detail would result in an irreversible calamity, wondering what, exactly, *de facto* meant. One of a series of veins pulsed against the skin where his neck widened into chest and shoulder muscles; another vein throbbed once at his temple. He worked the muscles of his jaw as if this might help him better hear the instructions over the rattling of the truck and the gear in its bed. In the fixedness of his stare and in the resolution of his nods, he resembled a paratrooper preparing to drop through miles of darkness into enemy territory, or an athlete before the game against the biggest rival.

"Go in at night, after they've left. They shouldn't suspect anything. Not yet. They think they're being covert. That's why they waited for the outcry and all those protests to quiet down before they tried this. What you'll be doing is illegal, as you know. But so is what they're doing. They're trying to get the cut started without announcing it or taking in any more public commentary. Even before the road they'll need has been approved. Later, it wouldn't surprise me if they use the fact that they've already begun as a reason to continue. I got a tip a few weeks ago from someone I have no reason not to trust. Cover your tracks. After the first night, a group might lay for you. Word is the FBI's been sniffing around Port Angeles and Forks. With this administration in power, the Freddies are cracking down everywhere like never before. If you're caught, they'll call you an 'eco-terrorist'—as if what has been and continues to be done to the earth in the name of progress doesn't amount to terror of a greater degree. They'll trot out that label, banking on its resonance since the Twin Towers, and the media will splash it around and get it in the echo chamber so the public will start to believe it must be true. But we won't let it come to that, will we?"

The young man didn't answer. They rode for a time in silence. Grass and trees and tire ruts flickered in the shifting light, tree tops revealed and concealed a three-quarter moon, before the older man began again: "Make sure you do some serious early damage. The more the better, so we can gain some time. It may be all you'll be able to do. In the meantime, I'll compose the communiqué, get the word out, anonymously, that the Temple Grove trees have been spiked. I know it won't be easy for you to drive spikes into those trees. It wouldn't be easy for me, either. It wasn't easy when I did it up in the Siskiyous back in the eighties. Remember, it's for the good of the trees. It may save them. Be sure you spike as many as you can. When you're out and it's done, we'll pray the gyppo loggers decide it's not worth it and leave the Park in peace. Forever. Amen."

The road ended. The headlights shone on a wide empty cul-de-sac of upturned stumps and underbrush—snarled root systems, fledgling silver fir, upstart alder, Pacific blackberry, fireweed, and foxglove—rising through the leavings of a previous logging show.

After the engine had been switched off and after the sharp report of the shut doors, the silence around them accumulated a hushed immensity. Far above the roots and stumps, on the otherwise denuded slope, the dim outline of a tree-filled ridge stretched black across a blueblack sky overspread with stars and the bright three-quarter moon. The young man looked up at the stars and thought that a silence as vast as the one adhering in the darkness around them was the sound made by a sky full of stars, in the same way—or so he'd come to think without knowing why—that the sound made by a rushing stream was a composite of the voices of the *tumanuwos* from his grandmother's and Uncle Jack's stories—spirits that could confer power but that had to be dealt with very carefully and at some risk.

He lifted the seventy-five-pound pack from the truck bed and slung it onto his right shoulder. With his left hand he pulled a headlamp onto his forehead, the unlit light in the center rounded by bunched strands of his long, black hair. He filled his lungs with a shot of chilly air and exhaled slowly, a part of him already bushwhacking through the slag toward the tree-serrated edge of the black ridge.

"It's over Rugged Ridge and to the west, as we discussed. Got your compass?"

He tugged at a leather string around his neck and pulled out of one of his pockets the GPS he'd bought with his discount from the outdoor store where he had worked part-time during the school year and most summers since he'd been fourteen.

"Fancy. Plenty of water? Food? Water filter? Bolt cutters? Spikes and hammer?"

He nodded.

The older man paused a moment. "Pistol?"

The young man nodded again.

"Meet me at the trailhead to Sol Duc Falls in three days. Failing that, we'll meet at the Hoh River ranger station in four days. If I fail to meet you there, go to the Llama Lady. She doesn't know to expect you or anything about this mission, but she'll know what to do if you need her."

The name conjured for the young man a dim image of a woman they'd once glimpsed leading a train of llamas across a distant ridge. The older man had spoken of her with reverential awe, as if she was the only person he knew who had figured out how to live her life the right way, off the grid, unbeholden to the pernicious currents of the wrong direction. She had a house on the outskirts of the Park where she raised llamas and rented them out for backcountry trips.

The young man snugged the pack strap around his waist, looked down at the dim shapes of his scarred boots on the mud of the road, then up at the older man with a fleeting grin, a momentary mischievous glimmer in his deep-set brown eyes. "I'll put it to 'em. For the trees and for the earth and what's right," he said, and grinned again. The extra intensity of the quick flashes of his white teeth and the somewhat exaggerated earnestness in his voice and something slightly staged in the way he carried himself constituted nearly undetectable nods (which the older man completely missed) to the fact that he was playing a part—pushing into a space of slight remove where he could watch himself performing this role—even though he mostly meant it.

The older man nodded back: "Godspeed," he said. He stood and watched the younger man turn and start up the ridge, moving between immense upturned roots that in the darkness and the sporadic light of the headlamp looked like the scattered innards and bones of some great leviathan eviscerated by something greater still.

The stars seemed to have been leant an extra shimmer by the cold, and they gleamed like pinpricks in the lid of a colossal jar through wisps of fog and between the limbs of western hemlocks, with their bent shepherd's-crook tops.

Paul bushwhacked through the loggers' leavings and tried to imagine scenarios that might await him, confrontations and their potential for calling forth bravery or cowardice. The going would have been difficult even with a trail and better light; bushwhacking in the darkness was torturous and had to be done slowly to avoid injury. The underbrush and limbs scratched his legs, arms, and face. He hiked through upstart conifers, scrambled up inclines of crumbling rock half-claimed by moss, and climbed ridges of pine-riddled dirt, sometimes needing to use his hands to gain any ground. He loved the way this kind of climbing woke up his body, challenged and pushed it to its best capacity, made his thighs sing and his blood thrum. Doing this, he sometimes thought, was the only time he felt truly alive.

Every year since he'd been working in the woods in the summers he'd bought a piece or two or three of new outdoor equipment. And for the past two years, even while he was in school, he'd been working part-time at Outbound, the outdoor equipment store in downtown Port Angeles, so he got good deals because of the discount and because Jim the manager liked him and sometimes comped him things. These gains, in addition to the gifts he got from his mom and Tom for birthdays and Christmas, had added up to an impressive collection.

Still, as much as he liked the gear, it was secondary to the experience of being in the woods. Some of the gearheads who rang the bell on the door of Outbound were more interested in the equipment than in where it would help them go and what it would help them do. Or, maybe it was simply that they had the words for the gear and not for the experience. He could understand that. Still, they underscored for him what was more important. For someone just eighteen, he was lucky to carry a surprising number of sustaining, refreshing memories of experiences of the mountains. He grew up skinny-dipping the lakes of the Olympics: Lake Angeles, PJ Lake, the lakes of the Seven Lakes Basin, no-name lakes where there used to be glaciers in the Bailey Range. Naked, with no audience but a bear and her cubs foraging up on Klahanne or some other nameless ridge, he dove from rocks into the breath-stealing coldness of the clear water and burst up for a breath of clean air, an activity that always reminded him of something he could never quite fathom but that made him feel as if he would be cleansed for months to come.

He caught and cooked brook trout whose reds, whites, and multi-shades of green on worm-tracked backs faded soon after he'd pulled them from the water. Their white bellies flashed as they darted to and fro over the logs that had slid into the clear water. They curled in the pan among the lemon and onions. Their flesh peeled easily from fragile white bones.

He slept under stars or under a tarp with tapping rain. He woke up to Pacific surfroar and hiss and looked out to see wisps of fog ghosting over the waves and around stacks on ocean beaches. He'd dropped into all the sandy beaches around the Cape and had hiked to all the ocean beaches in the Park. Sometimes he went with older friends, sometimes he went alone. Sometimes his mother or Tom went with him.

One time, at a potlatch for an elder's birthday party, an old-timer had asked him, "Those places speak to you?" and he'd nodded, but he wondered if they spoke to him in the way the elder had meant.

He had climbed Mount Olympus three times, once each in his fifteenth, sixteenth, and seventeenth years. Atop the mountain, he had looked out over the blue Pacific to the west, the Strait to the north, the snowy lesser peaks of the Bailey Range like a wall to the east.

All of the rangers knew him and had taken to giving one another reports on him, as if he were another animal they were monitoring and protecting in the Park—cougar, bear, mountain goat, elk, Paul Granger. Dan Kelsoe beamed with pride when he heard reports of these sightings. Some of the rangers who'd learned of Paul's Indian heritage and were goofing around among themselves in Chinook Jargon, took to calling him *tenas itswet*, which meant "young bear" in the trade language invented by Northwest tribes. They told one another in passing when they'd seen him, deep in the Park, lithe, dark-tanned, moving easily as if floating along.

He had long conversations with other campers, people from around the world, these woods an unlikely cosmopolitan gathering place. He'd shared meals, conversations, or sometimes a nod or a few pleasant words with people from twenty different states and ten different countries in the Park.

One day, hiking down from Happy Lake at dusk, he surprised a cougar that had jumped onto the trail to lope ahead of him. When it became aware of his presence, the cat wheeled gracefully to face him and, momentarily, stood watching him. Its sandy greys met the shadows cast by the trees and undergrowth. Eyes locked, they stood appraising each other for a moment. At first the cougar looked away into the underbrush, as if pretending nonchalance. When it turned to look at Paul again, it seemed surprised he was still there. It moved very slowly to straighten itself, then, in a stalking crouch, took three deliberate steps forward. Paul did not move or breathe as his heart slid to his gullet. The cougar's face looked to be made of a cool, chiseled stone; its eyes were large and uncompromising and seemed to burn at the outer irises with fear or perhaps rage at the interruption. It stopped again, watching him—then turned and leaped ten feet into the trailside underbrush, vanishing so completely that even moments later Paul wondered if he'd seen it at all.

On a few occasions he had seen a spotted owl, that small unassuming bird who'd caused so much controversy, locked away so much forest from harvest, flitting through the canopies of the rainforest hooting its little *to-who, to-who*.

He'd once seen a herd of elk making their way, single file, across a glacier, sending creaks and pings through it as they stepped almost gingerly, pausing as if to listen when the glacier responded.

But these had all been chance encounters, things that happened because he'd been in the right place at the right time. He'd never consciously hunted for any of these experiences, as he was now hunting the would-be destroyers of the same healthy forest that had provided all of the other moments that sustained him.

He carried in the pack on his back a lightweight camp stove, enough provisions for five days, 100 bridge-timber spikes, a single jack hammer, a pair of bolt cutters, a brown felt-tipped marker, a copy of *The Monkey Wrench Gang* and *Ecodefense: A Field Guide to Monkeywrenching*, both of which Dan Kelsoe had given him to read by penlight for inspiration and instruction before he slept. Also, in a pocket of his pack rested the pistol Dan had suggested he might use if he found himself in the stickiest of life-threatening situations—and only then.

In his breast pocket, close to his heart, he carried a portion of the tip of an antler barb whaling-spear blade, smoothed by age, which Uncle Jack told him had belonged to one of their ancestors who'd hunted whales. He'd given the spear tip to Paul at a potlatch that summer, just after he'd announced that he wanted to give Paul a whaling song. For Paul, the summons to the reservation came as a surprise. His previous visits were a happy, confusing blur of cousins and aunts and uncles and other more distant relations, a welter of names and family hierarchies he struggled to learn (brags from those who claimed to descend from whaling families, accusations of a descent from slaves leveled at others), whispers of "paper Indian" sometimes said more loudly to his face. Paul had looked back at Trace, who gestured him forward with her chin, the smile in her eyes indicating what an honor this was. The circle drummed and Uncle Jack raised up a high and plaintive voice that made Paul think of a lonesome stretch of windswept beach, pines on high stacks, and Uncle Jack pushing through fog in his gillnetter, wind in his hair and classic rock blaring as he gunned it for the halibut banks. Uncle Jack crouched and danced in a step-step, shuffle-turn dance that Paul watched carefully so as to begin to memorize it. Afterwards, his grandmother gave him a tape recording of the song. "I don't think I can do it," he said. "What did the words mean?" His grandmother told him the song was about a meeting place between the abovewater and the underwater worlds experienced by whale hunters who dived under the cold water to sew up the whale's mouth. The song was about plunging into the underwater world and experiencing those depths and about the return to the world abovewater with knowledge of the other world. The song celebrated this journey and acknowledged the difficulty of this passage and of assimilating the new awareness. Now, in an accessible pocket of the pack, Paul carried an MP3 player with headphones cued up to the whaling song alongside "Into the Dark" and "Good News for People Who Love Bad News."

Uncle Jack had said, "When you're up there in the woods, keep an eye out for spirits that might give you power. Since you're up there so much, there's a good chance you'll see something. Look out for things that should be by the shore, like a chinacap or a crab heading into the woods. Look out for blind snakes, unusual colors on animals, anything strange. If you see something, respect it, gather it up with something between you and it or leave something in exchange for it . . . but only if you think it's worth taking on." Then he placed the portion of the spear tip, wrapped in a purple felt Crown Royal pouch, into Paul's hand and told him it might give him power, lend him the help of this ancestor who'd been a whaler. He'd looked into Paul's eyes and said, "Keep this close when you're out-to-country preparing for the battles you need to fight when you're back in town."

His conspiratorial manner made it seem as if he knew what Paul was planning to do with Dan Kelsoe in the Temple Grove, as if he knew that Paul would soon need all the help he could get.

During the height of the Temple Grove controversy, when Paul had tried to explain to his grandmother what was happening with the protests against the cutting of the old-growth trees, she'd chuckled and asked, "Whose temple?" This made Paul think in a new way about the name the protesters and the earlier discoverers had given to the grove. The suggestion of a place of worship seemed apt given the solemn grandeur of the trees and the way the silence and the quality of the air seemed to push you toward a better self. Within that grove, standing in contemplation of the thousands of years the trees had stood silent witness, you felt more receptive to a higher power. It was no wonder that people read the presence of God or gods into the rich air and silence, the green and gold light filtering through the canopy. Just as his grandmother had made him question the idea of ownership and affiliation in the Temple Grove by asking whose it was, one of the protesters—a tall man whose name Paul never learned—had once pointed to his temple as he said the name of the grove. This, in the middle of a conversation about the wide disparity in views among the constituencies involved. This simple gesture left Paul reeling in his contemplation of the implications of *Temple* shifting to *temple*, the idea of a grove of trees named to honor the way what those trees meant shifted in accord with the interpretive and evaluative work going on in the brains, between the temples, of different beholders.

Visits to the reservation had often shaken him out of his mainstream assumptions. Whose temple? Whose language? Whose boundaries? Whose land? Whose fish? Whose whales? What would it mean to rediscover and employ the Makah terms, older ways of seeing and identifying the trees? He did not know, nor did his grandmother or Uncle Jack when he asked them, what the Makah (who'd been so carelessly named in the official record) had called these trees, now known as Douglas firs because Scottish botanist David Douglas had introduced them to Europe. Discussions with his relatives on the reservation made him think about the arbitrary dynamics behind names, taught him that solid-seeming assumptions and conventions could be deconstructed, laid bare, the way the name of a man known for cultivating a tree might be applied to that tree, and how this naming carried with it a whole hierarchy of values for what one should attempt to do with one's life. What was deemed valuable might ignore (in name at least) thousands of years of interactions with the tree that had come to be called Douglas fir before the new name came into common use. He imagined that the Makah name for the tree might carry with it some sense of the tree's practical role, and he vowed to learn that name and the uses the Makah had had for the tree. Learning things like this was not always easy as people had different ideas and recollections, told different stories about the old ways, which were often kept alive according to the idiosyncratic whims of the new interpreter, or irrevocably lost.

His Makah relatives adopted a bemused attitude toward the ways of the bubuthldithls (the "buchlids") that was part defense against a culture that dominated and threatened their own and part critique of the folly of mainstream white ways, the ways of these people who'd come so late to the land and seemed to want to make up for their lateness by throwing tremendous energy and self-righteousness into grabbing power and changing everything. This is what his relatives seemed to think, anyway, when they weren't adopting mainstream ways themselves.

Sometimes they juggled the worlds, integrating them or shifting between them. When Jack was still drinking and before he'd come back to Makah traditions, before he started singing and dancing again, he had pointed at the engine he was working on in his old gillnetter in the harbor at Neah Bay and told Paul and some of his cousins who were messing around on the docks that this engine was all he believed in and all that was worth believing in—internal combustion, well-oiled gears, turning pistons. "To hell with all that Indian mumbo-jumbo," he said so forcefully that Paul caught a whiff of his attempt to convince himself of something he didn't really believe. "Keep on Rocking in the Free World" was blaring from the speakers, and he was wearing a black-and-white AC/DC T-shirt. "Put your energy into the logic of smooth-running engines, boys," he said. "That's my advice." And he smiled his golden smile. These two Uncle Jacks were mirrored in Paul, who kept his selves separate, most of the time leaning toward the mainstream filtered through his love of the outdoors. He visited each self when it suited him, as if putting off a decision he assumed the world would one day force him to make.

The sun rose with him, up the ridge. By the time he'd reached the top, he was breathing hard and soaked with sweat despite the coolness of the morning. His arms and legs were scraped and bruised by the limbs and brush he'd had to clamber under and over. When he bushwhacked like this in the Olympics, he often thought of the Seattle Press Expedition of 1889–90, one of Tom's favorite subjects and Paul's favorite stories. It had taken the six men on that expedition, who were sponsored by Seattle newspapers, six months to go sixty miles into this country, which, at that time, no white men had ever seen. Despite the historical lateness of the expedition, due to the wildness of the territory they were entering, some speculated their party might find an undiscovered tribe in the Olympic interior, a lost civilization sheltered by the mountains, carrying on the way they had for hundreds of years in a pristine valley, oblivious to what smallpox and the engine fueled by Manifest Destiny had done to those like them on the outside. In order to beat a rival expedition, the Press party made the unfortunate decision of beginning their trip in December and of thinking they could raft up the Elwha's raging torrents. Paul loved the story because he loved any story in which the rugged wilderness foiled attempts to tame it.

Paul's grandmother and Uncle Jack told a story about a peaceful gathering of many coast tribes in a valley deep in the Olympics surrounded by mountains. Once a year, even warring tribes put down their weapons as they crested the peaks and went down into this valley to meet with the other tribes. One year a giant named Seatco, who was taller than the tallest trees in the forest and who could travel by air, water, and land, came to the valley. While the tribes were gathered to engage in contests and to trade, he summoned a great earthquake that swallowed up many tribespeople. Those who survived warned other tribal members, and the tribes never gathered in the valley again. Even though he knew it was impossible, Paul sometimes imagined encountering, in the deepest and remotest corner of the Park, perhaps in the valley Seatco had attacked, a civilization oblivious after all these years to the rampant taming and trampling of all things wild outside the Park. In these musings about a lost civilization, Paul saw himself throwing off all his connections to contemporary existence to join the tribe that, unlike his Makah ancestors, had avoided the blight—the rotting community-owned houses, the graffitied trailers overtaken by Himalayan blackberry and alder, the alcoholism, the depression and violence that he saw on his visits to Neah Bay. He hated the way these outward signs seemed so contradictory to the story the Cultural and Research Center wanted to tell about a past in which the Makah had lived in perfect, ingenious harmony with their natural surroundings for thousands of years. He sometimes thought of himself as the member of a new kind of tribe, somewhat dependent on technology, that would learn and teach others to respect and enjoy the natural world through close communion with its wonders.

When he was up in the mountains he also thought about the *oo-simch*, the purifying rituals Makah men performed before they went out to hunt whales in canoes. Before a great physical test, they would fast and rub themselves with cedar limbs. They'd lift heavy rocks, swim in cold lakes or rivers, walk underwater for ten or fifteen minute stretches weighted down with rocks and with lines tied from themselves to their wives, who sat as still as they could on the bank. All of this to prepare for the coming trials, to make themselves one with the whale, to gain power that would serve them well in battle.

Paul sat on the side of a fallen redcedar, ate an energy bar, drank some water, absentmindedly swatted mosquitoes, and thought of his mother back in the house on the bluff overlooking the Strait and the story she'd told him a little more than a month ago—a story he had never asked to hear but suspected he might when she was ready to tell it.

Some phrases from the story had played and echoed since he'd heard them, and some of them returned to play over the beating of his heart and the whisper of his breath as he made his way up the ridge and as he rested: *never planned to have you . . . on the banks of the Elwha . . . supposed to be a picnic but . . . he took what he wanted from me and left me, left us alone . . . when you do these things, it's him in you.*

He'd thought he might tell Dan Kelsoe on the way up about the story that had poured from his mother about this man, Bill Newton, whom he'd never met, who was supposed to be his father, but there was never a chance amid the steady stream of advice and the excited atmosphere of their mission in which he had such an important role to play.

He thought of the girl from school, Stephanie Barefoot (he hadn't even known she knew his name) and her powerful father, whose power apparently trumped Brink Forger's locally powerful father, and all those others who had taken his side against Brink Forger and signed the petition. The night before he returned to school, his mother had come into his room and sat on his bed. "Why didn't you say something?" she asked. "You shouldn't have hit him, no matter what he was doing, but I would've defended you if I'd known the whole story. I wouldn't have been so angry."

He told her he didn't know why he hadn't said anything and that he thought maybe it was because he had come to believe things happened a certain way, fair or not, seemingly at random, according to a preordained order, no matter what anyone said or did. The next day he'd returned to Roosevelt High under the watchful gaze of those who had signed the petition as well as those who thought his return to school so soon an unjust bending of the rules. Stephanie Barefoot stood in the entry hall in front of the trophy case to smile at him, as if she was certain Paul was the person he wanted to be but that he wasn't yet sure he was.

He stood, consulted his compass and the GPS, and continued to move to the west for a time, following the top of the ridge in the direction where the loggers' camp was supposed to be, though it would be quite a bit lower down in the Calawah valley. Signs nailed intermittently into the trees said *NPS National Park Boundary*. On one side, National Forest land, where limited logging was allowed, on the other side, National Park land where no one was ever supposed to cut down trees.

By midmorning, the sun was rising to better illuminate the thickly treed ridge across from him. As he was moving through a small meadow in a natural clearing, he heard for the first time, over the sound of his footfalls in the sedge, the distant *whaah-aaah-ing* of a chainsaw. He stopped to listen. The sound of his adversaries galvanized him in his mission. They were real and in the woods and already doing the damage he had set out to stop them from doing, not too far from where he now stood. If he had never agreed to take the mission, if he was clearing trails in the Park or working for Jim behind the register in Outbound, this would still be going on. They would cut down all the trees in the Temple Grove, destroying what had taken thousands of years to grow. They would kill off the complicated biome that relied on those trees and their roots systems—the owls, the salmon, salamanders and voles . . . things we didn't even know about yet, things that might cure diseases, thousands of species all told—because of a worldwide addiction to economic growth and rapidly expanding wastefulness and greed. Once they had the Temple Grove, they would set their sights on more Park land till they had wheedled it away to nothing but stumps so they could turn it into a monocultural tree farm overseen by Big Timber.

He would follow that sound, set up a hidden camp some distance from it, spy on the loggers to see what they were doing and how they were doing it, make his plans, and wait for his moment to go in and spike the trees. He would go in at night and do some serious early damage, just like Dan had said. He moved through the meadow, more conscious of the noise he was making, the swishing of his boots in the sedge, as he considered the next ridge and the best way to approach it. He wondered if he would die for the cause, if he would need to use the gun in his pack. He felt the spear tip of his ancestor at his chest and imagined the person who'd held it for his own battles with whales or against members of other tribes.

Dan Kelsoe stood watching the light from Paul's headlamp flashing on the limbs of downed trees as the boy made his way up the ridge. As he watched, he ran his right hand over his beard, occasionally letting his fingers stray up the left side of his face to trace the four wide pink furrows where the sow had marked him with the blow itself and, more profoundly, chosen him by sparing his life (a blow from a grizzly could decapitate an elk), infusing him with a passion to defend wild things for the rest of his life. Now, the story of the blow she'd administered that day fifty-two years ago had become his narrative in a way that nothing else ever would. Forever after, he was the guy who had been mauled by a grizzly when he was a kid. Whatever else his story might become, even if he'd gone on to teach physics in Copenhagen or peddled vacuum cleaners in Hoboken, his students would have looked up from their textbooks, the housewives and husbands from the informational brochure, and thought about the claws that had made those furrows on his face. Now, as a ranger since 1987, and earlier, during his covert days as an environmental activist, the mark was a godsend. People who liked wild things looked at the furrows and saw grit, character, authenticity, a tremendous capacity for understanding and demonstrating compassion for wildness, even as the scars distracted listeners from whatever his current message happened to be. Many times, he'd stop midsentence after noticing his listener was elsewhere, sometimes staring outright at the scars, wondering what it would have been like to be dropped to the ground by that blow.

When Paul's light was a quarter-way up the ridge and disappearing into a place where replanted hemlock had a root-hold, Dan got back in the truck and drove down the quasi-road they'd come up.

As he drove, he wondered for the hundredth time if he should have risked everything to go with Paul. He convinced himself again that someone needed to compose the communiqué that would alert the Park and Forest services and the media that some of the trees in the Temple Grove were being spiked and that the Forest Service and their ostensible boss, Timberforus Incorporated, a big timber outfit with international headquarters in an Atlanta high-rise, were planning to work through a small-time, local, independent gyppo contractor to take advantage of the current administration's gutting of the public appeals process to begin cutting down thousand-year-old Douglas firs, even without the proposed road. This, after they had caved in to mass protests a year ago and sworn they wouldn't go after those trees. Someone needed to get the word out—that was important—he assured himself, and it was also true that he shouldn't jeopardize his job as a ranger, which, oddly enough, had turned out to be the perfect cover for the actions he organized. But Dan knew there was another reason he wasn't going with Paul. He was sixty-two, and old-school monkey-wrenching was a young man's game.

Dan was frustrated with the new, most common mode of protest, which was more a media game than the stick-it-to-'em approach he preferred. He was delighted to find a protégé in Paul, who helped his crew clear and rebuild trails in the summer. They'd gradually come into each other's confidence and had increased their give-and-take till Dan found himself telling stories almost recklessly of his time in the Siskiyous and at Glen Canyon. The boy seemed eager to find a mentor, and Dan had never met anyone so passionate about the Olympics, especially no one so young.

Now, driving down the ridge, despite the training he'd given his young lieutenant—countless hours of hiking and trail maintenance in the verdant light among the thick columnar firs, climbing peaks in the Olympics, practicing driving home timber spikes, telling stories of his own environmental actions, including the time he drank beer with Ed Abbey at a rally against the Glen Canyon Dam—Dan felt a knot of guilt pulse in his chest for leaving Paul to carry this out on his own. He knew his own methods in the Park were outdated, that the trick now, among gentler outfits (he'd recently been in contact with some that believed in using any force necessary, even the most ruthless) was to get sound-bites on the news, images of big banners with clearly worded messages, to carry the fight with words and blogs and such, and maybe that's what he should have been teaching Paul . . . but it wasn't what he knew, and something needed to be done fast.

He especially regretted the gun, an old Smith and Wesson pistol. Three times before Paul left to climb the ridge and three times as Dan watched him make his way up it, he'd considered taking back the gun and come close to doing so. It used to be the case that no group he'd ever worked with in the past, not even the most radical, no environmental group he'd ever heard of, in fact, had ever used or suggested the use of a gun. But now the field was divided. Some organizations like ELF thought the only way to get noticed and make a difference was to use the weapons of the sanctioned terrorists who were in power against them. There was something to that, Dan thought. He reminded himself that he'd made it clear the gun was to be used only for defense, but he couldn't dismiss the possibility that it was dangerous for Paul to have a gun, regardless of whether or not he used it.

As he drove along beside the yawning drops to either side of the old road, catastrophic scenarios played in his mind—Paul shooting someone; someone shooting Paul; a group of loggers capturing and beating up Paul, their ire fueled by this capacity to do them harm—even as he tried to convince himself that Paul knew the Olympics too well to get caught, that he'd versed Paul in enough possible scenarios to ensure the effectiveness of the sabotage and the safety of his young protégé; that it was very unlikely Paul would need to use the gun and possible that the threat the gun could provide might even save his life. Still, it was clear that for the next few days he was going to swing back and forth on the subject of the gun till Paul returned safely and he could take it back and apologize to him for ever suggesting he use it.

Dan thought of the first time he'd seen Paul, the day he appeared in the ranger's office at Heart o' the Hills. Paul was only fourteen but already in possession of the almost impossible-to-pin-down *spirit* of affinity with Olympic and all it stood for. Even if Paul didn't articulate it at first, Dan could see it in him. From the moment of their first conversation, even though Paul gave brief, quiet answers during the interview, he could tell by the way the young man carried himself—the way he listened, the way he talked about his time in the woods with humility and respect for the place and the life it supported, punctuating his stories with a small, quiet smile—that Paul was the perfect candidate to carry on the protection of the Park.

At last! Dan told himself that day and again as he came to know the young man better: the next generation was stepping up to shoulder its burden! All was not lost. He confided in his closest friends that upon meeting Paul he felt like a sports scout discovering a great new talent—a basketball prodigy in a South Chicago project, a young soccer genius in a Sao Paulo shantytown. At other times, he compared his discovery of Paul to finding a species widely thought to be extinct. He had come to think that all young people ever liked to do was go to the mall, eat junk food, and play video games. Over time, Dan had formed fantasies in which Paul was a rising star who would one day shoot into glorious activist prominence, a warrior who would help save what really mattered.

When people who knew Dan well heard him talk in such glowing terms about Paul, they thought about Dan's former wife and their son who would be about the same age as Paul now. They remembered hearing that the wife and son were living somewhere back East—and how strange, they thought, that Dan never seemed to mention either one.

Paul worked on Dan's crew, clearing brush from the Hoh River trail that first summer, four years ago. From the beginning he'd done the work of two men twice his age, as if he'd been born to it. He possessed a steady energy that stood in opposition to the manic bursts you often saw in kids this age. He never seemed to tire, could shimmy up a tree or a rock face like it was nothing, carry over a hundred pounds of brush or tools a good distance, and he had a common sense about the best way to approach the obstacles you encountered in trail restoration. He was also willing to listen and learn. They made a game out of identifying the local fauna as they moved along a trail so that oxalis, Nootka rose, partridgefoot, youth-on-age, artist's conk, Pacific bleeding heart began to roll off Paul's tongue with precocious ease. Before the first summer was out, Paul knew many of the plant species they passed. From there, they moved on to the wealth of obscure amphibians and birds—the salamanders of the high lakes, the murrelets and harlequin ducks that swam up the rivers from the ocean every spring to breed. It was said that a single Douglas fir tree could house thousands of species.

Hiking down a trail after completing a maintenance project deep in the Park, they'd sometimes challenge one another to name the major rivers around the Park. Once the game was no longer a challenge, they sang the river names to whatever tune came into their heads: "Elwha, Sol Duc, Bogachiel, Calawha, Hoh, Queets, Quinault, Wynoochee, Skokomish, Hamma Hamma, Duckabush, Dosewalips, Dungeness." Dan said that the poet Richard Hugo had once written that the rivers of the Peninsula had good names, and Paul said he agreed. Once they'd sung all the major drainages, the whole wheelspoke of major river valleys coming off the Olympics, they sometimes sang the river names out of order and in hybrid combinations as they gamboled down the trail, high on the fresh air and endorphins, inspired in their earnest praise, exuberantly riffing in this new language and quite beyond their typical, off-mountain personalities.

During Paul's third consecutive year in the woods, at the end of the summer, when they were mid-descent and perched on a small shelf of a peak called The Incisor in the Needles Range between Mount Deception to the south and the Gray Wolf Range to the north, Dan looked down at Royal Lake and the sparkling ribbon of the upper Dungeness River and told Paul about the covert work he'd been organizing for years. Some tears came to his eyes as he talked. "It was all because of this," he said, pointing at the rugged view below them. A front was moving in and there was a low rumbling of thunder. As a federal employee whose job, let alone freedom, would be on the line for any deviation from Park policy, he had to be careful to keep a low profile, he explained to Paul, but he sometimes sought help. It took a constant vigilance to defend true wilderness, and he often needed the help of people who were not getting checks from the government to carry out actions for him.

"I'm thinking of doing something to make sure we keep them from making timber out of the trees in the Temple Grove," he told Paul. "I got a tip they're going to start cutting in there now that everything's quieted down from the protests last summer. I'd love to have your help," he said. "No pressure. It's a big decision. A risky one."

"Won't they back down if people know about it again and the tree sitters and everybody else comes in, like last time?"

"Maybe. But outfits like this only see dollars, and they'll always come back until they get what they paid for."

Paul was quiet for a time, looking out at the country below them, at the front moving in, a wall of grey clouds running almost to black. Again, there were some low mutterings of thunder. "I'll do it," he said, looking Dan in the eyes, then letting his gaze slide down the scar tissue on the furrows, then back to his eyes.

Dan clasped Paul's shoulder and nodded with great import.

During the fall and winter, while other kids in his class were playing sports and going to parties, figuring out how to get someone of age to buy them beer, Paul went up into the Olympics. He went every weekend, many times into the Douglas firs of the Temple Grove with their towering heights of almost 250 feet and their eight-foot-diameter boughs and their thick, furrowed bark. His purpose was to see if anything was yet afoot. Sometimes he went to other places, in the interminable rain, and, in the higher country, in the snow that blanketed the forests and the upper reaches of the mountains, slogging over muddy trails, gliding over wet snow on cross-country skis rigged with skids. Sometimes he went with Dan, sometimes he went on his own. When he went with Dan, Dan told Paul of the actions he'd accomplished in the past, the wild places he'd saved, or tried to, from the constant onslaught of extraction and development interests, his covert monkey-wrenching days in the desert southwest and the giant sequoia groves of northern California, and, again, about the day he met Ed Abbey at the Earthfirst! rally.

The current administration had set a high number for the amount of board feet that could be extracted from the National Forest in the region. In this case, there was also a "disputed territory." A zealous Forest Service boss with Washington, D.C., clout claimed to have discovered a surveying error that placed a stand of old-growth Douglas fir in the National Park under Forest Service jurisdiction.

It was unacceptable, unthinkable, this raid on the place he loved. To Dan's mind, all 1,400 square miles, some 900,000 rugged but delicate acres of the Olympics (and it should have been more than that, especially along river corridors and in the area to the west of the Park) and places like it and their continued protection were the greatest American endeavor. Protecting world heritage sites around the world was the highest cause, bar none. Protecting this place and places like it was more important than space exploration, more important than (but intricately related to) developing better health care, and certainly one hundred times more important than "growing the economy." People could live with less. If the economy had to grow, it should only grow in ways that benefited or enhanced the country's natural beauty and the intricate ecosystems on which natural beauty relied. He envisioned a nation of outdoorsmen and women, all with healthy bodies and a profound respect for natural beauty and the high that came only through close communion with a perfect natural ecosystem. His great sadness was the knowledge that this would never happen, and his great challenge was figuring out how to live, himself, in a world where this would never happen.

The federal attack on the appeals process and the cuts to national park budgets and the general direction in which the country seemed to be headed—*toward* a Las Vegas that was the fastest growing city in the country, *toward* a sport, also the fastest growing he was told, that celebrated noise pollution and buffoons plastered in corporate logos in an endless, idiotic circling of a concrete track, and *toward* breaks for big businesses that polluted rivers and spewed greenhouse emissions, and *toward* increased obesity—was anathema to this vision. It enraged him so much that a good friend had bought and hung from his living-room ceiling, not far from the television, a punching bag so he could achieve immediate release when he heard a plastic newsperson tell him in a saccharine voice where his country was heading, spouting on about the Economy as if it was some force to which humans were beholden, and not the other way around. He'd landed gut-crushing punches, absolute haymakers, on the president and vice president and the secretary of defense and direct hits to the noses of any number of pundits and gut punches to executives at any number of corporations.

People could change. Former loggers could run lodges. Cowboys could become dude ranchers. Mine operators could go into the salvage business or into researching and developing clean fuel options. Developers could harness their greed and turn their time and attention to developing blighted urban areas. People in general could define their sense of worth and personhood in areas other than from the stuff they could buy cheaply in box stores. The animals and the land, on the other hand, could not change; millions of years of evolution, snuffed out, could not be recovered. Old-growth Douglas firs, such as those in the Temple Grove, took thousands of years to grow and establish their enchanted biome. Hatchery salmon were a dim version of the wild.

Despite his rage and the need for action, Dan couldn't risk his own position as a federal employee (and the press that would follow) if it was discovered that for some time he'd been organizing small actions on behalf of the voiceless spirit of the Olympics. His anonymity was essential. He needed lieutenants to carry out the actions, which he had recently been expanding through new contacts. It was getting harder, not easier, in this supposedly enlightened age, to get help in the Park with clearing trails and manning stations, let alone to find anyone willing to participate in covert action. Over the years he'd planned a number of actions, always behind the scenes, usually after finding someone else to carry them out. He'd organized the burning down of a controversial storage structure that had been helicoptered into a campsite in the Enchanted Valley. He'd written anonymous letters to the editor at the *Peninsula Daily News* in favor of the reintroduction of wolves into the Park, the removal of dams from the Elwha, and the extension of the Park to include all the river systems in their entirety from headwaters to ocean mouths. On countless occasions, he acted like a company man, then did whatever he felt was best for the Park in its wildest, most natural condition.

The Temple Grove controversy was a familiar subject on the Peninsula. For an entire year, two years ago, a good amount of space every day in the *Peninsula Daily News* was devoted to the National Forest's controversial claim that a surveying error meant a swath of National Park land on which stood a grove of tremendous Douglas firs was actually National Forest land, and, as such, available for harvest in order to help the National Forest reach its stated timber quota. The forester now in charge had vowed to reach the maximum quota. Timberforus

Incorporated, a big player in the timber industry, had been awarded the contract. These interests seemed to have backed down after a wave of noisy protests that played out in public hearings and newspaper articles and editorial columns that split along predictable lines. The timber companies said it would be good for the economy, would give folks jobs and provide timber for use in American homes and for export overseas. Several environmental and Park watchdog groups vowed that any harvesting in the Park was an outrage. They organized campaigns to stop it. Some groups vowed action. A group of tree sitters set up camp in the area and took to calling it the Temple Grove. Timberforus Incorporated and the National Forest Service officially backed off, but they did so while reminding people of their legal right, given court decisions, to go in after the millions of board feet. They made their decision not to go after the timber sound like a noble sacrifice. Placated, the tree sitters went away. The Park watchdog groups sighed their relief.

With the backing of a current federal administration more friendly to extraction economies than to preservation, Timberforus was making a quiet, unofficial incursion into the Park after removing the appeals process that might question such an incursion. For a time, Dan had thought it best to alert the press to this tip, but it sickened him to think of another round of hearings and press conferences, this time with all eyes on him as he tried to shoulder the burden of proof for something a repentant logger had whispered in passing only after hearing Dan swear to protect his anonymity. That would be time of his life ticked away, time when he'd be stuck in the squalid, airless land of bureaucrats. Something like that could rot your soul, ensure that an entire chapter of your life passed indoors. He decided to respond to their covert attempt in kind, to fight the silent, private attack with a silent, private response. When there were spikes in boughs of some of the biggest Doug' firs in that stand, he would anonymously alert the media.

As Dan rounded one of the last bends in the winding gravel road, not far from the place where it joined 101, headlights appeared in front of him. A dark SUV was parked at a diagonal, blocking the narrow road. Someone was getting out of the passenger-side door.

Dan stopped the truck and started to put it in reverse. Light and shadow suddenly filled it from behind. More headlights. Another black SUV—where could it have come from?—blocked his retreat. Dan looked at the steep, forested ridge to his right, the gully to his left. In front of him and behind him were men he could see only in silhouette.

The man who'd stepped out of the first SUV had a megaphone. Other men beside this man had drawn pistols. Men with drawn pistols had also stepped out of the SUV behind the truck.

One of these men was a new agent fresh from Quantico named Brent Sawtelle. He'd been given notice that he would be on the case two days before his two-year-old daughter's birthday, and he was calling home whenever he could to have long conversations with his wife, Sandy, about whether or not it made sense, considering their young family, to stay with the Bureau. He had grown up in Eugene, Oregon, where he was raised by a mother and stepfather whose off-the-grid home-schooling pushed him in the opposite direction of what they intended. He'd taken up football in high school, then played free safety for the Ducks for four years before further dismaying his parents by taking the necessary tests to become a federal agent. Now, he was standing on an old logging road on a cold, clear night beneath brooding western hemlocks, a silhouette with a gun, because his superiors thought he could provide some Pacific Northwestern know-how to this case. He was thrilled by the terrain around them and by this contact with an adversary who had up to this point been just a name in a dossier. He clutched his pistol and waited to see what this Dan Kelsoe might do—this man who had gone rogue in order to put innocent United States citizens in harm's way, this traitorous man they thought might be connected with, if not directly involved in planning, bombings at a University of Washington laboratory and at SUV dealerships in Seattle and Portland.

The man with the megaphone called out: "Dan Kelsoe! This is the FBI. You are under arrest. Step out of the vehicle with your hands behind your head."

4

Bill Newton drove out of the Albertsons parking lot, casting worried glances in the rear-view mirror, his heart racing from the encounter with the Makah girl whose image he'd carried with him for so long in memory and dream that seeing her again in person felt like it might wind up being the messy end of him.

She'd looked nearly the same as her imagined avatar—a little heavier, perhaps, more wrinkles around the eyes. The collision between the psychic and real versions of the girl had set a mechanism whirring in his chest that cycled his blood so emphatically he thought something would burst if he didn't find release. He hit the dash with his right fist and damned the thirty joyless seconds nineteen years ago that had so altered the course of his life. Then, feeling guilty for the outburst and for the memory of moving up the trail in the wobbly legged aftermath with the wind roaring after him up the valley, he ran the fingers of his left hand over a scrimshaw bear he kept in his left shirt pocket. Over the last few years, ever since he'd carved it and it hadn't sold, he'd taken to worrying it behind a threadbare section of his shirt pocket, a touchstone to accompany his prayers for better luck. He wondered, now, if fate had led him to the girl at the mouth of the frozen-food aisle due to inattentiveness to this bear, or whether he'd seen her due to some deeper flaw in his faith, or if something else he could never imagine or understand, no matter how much he tried, had left him vulnerable to this re-encounter. He said again the words he'd tried to say to her, whispered them to try to slow the panic: "I'm sorry for what happened. Please forgive me."

He maneuvered the pickup through the curves of the road to the west of town, reminding himself not to arouse suspicion by driving too fast. He didn't want to go back to Alaska. This place felt like home in ways Alaska never would. He would need to shop somewhere else to provision himself for the godsend of a job he'd landed, good work up in the woods, and when the job was done he would need to find somewhere else to live. He stopped the truck on a gravel turn-out, sat breathing for a time to try to settle his nerves, then turned the truck around and drove back in the direction of his mother's house where he planned to call the gyppo Smitty. Once he'd checked in with Smitty to see if he could start the job early, he would drive on to Forks to provision himself. After the job, he would need to leave town again—maybe go to work with his brother at Seiku, maybe head back east. Maybe . . . who knew what he would do?

He found some relief in the fact that he would be able to get away for a while in a place where he could think about his next move and told himself he was lucky to have run into the gyppo Smitty at his mother's funeral at the cemetery overlooking the Strait.

On the night when he first met the girl, Bill Newton had rappelled down a sandy cliff face with a sycophantic pseudo-friend named Shoot Morely. They were taking a shortcut to an ocean beach in Olympic National Park. Shoot, who knew the area because he sometimes stole things from hikers' cars at a Park trailhead, kept shouting, "What's the word?" and answering himself, "Thunderbird!" a pint of wine of that name clutched in the hand that wasn't holding the rope. "What's the price?" he howled into the night, into the driving spears of rain. "Dollar twice!" he answered himself.

Earlier that day a bunch of Hells Angels had come up 101, two by two, hogs rumbling, roaring, spewing exhaust into the air for the cedar, hemlock, and spruce to ingest and purify, if they could, for a cougar following strong deer scent through thick sword fern on a ridge above the Bogachiel to sniff at and frown over, for the verdant, rain-soaked land to deal with how it would.

On a logging road 300 yards up a ridge, a man in a flannel shirt and stagged-off overalls climbed into the cab of his truck and picked up his CB: "Here they come," he said, and started it up.

Ten miles from the spinning wheel of the lead angel's Harley, their convoy of fifteen trucks rolled into motion, turned onto 101, and headed east. Bill rode shotgun in the lead truck, his arm out the window, flannel hickory shirt folded up on the forearm, curly black hair waving in the wind, deep-set brown eyes fixed down the road, his face inscrutable as an iron door.

At a preordained place, the driver stopped the truck and maneuvered it so that it blocked both lanes. The men in the other trucks got out and stood in the highway. Some friends who worked on road crews had set up orange cones to stop any other traffic both ways.

The angels numbered more than twenty and seemed comfortable in their velocity. One or the other of them drifted ahead, fell behind. They came in a line, of a piece, like a great snake, swallowing road en route to a rally in Sequim, "the hole in the sky," where, due to an anomalous flow of air currents off the Strait of Juan de Fuca up to the peaks of the Olympics, it rained less than it did in Phoenix despite its proximity to rain forests. Sequim was also where "the Duke" had had a home, and some of the angels thought that was all right and others thought John Wayne was a Hollywood pussy.

Their arms were festooned with tattoos—*Shelly Forever* x'd out, *Mom* (heart and arrow), dragons, demons, skulls, *Angelica Forever* jolly-rogered out, Vietnam platoon numbers—and some of their girls clung to them like baby raccoons. They'd come up the Pacific Coast from California and leaned into their turns along the curvy road. Above them, the peaks of the Olympics, rising beyond ridge on timbered ridge, looked down—solemn, unreadable, impassive as gods in the distance.

The lead angel saw the truck blocking the road before the rest. He raised a black-gloved hand in warning. The riders squinted to better see the nature of the obstacle: likely a wreck, they thought, deer run out in front of a truck.

But if that were the case—one or two of them must have been wondering, as, nearing the obstacle, they slowed their bikes—then who were these men standing in front of a truck filled with stripped timber, thick arms folded across barrel chests, nearly to a man dressed in hickory shirts and overalls with the cuffs stagged off well above caulked boots the angels would feel before the day was over.

The angels stopped and stood off their bikes a hundred feet from the truck.

Loggers and angels fanned out across 101, at either side of which the trees were thick and tall and rose from the road on steep ridges, the tips pointing up at the grey sky.

None of the combatants who flung themselves into the melee did so with as little regard for his own safety as Bill Newton. For its duration he remained in the thickest part of the fight, manhandling men who had thought themselves invincible in a hand-to-hand scrap until the very moment they found themselves moving in unexpected directions.

The local authorities—family, friends, classmates of the loggers—looked the other way. Angels hitched and limped into Port Angeles, Joyce, and Sappho, some of them several days later. Others hitched back to California, vowing revenge.

After the fight, Bill roared in glory into Skidders Tavern on the outskirts of Forks with the other victorious lumbermen and some bandwagoning locals who hadn't been there but claimed front and center status. The men drank their fill of Rainier, Olympia, and Old Grand Dad.

"Kicked their asses again," they said, "just like we did at the Hang-Up back in '79."

Bill stood at the epicenter of the celebration, a head taller than anyone else in the room's fugged space, and listened to the wits among their crew hail him as the battle's great hero. His curly hair grazed his shoulders; his eyes glanced at his admirers who clamored to buy him beers. A beard almost hid his mysterious smile, which was friendly seeming when it opened on occasion in the otherwise inscrutable wall of his face. Adrenaline from the recent fight coursed electric through him, and, though he didn't say anything, his thoughts turned to the possibility of even greater pleasure from this night, even though in another part of his mind he knew it was foolish to expect a crescendo in pleasure from such or any night. With this realization, each drink he took was an early, half-conscious attempt to stave off a little longer the inevitable coming down from the rush of the fight and going home alone to fall asleep to rain on the roof of his single-wide at the Alder Grove Trailer Park.

A hapless angel, by the looks of him, and the girl with him opened the bar door, and both of them looked with surprise upon the scene they beheld—large men in overalls and flannel shirts, wild-eyed in celebration. For only a moment, the man's eyes met Bill's, and Bill opened his wide, unexpected smile in the wall of his face. A few silent seconds were followed by a great hubbub of voices as the loggers recognized the angel as one of their defeated adversaries. The door closed and some of the hangers-on, eager for a greater part in the tale, opened it and gave halfhearted chase in the drizzly night only to return a few minutes later to report that the man and his girl were running along the side of the road like a couple of wingless spotted owls.

The appearance of the angel heightened the festive atmosphere in Skidders. The men turned their imaginations back to the fight. They told Bill's part in the tale, exaggerating liberally, and bedecked him with a warped chrome rim. Bill stood in the midst of the men in the bar, the metal rim resting on his great shoulders, saying not a word, as those who had done much less in the fight grew louder. Over time, their loudness and the drinks they handed him, one after another, intensified his inwardness. He smiled at their jokes to keep them from asking "What's the matter, big fella," which, depending on their tone and his mood (as the ones who knew him knew too well) in the particular moment, might have led to blows.

Though you could rib him about it, and many of them did when he was sober and eating lunch at the jobsite, you especially did not want to say anything when he was drunk or in the wrong frame of mind about the fact that he was a virgin.

An old-timer at the bar thumbed toward him. "Billy there's a thoroughbred of a logman. Real crackerjack fernhopper. Traces his roots back to 'High-Wire' Jim Newton, who worked for Merrill and Ring in the Pysht around dubya dubya one."

"That right?" said his companion.

The man nodded. "Old Jimmy helped 'em cut down two-billion board foot of timber. Mostly spruce. Used to free climb 250-foot trees—harness and chains be damned. He'd saw off the top of a tree and stand on the cut surface, a-swaying with the unsettled trunk. Crazy bastard. Used to run barefoot through blackberry bushes on a dare. Climbed peaks in the Olympics with no special equipment during the day, and high-tailed back to Forks to dance all night. They say one time he fell a hundred foot from the top of a Sitka spruce, landed in the mud—walked it off—no damage but bruised insteps." The man nodded again, his face growing red, smiling, getting worked up by the telling. He became suddenly somber: "Died when a crane fell over while he was working on the Grand Coulee." Then he whispered to his companion with a nod toward Bill. "He's a good kid. Had a tough go of it. Family's been a bit troubled since Old Jimmy passed and that was some time ago. The father was a bad drinker. Didn't kill him though. Died in the woods when a big gust sent a spruce back at him. That boy there could have probably wrote his own ticket in football but chose to start making money in the woods as soon as he could."

Spifflicated loggers spilled out of Skidders, started trucks, and dispersed into the drizzly night. Bill and Shoot Morley stumbled into the gravel parking lot after the others. To Shoot's way of thinking, it seemed a shame the night had to end when he felt like howling and there was only bachelor filth and gloom in his camper near the Quileute.

"M' on," Shoot said in a nasal rasp, his nose having been broken in the brawl, his flannel shirt splotched in a new world map of blood. "A man that won't fuck won't fight and vice versa's what I say. Seeing as we had the latter, I know a place where we can go to find the former."

Bill stood in the rain, tottered in the gravel. "I'm not going to a whorehouse . . . or any kind of freelance whore," he said.

"M' on," Shoot repeated. "This is different. Real, actual girls, if you don't mind Indians." The neon Rainier Beer sign in the window blinked a red tinge to the parking lot puddles. Shoot smiled, revealing a set of teeth full of gaps. He grabbed Bill's shoulders, and steered him into the passenger side of his truck, which tossed along the road like a spawning salmon nearing its death throes, taillights making standing rainwater in the unevenness of the wet concrete look bloodfilled and portentous.

Bill passed out, his black-maned head swaying with the motion of the car as Shoot weaved them into the rain across and back over the yellow lines, beneath hills filled with stumps and snarly patches of clear-cut slopes, beyond further hills arcing higher and higher until they became the peaks of the Olympics.

The truck's headlights briefly caught fire, threw sparks—one then the other—and Bill, awakening, mumbled as much to Shoot, to which Shoot replied with a ramshackle grin and high coyote cackle, "We don't need no god-damn *lights*!"

Bill looked into the focusless blackness, frowned, shook his head, went back to sleep, and dreamed of a girl of irenic stillness in a light-blue sundress walking through the doors of Skidders. She fixed her pale green eyes on only him and took his hand and led him out of the bar in front of all the men under a sky full of stars.

Shoot dead-reckoned them into the spears of rain. When they were at the trailhead, Shoot nudged Bill awake. They stumbled out of the truck into the forest through the rain, at a certain point using a rope to descend a sandy cliff, cussing when they slipped. One time, Bill swung over on his rope to try to sock Shoot for getting them into this.

Shoot swung out of the way, his laughter cut up by the rain. "Short cut," he said.

At the bottom of the cliff, they felt their way into the darkness, through trembling leaves. Bill was sobering up, and the soberer he got, the meaner he felt. The glory he had won in the fight with the angels and its celebration at Skidders was already fading. Here already was the coming down. He took the rim which was still around his neck and hurled it at a nearby tree. It whirred through the air and hit the bough with a dull thud, shaking rainwater down on them.

"That's using your head," said Shoot, and Bill turned to face him with belligerent intent. Thinking quickly, Shoot offered Bill the flask of Thunderbird and was relieved when Bill accepted it. Bill took a long pull, letting some of the harsh liquid drip down his black beard.

"That's awful," he said.

Shoot watched him with a sort of reverent awe. He crouched low and bent his knees: "What's the word?" he sang, dancing around Bill in sudden and inexplicably gleeful anticipation.

Bill shook his head and started walking.

"Come on," Shoot repeated. "What's the word?"

Bill kept on.

"Thunderbird!" Shoot answered himself. "What's the price?"

Bill did not answer.

"Dollar twice!" sang Shoot. He laughed and added, "My old man's favorite rhyme."

As they continued to push through the underbrush, Bill felt a pleasant pressure return to his head. After a time, they saw the glow of a campfire twenty-five yards through the trees. Its flickering light fell on flecks of rain, seven or so glowing faces broken by face-bound beer cans, scattered driftwood and logs, a portion of beach, and—farther off and dimmer—the sheen of thin water spread across sand, the white foam of broken and breaking waves. They heard voices, laughter interspersed with surfroar.

"What I tell you?" said Shoot, crouching down. Cackling under his breath, he looked up at Bill, whose black eyes were fixed in an attitude of stupefied hunger on one of three girls gathered around the fire.

She was no more than seventeen. Her cheeks burned in the firelight. Her eyes sparkled when she laughed, and her long black hair, under a lavender woolen hat, fell down over her shoulders.

Bill stood up, ignoring Shoot's whispered remonstrances, and strode the distance between himself and the circle of faces around the fire, keeping his eyes on the girl.

5

Trace unlocked the door of the Marine Life Center and walked into its main room, which was filled with tanks and human-made tide pools, charts and illustrations of marine flora and fauna, glass cases of shells and bones. It smelled salty and dank, the air alive with the bubble and buzz of filtration systems.

She stopped and peered into a rectangular glass aquarium near the door and took some time to find Pishpish, a giant Pacific octopus a fisherman had brought in six months ago in a rusty coffee can.

Pishpish was in the corner of the tank, just outside the cave they had made for her. Water filtered through the funnel below her eye and cheek, and ripples ran through her amorphous body which was, for the moment, a grey and brown patchwork, a contented color. Her horizontal slit eye—shaped like a slight, enigmatic smile—fixed on Trace, suggesting an intelligent regard and a capacity for mischief.

On some days Pishpish remained a depressed darker brown for long periods of time and sulked in the corner, curling and uncurling the end of one of her arms and ignoring Trace, scarcely moving even for a squid or abalone.

One day, after Pishpish had been in the Marine Center for two weeks, Trace was surprised to feel a sudden squirt of water hitting the back of her neck and wetting the back of her shirt as she walked by the tank. When she turned to look, Pishpish was sinking beneath the surface, the wet circular mark of one of her suction cups still on the outside of the glass of her aquarium, the tips of three of her legs in motion, an undeniable smirk in her eye.

When groups of children came through for their second- and fifth-grade visits, Trace told them about Pishpish, feeling as she did so, that she and Pishpish were a team, working together in a performance. Trace gave the kids her octopus speech, told them that Pishpish was three-feet long and growing almost a pound a week; that the biggest octopuses in the world lived under the water of their very own Strait of Juan de Fuca, sometimes growing as long as twenty feet and more than 100 pounds; that they were as intelligent as house cats (*pishpish* meant cat in Makah); that Pishpish liked to eat red rock crabs, oysters, scallops, and abalone; and that her diet in the Marine Center was a crab a day.

To the older kids, Trace described, in quick, vague terms in an often unsuccessful attempt to avoid wisecracks, how octopuses mated. The male octopus passed spermatophores (sperm packets) through a groove in its third right arm into a spoonlike appendage at its end called a hectocotylus, which he used to deposit the spermatophores in the female's pouchlike mantle.

Trace didn't tell the kids who came through on these tours that sex between octopuses was an intense emotional experience judging from the rippling rainbow of colors they exhibited during the act, which could last as long as three hours. After the male used an arm, (part of which he lost) to deposit the spermatophores in the female's mantle, she got to choose when and if she would use one of her own arms to complete fertilization, a process that would culminate in 50,000 octopuses, each no bigger than a human eyeball, and in the mother's starvation and death. The death was sad and colored by the poignancy of this sacrifice, but what amazed Trace and what she often thought about when she looked in on Pishpish, seeing her own reflection in the glass of the aquarium if she shifted focus, was the choice the female octopus had. She chose when and if to impregnate herself after the act, chose the fertilization and her own death for the perpetuation of the species.

Maybe that's why her mother and the other Makah elders called the octopus the "devilfish" and said it was bad luck to look at an octopus when you were pregnant. Now, Trace wondered if this warning had filtered into the common pool of wisdom because looking at an octopus, with its amorphous shape and all those arms with their suction cups, could remind you of the choices you'd made and couldn't reverse and the more limited choices you still had.

When Paul made his fifth-grade visit to the Marine Life Center, Trace had been especially careful not to embarrass him in front of his classmates. She'd noticed how he seemed withdrawn, unwilling to acknowledge knowing her. She decided not to blow his cover, although once, when it seemed no one else was looking, she crossed her eyes at him and he smiled in spite of himself.

Trace dropped a red rock crab into Pishpish's tank and watched as Pishpish rippled gracefully over to engulf it. The octopus would subdue the crab, pierce it with her radula, turn it into an ingestible liquid, and slurp it in.

When Trace looked up from the tank, she noticed a girl who looked vaguely familiar standing in front of the Center's glass doors.

Trace opened one of the doors and said, "We're not open yet. You can come back at nine."

"Oh, sorry," the girl said. "But I'm actually here for something else." For a moment the girl looked as if she was going to leave, but then she said, "Are you Paul Granger's mother?"

"Yes," Trace answered and suddenly recognized Stephanie Barefoot, the girl who had organized the petition to save Paul from expulsion. Trace had made a point of noticing her when her name was called at Paul's graduation ceremony and had thought, as she saw her take the stage, there she is, the girl who was kind and brave when she didn't need to be.

"Well, I, we, some of us, were wondering where he is," the girl said. She was tall and thin, slightly leggy and awkward-looking. She had long, straight brown hair and wore a T-shirt advertising a wooden boat festival in Port Townsend.

"You're Stephanie, right?" Trace said. "The one who helped him out. That was a big deal for us."

"Yes—I mean, good," the girl answered and smiled. "He deserved it. It was totally the right thing to do."

They stood in silence for a moment. "Well, I haven't seen him at any of the graduation parties or anything," the girl said. "And nobody knows where he is. So, I thought I'd try to track him down."

A chorus telling her she was a bad mother had plagued Trace from the day of Paul's birth. Its volume had only increased after his fall into the Elwha, and here it was again. It was always at its most acute when she was facing someone else or when she was forced to compare herself with other mothers, but even when she was alone the question arose with an often staggering directness.

To tell the girl the truth and admit she didn't know Paul's whereabouts was to admit she was a bad mother. To make something up was to run the risk of seeming suspicious and strange. "He's away for a while," she said, hoping that would be enough and the girl would go away.

"Oh," the girl said. "Away." She screwed up her face as if that might help her squeeze the word to extract more meaning. Even if the word worked, temporarily, it was clear the answer hadn't satisfied the girl. It's because she saved him, Trace thought. She expects more in return, proximity, knowledge.

Without saying anything else, not even thanks or goodbye, the girl turned and left Trace feeling as if she hadn't properly thanked the girl for all she'd done for Paul.

The next day, a few hours after Trace had opened the Center, the girl was back. Trace had just spent some time communing with Pishpish, who had remained a contented grey all morning, and was cutting up some herring to feed to the red rock, Dungeness, and spider crabs in the tidepool when suddenly the girl was saying, "I know you said he was away, but I was wondering, we've been wondering, some of us—where exactly is he?"

Trace wondered how she'd missed the tinkling of the bell on the door. She stared at the girl for some time. The girl's eyes looked clear and honest, if a bit indignant and mistrustful, perhaps perched on the brink of some kind of accusation. "I was about to close up and get lunch," Trace said. "Maybe you want to come with me?"

The girl gave Trace a quick, suspicious glance, then said, "Okay. Yes."

They went to a café and bookstore called "C. C. Gulls" in downtown Port Angeles. Trace leaned in over her club sandwich: "Thanks for doing what you did for Paul," she said and was surprised when it seemed as if she might begin to cry. "Like I said, that meant a lot to us."

"I had to do it," the girl said. "Otherwise it would have been so unfair. I was there when it happened. Brink Forger was holding Jason Parks's nose and mouth down in a bowl of noodle soup. Paul had warned Brink just two days before not to do anything to Jason Parks ever again. I sit at that table, so I saw him give Brink the warning. He was like, 'If you bother Parks again, you'll regret it.' And Brink was all tough like, 'We'll see about that.'"

Trace nodded and looked down at her plate. "I don't know where Paul is," she said, then continued, quiet and low, "I wish I did, and I wish he wouldn't do things like this to people who care about him. A few days ago he just left. He called, but he didn't tell me where he is or where he's going."

Stephanie nodded in an appreciative way, glad to have Trace's confidence.

Trace looked more closely at the girl in front of her, feeling, oddly, like she wanted something from Stephanie, that that was the real reason she'd asked her to lunch, but unsure what that could be, now that she'd already thanked the girl for helping Paul.

"So, he's missing?" Stephanie asked.

"No, no, he's not missing. Like I said, he called a few days ago to say he was all right and not to worry." Since the Brink Forger incident, she had a fear of revealing a lack of faith in him.

"But he didn't say where he was or what he's doing?"

Trace shook her head.

"That's *so* mysterious," the girl said. A faraway look animated her eyes even as they flashed at Trace. "It seems like that's the way he is. Is it? He doesn't talk a whole lot all the time and make a lot of noise all the time, like some, well, like most boys," she said. "I can't ever tell what he's thinking. I don't know what category to put him in, when most people are easy to peg. Some people say all he cares about is going up into the mountains."

It was peculiar to hear Paul characterized by someone his own age. She sometimes worried about him because he seemed not to have many friends except for the random hikers he met in the Olympics with whom he sometimes corresponded, people from all over the world, who were usually older than he. He gave monosyllabic answers to her questions about school. It was always fine, okay, all right. He was even more quiet with Tom, especially since he'd found out about the controversy surrounding the spill and the job with the old ships in India. She often found herself wanting to get more out of Paul, to hear him talk about what it was like to go to this mostly white school.

"Well," she told the girl, "that's not *all* he cares about," but she wasn't sure that was entirely true.

On weekend nights when cars full of kids out for a good time cruised along Front and First streets, the one-way thoroughfares into and out of town, east and west, whoops coming from the windows, she worried that Paul wasn't living it up like he ought to be, that in his apparent seriousness he was squandering his youth in much the same way she'd lost hers after his birth. More often than not he was off on a hike by himself up in the mountains—at one of the lakes or down in a river valley in the Olympics, winter and summer, cross-country skiing, mountaineering, clearing trails, building cedar walking-planks, helping capture mountain goats to be helicoptered out of the Park. For a time she'd tried to stop him from going up into the Park so often. She'd even enlisted Tom's help, but neither of them could stop him. There was something about his silent, dogged resistance that unnerved them, made it seem as if his passion was based in some beyond-his-years sort of wisdom they had better attend to and respect. At least he wasn't drinking and carousing. At least he had jobs in the summer. He'd sneak out and leave a note whenever they tried to keep him close to home. Finally, they gave up. They let him go and took to saying they only wished he wouldn't go alone. Sometimes, reading one of his notes—*Mom, Climbing Mt. Olympus with Dan. Be back Sunday night*—she remembered his baptism in the river and wondered if she would ever tell him that story.

"Tell me more about him." Stephanie asked. Trace was surprised by her directness. It occurred to her this was the very question she wanted to ask Stephanie.

The girl filled the space of silence before Trace could decide what to say: "I mean he's so quiet. And he doesn't hang out with anyone at school that much. He usually takes his lunch to one of the picnic tables outside and eats facing the mountains, even when it's cloudy and you can't see them. I heard the football coach wanted him to go out for the team because he's so big and strong and in shape and stuff, but he wouldn't do it. Most guys would kill to make the team. And he didn't ask anyone to prom or anything. And, when you talk to him, he waits, like, a couple seconds before he says anything, but it isn't because he's slow, it's because he's thinking and when he says what you're waiting for it's usually not that much but it's kind of surprising and right on target what he ends up saying . . ."

Trace wanted her to keep going, but it seemed inappropriate to ask someone else to tell you about your own son. "He's special," she heard herself say, regretting the word as soon as it was aired. "I mean, he doesn't care about a lot of the things most kids care a lot about. But he's steady and strong in what he does care about."

"What does he care about?" Stephanie asked.

Trace paused to think. "Well . . . ," this girl was going to make her work . . . "like you said, he loves . . . the mountains and the rivers and wild animals," she said. "He's up in those mountains every chance he gets. He's going to Oregon State in the fall, to study forestry." Trace paused a moment to worry that there wasn't readily something else to add to the list. She wanted to tell Stephanie something else, something only Trace knew, maybe a story that would illustrate how silly he could be. She remembered him at four or so running around the house with a colander on his head armed with a slotted spoon and at twelve playing "Purple Haze" on the CD player and mimicking Jimi Hendrix playing, smashing, and burning his guitar. She remembered his shy smile when he saw that she and Tom had seen and enjoyed his performance. When they were in Seattle one time, Paul had made them go to the Central District to find the house where Hendrix had grown up. Now Paul was into Death Cab for Cutie and Modest Mouse, she thought that was it—

unless it had changed, the way it did. Their relative closeness in age meant that their taste in music sometimes overlapped. But it seemed too soon to launch into all of this and more with the girl in front of her.

"I live up on Mt. Angeles Road with my father," Stephanie said, "and I've seen him riding his bike past our house with a humongous pack on his back. So big that the bike, like, teeters and totters."

"When he can't get a ride to a trailhead, he rides up to them himself. I tell him not to hitchhike, but people have told me they've seen him doing that, too." He'd gone through his truck phase, his dinosaur phase when he was younger, but from early on it was all about those mountains, getting out and getting up onto a trail into the wild.

"That's probably where he is now then? Up in the mountains somewhere?"

"Yes, I hope so. But he said he couldn't tell me where he was. Which is . . . strange."

Stephanie nodded.

"You've already helped him so much. Why are you looking for him?" Trace asked. "Why do you want to talk to him?"

A wild expression passed over the girl's face, and Trace realized what she should already have suspected. Stephanie's face flushed pink, and she shook her head. She looked down at the table, exhaled, and blushed more deeply.

Trace smiled.

"I want to get to know him better," Stephanie said, partially regaining her composure. "I've noticed him at school, and I thought this summer might be my last chance because I'm going away to college in the fall. If nothing else, I just want to say goodbye and I hope he'll keep in touch."

Trace chuckled and shook her head. Perhaps you also want to gloat a little, she thought, come see about the boy you saved. For a few years Trace had wondered when and if Paul was going to show an interest in girls. She'd suspected the interest was there, but he never revealed any evidence to her. It was as if every bit of interest and energy went into the mountains.

As they were walking up the sidewalk, Stephanie said, "I know who we could ask about where Paul could be. I doubt he's there because this place is . . . not such a good place. But we could go and look if you want, just to make sure he's okay."

For the rest of the slow day as Trace cleaned out tanks and fed some of the creatures in them, she wondered if anything would come of the girl's lead. She couldn't keep her suspicions about the girl completely at bay, even though she pushed them back when they arose.

That morning Trace had gotten an e-mail from Tom. The message had bounced around in cyberspace for a week, as all communications from the doomed ships seemed to do, before landing in her inbox. Sometimes e-mails from these ships never arrived, as if the ship itself had found a way to seek revenge for its own dead-letter mission. The e-mail read: *How're my two favorite people? We just stopped in Cape Town. Beautiful coastal city. Bringing home a Krugerrand. Hope all is well. Love, Tom.* She googled "krugerrand," and shook her head at the great variety of things that came up. She e-mailed him back a brief message—*Miss you, too. Be safe!—T.* She imagined him holding a gold coin—her nerdy mechanical whiz pirate, pleased with this savvy investment treasure—but she didn't mention Paul's absence because she knew these trips to Alang's ruined beach, with its dark, oily water, smell like warm mayonnaise, and jagged hulls of dead ships, upset him enough. By the time Tom got home, Paul would be back.

6

Bill Newton stopped in at his mother's house and called the gyppo Smitty to see if it was all right if he went to the site in that Doug' fir grove a few days early. His brother Troy had already stuck a *For Sale by Owner* sign in the front yard listing his Seiku number and gone back to work. Bill was relieved there was still a dial tone when he picked up the phone in the kitchen. Smitty sounded surprised by Bill's eagerness to get up in the woods earlier than planned, especially given his recent loss, but told him he guessed it would be all right if they went a little early and that his second faller would be Smitty's own nephew, a kid named Lincoln Maxey who was pretty green but stout. He reminded Bill of the necessity of keeping a low profile and of making up a story for anyone who might come by, aside from Forest Service workers, who had already surveyed the grove and were expecting them to begin working there. He reiterated the necessity for silence and reminded Bill not to mention his name or to say anything about Timberforus.

When Bill called him later that afternoon, the Maxey kid said, "What's your hurry? My uncle said you might not be going up for a while because of your mom just passing away."

"Changed my mind. Drive out and meet me in the parking lot of Jerry's Rentals on the south side of Forks." He gathered together some of the old camping gear that was still in the garage—an old frame pack, a few changes of clothes, his hunting knife, a Coleman lantern and stove covered in cobwebs and dust—and the Stihl with the 20-inch guidebar he'd already tested out on some unruly alders in the back yard, and five extra chains and plenty of oil. The Maxey kid, who was staying with Smitty's ex-wife, it turned out, was in his late teens and had a linebacker's build, hair cropped nearly bald in a number-one buzz, and a baseball cap that said *KCMHS Grunge*.

They rode away from Jerry's Rentals for a time in silence before Lincoln said, "My uncle tells me you been up in Alaska a long time."

Bill nodded.

"Good country up there. I worked on a crab boat in Bristol Bay last summer. What'd you do up there?"

"Worked on the pipeline a few years. Logging, when I could get it—near Ketchikan. Gill-netting salmon, herring, some hunting, sold a little scrimshaw. Worked maintenance at a . . . camp toward the end."

"What'd you hunt?"

"Brown bear, wolf, moose, caribou."

"My uncle says your dad and his dad and even his dad all worked in the woods."

"We've been at this a while."

"My family too," the boy said and looked out the window at the passing timber. "Why's it you left the first time, and for so long? I think some people were saying something about it one time."

"I was hoping you wouldn't be so much of a talker," Bill said.

"It's all right if you don't want to set the record straight. A lot of them say you got a raw deal from a half-Indian girl."

Bill gazed down the road, dappled in tree shadow.

The Maxey kid looked at Bill for a time as if considering pressing further, then pulled his cap over his eyes and went to sleep.

Bill drove on, eventually leaving the paved road for dusty gravel winding up into the woods. His mind lit on a time after the funeral when his mother was three days in the ground. About a dozen condolence cards were arrayed on the kitchen table. His brother Troy was passed out on the couch in front of the TV, having rationalized a three-day drunk. Bill decided to go to the store to get provisions for the woods, not realizing that what he saw there was going to end his hopes of making a fresh start back in the lower-48 by reminding him of the constraints that had driven him away in the first place. In that moment before he'd seen her in the store, he could still pretend a fresh start or something like it was possible.

As soon as he had arrived in Port Angeles from Alaska aboard a fishing boat, and three days before he saw the girl in the Albertsons, he'd hitched a ride to the Strait View Cemetery. He stepped out of a red truck onto a gravel turnaround and stood in the rain facing a field overspread with clusters of roses, American flags, headstones. In the distance, a small gathering in blurred rain jackets stood under a canvas tent on a patch of Astroturf near a casket and a fresh mound of brown earth. Beyond them, the field gave way to a cliff below which the Strait churned and roiled. The Olympics to the south were completely lost to cloud, grey on grey.

The truck idled, expelling exhaust. Bill looked across at the assembled, whose backs, with the exception of the reverend, faced him. He turned, and mumbled his thanks to the driver, a man who was retired from Weyerhaeuser, slung his olive-drab bag onto his shoulder, and shut the door. The truck crunched away on the gravel and sped up when it hit asphalt.

He pulled the hood of his black rainjacket over his head, looked cautiously both ways as if he might have been about to cross a busy street, and walked between the headstones toward the small gathering of folks with bowed heads.

Before he'd left for Alaska, the last time he'd been in the lower-48, he'd knocked on the door of the house and it had cracked open to reveal her big-jowled face, her sleepy eyes squinting down. "What is it? What's the matter, Billy?"

"Something's happened," he said. "And I got to go away for a while. Maybe a long time."

"Oh, whad'ya do? Whad'ya do, Billy?"

He shook his head. His shaggy black hair, covered at the crown of his skull with a bandage, rustled in the close room, smelling like smoke and rain.

"Billy, what's happened?

He shook his head again. "I can't tell you. Others will, so you got to stop asking," he said. "Hold out your hand," he said, and she did and he pressed a wad of soft bills into it. "I'll send more when I can," he said.

"Where you going? Come in, Billy. Come in."

It seemed to him she was putting on years in months. She still looked sleepy, but she was coming awake with worry, her wispy, greying hair wild above her head, her face overwritten with wrinkles, some of them, it occurred to him, attributable to worry he had caused her over the years, others his brother's to claim, still others their long-departed father's. Some were entirely her own stupid fault. He stepped toward her and started to embrace her, kiss her goodbye. But a sudden mixture of guilt and a feeling of unworthiness—a fear that he might infect her with his own bad luck and fundamental wrongness—made him stop. He turned away, walked across the gravel, ignoring her calls. "Billy. Tell me. What is it, Billy? What's going on? What's happened to your head?" Then, muttering to herself, "My big boy, my big baby boy."

That was the last time he'd seen her alive.

Many of the faces gathered around the grave looked familiar. From a distance, he looked from one to the next and tried their names in his mouth when he knew them. Many of them were his mother's friends from church, but there were also several men from the industry, some of his father's old buddies from Merrill and Ring. They were a pretty tight-knit community, united too often in their sorrow over lost jobs and uphill battles against the federal government and rich, latte-swilling urban environmentalists who wanted old trees as the playgrounds of their protracted youth.

Troy swayed a bit in the rain. He looked much older than Bill's memory of him. He had always been quite a bit smaller than Bill, and he was wearing a beard closer-clipped than Bill's and capped by a Buffalo Bill mustache. He wore thick lenses with big frames, dark-tinted despite the rain, that gave his eyes a magnified aspect. Bill also picked out and let his eyes linger for a time on Smitty, the old gyppo who was known for finding jobs in the woods even when they were scarce.

"Here lies a good, warm-hearted woman," the reverend was saying.

When the service was over, and as the crowd was slowly dispersing through the steady rain, Troy paused in front of Bill in a way that suggested he'd sensed something familiar about the hooded form lingering on their periphery, something familiar in it if it was not a shadowy figure from the great beyond come to shepherd Matilda Newton to her afterlife. Troy came around from the side and tried to peer under the tightly drawn hood to see the dark figure's face. As he made the attempt, Bill turned his head in a playfully furtive manner so that Troy had a difficult time.

"God damn. Billy!" Troy said. He threw his arms around his brother and squeezed hard.

"Had to come back for this."

Some of the other men—the gyppo Smitty and another man who had known his father in his Merrill and Ring days and their wives—had heard the reunion. Several of the slowly departing mourners looked over at them and whispered. Others stopped and stared. The man with Smitty, a skinny old man in a camouflage jacket, whispered something to Smitty and said to Bill, "I'll be damned. We figured you for a goner. We're sorry for your loss."

"I thought you might show up. I almost *knew* it," Troy said, casting a glance around to see if anyone present might make trouble for his older brother, his eyes tearing up. "I started looking for you in town soon as I got back."

"See you back at the house?" Smitty asked.

Bill nodded.

"How long can you stay for?" Troy asked.

"Don't know."

"We never told them *nothing*," Troy said. "They don't know *jack*," he said. "Hell, we didn't know jack. And we know you don't neither."

Bill nodded, frowned.

The reverend was waiting to speak to Troy.

"I wish you could have seen her before now," Troy said. "She wanted to visit you up there. So did I, but it never quite worked out."

Bill nodded. He caught a hint of liquor on his brother's breath. Troy turned to speak to the reverend.

Bill always thought he would see her again. He was glad he'd sent money back to her as he'd promised he would. When most of the mourners had left, he knelt before the grave and tried for a time to come up with something profound, something from the Bible he'd learned at the New Way Peak Oil Commune where he'd lived the last year. In the end he let the silence speak for him, imagining that now she could divine his feelings, even if he couldn't express them.

Bill rode in the front seat of his brother's truck to the house.

"So, where're you living now?" he asked.

"Out in Seiku," Troy said. "I work at Olympic Auto Body over there. Trying to save up to buy a boat. God damn, Bill. I can't get over you being back," he said. "Are you back to stay?"

"Don't know," Bill said. "Might see if there's any work around, something up in the woods."

Troy shook his head. "Pretty hard to come by nowadays with all the goddamn regulations."

Bill stood in the living room of the house where he'd grown up. He looked around at the décor, which hadn't changed much since he'd left, and occasionally glanced out the window at the rain falling on the driveway and over the rust-colored landscaping rocks on either side. A shelf of her Hummel figurines vibrated as mourners walked the floor. On the wall facing him was a laminated poem his mother had tacked up. It was by Luke Betts and had been published in *Loggers World:*

> *The Sins of the Logger*
> Oh, we have sinned and are not good
> Forgive us for these things we have made.
> Your house within which you live,
> Your toothpaste you use and most gifts that you give,
> Forgive us for our long hard days,
> Please take pity on us for our sins,
> For the paper you use,
> And your kindly abuse,
> For the posters and cards,
> For your boxes and boards,
> Even for your toilet paper too,
> This we have done, it is all true
> And for our families we work for,

For our kids to survive,
Forgive us for this,
But we can't live in your ignorant bliss.
For the money we raise for charities,
For the love of our profession,
For our work through good and bad years,
For ignoring your unjustified fears.
For replanting more than we ever take,
For not protesting you in your line of work,
For not telling you, you're polluting when you drive,
For not telling you you shouldn't survive.
Forgive us for making your protesting signs,
For making your holiday gift wrappings,
And definitely forgive us for your Christmas tree,
And for asking for peace between you and me.
Forgive us for building your home.
Forgive us for improving your forest,
Forgive us for our evil ways,
Forgive us for working for you through those long hard days,
But the next time you protest what you don't understand,
And refuse to educate yourself my friend,
Remember the sins of the loggers and for what they stand.
For supplying you with what your survival will demand.

On the refrigerator she'd hung up some editorials she'd written and published in the *Peninsula Daily News,* a new, somewhat surprising turn for her. One protested a proposed expansion of the National Park:

"Whenever I hear about the Park asking for *more* land, it makes me sick. I feel like I'm living in a country that doesn't believe in freedom and democracy where the government can just take whatever it wants and the people have no power to stop it. This Peninsula needs more, not less, job opportunities and locking up more land in the Park means fewer timber industry jobs for the good people of this Peninsula . . ."

Another she'd written to weigh in on the Temple Grove controversy: "Finally, the government is getting some sense about timber management and refusing to cave in to out-of-touch enviros. For too long too much land has been locked up in stupid regulations. Those trees in that Temple Grove everyone's talking about, which they proved are really in the National Forest not the Park because of a surveying error, will finally be used in the manner God intended when he created them for people to use. Anyone who says otherwise should join all those hippies out there making such a fuss and sit up in one of those trees with all those other tree huggers and ride a big fat Doug' fir to the ground when they cut 'em down!!"

An older woman approached him from across the room, the mother of one of his high-school classmates. In a long letter Bill's mother had written to him when he was in Ketchikan, she had told him that this woman's son had joined the navy after he and his father lost their jobs at the mill. Now, her son was living in Tacoma, working for the lazy B (a nickname for Boeing). "Hi, Billy," the woman said conspiratorially.

Seeing how much she'd aged, he realized how long he'd been gone.

"We know you didn't do it," she said. "Your mother loved you. It broke her heart when that Indian accused you of doing that *thing*. Must have been on peyote. Surprised she didn't say Sasquatch did it to her." She waved her hands and scrunched her face to indicate unspeakable injustice and the difficulty she would have had saying the thing of which he had been accused. "We know you're from a good family," she said and clasped one of his hands in both of hers.

Bill thanked her.

Troy was talking in close proximity and in low whispers with the gyppo Smitty and the man with him. Both men looked over at Bill on occasion and nodded. When they were finished talking, Troy came over and said, "Good news. Believe it or not, he said he can use you for a job that just come up, as long as you don't tell no one. Says in fact you might be the perfect one for it. Head faller on a two-man crew. He said he was taking a chance on you, 'cause of how he felt about Mom and Dad and because he remembers how good you used to be, but you got to keep it a secret."

Bill looked over at Smitty, who was talking to an elderly woman across the room. He nodded and Smitty nodded back. "When?"

"He don't know yet," Troy whispered. "Wants you to call and check in in a few days. It's on that grove there was such a stink about. Land they say is in the Park but shouldn't've been."

Bill pointed at his mother's editorials on the 'fridge.

Troy nodded. "Yeah, that's it."

A man from his father's era, who had run a feller-buncher in the Pysht came over. "Your mother's gotten pretty tight with Jack Ratner's wife, Phylis." When it was clear it hadn't registered with Bill what this meant, he said, "Retired police. Probably saw you at the cemetery. Kind of a do-gooder. Still close with some of the boys and might feel duty bound. Likely coming over. I imagine you must have a statute of limitations on your side in this, not saying you did anything wrong, now, but you never know."

Bill nodded his thanks, put on his coat, and went out the back door into the rain. Troy followed, gave him the keys to their mother's truck, and told him to call before he came back.

Just three days later, after his brother sobered up and went back to Seiku, Bill risked driving to the Albertsons to get some food to pack into the woods and saw Trace in the frozen-food aisle.

7

When Paul was three and Trace had some time off from her tables at Bushwhackers Restaurant and her new job as assistant at the Marine Life Center, and was between deadbeat boyfriends who'd come in a calamitous, if sometimes recklessly fun, series four years before she met Tom, she took Paul to see the tide pools on a beach on the Cape—the same place where Bill Newton had crashed out of the woods with Shoot Morely that night.

On the way to the trailhead, Paul pattered her with questions about the exact source of the opalescent color of the sky and why the yellow marks in the center of the road were sometimes dotted and sometimes a continuous line and why there was stripped timber in the logging trucks filled and speeding with abandon down the narrow road and why there were little trees growing out of the great stumps and why the dirty deer sleeping on the side of the road didn't move, and a hundred other why's.

They rode through Neah Bay to what everyone who lived there called "out-the-country" through a persistent drizzle, parked under a colossal Sitka spruce, and hiked three miles to the beach past salal, sword fern, skunk cabbage, and banana slugs trailing nacreous slime. It amazed her that he didn't get tired or complain of the distance, especially since some of it took them through long patches of mud. It seemed, instead, as if he was being patient with *her* pace—one of many amazements he'd brought her. When they neared the ocean, their feet impressed sand along a slender, tea-colored, inch-deep stream bordered by huckleberry—the pale red, slightly translucent berries ripe against green leaves dotted with drops. Beyond that, their first glimpse of Pacific surf—arches and stacks topped with scraggly shore pine.

She knelt to lift a handful of sand and let it sift through her fingers. "This is what the ocean does to big rocks and shells over eons of time," she told him. "It breaks them down to this." Sand fell on sand in a soft hiss. She watched him to see what he thought of that.

He lifted his own handful and let it fall. "Big rocks?" he asked.

She nodded.

"This?" He brought his hand to rest on the sand.

She nodded.

"Ee-ons?" he frowned.

"So many you couldn't count that high—even if you counted for the rest of your life."

He walked ahead of her, erratically counting the numbers he knew, and she wished him time enough to count an eon.

Farther down the trail, she thought she saw for just a moment in a copse of thin trees an intent face, a black beard slick with rain. She sat down in the sand and stared for a time at a crushed Rainier Beer can caught in twigs at the margin of the stream. In a bent indentation in the middle of the can, a rusty, crescent-shaped hole gurgled with the passage of water.

Paul stopped counting, came back, and brought his face in close to hers. He seemed to know it was best not to say anything. He sat next to her while she breathed out of it.

"I need a minute," she said, not looking at him so she wouldn't have to see his eyes. "Can you give mama a minute?"

He didn't protest as she expected. Something in her tone.

After she'd recovered, they crossed the beach to the glittering tide pools and peered down into the wavering clarity atop which their reflections rippled when the wind picked up, making them seem unformed, in question: flesh morphs below rippling tufts of hair black as mussel shells above reflections of bright orange ponchos.

She told him, "Everything in here, except the rocks and sand, is alive." It was something she had recently officially learned at the Marine

Life Center but it was also second nature from growing up Makah. She looked to see his reaction.

He creased his brow, cocked his head, and stared down into the water.

She watched him and wondered how he was turning out and how she was doing and whether his fall into the river had scarred him or marked him as blessed or neither or a little of both. She wondered about the presence and capacity to linger of the *tumanuwos* she'd felt in the aftermath, and how much of his father was in him and what that amount might mean for him and for her. She looked back at the place near the creek where the memory had seized her and, as she often had to do when she was with Paul, willed a distance between present and past in the hope they might never meet again.

They climbed up and sat on colossal beach logs bleached white and worn so smooth they seemed the bones of trees, so that it was a difficult thing to imagine the logs had ever been real, rough-barked trees pushing their lengths at the sun on a ridge. They ate sliced apples smeared with peanut butter and washed it down with grape Hi-C.

"Why did all these big trees come to the beach?" he asked.

She thought a moment. "They fell over in a storm, maybe. When the snow melted, a big river carried them to the ocean. The ocean stripped off the limbs and bark. Then, another big storm came and washed them up here—so now we have a place to sit and eat lunch."

She watched his eyes shift in comprehension as she talked. He looked pleased with her explanation, which pleased her. What a powerful, frightening thing it was to be the one who knew things.

After they'd eaten, Paul stepped into one of the pools, grimacing till his feet and ankles numbed. Flounder fluttered to glide after he'd startled them with his sandals. Each time a new one alit to flurry, he shrieked with delight. He pointed down into the pool and looked back at Trace. She sat a short distance away gazing over the empty beach to the surf beyond, one hand stirring swirls in the sand with a piece of driftwood, the flat of the other hand erasing what she'd skritched.

He lifted rocks in the shallowest parts of the pools to reveal scores of tiny purple and green bellicose crabs raising dukes to bluff escapes.

Orange sponges and white anemone breathed, cilia dancing. Gooey limpets in their chinacap homes clung to the rocks; transparent, round jellyfish, like rubber ashtrays, oozed into the water through his fingers. Blood stars ambulated surreptitiously with their hundreds of legs over barnacled rocks.

Trace pulled herself from her reverie to tell him their strange names. She wasn't sure all the names belonged to the creatures she pointed out, but she liked the names because they were fresh in her mind. So, she named them for him and told him her mother would someday tell him the Makah names for these things, which she wished she'd been able to remember but did not. She also told him about the smooth glass floats used to buoy Japanese fishing nets that sometimes drifted hundreds of miles to wash up on a beach like this, and that they had one in their apartment back in Port Angeles.

When the wind came up, the cornucopia blurred under a crossweave of ripples. She pointed over the stretch of beach. Beyond the surf and land formations—the arches and stacks—the glittering, protean expanse of the ocean rolled. As far as they could see, ridged swells rose and fell with the ocean's ceaseless breath. She imagined her ancestors, their ancestors, heading out to sea in redcedar canoes carved out of whole boughs after whales or seals. An obvious thought that felt profound came to her as it often did when she watched him: *I am his mother and he is my son.*

In the last three years, she had worked very hard to raise him, following a vow she'd made him on the way out of the Elwha on the day of his miraculous salvation when she'd clutched him to her to warm him and found a thin trail up the bluff. As she hiked to the trailhead where the old Dodge was waiting, she was filled with a new energy. Moving through a portion of forest filled with trees that still showed evidence of the fire that had whipped through and burned their lower boughs in the early seventies, passing hikers on their way in, some of whom made little waves at Paul, her mind wheeled to the resolution that if she did not manage to be the best mother the world had seen, she would at least be numbered among the best. She would, with a rare, saintly diligence, raise this boy whose weight she could feel against her, this boy the river had elected to save. Was this strength lent her by some powerful *tumanuwos*? She felt as if she were walking above the ground, hovering over the trail as if by an inflation of heart. She felt as if, all along, the thing that could set her free was not casting him away but keeping him, supporting him, until he could support himself. Paul responded with a gurgle, telling her something, and she agreed with him, whatever it was. She floated down the trail, apologizing, making him promises.

There had been difficult times and nights when she had awakened with an image seared onto the back of her mind: Paul plummeting into the white water at the bottom of the gorge. In these dreams, she fell with him and, for a few terrifying moments after she had awakened, it was as if she had lost him that day and everything since had been a dream.

When he was two and now that he was three, it amazed her to see Paul learning the world. She marveled at the intensity he brought to noticing small, new things. She loved the way he would stop on the street to observe, with wide-eyed reverence, the awkward phenomenon of a man on crutches, the way he'd pick up a pine cone or leaf and carry it to her with a grunt that asked for her appraisal. She loved watching how he crawled along, head to ground, to more closely monitor a woolly worm's slow progress between cracks in the sidewalk, how he looked from the thick-coated worm up to her to make sure she was seeing this wonderful thing in the world. On the bus, he had once reached out, transfixed and helpless against the urge, to touch a woman's dangly, silver earring after it had caught the sun. She loved the way he would reach out, as if spellbound, for tangible knowledge of what had caught his interest. For a time, everything went into his mouth; he had to taste the world. And she especially loved the way he included her in his discoveries, the way he turned to look at her, as if to say, *So there is also this in the world? Did you know about this*?

There were other times when Paul gave the impression that he was worrying over great conundrums. When she noticed this darker concentration with no discernible object, Trace wondered if this too was evidence that Paul was putting great thought into the assimilation of the newly encountered, or if something more troubling accounted for his thoughtfulness. She wondered at these times if, in addition to his capacity for wonder, there might also be something dark wound into him. How much of him would remain mysterious to her till the end? Something in his farawayness at these other times worried her. She would watch him carefully when he was caught up in these moments, lost in thought and frowning at she knew not what, and hope that a developing intelligence and not a burgeoning malevolence accounted for these interludes. Looking at his clouded-over visage at these times, she couldn't help but wonder about his father.

We are caught in a cycle, she thought, watching him leaping after something in the pool, the displaced water also seeming to leap up. She had not known her father; Paul would not know his. Her mother had told her with no preamble when Trace was thirteen and they were sitting on the porch of the little house on the reservation at Neah Bay and the sky was an assembly of greys: "Your father," she said, "was a hippie." She chuckled at that word and what it meant—a survivor's chuckle, not so much armor as the long view. "You know what that is?"

Trace shook her head, no, though she thought she did.

"Long hair, no job. Peace and love and back to the land. He used to camp out with some of his friends. A whole community of them were over there near Shi Shi. They called it 'dropping out.' Didn't want to be part of the 'system.'"

"Did you love him?"

She paused a few moments before answering. "Yeah. He was funny. And I was very young. He shrunk up the universe and made me feel like I was at the center, for a little while."

"Where is he now?"

She shook her head. "Might be in Iowa or someplace. Far away from any ocean. Teaching at a college. That was the last I heard. Years ago. Sorry, Tracie."

She looked back at the place near the stream where the rusting can was gurgling with the passage of tea-colored water. When the time came, she knew she would tell Paul what little she knew of his father. When the perfect time came, when she thought he was ready to hear it, she would recreate the event with words as carefully as she could.

Paul walked across the sand, carrying the shell of a red rock crab in both hands. He sat beside her and looked closely into the crab's hollowed eye sockets and former eating mechanism. He held the crab up a little for her admiration.

"This is the crab's skeleton," she said, lifting off the back of its shell. "They wear it on the outside. See? Nothing inside. The real crab shed it and grew a new one when it was ready to grow bigger."

She told him about bigger animals under the surface of the ocean that sometimes breached to breathe: harbor seals, sea lions, Dall's porpoises, killer and gray whales. She reminded him how his brave ancestors had hunted the whales in long boats carved from redcedar and told him that deep under the water the biggest octopuses in the world crawled over the rocks and changed color to match the seafloor and squirted dye when they were in trouble and were intelligent and never breached. And she told him how the great ships crawled across the surface, riding high when empty, low when weighed down with cargo—lumber, the main reason, once the otters were gone, the white settlers had come to the Peninsula to take the land and the fish and the game in the first place—heading all over the world.

"Tell again how they hunted whales," he said.

She used a stick to demonstrate. "They threw a harpoon, a sharp spear with an antler or mussel-shell blade attached to a woven cedar rope, into the whale and let it drag the boat on a long ride, until the whale was tired out and . . . dead. The rope was attached to floats made of seal skin that slowed the whale down. Sometimes they had to follow the whale for days. When they brought the whale to the village, everybody said, 'They return. And they bring a guest!'"

"The whale stayed with them?" he asked.

"They ate it."

He widened his eyes. "Mama? How did they eat a whole whale?"

This had become a ritualistic conversation, each of them playing their part. He loved to hear about it and often played at whale hunting in the bath. "All the people shared the whale. And the great whale hunter gave out parts of it as gifts. The oil, the blubber . . ."

He lingered on that for a moment before his eyes turned to the next question. “Sea *lion*?” he asked, setting the crab shell down.

She imagined him imagining an African lion with a thick mane living in the water, sporting as if it had been born to it. “It’s like a seal,” she said and watched him assimilate the thought, wondering what he was imagining. She wondered how he would do in preschool in the fall. She thought perhaps he asked too many questions.

He frowned. “What is breached?”

She looked at him and thought about his miraculous survival despite her, and how she could never anticipate what he would feel he needed to know about the world, and that that was only one of the things about spending time with him that made a thousand vicissitudes associated with having kept him melt to joy. “Break the surface,” she said. “Come up for air.”

Later that afternoon she watched Paul pick up a stick, hold it like a harpoon, and throw it into the sand. Then, he pretended to be a whale swimming under the water. He picked up the stick and came up to an imaginary surface. As he was breaching, he simulated the harpoon finding its mark and writhed in the sand, holding the stick to his back. After a time, he stood up again and pretended he was a proud hunter standing in a boat celebrating a successful throw.

On the way home, just before they left the beach for the trail up the bluff, she lifted him up and nuzzled her nose and cheekbones into his chest and ribs till he laughed, then she lowered him down and hugged him with her face in his hair, till he squirmed and said, “Mama, let’s go.”

8

Bill Newton and the Maxey boy unlocked a gate and traveled an hour over a teeth-jarring Forest Service road to its end near the place where the National Forest and Park boundaries met. At several moments it sounded as if the old truck would be reduced to a pile of metal and bolts, so severely did the road shake it up. Now, Bill was looking at the map Smitty had left in his mother's mailbox along with the key they'd used to unlock the gate and notes about how to begin the job. At the bottom of the map Smitty had written, "Get 'em down quick, clean, and quiet. We'll take care of the rest. Anyone asks, you don't know nothing. If they press, you take the fall, so don't get caught!! Burn this note."

Before they started up the trail that would take them to the top of the ridge, Bill bowed his head and thanked God for the opportunity to work again in his home woods and asked for guidance. His old caulks with spiked soles dug into the mossy earth—decaying fallen redcedar and Douglas firs, many of which had become nurse logs, fern, liverwort, and young hemlock sprouting out of the rot. At the top of the ridge, they moved past the signs stapled to some trees demarcating the boundary between Forest and Park land. They saw the check-in point for hikers headed into the Park's backcountry and the sign that said it was illegal to bring in firearms or pets. They crested the ridge and headed down into the Park, which, if the surveying error the head of the Forest Service had caught was accurate and the court ruling that held it up was to be believed, was not really in the Park at all.

After they'd gone a distance down this trail, they left it to cut over a few miles to the west above the Calawha River. Due to the density of the undergrowth, the going was slow, and it took them some time to arrive at the orange Forest Service markings on the trees of the Temple Grove.

Bill was impressed. It had been a while since he'd cruised timber, but you didn't have to be an expert to see that this was a magnificent stand of trees, probably 140,000 or more board feet per acre in its heart, he guessed. Some of the wood could be rotting, but most of the trees looked sound and firm. They were, for the most part, straight and perfectly rounded, like columns fronting an important building—a courthouse, church, or fancy school—their thick, gnarled bark making them look irregularly fluted, the first branches, in some cases, a hundred feet from the ground. Though he had never been in an ancient temple or to a fancy school, the name that had been given to this grove seemed appropriate, even if it had been deliberately coined by environmentalists trying to make anyone who wanted to fell the trees seem like desecraters of sacred ground. More than five-thousand goods came from timber products, things you'd never think about like toothpaste and tires. He wondered what the protestors would say if all the goods in their lives connected to trees were to suddenly disappear— paper towels, diapers, popsicle sticks, filters for their coffee and bags for their tea, other goods they'd never imagine had any connection at all to the trees they wanted to save but which they would miss the moment they were gone.

It was invigorating to be in the woods again, despite, perhaps *because* of the steep gradient, the snarliness of the undergrowth, the near impossibility of extracting wood from the ridge without heavy machinery. He gave the Maxey boy some orange flags for tagging the best trees within the boundary Smitty and the Forest Service had marked with orange X's. He told him to look for larger, straighter specimens that didn't look like they were decaying so much they'd bust up when they hit the ground, and he directed him to start a half mile or so to the east and come back to the west so they could meet in the middle.

After two hours of marking trees in the grove, Bill met the Maxey kid a little over halfway across the ridge. Both of them were sweating and had added new scuffs to their stagged-off pants and chaps.

"I don't know how Smitty's going to get these out after we cut 'em down," the Maxey kid said. "I mean, we're in the middle of nowhere down here."

"They'll probably punch in a road up over this ridge, then set up a Cat operation to yank 'em up. Maybe they'll 'copter 'em out. I've seen worse. Anyway, we'll let him worry about that. We're the thin end of the wedge. By the time we get these down everything'll probably be cleared up. First thing we need is a strategy for getting 'em down. Try to find a way to make it easier to get 'em out. We'll work up from the bottom and try to keep it clean."

That night back in the camp they'd set up on the saddle beside the road, as Bill lay listening to the Maxey boy's snoring, he remembered his first meeting with the Makah girl. He tried to bring the night back to life, the cat-o'-nine tails with which he kept in contact with the version of himself he hoped he'd left behind but which sometimes returned to surprise him when he least expected it.

Emboldened by all he'd had to drink that night with Shoot Morely, he had tried to talk to the girl in the lavender hat but, finding he had little control over what he was trying to say, he cursed the Thunderbird wine. Behind them, high tide surf pounded the ocean beach as if mulling the grist of the ages.

Five young Indians—two guys around his age and three girls—were seated on an L-shaped configuration of thick, smooth-worn Sitka spruce logs facing a fire. Their tents were set up just at the edge of the firelight, below a bluff beside a small tea-colored creek. Some appeared to Bill to be full Indian and some looked to be mixed, like Shoot, who claimed whatever tribal affiliation suited him in any given moment. Answers to Shoot's loud questions revealed that they were there for a big low tide in the morning and planning to gather mussels and clams, as they were allowed to do on Park land according to the 19th-century treaty the tribes had signed with the U.S. government, which was reasserted in a 1974 federal court decision.

"Ah, Shoot—you told us you wouldn't come out here tonight," said one of the young men on the log.

"I came here to tell you a story," Shoot said, as if hurt by the non-greeting, stepping into the firelight. "Besides which, I'm your cousin, Jesse. Your blood, your tribe." He clutched his arm to his chest.

"What the hell happened to your face?"

Shoot grinned as if to better show missing teeth in addition to the crooked nose and other wounds, bruises, and abrasions—the earlier fight's cheerful ambassador.

The three girls looked from Bill to Shoot. A chubby one looked down, shook her head, then looked at the girl to her right, and they both shook their heads. "Get your ass kicked again, Shoot?" she said.

Shoot smiled at her and worked his eyebrows. "That's the story," he said with sudden glee.

"I thought you were on parole or house arrest or something, Shoot," one of them said.

Shoot shook his head, as if to dismiss a painful subject.

"No, Shoot," Jesse said, "I'm sorry. You got to leave." He looked at Bill. "Your friend, too."

Shoot smiled at the girl who'd spoken to him earlier. "Whupped a bunch of Hells Angels," Shoot said. "Didn't we, Bill? And I came here to tell you the story. If you'll let me . . . ," he said. He walked to the fire, tripped over a piece of driftwood, and fell on his face and hands in the sand and warm rocks, sending another piece of driftwood into the flames so that a flurry of sparks ascended, as if to mark a punchline, into flight. The girls laughed derisively. Except for the girl in the lavender hat.

"What's your name," Bill said to the girl, who, either because she didn't hear him or was ignoring him, didn't answer. Bill took a deep breath and nodded as if in painful acceptance of her rebuff.

Shoot settled onto a log. "So, here's how it went down. Toss me one of them Rainiers—you're too young to drink," he said.

One of them grudgingly tossed him a beer.

"Well, you heard how them Hells Angels were coming through town, right?"

None of them had.

In response to Bill's second jumbled attempt at speaking to the girl, delivered as with a newly issued tongue, the girl smiled a smile surprising to Bill for its apparent beneficence and said, "Easy for you to say."

Shoot told the story of the fight with the Hells Angels, using broad gesticulations and embellishments in his favor, giving an occasional nod to Bill's part in the melee as if offering tribute to ward off any physical corrections Bill might choose to make.

"I think you were promised to me . . . in a dream," Bill slurred, thinking of the girl in his dream who'd found him in Skidders, and wondering if his words had come out in a better order this time. He stared at her with imploring eyes. The girl narrowed her eyes but didn't say anything in response. Just after he spoke, a tremendous tiredness hit him like a blow, the exertions of the fight and the climb down the cliff catching up with him. He couldn't remember ever being so tired.

One of the girls started singing a strange-sounding song to drown out or accompany Shoot's story, or maybe Shoot's story was long over. Some of the others joined in. Bill laid his head down in the sand at the girl's feet and listened to her voice rising in the strange song above the rest.

Bill's remembrance was interrupted by a sound he heard for some time before he realized he was hearing it, a dim echo that for a time seemed an accompaniment to the remembrance. He got out of his sleeping bag, stood up from the cot, walked out of the tent into the cool night under the stars, and listened up and over the ridge where the mysterious sound seemed to be originating. A distant clang, faint and lonely as a cowbell on a lost cow a mile or more away. Someone in the wilderness ringing a bell or hammering something. It sounded three times, then stopped. During the pause he wondered if the ringing was only in his mind—the distant sound asking him to mark the moment—some warning or portent. After a pause of five seconds or so, it started up again with a steady insistence—clang, clang, clang, clang. Difficult to tell where it was coming from—a ridge, maybe two ridges, over. Sound traveled strangely in the mountains, vaulted, echoed, and bent. He stood for a time with a creased brow, wondering at the sound, thinking how, when he was younger, he might've charged into the woods without a second thought to see what it was. How strange it was that anyone would be this far out, working on anything, at this hour.

He took a few steps toward the edge of the forest and stood listening for some time, eyes scanning the tree-filled darkness—what could that be? Comfortable as his sleeping bag on the cot had been, he thought he'd better go in, up and over the ridge, to check it out, find its source. But just as he was about to make good on this thought, the clanging stopped, this time long enough for him to turn, go back into the tent, and settle back into his sleeping bag.

As soon as he'd pulled the top of the sleeping bag up under his beard, the clanging began again. He listened to it for a few moments, deep internal receptors noting it, telling him to mark it *important*, even as he let the clangs recede into the background of his consciousness so he could better resume his remembrance.

Sand stuck to the side of his face. Shoot was nowhere in sight, and the girls from the night before were fanned out in the tidepools across a shimmering expanse of wet sand, gathering mussels from rocks in some of the tidepools and digging for razor clams in the sand. The surf, which had beaten the sand so close to camp the night before, was a white line a half-mile away—the lowest negative tide he'd ever seen. A chilly wind swept in off the water over the wet beach, and the bright sun was higher in the sky than Bill wanted it to be. The fire pit was covered with sand and littered with beer cans.

He made his way across the wide beach, his boots sinking into the wet sand. He needed to find a way out of there and back to his trailer on the outskirts of Forks, and he couldn't believe he was about to ask some Indians for help. He had a day off, but after the exertions of the day before he wanted to use the remainder of the day to rest up so he would be ready to work the stand they were cutting near Mount Octopus by tomorrow. He approached the girl, unable to remember what had happened and hoping he hadn't been too bold the night before. "I'm looking for a ride out of here," he said. "Can you help me out?"

She looked up at him in silence for two or three seconds. Then shook her head and looked at the girl who had been feverishly digging beside her but was now also looking at Bill, waiting to see how Trace would answer. "He crashes our camp with a man who's probably stealing the radio from my car as we speak. He snores when we try to sing. And now he's asking for our help." Trace looked at him impassively.

"Go figure for a long time," said the formerly digging girl.

He wanted to say something back to them, something winning or scathing, but he drew a blank. His seething bigness was enough for the men with whom he spent most of his time but didn't seem to have much effect on these girls.

"Where are we taking you?" she asked.

"Not too far. Just outside Forks."

"You pay to fill up my tank when we get there," she said. "Plus twenty bucks."

Her friend frowned, shook her head, and looked back, squint-eyed, at Bill.

"That's a rip-off, but you got a deal," he said and looked at the friend. "I'm harmless. Mostly," he said.

"Yeah? Tell that to those Hells Angels Shoot was talking about last night," Trace said.

The wall of his face opened into a smile.

She told her friends she'd be back in a few hours and set off on the trail toward her old blue Dodge with the strange, burly boy-man. They hiked four miles to the trailhead in the damp coolness of the coastal forest, Bill behind her, watching her long black hair, the sway beneath her shorts, through sunlight and variegated shade and the rustling of the leaves and needles of the spruce, hemlock, and fern.

"How do you know Shoot Morely?" she asked.

"He used to be the assistant gut-robber at a real remote old-fashioned logging show I worked at," said Bill. "Now, I don't know what he does. Turns up when there's trouble I guess. Like yesterday."

At the trailhead, they climbed into her car, and she drove them to Forks.

"What was that song you were singing last night?" he asked. "What did those words mean?"

She laughed. "Are you serious?"

"Yes."

She laughed again. "'Material Girl.' I think later we also tried to sing 'The Boys of Summer' and 'Every Time You Go Away.' But you were passed out by then."

"I thought you were singing old Indian songs."

She shook her head. "You wouldn't ever be around to hear any of those songs. The elders sometimes do that—I know some," she said. "But, no. Last night, it was Madonna with a few hey-ah's thrown in." She chuckled.

They rode for a time in silence. "So, what tribe are you?" he asked as they crossed the Sol Duc just before it met the Calawah and Bogachiel to form the Quileute.

"Makah. My mother's Makah. So I guess you'd say I'm half."

"Which half?" he asked.

"Ha, ha. You're funny," she said. "The broke half," she said.

"It's a good mix," he said.

She let him get away with it because he sounded, when he said it, like a little boy, which was incongruous with his size. She smiled and looked at him out of the corners of her eyes. "This how you talk to all your taxi drivers?"

He paid to fill up her tank at a station in Forks and unfolded from his overall pocket a wrinkled twenty that he was amazed to find there after all the drinks he'd had at Skidders, and she drove him to his leaky single-wide in the Alder Grove Trailer Park where he lived alone and stashed the cash from his monthly Rayonier checks in his high-school football duffel bag, sending some home to his mother, as did his brother, who was on off-bearer in the mill at Port Angeles. "I'll keep cutting 'em down and sending 'em to you, if you keep getting 'em ready for the world," he'd told Troy the last time he'd been home. On that visit, their mother had wept and told them how proud she was of her boys for working so hard and keeping folks in wood products and herself afloat since their father had departed earlier than any of them had ever had any cause to expect.

"You got a phone number where someone could call you sometime?" Bill asked the girl, surprised himself he was saying it, his voice catching between *some* and *one*. He'd found the girls around Forks mostly already spoken for by guys they knew from high school, and despite the fact that he'd kicked a few of their asses, the men were ribbing him worse and worse.

She looked at him for a time, then smiled, told him a number, and said, "I live with my mother by Washburns in Neah Bay. We don't have phone service right now, but if you call the pay phone at Washburns, sometimes, if they feel like it, someone'll answer who'll come get us."

She drove away.

Saying the number again and again to himself, he opened the door as quickly as he could, looked around the trailer for something with which to write it down, and wrote it across the bare breasts of a woman on the cover of a magazine.

9

The next day, after Trace closed the Marine Life Center, she and Stephanie drove to the east side of Port Angeles and the Elk Antler apartment complex, which squatted under an eroding bluff covered in Himalayan blackberry and clubfoot.

On the drive over, Stephanie had told Trace that the two-bedroom apartment was inhabited by five newly graduated students from Paul's class at Roosevelt High whose parents had told them it was time to live on their own. Two of them had jobs at fast-food restaurants in town, three were still looking for work.

"So, why do you think they'll know anything about Paul?" Trace asked.

"These guys were talking about hiring Paul, I heard. As a bodyguard or something. After the thing with Brink Forger. I heard it from someone who sometimes goes to their place."

What did a bunch of kids who work at fast-food joints need with a bodyguard? Trace wondered. She was having misgivings about this investigative jaunt, and wouldn't have agreed to go if worry about Paul and Bill Newton hadn't become such a steady presence in her life, an undercurrent threatening to sweep her legs out from under her and carry her away. Paul's having gone missing meant something different since Bill was back.

Stephanie knocked on the door of unit 9C, and a few moments later a spiked head of hair and a pimpled face appeared in a crack in the door above a black t-shirt. A boy in his late teens who looked vaguely familiar (she'd probably seen him around town) looked first at Stephanie with a smirky smile, then at Trace, who stood, as if unready to fully commit to the visit, behind Stephanie on the sidewalk. When he saw Trace, the boy's face sobered and he looked back at Stephanie somewhat imploringly.

"This is Paul Granger's mom," Stephanie said. "She wants to ask you guys some questions."

The boy mumbled something, told them it would be a minute, and shut the door. Nearly three full minutes later, he opened it again onto the living room of a two-bedroom apartment. Two boys sat on the couch grasping and jabbing their thumbs at video game controls. Trace wondered if their thumb muscles grew outsized from all that jabbing. Sometimes she wished Paul would stay home more often and hang out with friends like a regular kid. Maybe this wish was misguided, she thought now, if this was what staying home meant, if this was a good cross-section of potential friends.

"Hey, Steph!" one of the players called out after glancing over.

On the screen, two tanks barged down the streets of a crumbling city, destroying everything in their path, enduring a firestorm, the crackly voice of a walky-talky representing the voices of the tank drivers saying, "I've been hit. I need back-up!"

Trace recognized the boy who'd called out to Stephanie as Lee Hepner. He'd called Paul on the phone a time or two to ask about homework assignments and things like that, but he wasn't a friend. She had seen both of the thumb jabbers before, around town, usually looking like they were about to get into, or had just narrowly escaped, some kind of trouble. She'd often seen them hanging out on the corner or at the new skate park, cackling over something they found funny, which, if she knew what it was, she was certain she wouldn't find the least bit amusing. They reminded her of some of the young toughs back at the Bay who cruised up and down Bayview, gangsta music vibrating the windows of cars they spent hours souping up.

Pizza boxes and soda cans were piled up beside an ashtray on the plywood-and milk-crate coffee table. As the boy who'd let them in walked past a dirty gold recliner leaking stuffing, he snatched up a blue bong (forgot to hide that, Trace thought) and continued with it back to one of the bedrooms.

The place smelled strongly of cat urine, though there was no evidence of a cat. Even when they'd been outside, Trace had recognized a scent that took her back to certain corners of the reservation. She couldn't immediately place it, but it carried an association of danger and dis-ease. The clutter of the place and its size reminded her of the apartment she'd crowded into with a group of young people from the reservation, all of them trying to make it in Port Angeles. But their place had never been so dark and had always seemed animated by their hopefulness, the way all of them, even the two girls who didn't yet have kids, thought of the infants first in making their decisions. One of the girls was now back in Neah Bay, raising her daughter there. She'd lost touch with the other two after they moved to Seattle.

"This is Paul Granger's mother. She wants to ask you some questions," Stephanie repeated to the room.

The sheepish teen who'd let them in returned to lurk in front of the counter separating the living room from the kitchen. Behind him on the countertop rested one hundred or more bottles of ephedrine. Who would ever need that much aspirin? Trace thought. The garbage can at the border between the kitchen floor and the carpet was overflowing, an empty, folded-up package of lye resting beside it. Beside that, a bag full of rock salt. The smell of the place flushed the memory of the trailers out in certain corners of the woods back at the Bay. The plan to hire Paul was beginning to make a gloomy, terrifying kind of sense. These stupid boys! she thought. She hoped Paul had never set foot in this apartment and wondered how Stephanie knew this place even existed.

"So you're Paul's mother?"

She nodded.

"No offense, Mrs. G, but your kid's kind of a wackjob." The boy turned his eyes from the video game without moving his head or neck to see how his comment had hit her before continuing. "Don't worry, though, no one fu— messes with him much because he's such a big, like, burly mountain-man kind of a guy. Especially since he beat the crap out of Brink Forger. Everyone's his good buddy since then. Except

Brink and them." The boy smiled in a wide way that was meant to be, and perhaps in some quarters succeeded at being, charming. His confidence in the smile and the length of time he held it had the effect of undermining this expectation.

Who was this punk, this gadget-jabbing couch jockey, to make pronouncements about anyone's saneness? If this was the sort Paul had to choose from, no wonder he hadn't developed any serious friendships with kids his age. She tightened her eyes on the boy, preparing for battle, or outright war, if it came to it, once again recognizing something building in herself, the undercurrent threatening to become a torrent.

"For real," he continued. "He's developed a serious reputation. He doesn't have many friends. If he wants some friends, tell him to come over here sometime. If he had more friends, people, like especially his mother, would know where he was all the time, right?" The boy looked around to see if he'd impressed anyone else with his logic.

Tell him to come over here sometime implied a lack of knowledge of Paul's whereabouts.

"You never know, we might make him rich," the boy continued.

"How would being friends with *you* ever make him rich?" Trace said.

The boy mumbled something she couldn't hear, that nonetheless carried the meaning of *just wait and see*.

"I heard," began the sheepish kid from his perch by the counter, shying when he found he'd gained the room's attention, "I heard he was working up in the Park. My dad drives concessions up to Hurricane Ridge. He told me he saw Paul with some ranger guy up there not too long ago. That guy with the, like, clawed-up face."

Trace glared at the boy. Feeling the force of her stare, he looked to the ringleader on the couch, who was still thumbing the video game and had for the moment retreated too far into his dreams of riches to join the actual conversation.

"Thanks for the tip," Trace said with some sharpness. "When did your dad see him?"

The boy shrugged. "A few days ago, I don't know."

It made perfect sense that that's where he was, but why had Paul felt the need to keep it a secret this summer? He'd worked with Dan clearing trails, when he wasn't working at the outdoor store for Jim, for the last four summers. Why wouldn't he have been able to tell her that?

Looking at the two boys on the couch thumbing their controls and staring at the screen, Trace wondered if they would have been so rude had one of the big-shot white ladies in town come to see them, and decided these boys would have acted this way if the president of the United States came through the door. She looked at the pills on the counter, the rock salt and lye.

The sheepish boy saw Trace noticing these items and cast another nervous glance at the boys on the couch who seemed to have completely forgotten their visitors. Trace grabbed the boy by his shirtfront, which made him seem as if he wanted to jump out of his skin and run skinless out the door and down the street. "Paul's never been to this house? You swear it?"

The boy shook his head, no, vigorously.

"How well do you know those guys?" Trace asked as she drove them away from the complex.

"Not very well at all, I promise. I'm glad Paul wasn't there."

"Did they send you to find him so you could get him to work for them?"

"No. I was hoping he wasn't with them."

So many dangers could bring someone down, Trace thought. It was an ever more complicated world, and the faction that saved you could be worse than the faction that threatened you.

Stephanie told Trace her father had dropped her off at the Marina, and Trace offered to drive her back to her house, which turned out to be one of the fancy houses, most with views of the Strait of Juan de Fuca far below, up Mt. Angeles Road. The girl indicated a driveway, and Trace turned into it. They passed a sign near the front of the driveway unreadable from the road:

Olympic Think Tank: Smart Transitions for a New Era

"My dad runs a consulting business from up here," Stephanie said. "He calls this his aerie. He works with people who want to find out how to be environmentally friendly while still making money. He's a green capitalist." She said the phrase with pride, as if these two words represented the best thing anyone could say about anyone else.

They took a curve on the driveway between cedars and western hemlock. The house was a complex assemblage of wood and window, multiple levels spilling down the slope. The roofs were full of solar panels canted up toward the sky. In the driveway in front of a walkway sat a strange model of car unlike any Trace had ever seen, an extension cord running from its side to an outlet that looked like a battery.

Stephanie noticed Trace looking at it. "It's electric and it runs on vegetable oil," she said. "We go collect oil from fast-food places in town. It's also partially solar-powered. Do you want to come in for a tour?"

Trace hesitated a moment before surprising herself by saying yes.

As they walked into the house, Stephanie called out, "Dad! Anybody home!" and when she didn't hear an answer said, "We moved out here two years ago. We still have a house in Bellevue, but we mostly stay up here now. My parents are split up. My mom moved back to Palo Alto. It was either go to a totally new place or stay out here with my dad. I chose to stay out here."

They walked on black slate tile into a foyer that opened quickly into a large kitchen with copper pans hanging from a rack over an island of recovered blonde maple. To the left of the kitchen, a living room sank below a ceiling thirty-feet high. The wall facing them was all windows, in front of which a section of trees had been topped to reveal a view of the Strait far below. Trace became aware of a whirring sound that grew louder as they continued through the kitchen into a large room on the other side where Stephanie's father (Trace guessed) was gliding back and forth on a kind of rowing machine attached by wires to a device set against the wall. The man, who was dressed in shorts and a shirt fashioned from what looked to be some state-of-the-art sweat-wicking material, slowed, then stopped rowing. He smiled up at them.

"Dad, this is Mrs. Granger, Paul Granger's mom."

"Oh," he said, slightly out of breath. He stood up from the machine's small seat and kept unfolding till he towered over Trace. "Paul Granger," he said. "Okay. I won't embarrass you by telling Paul Granger's mother that I know who Paul Granger is," he said and winked at his daughter.

The veins on his neck were well defined and his wiry build suggested he spent a lot of time on this machine.

He offered his hand. "Spears Barefoot. I was just exercising. Also, if all is going according to plan, I was generating a little energy for the house. This," he indicated the rowing machine, "if you can believe it, is hooked up to an energy-storage unit. A little experiment in exercise-generated electricity. It won't amount to much. But can you imagine the benefit to the country, if we're all generating our own electricity through exercise? It'd kill two birds with one stone."

Trace nodded. "Sounds like a good idea." Whenever she was permitted entrance to a house like this it made her wonder all the more what went on in all the other houses she passed and never got to see. People, she thought, make and live in worlds as different from one another as the sea creatures in the aquariums at the Center. It's a wonder they're ever able to communicate with one another at all. She thought of the shipbreakers at Alang, Tom with his kruggerand, the boys they'd just visited at the Elk Antler apartment complex—all so much in their own worlds it was amazing these worlds were in the same world.

"Mrs. Granger works in the Marine Life Center," Stephanie said. "She runs it."

"Wonderful," said Spears. "You must know Claire Wittington, then."

"She's my boss," Trace said. "I took a marine biology class with her at Peninsula."

"That Center's a good thing for this town," Spears said. "Teaches kids to respect what they've got so there's less chance they'll grow up to squander and destroy it indiscriminately. Our oceans are in a heap of trouble." He looked at his daughter. "Stephanie's my right-hand girl around here," he said. "She's edited my newsletter since she was a sophomore, has a knack for language—quite the grammatical snoot. I'll be in trouble when she goes away to college this fall."

Trace nodded. "I've enjoyed meeting her. We were very grateful when she organized the petition for Paul." Again, inexplicably, she felt choked up and close to tears when she said it. Was it because Paul was gone?

"She can be very strong-willed and persuasive when she wants to be." He smiled at Stephanie, looked at Trace for a moment, then said, "Well, Trace, I'll tell you a little about what we do up here."

Had she asked what he did? She hoped he wasn't one of the ones who fawned over Indians.

"I was fortunate enough to be an attorney at Microsoft not far from the ground floor. Worked for the company up till a few years ago. Especially in the area of identity theft. I know both B.G.s, Jr. and Sr., pretty well. I grew up over on the dry side, across the Cascades, outside of Yakima. I loved it there, but I've always found this region to be breathtakingly beautiful with the big jumble of mountains rising up so close to this arm of the sea. So, after I wound things down at Microsoft, and when Stephanie's mother and I were having our differences, I decided I wanted to live the mountain lifestyle and set up a think tank here on the side of Mount Angeles."

Trace wondered why he was talking to her as if she might invest in his company and decided this must be how he talked to everyone he met. Over his shoulder and behind him she noticed the *Coho*, small as a bathtub boat, returning with its passengers from Victoria, inching into the harbor. She caught herself drifting, the tendrils her mind had had to worry of late clamoring like untended creatures for attention—Paul probably up in the mountains, Tom chugging toward Alang, Bill Newton back in Port Angeles—and made herself return to focus on what the man was saying and to notice that Stephanie was looking at her father as he delivered his spiel with what seemed to be great pride in his missions and accomplishments.

"So far, we work with conscientious small businesses that don't want to harm the earth to turn a quick and dirty little profit. Our goal is to find ways to make it more profitable, even in the short term, for companies to be eco-friendly. We do a lot of work with emissions folks and with people trying to broaden the scope of which resources are renewable. I act as a liaison between the consumers and business people who want to do a better job, and the science folks, the inventors and innovators who are figuring out how to get us there. It's a simple fact that we're dealing with finite resources and an economic policy of infinite growth that's in terrible denial of this fact. We work with a number of former extraction communities dealing with how to get their laid-off workers transitioned into a recreation or some other kind of economy. And we're interested in smart growth out here; this area will double in population in the next ten years. We think companies should be taxed according to how much damage they do to the earth and rewarded according to how little impact or how much they improve the earth. We don't think that should be a radical concept at all. We actually have clients all over the world. We're riding what feels more and more like a zeitgeist, a real wave for change."

"When you say we, you mean . . .?" Trace asked, playing along.

"I employ about seventeen people right now, not including Steph here. And not including the inventors and entrepreneurs we work with. None of them live here, none of them come in to work at this site. They're spread out across the . . . world actually. We communicate remotely. Well," he said, suddenly, his attention already shifted, "I have a conference call at six, so I'd better run. It was a pleasure meeting you, Trace. I hope your son turns up soon. If you'd like my help, please let me know. I'm sure he's somewhere up in the mountains having fun and he'll turn up dirty and happy in a couple days."

For a moment she wondered how he knew about Paul's absence (she'd been trying to keep it a secret herself) before realizing that, of course, Stephanie had told him because that's how it is in a family. "Thanks," she said, "but he's not really missing." She was about to go on and tell him more—how much, she couldn't say—but stopped herself. Did she want him to set his think-tank skills to work on her case? She chided herself for thinking of letting this man know what it was like to feel the absence of the two missing men in her life and the recent return of the man she'd hoped would stay gone. There was something running deeply in her. If she wasn't careful, it would all spill out the way her confession had spilled out to Paul.

Spears smiled. "I'm sure you're right. I'm sure he's not missing," he said. "I bet he'll be there waiting for you when you get home." Then he said goodbye, turned, and started to move up a spiral staircase.

"He's quite a talker," Trace whispered to Stephanie as she walked Trace out to her car. "A lot going on up there, huh?" she said, pointing to her head. "Saving the world from right here on Mount Angeles."

"Yup," Stephanie said. "He's pretty good at convincing people the world can change for the better."

10

Bill called the number the Makah girl had given him three times before he finally reached her. The first time no one answered at all. The second time, the person at the other end said, "Jerry Peak, that you?" and hung up when Bill said he wasn't. On the third try, a young voice answered and told him, "Wait a sec, I'll see if I can get her."

Her voice came on the line ten minutes later, seconds before Bill would have given up.

They went on two dates that summer—one to Sully's in Forks for burgers and milk shakes, one to a gathering another young lumberman was having in Forks—before their last long date. On the morning of the long date he showed up in Washburns' parking lot, the same place as for the other two, in his new black Ford F-150 pickup at ten on a Saturday morning. Her mother watched them leave, frowning with motherly intuition on the front porch. On the phone he'd asked Trace if it was okay if they made a day of it and told her his plans to take her to see *Crocodile Dundee II* all the way over at the cinema in Port Angeles. On the way, he told her they'd stop off and have a picnic at a place he knew. He said the word "picnic" in a way that suggested he expected her derision and was ready to amend the itinerary accordingly.

She told him that sounded fine. She hadn't listened to her mother or her friends who insisted that anyone hanging around with Shoot Morely was bound to be bad news and wasn't this date kinda long? All the way in town? Port Angeles was an hour and a half away. The movie wouldn't get out till ten. She wouldn't be back in Neah Bay till after midnight. How well did she know this Forks logger?

From the beginning Trace had seen a good-boy-pretending-to-be-a-bad-boy potential in him. She'd had fun on their other two dates, and nothing had happened. He hadn't even tried to kiss her yet, though their partings following the dates had been awkward. If she hadn't seen something in him, she would never have gone on the crazy trip all the way to Port Angeles to see some movie.

Despite their self-conscious silence as the truck negotiated the fierce curves along the coast and the shores of Lake Crescent and Lake Sutherland, she appreciated his effort—the new, clean truck, his combed hair, the fact that a guy who was supposed to be so tough had planned a picnic because, presumably, he thought that's the kind of thing girls liked. She thought she smelled a hint of cologne on him, a smooth, deep, amber liquor-like scent along with the new truck smell that could as easily have been the smell of the woods—sawdust, sap, and pine tar.

"So," he said, "Trace," and stopped there, as if this was a full thought, or a question to which she could respond.

"Yeah?" she said.

"Trace, Trace, Trace," he repeated.

When it was clear this was as far as he was going to go, she shook her head and laughed: "That's my name; now go proclaim my fame."

He chuckled and went silent for a time. "So, you're a poet," he finally said, after a full curve in the road and into the next one. He was grappling with the realization, yet again, apparently to be renewed on each of their dates, that the real person sitting beside him wasn't saying or acting the way he'd imagined she might, and the fact that she had the power, just by being herself and not the anticipated projection, to make him wonder who *he* was.

She shrugged. "I've been known to make a rhyme, but only at the appropriate time. Which, apparently, is now. I don't know why, but I do know how," she said and smiled. This was a set collection of phrases she aired from time to time when she was being silly with her friends. She smiled and looked at him, this hella-big boy with the beard and the hard-to-read face and eyes, internally wheeling to find the right thing to say to such a thing even as they were fixed on the curves in the road.

He nodded and blushed: "Pretty good," he said after another curve and into the next one. He glanced at her out of the corners of his eyes, leaving her to wonder what he had meant to ask, if anything, following the initial recital of her name.

Starry gleams winked out in the Strait and from the surface of Lake Crescent and Lake Sutherland as they passed these bodies on the dragon road. Trace thought about telling him about Wiki-baquak who returned and helped her people, or Nahkeeta who went too far, but decided to save these stories for later. The air from the open windows was cool under the warmth of the bright sun and the sky was a scrubbed blue.

They stopped to pick up burgers, fries, and blackberry shakes from the to-go window of a diner called Granny's, then drove into the Park along the Elwha and up the winding gravel of Whiskey Bend to the trailhead. Sipping the shakes made the silence that had crept into the truck following their first attempts to stoke a conversation (his repetition of her name, her silly rhyme) more comfortable to bear. The banter of their first encounter three weeks ago, during the ride she'd given him from the beach to Forks, and the relatively easy if shallow rapport of their first two dates, was replaced, on the ride to the trailhead, by a weight-accumulating silence that threatened to topple any hope for their future together.

"I came here once with my father," he attempted, the gravel of Whiskey Bend crackling under the tires. "Ten years ago." He almost but didn't tell her about the twenty-inch Dolly Varden they'd caught that day and taken home to his beaming mother.

"Oh. Okay," she said. The green sunlight splintered through the trees. He tried to find a radio station, suddenly, as if that was the thing they were missing, and found a newscast on a Victoria station which played for thirty seconds before it was lost to static.

They hiked the trail in almost complete silence. Once, near Elk Overlook, looking at his watch, he apologized for how long it was taking them—he hadn't remembered it being this far—and Trace told him it was all right, she was fine.

When they reached the meadow at Hume's Ranch, he spread out an unzipped flannel sleeping bag, and they sat on it atop a bank overlooking a minor side channel of the river laughing under and against a log jam. They ate the burgers and fries, which had gone cold, in the shadows of alders and a moss-covered bigleaf maple and struggled to find things to say. Their voices quavered when they mentioned the strong wind sweeping through the valley, trying to carry the butcher paper wraps around their burgers away from their hands and into the meadow. Twice, Bill stood to grab one of the errant white wrappers before it had gone too far while Trace chuckled to see this big boy move so fast.

Then, from somewhere, somehow—it was mysterious to both of them then and in the many years after, how it happened—there was a tear in the fabric of the afternoon that had something to do with the feel of the warm sun and an inhalation of conifer scent and dry dust and intoxicatingly clean air and a too-blue sky and the roar of the river. A great rift in the fibers that had formerly held the afternoon together brought on by the down-valley gusts, somehow suffocating for the wildness through which the wind had swept, the river mist and brooding moss and screaming needles—bear breath, elk hide, cougar gaze—before it found their lungs, pushing across Trace's forehead and over her eyes, a wisp of dark hair she kept tucking behind her left ear and the wind kept releasing.

On the drive up Whiskey Bend and on the hike in, he'd stolen a number of quick glances at her—the dimpling of her cheeks when she smiled and the tops of her breasts in the sundress and the shadowy-switching flex of the fabric at its seat and the definition of the muscles in her bare legs and at her feet through the straps in her sandals. Back in his trailer in Forks he kept a stack of girlie magazines (of which he was ashamed and which he repeatedly vowed to throw away) hidden with a pile of Rayonier money under the bed. The images in these magazines joined the images in current reception, and the fact of his virginity and the echoes of his co-workers' taunts when they'd found out he was a virgin (sensed it in him because he was so quiet when they told their stories and wouldn't let him forget it because they marveled at the fact that he was a virgin since he was the most competent young lumberman of his generation, and, since the Hells Angels episode, famous for knowing how to handle himself in a fight)—all of these joined one another and compounded to push him into a kind of delirium.

He sat in the shadows of the alders and the twisting branches of the moss-covered bigleaf maple, watching her as she stretched her brown legs and rested the weight of her body on her extended arms and closed her eyes to bask in the flashes of splintered sunlight.

A short time later, he fell as if drunk on the ripping fabric of the afternoon, like grabbing a high limb on a spar and feeling it give way, toward her and kept falling.

She opened her eyes to see him falling and felt his rough beard on her chin, smelled hamburger and blackberry shake on his breath, before she'd had time to decide what the movement meant. She decided some kissing was okay, for now, but not like this. Then it sounded like he said something followed by, ". . . what I want . . ." in a kind of growl as he morphed from shy boy to impatient man to enveloping force.

Before he fell on top of and over and in and all around her, she'd been trying to fill the silence with talk. Now, she couldn't remember what it had been about any more than Bill could. Maybe she was talking about how the Elwha Klallam tribe was a traditional enemy of the Makah, that Makah warriors sometimes returned to the Cape with the heads of Klallam on spikes, their women as slaves, and sometimes a place remembered things like this and tried to transmit this remembrance to visitors. Perhaps she told him she was on doubly dangerous ground because all the coast people of the Peninsula thought powerful spirits, not all of them good, and requiring careful reception, lived in the mountains and for that reason the people mostly stayed close to the water. Maybe she was simply saying how good the sun felt through the leaf shadows on her face and body, or talking about the movie they would see after the picnic. She may even have been flirting with him, trying to get him to open up by teasing him a little—asking what kind of person takes someone on a date to a place like this, on this kind of a marathon date, or maybe she was finding out about his other trips to the river, getting him to talk about the time when he was ten and they'd caught the twenty-inch Dolly Varden, if he'd brought himself to mention it to her by then.

A tear in the fabric of the afternoon, like losing his grip attaching the cable to the spar, puzzling then and years after to both of them. If they'd been able to talk long enough and in the right way in the frozen-food aisle of the Port Angeles Albertsons or elsewhere, they might have wondered together how it was they went from the halting banter in the car, to the side of her face in grass and dirt and twigs, her mouth open and mute, the sundress yanked up from below and down from the top, the sunlight dappling through the alder and maple leaves. His huge hands and his body, hardened by hard work in that rugged country with its great conifers, all around and on and in her and his beard coarse as dogfish skin on her neck and shoulders and a part of him inside her, unmaking her, rippling and scrambling her like stones or hail in her reflection in a pool moved by wind—how did that happen? How was it that she, who was so fierce and took no shit from anyone on or off the reservation, in Neah Bay, didn't struggle but let this happen (did she let it happen?) in silence except for strange guttural grunts that she thought of then and now as blunt push-off points for inverted shrieks traveling great distances and over long periods of time inside her. She groped with one hand in the grass and dirt and found a smooth stone.

Bill exhaled (immediate undistilled regret and guilt and disappointment along with the physical release) and tensed behind and around and on and in her in the same moment as she brought the stone down on his head.

At the same time as his tensing and the fall of the stone, it seemed, precisely, someone else exclaimed. Two hikers, a couple from Seattle who had been dating for only a few weeks and were on their first extended trip as an official couple, were coming down the trail from the cabin and had seen them there, coupled like wild animals. Their initial reaction was to turn the other way on the trail, as if they'd stumbled into someone else's hotel room and were surprised to see nothing but trees when they turned as if to double-check the room number.

Bill was buttoning and zipping his jeans then standing and leaving, a line of blood running from scalp to his upper lip. He was aware of little but the need for immediate flight because he didn't know what to say, hadn't thought out this part of it. Trace stared into the Elwha's minor rivulet, just a touch of the turquoise its partial glacial source gave to the main river, down the small bluff, rippling beyond the alders and the bigleaf maple under the log jams, then turned her head to see the hikers' boots stepping off the trail to let Bill pass, what Bill remembered best now, the unceasing guilt of the wobbly-legged aftermath, the roaring of wind in the trees.

"Hey!" the man said. "What's going on?" as he watched Bill moving away. After a pause, the woman asked Trace, "Are you all right?"

Trace began to gather herself, managed a strange smile, and began walking. She was dizzy and the alders at riverside and the trees higher up on the ridges seemed to tilt and wobble as if something was shaking the earth. The gusts continued to pour down the valley, one after another, rushing through the trees upriver like a great sigh that might carry her away as casually as the scraps of butcher paper around the burgers. She'd walked halfway across a suspension bridge spanning the Elwha when she realized they hadn't crossed a bridge on the way in. When she turned, she saw the couple who would give her a ride back to Neah Bay, standing and watching her with some interest on the other side. She looked down into the turquoise pool some distance below the rapids under and above the bridge, more rapids churning white downstream.

11

Tom Granger arrived at the Hi-Lo Apartments in his red Chevy pickup precisely at eight. Trace had watched him circle the block twice. When he finally stopped on the street below, she walked down the steps from the second-floor apartment and climbed into the truck.

"I was going to come up," Tom said.

"Well . . . I saw you, so I came down," said Trace, arranging herself in the passenger seat, shutting the door.

"I'm glad this worked out," said Tom.

Trace nodded and smiled, thinking nothing had worked out yet. She caught a minty medicinal hint of aftershave; her stomach did a turn; it felt wonderful and awful to be on a date. Tom put the truck in motion. The radio played a song by the Rolling Stones. Tom turned it up, then turned it down, then turned it off.

Through the kitchen window Paul watched the red truck pull away.

The restaurant was on the second floor of a wharf supported by barnacled pilings running down into the water of the Strait of Juan de Fuca. While Trace and Tom were waiting for their table to be prepared, Trace watched a dozen Dungeness crabs, their claws fastened by red strips, crawling at the bottom of a long, lighted tank in front of the well-stocked bar. Watching them, she was glad the crabs they served at Bushwhackers were frozen. It occurred to her, too, that if one of the crabs at the aquarium died, she might be able to get a live one from the restaurant—save one of their lives.

"You ever had one of those things grab your finger?" asked Tom.

"No," said Trace. "You?" she asked, expecting a story.

"No," he said as if he had expected a story from her.

Trace chuckled.

They were seated at a table with a view of the harbor. A white candle flickered atop a burgundy tablecloth. Out the window, the cold slate water, rippling and glazed in the light of a newly risen half moon, stretched away toward Canada. Trace and Tom's dim reflections in the window made it look as if they were suspended over the water.

For a time Trace was conscious of the servers bustling about the room. She had to remind herself to relax, that she was not responsible for anything. Over time, the hushed light and low babble of conversation calmed her. She decided she was glad to be warm, inside, in this place, if not yet with this man, when the water of the Strait out the window was so deep and cold.

Tom ordered a bottle of wine.

"I'm not dressed up enough, I think," she said, looking at a man in a coat and tie, a woman in a black dress following the hostess to their table.

"You're fine, you're great," he said. "If you feel uncomfortable, though, we can go somewhere else."

"No," she said. "I think we should stay."

"Good," he said.

The server brought the wine, poured a dollop—so red as to be almost purple—into Tom's glass, waited a few seconds, cleared his throat. "Oh," said Tom, and took a sip. "Good, fine, great," he said and nodded, flushing. Trace smiled. The server poured wine into both of their glasses and placed the bottle on the table.

After a time Tom said, "So—do you think it was too forward of me to ask you out . . . so soon after meeting you?"

She shook her head, no. "It's actually kind of flattering," she said.

"You must have all sorts of guys after you. Passing through the aquarium."

"Not so much," she said. "A few." The glint of the candlelight in his eyes made her think it would be more difficult than she thought to fathom what sort of man he might turn out to be.

"It's a lot of responsibility, taking care of all those animals, I would think," he said.

"It can be," she said.

"What's your degree in? Biology?"

"G.E.D.," she said. "But . . . I've learned a lot from Claire, my boss. She's a marine biologist, from the U-Dub."

"Oh," he said. "Well, I don't believe you—about not having guys interested," he said, giving her a smile full of implication and intended charm that missed its mark.

"I have a nine-year-old son," she said. "That's something you should know about me."

For a time, he was silent. He looked into the candle flame, took a sip from his glass. "But you're so young," he said, and looked up.

She shook her head. "Not really." He took her meaning and was quiet.

Not long after their meal had arrived, the *Coho* appeared on the horizon, coming toward them from Victoria, its lights shimmering like manifest chills in the distance. When it had crawled close, the great ferry released a loud low bellow that sent a slight tremor through the window in front of them.

"Let's see how he does," said Tom.

The ship's rusty black-and-maroon side swung slowly around, churning bay water. Passengers milled and huddled on the deck, ready to disembark. Dock workers on the landing, wearing jumpsuits and orange vests with white and yellow reflector strips, handled the massive ropes and chains. When the ship had been secured, people streamed off—first a handful of bicyclists, then car after car, headlights jostling as they bumped over the ramp onto terra firma. The cars seemed eager to get where they were going—maybe home, maybe far from home. Facing the ship, another group of cars was poised and ready to board and head the other way. Watching the cars unloading and boarding with equal urgency raised the question of why anyone went anywhere.

"Well, how did he do?" asked Trace.

"He did fine," Tom said and poured wine into her glass, his glass. "It's a pretty tight squeeze here, too."

"Are the ships you drive this big?" she asked.

He looked surprised, shook his head. "Much, much bigger."

"What kind of cargo do you carry?"

"None," he said and smiled coyly.

"None?"

"I serve as first mate on ships that are on their last trip—ready to die. We take them to beaches in India and Pakistan and run them aground in old-ship graveyards."

"What happens to them then?" Something told her that she would have appreciated it more if he had answered that he carried any sort of freight in these boats.

"They're broken down for scrap. Workers swarm out of these shantytowns on the coast, where they live. They pour out onto the beach and cut the ships apart with acetylene torches."

"Ah," Trace said, an image of antlike workers with glowing torches playing in her mind. She took a sip of wine, surprised to find her glass so full. Tom looked better in association with the sea—despite the strangeness of no freight—travel to exotic locales, maneuvering great ships "much, much" bigger than the ferry now disgorging car after car onto shore. The association lent him possibility and dimension; it changed him, suddenly, in Trace's estimation. He had simply been balding, a little chubby-cheeked, perhaps too wobbly in the world. Now there was the possibility that he was weathered, competent, had some measure of wisdom. Maybe it was the Makah in her; she couldn't resist an oceangoing man.

At the end of the night, Trace stood on the sidewalk in front of her apartment, saying goodnight. "I had a good time," she said.

Tom looked at her. "I'm glad," he said. "I did, too."

She turned to go.

"Trace," he said.

She turned.

"I think I'm a little bit smitten," he said.

She gave him a peculiar smile, turned, and walked inside. She pulled a dictionary from the shelf to be sure she knew what he had meant: *Smite: 1. strike heavily or kill. 2. affect strongly.* Thinking about it, she shook her head; men were tricky to comprehend. She searched her memory for any sign in his eyes of a potential for violence and contented herself with the thought that she had not sensed it when she had been with him.

She looked for Paul in his bedroom and, not finding him there, she called for him. When he didn't answer, she checked the roof. He was sitting on the sloping shingles, looking up at the sky. She climbed through his bedroom window and up onto the roof with him. He looked over when she shimmied up, then returned his eyes where they had been.

"What are you doing up here?" she asked. "It's cold."

"Looking," he said.

"What are you looking at?"

"The mountains and stars," he said. She looked where he was looking—at the silhouettes of the Olympics where their great forms rose above the gradually inclining lights of the town. The mountains were a few shades darker than the sky in the half-moon light. Most people who lived in the shadow of the mountains tended not to notice them after a time, to take them for granted. They left it to the tourists to make a big fuss over the mountains, to remind them how magnificent the mountains are. But even though he had grown up in their shadow, Paul was steadfast in his awareness of the Olympics. He let her know when the upper peaks had been dusted with new snow, and he awakened her when a particularly thrilling sunrise blazed red behind them.

She looked up at the mountains for a time. "You do your homework?" she asked.

He nodded.

"Aren't you going to ask about my big fancy date?"

"No," he said.

"Paul," she said.

"Is he going to be my father?" he asked.

She looked at him for a time and said nothing. "We ate at a nice restaurant. He's older than me, and he's kind of silly, but he seems like he cares about good things. He has an unusual job. You know what he does? He helps steer big ships that are really old and ready to be junked up. And you know what he does with them? He crashes them into the beach."

Paul looked away from the mountains, at her, and creased his brow.

She nodded to let him know he had heard her correctly. "Strange job, huh?" she asked.

He allowed that it was.

Two weeks later, on their fourth date, Tom drove Trace and Paul the thirty minutes from Port Angeles up the road to Hurricane Ridge. It was a clear day and from the Visitor's Center they could see the blue-black swath of the Strait, the mountains of British Columbia on the other side. Tiny boats close to shore trailed white wakes; a small armada of sports fisherman were going for Kings off the curved, fingerlike tip of Ediz Hook. Thousands of feet below, between the foothills and the water, the tiny, haphazard buildings of Port Angeles dotted the landscape: the marina, the pier, the smoking stacks of the mill, the gridded streets lined with houses rising up the hill.

On the deck of the Visitors Center, they listened to a ranger give a talk about the Olympics, its geography, flora, and fauna. At first it was difficult to pay attention to what the ranger said, so badly disfigured was the man's face. There were four wide, pinkish-brown slashes running in a diagonal across the left side of his face, barely sparing his left eye.

The ranger told the small crowd that the ridge had been named for the winds that played havoc with the scraggly trees in the winter. He talked about the campaign to rid the park of mountain goats, which were not native to the region, and about the discussion surrounding the reintroduction of wolves. When the ranger had finished, he asked if there were any questions.

No one said anything.

"You're probably wondering what happened to my face," he said. There was some squirming among the members the crowd, accompanied by a noticeable increase in the level of interest.

"This is the result of a run-in with a grizzly bear at Glacier National Park," he began. "I was ten years old and visiting the park with my parents. We were standing with a group of people, much like yourselves—visitors to the Park. We'd pulled over to the side of the road to see why everyone else had pulled over. We soon saw the reason. A mother grizzly—a sow—and her cub were moving slowly toward us across a meadow, grazing at the grass. The mother was keeping herself between us and her cub. People were clicking photographs. With no real warning the mother bear, probably perceiving a threat to the cub, charged us. Everyone scurried for their cars, my parents included. They assumed I would run, too. But I didn't. I had read somewhere that you shouldn't run from a bear if it charged you. So, I stood my ground. Well, the big sow bear focused on me. I stood still while she stood up. I could smell her breath. She brought the claws on her right paw down across my face. I don't think you need me to tell you which side she swiped," he said. He smiled as best he could, a half smile. "I might have been mauled to death if my own mother hadn't come out of our car, yelling and distracting the bear just as it swiped. She hit the bear across its snout with a tire iron."

The crowd shifted nervously.

"Well, you're probably also wondering why I'm here today—why I became a ranger after that. I don't hold a grudge against the bear. She was a mother following her instinct to protect her cub. I forgave her. In fact, I think I'm standing here in this uniform because of her. I learned something that day about wildness, and I carry its mark on me with pride," he said, and his talk was finished.

The crowd applauded. Paul stared at the ranger's face. The scars looked malleable, like raked clay—claw-made furrows, vivid brown and pink. Tom put his arm around Trace's shoulder and squeezed. Trace looked at Paul, who took his own hand up to his face and brought it across and down.

12

Paul woke to birdsong in the bunchgrass meadow where he'd pitched his tent near a small creek chuckling down to swell the south fork of the Sol Duc. He lay in the tent identifying the songs as swallows, the tight rasp of the Vaux's swift, occasionally interrupted at closer range by the unmistakable caw of a Steller's jay.

He was bone-weary from spiking so many Douglas firs in the Temple Grove the night before, pounding the bridge-timber spikes with his single jack hammer, cutting off the heads with the bolt cutters, driving the headless nails farther into the tree, then coloring their tips with a brown felt-tip marker to disguise his work. He'd lost count of how many he'd done—maybe fifty of the trees the lumbermen had tagged.

The ridge was in almost total blackness, broken only by the cloud-shrouded moon and a few stars barely visible through the forest canopy. Paul felt as if he was hovering over himself to watch himself work, as if he had been divided into the tree-spiking crusader and another self with the ability to watch the crusader at work on the ridge in that magical grove, violating the sacred silence with clang upon clang from his hammer as the spikes disappeared into the boughs. Dan was right. It had been a painful thing to do, especially the first breaching of the wood. He had to remind himself—or, at times, it felt as if he was reminding his other, crusading self—that it was necessary for their salvation. Each time he finished with a tree, he flattened his palm against its thick rough bark as if he were soothing a horse or some other large, gentle creature suffering from an incomprehension of the human logic or illogic dictating the course of its life. The trees around him creaked and swayed in the silence between clangs. He practiced the same ritual before striking the first blow to the spike on the next tree, resting his flat palm for a moment against the thick bark that protected Douglas firs from forest fires when lesser trees perished. As on many previous occasions in the Olympics, he felt that these trees were creatures assembled to listen and give advice, whose incomparable wisdom was based in silence, and he thought how sad it was to live in a world where it was necessary for the loud clanging of a hammer to drown out the trees' silent council, a world in which, in order to save something, you had to pierce it with metal.

He climbed out of the tent, ate an energy bar, and set some water on his pocket stove to boil (timing it to see if it really took only the advertised three minutes to bring water to a rolling boil) in order to make oatmeal. He had sold many of these little stoves to customers at the outdoor store, and he wanted to see for himself if what Jim had told him to tell them was true. It took 3:25. He'd conduct another trial later on and take the average. He wanted to focus on gear as little as possible, as he felt it detracted from the wilderness experience. But in order to keep from thinking of gear too much, the gear needed to work quietly and unobtrusively.

He listened down the ridge to see if he could hear the plaintive growl of a chainsaw, but he heard only birdsong and wind, the whine of mosquitoes, the close-then-far buzzing of flies. He decided to leave his tent and his big pack where they were and he pumped water through his filter into his green Nalgene bottle from the tiny rivulet and started down the ridge, sometimes at a crawling pace, wicking sweat from his forehead and pushing aside underbrush.

When he'd climbed down the first ridge and had reached the top of a second small ridge, his heart was pounding in his chest. He sat on a great soft fallen redcedar in dappled shade and drank ravenously from the bottle, scanning the forest below for any sign of movement or color. He wasn't sure what to expect, and he hit on the strategy that if he was seen, he would pretend to be a surveyor for a new map or a lost hiker, then carry out his disruptive plans anyway. There was no sound of any activity, and the trees and undergrowth on this side of the ridge, while not quite as thick as on the other side, were still so formidable and shadowed that he couldn't see any more than twenty or so feet down or back up the slope. After making his way about fifty yards farther down the ridge, he would stop again to listen. Sometimes the sounds he made in breaking through the underbrush made him think he was hearing someone else disturbing limbs nearby. Once he stopped and, hearing nothing but birdsong and flybuzz, the beating of his own heart, he carried on.

When he'd made it halfway down the ridge, past the buffer zone between Park and Forest land and back into the National Forest where the trees were appreciably smaller, he heard a chainsaw start up and bite into wood. The sound was coming from back over the ridge in the Park, in the area where he'd been the night before.

Evidently, the work he'd done last night wasn't stopping them from doing the damage the saw was doing right that minute. He wondered if Dan had gotten the communiqué through to the right people yet, and he decided to continue on toward their camp to see about leaving a note while he knew they were occupied, lamenting the trees they would cut down while he was doing it.

After he'd reached the top of the ridge and started down the other side, he came to a clearing, a brief saddle in the mountain, before another drop-off, a place that had probably been logged and re-seeded in the eighties—trees here, roughly his age. A black Ford 150 was parked in a cul de sac at the end of the rutted dirt road. A large blue cooler, a few pairs of canvas gloves, an orange water cooler, and an assortment of axes, saws, awls, a toolbox, and a canister of saw oil rested in the truck's bed beside two empty, black chainsaw cases and one shut orange chainsaw case. He was surprised there wasn't more equipment, prepared as he was to pour a mixture of grit into the engines of bulldozers, backhoes, and feller-bunchers. Maybe they would come later. For now, he stood looking into the truck's bed, feeling somewhat overarmed for his adversary. This made it harder somehow. While he was thinking, his eyes fell on two tattered stickers from the nineties riding the truck's bumper: one read *Save a Logger, Kill an Owl.* The other featured a drawing depicting a hand holding a bedraggled owl heading for someone's ass. It read: *Clinton's Toilet Paper.*

An olive-drab tent had been set up in a cleared-out area of sawdust and tamped grass beside the road, two cots set up in it. Three pots and two pans rested on a planed-off board spanning two stumps. A circle of rocks surrounded some blackened ashes.

What good would it do to damage the truck? It wouldn't help the trees to strand the loggers there. It would be better if they left. He picked up the full chainsaw case, carried it a distance and threw it into a thick stand of alders hugging a little creek trickling down the drainage on the other side of the saddle. He made a mental note to come back and get the saw later. He put the container of oil into a pocket of his pack and looked around to see what more he could do. He opened the cooler and put the food in it—some cans of chili and soup, some sausage and jerky, bread and peanut butter and jelly, some apples, a box of pancake mix and several packages of pink Sno-Balls—into a black garbage bag and hauled everything out of the camp up the ridge. When he reached the place where the trees began, he looked back, considering what else he might do to disrupt their progress. He decided this was enough for now.

Before he left, he set down the bag of food and wrote on a cardboard box: *There are spikes in the trees in the Temple Grove stand. Leave them alone! Go home! And don't come back!*

The Maxey boy wasn't as green as he'd seemed in the truck on the drive over or as Smitty had made him sound. He'd worked as a choker-setter outside Aberdeen for Weyerhaeuser for two summers and he seemed to have learned quite a bit during his time there. He was a smart kid, had graduated from high school earlier in the summer, he told Bill, from Kurt Cobain Memorial High, where he'd played a mean free safety for the KCHS Grunge. He had planned to go to WSU in the fall, where he thought he had a good chance at a walk-on scholarship, but his girlfriend got pregnant, and, with her family putting pressure on him, they'd gotten married and he'd started working for gyppo operations like his Uncle Smitty's.

Bill told the Maxey boy that he sometimes wondered what would have happened if he'd taken a scholarship and gone to college to play ball instead of going to work right away. "It was a different time, then. My dad was dead and you were crazy if you didn't go up there and get some of the money to be made in the woods. The work and the trees and the money seemed like it would never end."

They'd identified the best trees in the stand in terms of felling them, getting good lumber, and getting them out when the time came, when Smitty and the Forest Service would have to worry about how to move them from the ridge. Bill wanted to work cleanly and efficiently, but you could never predict exactly what would happen when they fell in a forest like this. You could get into some serious messes in no time. You could ruin the timber or wind up a bloody smudge on the hillside (like his father) if you didn't think carefully about every move.

The trees in the grove reminded him of a few rare stands he'd worked in the eighties when they were at it all day and with lanterns blazing well into the night getting out the cut and he and his compatriots were the undisputed lords of little towns like Forks and Joyce all over the West End. He looked up at the god light filtering through the upper canopy and again said a prayer of thanks for the opportunity to be in the woods and for the gift of this new challenge, this opportunity to help get all this good wood that would otherwise have been locked up to rot into people's homes. Good lumber improves folks' lives.

"All right. Let's get'r done," the Maxey boy said, and Bill smiled and nodded.

Bill always experienced a rush with the first tree. For most of the day and the day before they'd been clearing from a small area of the grove as many snags as they could, getting rid of obstacles—blowdowns, lesser trees, and anything else that looked like it might break up one of the Douglas firs when they fell. They'd been further delayed by the note a protester had left about spikes in the trees, and the Maxey kid had had to drive into Forks for more provisions. Nonetheless, Bill was determined to carry on with the job until he got word from Smitty to stop.

Trees like these sent chills through you when they thundered to the ground. Like an important move in a chess match (Bill had played a lot of chess with an Alaska foreman when he worked on the pipeline), the first one you fell established the rhythm for the rest of the project. You had to think ahead three or four moves to keep from snarling things up or ruining the wood. He looked at the trees in front of him and singled out a particular Douglas fir that looked to have a cleaner place to land than some of the others and that wouldn't be in the way once it fell. It was straight, about 150 feet tall and 6 feet in diameter. He estimated if they got it down clean it could amount to about 5,000 board feet—enough in one tree to build half a good-sized house. He looked at the tree and the area around it for a long time, walking up the ridge then back down. He looked up the bough and stopped to notice the wind and started his chainsaw with one pull and tested it briefly on the bark, then he made a horizontal cut about halfway through the bough. He went around and finished the horizontal cut on the other side, looked up the bough again and up the ridge and made a motion with his arm for the Maxey boy, indicating an invisible swath where he planned to lay it out. He made a diagonal cut from the other side to meet the first one, then completed the diagonal cut on the other side and stepped back.

The tree tottered, stayed still a moment, then slowly, and with greater and greater momentum, tipped and fell up the ridge, just as Bill had planned, missing its marked neighbors, and landing completely intact with an earth-shaking thud that seemed to startle the forest into a quieter stillness after it had fallen and the shaking of the fir had subsided.

"Nice one!" yelled the Maxey boy.

"Still got it," Bill said and held up his saw and revved it twice.

When he turned back to look at the downed tree, he noticed a splash of color among sword ferns and huckleberry about twenty-five yards to the right of the tip of the just-fallen tree. He pulled his goggles up onto his helmet and stared to confirm what he thought he'd seen. He took a few steps up the ridge in the direction of what appeared to be a human form. "Can we help you?" he called and again, "Can we *help* you?" wondering if the tree could have hurt someone even as he told himself this was impossible.

The Maxey boy turned around to see who Bill was addressing, pulled his goggles up onto his helmet, and after some squinting also saw the form among the sword ferns and huckleberry. "What's he doing, you think?" he asked Bill. Then more loudly in the direction of the form: "We can see you, y'know?"

Paul lay frozen on the ground, incredulous that they'd seen him so soon into his surveillance. When the tree fell, it had flattened some of the underbrush that had been concealing him where he was waiting for the appropriate moment to deliver in person the news of his spiking work to the loggers, since the message he'd left on the cardboard that morning seemed not to have gotten through. He'd been steeling himself to stand and do it before they cut down any more than just this one tree.

"Hey," the Maxey kid yelled. "If you're the one who fucked with our gear and left that fuckin' note, you better hope you got wings to fly outta here."

Bill put the back of his forearm against the Maxey kid's chest and shook his head. There was a time when he would have charged through the forest and cuffed this interloper, whoever he was, so he was surprised to find himself in the cooler role some of the old-timers had adopted when he started working in the woods. Bill began to make his way up the ridge toward the form. "Are you hurt?" he asked and added in his mind, *if you aren't and you monkeyed with our gear, spiked these trees, and're snooping around to cause more trouble, prepare for the beating of your miserable life.*

The Maxey boy released a grunt of incredulity at this apparent evidence that they might give their guest any quarter at all, especially in light of what had been done to their camp and the claimed spiking of the trees, the missing chain saw, chains, and oil, the extra trip he'd had to make into town in Bill's truck (because Bill had refused to go himself) to get more food. Bill could feel the Maxey boy's bristling energy and understood it and knew he'd need to try to control it. If this was a lost hiker or even an innocent person spying on the work they were doing, a report of their activity could jeopardize the job.

Paul felt around in his pack for the ski mask he'd brought and couldn't find it. He cursed himself for being so careless, stood up, and held up his hands, realizing that if he didn't stand, they would walk right up on him. He'd wanted to see them working and to wait for his moment to make sure they knew—since the note seemed not to have stopped them and where was Dan's communiqué?—that many of the trees were spiked and to ask them in person if they wanted to risk sending the trees to a mill. "Sorry," he said. "I'm just a hiker. Guess I got a little lost." Paul's right hand strayed up to touch the spear blade through his shirt pocket.

What kind of a hiker, thought Bill, identifies himself so directly as a hiker.

"Yeah," said the Maxey boy, "I guess you sure as hell did. What are you looking for up here? Why were you lying down? Were you sleeping through a chainsaw?"

"Looking for Camp Hyak. In the Park. Got off track and then I just got tired and took a rest here. Now I'm better. I think I know which way to go now. So . . ."

Bill and the Maxey boy were still moving up the ridge toward Paul, closer now, about twenty-five feet away. "So you just hiked right up this fuckin' ridge after you hiked up and down another one to help you get unlost?" asked the Maxey boy. "And I bet you also put some spikes in some trees to help you find your fucking way."

Bill made a motion for the Maxey boy to calm down.

Paul shouldered his day pack.

When Bill and the Maxey boy were close enough to see Paul's face, all three of them froze. Even though it was so strikingly clear, so singular and strange as to beg for commentary, there was no good way for any of them to name right away under these circumstances the resemblance between Paul and Bill. Even though it went unspoken in the moment, it made such a strong impression that no one said anything for a few seconds. Paul was a younger, lither, darker-skinned version of Bill, complete with a beard that was less developed but on its way to becoming as full as Bill's. Their eyes were set in their faces the same way and were identical in shape and color. Both Paul and Bill were momentarily stunned by the recognition. Bill took a step back, staring as if he'd been surprised by a blow from an invisible hand. Looking at the kid was like staring into a mirror through eighteen years.

The Maxey boy looked from Bill to Paul twice, started to name the extraordinary resemblance they were all seeing, then stopped himself because it seemed too absurd a thing to witness under the current circumstances.

Paul broke away from the shock of the odd coincidence first, spurred by the need to find a way out of this, though he kept his eyes on the tall burly man with the mane of a beard in the grey hard hat with more hair curling out of it, a hickory shirt and staged-off overalls with faded red suspenders and a face and eyes so like his own: "Sorry to disturb your work," Paul said and tried to reinforce this with another jaunty smile. "Guess I'll try to head back down the ridge and see if I can find the trail." He indicated the direction he meant, and made to start moving down the ridge right away.

Bill noticed the hammer and bolt cutters affixed to the side of the pack. "Hold up," he said and took a step forward.

"Yeah, wait up a fuckin' minute," echoed the Maxey boy.

Paul considered running away, a dangerous proposition in this rugged forest, especially with so short a lead.

Bill and the Maxey boy climbed over a nurse log supporting three western hemlocks and were ducking under a leaning moss-covered vine when Paul reached back, unzipped a side pocket of the pack, and let his hands find the hard steel of the pistol.

When they'd both ducked under the branch and were fifteen feet from the ferns and huckleberry in which Paul stood, Bill stopped the Maxey boy's progress with a hand.

Paul stood facing them with the pistol drawn, finger on the trigger.

"Jesus Christ!" said the Maxey boy, ducking and flinching when he saw it. Both he and Bill held up their hands.

"That's not a good idea," said Bill. Looking at the boy's face with its several day's growth beard, it occurred to him he had entered some bizarro world in which he was facing his younger self. Nothing was easy. No easy road. "We're just doing our job," he told the boy. "Just doing some salvage here. It's all pre-authorized by the Forest and the Park."

"I don't like your job," Paul said and dimmed his eyes at the two men, effectively masking his own fear and lack of control. Could he shoot someone over this? How had things gone so wrong so quickly? He concentrated on keeping tremors from rioting up and down his arms. Aside from the time when he'd taken it from Dan to put in his pack, he'd never even held a gun.

"What're you gonna do?" asked the Maxey boy. "You're not gonna do *nothing.*'"

Bill put out a hand to try to get the Maxey kid to settle down.

"Turn around," Paul said. "And go all the way back down to your camp. If you turn around to look back, even once, I'll shoot," he said and added "to kill," as an afterthought, something apparently waiting to fall out when he opened his mouth.

"For a bunch of fuckin' trees. That we're getting out to make stuff people *need,*" the Maxey boy said.

"Let's go," said Bill placing one of his big hands on the Maxey boy's shoulder, experiencing the strange sensation that he was obeying his younger, ideologically altered self.

Paul watched and heard them moving across the ridge, the big logger silent, moving steadily, the younger one, who was stocky and strong himself, erratic with rage, snarling, cursing, and whining his way across, fulminating about trees and tree huggers, and the right to work to earn a decent wage to give people things they needed. When they were almost out of earshot, Paul shouted after them, "Don't come back!" When he could no longer understand what the boy was saying, he consulted his GPS and turned and moved quickly in the direction of his camp, his heart doing somersaults from his stomach up to his throat.

"God I'm all stirred up!" said the Maxey boy as he and Bill neared their camp. "He's probably smashing the stuff we left up there. We gotta get the Forest Service up here. Call the cops. Get that loony toons caught and committed. Or . . . we round up Uncle Smitty and some of those other old boys and some of my buddies around there and go get that tree-hugging son of a bitch. String him up in one of his trees as an example. The son of a bitch had a gun! Do you think there are other ones? God!" he shouted. "And, Jesus, Bill, is it just me or did he look a hell, I mean a *hell* of a lot like *you*?"

Bill couldn't bring himself to agree aloud. He was waiting to wake up from this dream and thinking of the clanging he'd heard up the ridge.

"Bill?"

Bill shook his head.

They were coming into camp.

"Well, I'll say it, he looked just fuckin' like you. That is some weird shit. Let's go into town and come back loaded for bear . . . not that I need a gun. He's almost big as you, but he's a fuckin' environmental terrorist pussy, so I'm sure I can take him. Grab him by his North Face and twist."

Bill sat on one of the stumps around the fire pit.

The Maxey boy stood by the passenger side door of the truck. "What are we waiting for? Let's go!"

"We aren't doing nothing," Bill said.

"What do you mean we aren't doing nothing?" He rushed toward Bill. "That son of a bitch up there just fired the first shot in a fuckin' *war*!"

Bill sprang from the stump and had the Maxey boy in a tight half-nelson before he could protest. The boy struggled for a few seconds till Bill tightened the hold to let him really feel it. "We're not supposed to be up here, first of all," he said. "So this has to stay quiet. Second . . . it's not in my best interest to speak to the authorities around here about anything."

"God damn. Le'me go. I can go to town. Just like I did for the food. No telling what he'll do next. How can we work with him on the loose and talking about shoot to kill? We only got one tree down!"

"I need to think a while. When I let you go, you need to settle down and don't disturb me while I think what to do next."

A half hour later, Bill went to talk to the Maxey boy who was lying on his cot and still fuming. "If you feel up to it," Bill said, "go ahead and drive my truck back into town and let your Uncle Smitty know what's going on. If he wants to let the cops and the Forest Service know about this and tell 'em we were up here doing something different from what we're doing, then you make sure you get back up here before anyone else to give me some lead time to get the hell out of here too."

The Maxey boy looked pleased. "Thank god," he said. "I was sitting here thinking about walking away, or stealing your truck. We can't work with some nutcase out in the woods. I'm not doing it," he said. "I've got a kid about to be born." A few minutes later he hopped in the truck, started it up, and drove down the road leaving Bill to the silence of the camp and wondering what Smitty would make of the situation.

13

Trace held in her hand a crumpled scrap of paper on which was written a phone number Paul had given her four summers ago, when she'd asked him who she should contact in case there was an emergency. He had given it to her reluctantly, as if any connection between them diminished his fragile young manhood and independence. It was nearly miraculous the scrap was still in a kitchen drawer among rubber bands, paper clips, old coupons, receipts, and post-it notes.

Phone in hand, she hesitated for a few long minutes before dialing, wondering if to call and check on Paul amounted to a breach of trust no different from her lack of faith following the Brink Forger incident. Since Paul had told her not to worry, did she owe it to him to trust that he would be okay?

Since Paul had been gone, before she went to bed at night, she'd taken to using the bough and a branch of a Pacific madrone beside the house to climb onto the roof, where she would lie on the shingles and look up at the silhouettes of the Olympics. This was something Paul had often done. The roof had become one of the places she looked for him when he wasn't turning up anywhere else. When he first got his growth spurt, he climbed there with snacks to eat as he gazed up at the peaks. On a few occasions she'd joined him. He'd acted as if he didn't like it but he seemed, secretly, to enjoy her presence. Climbing onto a roof was such a refreshingly unmotherly thing to do. She and Tom preferred to look through the windows in front of the house out at the Strait; Paul preferred to gaze up at the mountains from the rooftop. On these nights, she'd been casting her feelings and intuitions toward the dark shapes suspended in the last light to see if she could get some kind of signal from their massive forms. On a few nights she felt she did receive an answer, a feeling of benevolence, as if the mountains meant to tell her *we are watching out for him and all will be well.*

In spite of herself, she dialed the number on the scrap of paper. When Dan Kelsoe didn't answer his work phone at the National Park office, she looked up his home number in the Port Angeles white pages and tried him there. When she got his machine, she hung up and tried the main number for the National Park.

She asked the woman who answered this number if she could speak to Dan Kelsoe. After a long pause, the woman said, "I'm sorry he's not . . . in. Can I take a message?"

"No," Trace began, then reconsidered. "Tell him Trace Granger called."

"Oh . . . Trace," the woman said. "This is Bonnie Jones. I know your son. And, well, I'll tell you this because your son and Dan have worked together the last few years and you should know. Dan was picked up by the FBI early in the morning a few days ago on some DNR land over near the Sol Duc. We don't know exactly what's going on." She paused, as if to let that sink in. "Apparently, they're holding him for questioning. We think it may be concerning some kind of sabotage of the cut in the Temple Grove, but we're not sure. I mean the cut wasn't supposed to happen anyway, but . . ."

Trace wasn't sure what to say. "Thanks," she managed, remembering Paul's voice on the machine—*I can't tell you what I'm doing.* "Dan was alone when he was picked up?" she asked.

"As far as we know. Is Paul all right?"

"I'm sure. I mean, yes, I know he is."

"He's at home then?" she asked.

The bad-mother chorus that had plagued her since his birth, despite her vow to be the best mother she could, voiced its phrase in her head. "Do you know where they've got him . . . where Dan is being held?"

"I haven't heard."

"Thanks for the information," Trace said. After she hung up, she sat for a moment wondering what all of this could mean—how all these strands might connect, because they all seemed related, somehow, the product of forces beyond her understanding. She felt she would be able to discover the connections between the strands if she was able to concentrate long and hard enough—Paul's disappearance, Bill Newton's return, Tom's job overseas, the girl Stephanie's sudden appearance, Dan Kelsoe's arrest.

She went down the white-carpeted stairs to Paul's room in the basement. A window near the ceiling let in plenty of light, especially in the morning. On the wall hung a poster of an athlete, a bicyclist with bulging calf and quadriceps muscles traveling up a mountain road. The caption under the bike read, "What to drive when you're the engine." Beside that hung two black-and-white portraits of Billy Everett and Boston Charlie, two half–Native American explorers of the Olympics around the turn of the century who eschewed life in town to tramp around the mountains all year long. Paul had adopted them as unlikely heroes. Other kids had rock stars and sportsmen, Paul had Boston Charlie and Billy Everett. Boston Charlie had a camp in the Olympics named after him. Billy Everett had a peak. They said Boston Charlie sometimes paddled a canoe seven miles across the cold, rough currents of the Strait to sell turkeys in Victoria. Billy Everett, "the mowich man," was supposed to be the greatest deer hunter the Peninsula had ever seen. In his photo, Boston Charlie had a long white Confucius beard and a wise smile. Billy Everett carried two trussed deer, one on each shoulder. Both photos had been gifts from Tom, who loved to feed Paul lore about the Olympics.

Below these photos, above his bed, Paul had hung a map of the Olympic National Park. All over the map, almost completely obscuring the place names, he'd highlighted the routes he'd taken in green and yellow and written notes in a kind of shorthand about specific things that had happened to him: *7/15—Cougar! coming down from Happy Lake. Took steps toward me, then leaped ten feet into the brush and completely disappeared; 10/11—blocked in by the high tide at the headland, fog and rain all three days. Portland girl at Alava.* Atop Mount Olympus he'd drawn three stars and written dates inside, one for each ascent. There were also stars atop Mount Anderson, Mount Duckabush, Mount Eleanor and many others. Next to the star atop the peak named The Incisor, he'd written *Dan asks*.

Asks what? Trace thought. What had been the answer? Who was *Portland girl*?

His graduation cap and gown were draped over a chair in front of the desk where he did his schoolwork. On a shelf above the desk sat a wooden triceratops he'd had since his dinosaur phase, not long before she'd married Tom. She fingered the tassel attached to the mortar board. What was she looking for? She looked at the articles he'd clipped from the *Peninsula Daily News* about encounters between people and cougars in the Park; and articles about the Temple Grove controversy at its height, when tree sitters and timber company workers were squaring off almost daily; and articles about plans to tear down the Elwha River dams to restore the runs of steelhead and salmon; and several articles about contentious hearings to discuss reintroducing wolves into the Park, at which some old-timers vowed to kill any new wolves if they ever saw them, just like their homesteading ancestors who'd eradicated the original wolves.

She picked up a photo of Tom, Paul, her mother, and herself that had been taken on the porch of the house on the reservation at Neah Bay not long before the wedding ceremony. She remembered ten-year-old Paul sitting on the couch listening while Trace's mother told him the kind of story he loved to hear about traditional Makah preparations for a whale hunt. One involved a harpooner going to a secluded freshwater stream or pond, diving in, and staying under for a long time. When he came up to the surface, the hunter would breathe like a whale—*hooo*! Trace listened to the story with a sense of relief that the burden of Paul's cultural learning didn't fall solely on her shoulders, pride that he wanted to hear the story, and contentment that he could now pass this along. This was the summer of the first successful whale hunt the Makah had conducted in seventy years, so the power of this kind of story had been rekindled and seemed alive again. Uncle Jack had participated in the cleansing ceremonies the whalers underwent before they set out, and he'd been in one of the motorized support boats that accompanied the traditional whaling canoes. He'd helped protect the whalers and Neah Bay from the protestors who came to try to stop and later to decry the hunt. As soon as she heard about the capture, Trace's mother had called the house in Port Angeles to tell Trace in a voice full of pride, "They got one! The Hummingbird has landed!" and Trace, Tom, and Paul had raced out to Neah Bay to participate in the celebration. They arrived in time to hear the prayers said to release the whale's spirit, to see groups of men hoist the whale onto shore to a cadence, and to watch the butchering. Later, they received a portion of the meat and some oil.

To go with some of that smoked whale meat, Trace's mother cooked up a batch of ozette spuds, the sorry little potatoes that grew on the rez, a relic from the Indian agent's attempt to move the Makah toward agriculture, a time when tribe members had famously bent their pitchfork tines into halibut hooks and held secret potlatches on Tatoosh to keep their culture alive.

Trace remembered a small fight she'd had with Tom at the time over the tribe's decision to exercise their treaty rights and go after a whale. Even at age ten, Paul had expressed an ambivalence that Trace, her mother, and Jack didn't share. They understood how important this hunt was to the Makah's cultural identity. At dinner one night, Tom had questioned the necessity of the hunt. Why did they need to do it now, he asked, when the Makah didn't have to have the meat for sustenance and when whales were just barely off the endangered species list? She'd gathered that his relatives were even more opposed to the hunt, and some letters to the *Seattle Post-Intelligencer* were violent in their opposition, the worst of them suggesting that if the Makah could renew their traditional hunting of whales, whites should be able to renew their traditional hunting of Indians. Tom told her he didn't understand the use of a high-powered rifle and contemporary support boats if this was meant to be an exercise of traditional rights and ways. Trace had argued for the cultural and religious importance of the hunt, in the end telling Tom he didn't know what it was like, how closely this was linked with tribal identity. She surprised herself when she said it, given her former ambivalence about these things, along with her job at the Marine Life Center. Tom had backed down, admitting he hadn't considered that part of it, though his stand had raised some doubts about him in Trace's mind at a time when they were getting more serious. Paul had remained silent during their discussion. Perhaps he was weighing both sides.

Paul had joined some other children gathered around the whale's head at shore's edge. He ran his hand over the whale's smooth skin, covered in places by white barnacles, and he looked into its eye. He later told people who asked, hikers he met in the mountains who wanted to know more about it once they learned he was Makah, that the eye seemed knowing and kind, full of good wishes. He sometimes wondered in the years since if perhaps these good wishes were for the Makah to whom the whale had willingly given itself, or if what he had seen was a potential for goodness lost when the whale died. Paul was the last of the children to leave the whale's side. Throughout the celebrations that followed he seemed pensive and subdued even as he was very interested in anything he heard about the hunts and preparations for them in stories such as the one his grandmother was telling.

Later that night a sudden thud had sounded against the wall—something had hit and shaken the little Neah Bay house where she'd grown up. Trace opened the door to reveal Tom, standing ten feet away in the gravel between Uncle Jack and Cousin Hank. Tom was wearing a hemlock crown, a dyed redcedar vest embossed with abalone, and an expression that was at once proud, hopeful, and bewildered. Some people came over from Washburns to get a better look. Tom snuck a nervous glance at both of his companions, who looked as if they were trying to keep from laughing. Trace's mother and Paul came to the door to see what was going on.

A twelve-foot yew harpoon protruded droopily from the wood beside the door.

"Jack, what the hell do you think you're doing?" Trace's mother asked.

"It was all his idea," Jack said plaintively. "He said he wanted to do everything traditional. We just encouraged him a little." Cousin Hank, who'd been in the Hummingbird for the hunt, laughed behind a hand.

"Go on, Tom," Jack said, barely managing to get it out before it was lost to laughter. "Don't you have something to say?"

Tom looked from one to the other of them. "I've come for Trace," he said in his gruffest voice. Jack and Hank gave in to the laughter they'd been holding in.

Trace's mother shook her head, then started to chuckle. Trace, whose face was composed with concern for what Tom might have had to endure with Jack and Hank (they had told her they were taking Tom halibut fishing in Jack's old gillnetting outfit), stepped out of the house to examine the harpoon. Trace had hoped that sometime during their day, Tom and Jack might get on the subject, beloved by both, of boat engines, about bilge pumps and pistons, electrical systems, and machine oil. Paul peeked around the door and looked at the old harpoon jutting at a precarious angle from the wall. "A little dicey," Trace said, fingering the wobbly shaft. "But I guess it'll do."

She walked down the steps. Tom stepped forward. When they hugged, Jack and Hank raised a whoop. Then everyone, including Paul, whooped. So, strange, this whooping, a performance for Tom, heartfelt, jubilant, playful, but with some distance too, an acknowledgment that in some ways he was not one of them but also that they were not fixable in any old ritual whose authenticity was dubious. It was endearing that Tom took it so seriously, that he wanted to believe in it, when the rest of them were ready to laugh.

Trace's mother went in for a camera, and Jack snapped the photo of all four of them on the front porch. Tom had been such a good sport, she thought, so eager to please, so naïve in his thinking that the secrets of the tribe might be so readily accessible, that he almost erased himself in his attempt to comply.

Tom had already proposed in his own way. When he came back after going out to sea for two months, he and Trace went digging for clams. Paul stayed with his grandmother at Neah Bay while Tom and Trace walked out to the thin sheen the waves left over the sand at a beach near Sequim and watched intently for a tell-tale spurt of water.

When they saw a spurt, they rushed to it and dug as fast as they could to catch up with the clam, which was itself racing to dig away from them. Trace had been doing this since she was a girl, so she was adept at displacing the wet sand to catch the descending clam. Tom laughed in amazement at her ability. By the end of the day, they had a bucketful of butter clams.

Back at Tom's house, they steamed the clams and melted some butter. When Trace opened her third clam and was about to fork out the contents, she saw a ring sitting in its moist flesh; the twinkling of the small diamond outshone the shimmer of clamflesh. She gasped; it was beyond unexpected. She told him she needed a few days to think it over.

They told Paul he would be their ring bearer, and he was thrilled until they showed him the suit he would wear, and he realized they had said "ring bearer" instead of "ring bear." He had formed an image in his mind of himself in a bear outfit, pacing and growling around in a ring. When he found out the real meaning, he thought for the first time that the adult world was never as exciting as it should be.

Now, eight years had passed since their wedding.

That morning she'd had another e-mail from Tom. He'd written to say he was overseeing the cleaning of the tanks on the ship, the *Melinda Rae*, and that they were moored not far from the ship's final resting place at the Alang beach in the Gulf of Khambat in the Arabian Sea. In this e-mail, he went on at some length because, following the cleaning, they were merely waiting for the signal to rev the engines and beach the ship. *The currents are very strong*, he wrote, *and our rusted anchor chain is stretched tight in the wind. Anchored all around us are old Russian ships, including, until early this morning, an especially beautiful one named the* Illya. *All of the ships will meet a similar fate as the* Melinda Rae. *With its icebreaker bow and fresh paint, the* Illya *looked like it ought to have had a long life, a respectful second or third act. Its owners must be desperate for cash. Early this morning, about five or so, I watched as the* Illya *churned off toward the beach. An hour later, we heard on the radio that the* Illya *was no more. I wonder if I'm the only one who thinks these old ships have souls.*

Once again, when she answered this e-mail, she didn't let Tom know about Paul, feeling this time that not telling him was a sort of betrayal. She wondered what was in this deception by omission and decided it was a kind of denial founded on the strong hope, even now that the possibility of Paul's involvement with Dan Kelsoe had come to light, that everything would work out before Tom returned.

Trace put down the photo and opened and closed Paul's clothes drawers, seeing nothing unusual. Did she want to find a diary? For what kind of clue was she looking?

A series of knocks sounded—four emphatic pounds like four stones hitting the front door—that froze her in place for a few seconds. Irrationally, she thought of the harpoon.

She walked upstairs and put her eye to the peephole. Two men she' d never seen before, dressed in jeans and plaid-patterned collared shirts, were standing on the front step. Slowly, she opened the door.

"Hello, Mrs. Granger?"

"Yes?"

"I'm Clark Duncan and this is Jim Lassiter. We're with the Federal Bureau of Investigation. We have a warrant." He flipped open a wallet and flashed a badge. "We'd like to ask you some questions about your son Paul, if you'll give us a few minutes of your time."

"Or, if he's here," Jim Lassiter added, "we'd like to question your son himself."

Trace nodded and opened the door.

"*Is* he here, Mrs. Granger?" Jim continued.

The bad cop, thought Trace, and shook her head, "No. He should be back . . . soon."

"Is there somewhere we can go to talk for a few minutes?"

Brent Sawtelle sat in a black SUV down the block. They'd decided he'd be covert in this part of the mission. He was to watch for anyone exiting the house and to be on call in case they needed him to pursue a car fleeing the scene. He listened to Marvin Gaye on the radio and wondered what progress his fellow agents might be making. He'd taken an interest in the profile of Trace Granger's son Paul, whom he'd begun to see as a kindred spirit—his expulsion from school for defending kids who'd been bullied, his work in the Park during the summers, his summits of peaks. Brent knew he should remain objective, but he couldn't help hoping the kid was innocent, or, if he was guilty, that he'd cooperate and help them nail down their case against Dan Kelsoe. *What's going on* went the chorus as he watched the nice house on the bluff set off by Scotch broom and a tall Pacific madrone. Through cracks in the foliage, he could see slivers of the Strait.

Trace nodded and led them into the living room.

"Quite a view," said Clark.

"Amazing view," echoed Jim.

"It's always changing." Trace sat on a chair. "Never the same."

The two men sat on the couch.

"Do you expect him back soon?"

"Yes," she said, nodding, "very soon."

"Where is he?"

She shook her head. "He goes camping like this all the time. Up in the mountains." She gestured vaguely in the direction of the mountains and thought of Paul's message on the answering machine and made a mental note to erase it. Did they already know? Had they wired the house? So many worlds in the one world. Or perhaps these men were more like aliens from another world who opened up a door and changed your world when they entered it. Be careful, she told herself. They can change your life. Think about Paul at all times. Keep his best interests in mind.

"Where is he camping now, do you think?"

She pointed in the direction of the mountains again beyond the front door they'd just come in. "Don't know. Just somewhere . . . up in the Olympics. Like I said, he does it all the time."

"How long has he been gone?"

What was the best answer for Paul? Was it best to be honest? How much did they know? What was there to know? What had he been doing? What did he get himself mixed up in? "I'm sorry," she said. "Why are you here?"

One of them looked down at the white carpet—Clark or Jim? She'd forgotten which was which. The other—Jim? Clark?—put on a reassuring expression and began nodding. "That's a fair question," he said. "You're entitled to an answer. We're afraid Paul may be in some danger. He may have fallen under the influence of someone engaged in illegal activities."

"What kind of activities?" she asked.

"Domestic terror. Conspiracy to tamper with a legal timber sale on federal land. Organizing the bombing of dams. Burning down shelters in the National Park. Perhaps helping to organize the bombing of SUV dealerships. This sort of activity."

"How long has Paul known Dan Kelsoe?" the other one asked.

"A few years. Three or four years, I think." She thought of the first time they'd seen him up on Hurricane Ridge longer ago than that, of all the time Paul had spent with him.

"And how would you describe their relationship?"

"Paul works for him in the Park. Clearing trails and repairing bridges."

"Has Paul ever mentioned the Temple Grove, Mrs. Granger?"

She shook her head and said, "No," though she remembered how closely he'd followed the controversy when it had had the whole community choosing sides. Even though he posted those articles on his bulletin board and displayed a quickening interest whenever a story came on the television about the stand-offs between loggers and the activists who'd come from all over the country to sit up in some of the trees in the grove, she couldn't remember him ever saying very much about it. That wasn't his way of being in the world. You had to watch what he did, not what he said, to discover what he cared about.

They looked at each other. One nodded to the other. "Do you mind if we look around a bit?" the second one asked. "May we see his room?"

"Yes . . . no," she said with a quiet sharpness, the undercurrent gaining force in her. "But you will anyway, won't you?"

"We do have a warrant, Mrs. Granger," one of them said.

14

Paul lay awake in his tent thinking he should have talked his way out of the situation on the ridge, had a better story ready, or been more careful in his spying—anything instead of resorting to the gun so soon. Anything but getting caught.

Sleeping was often a difficult prospect when you were alone in the woods. In the confines of his tent it was easy to imagine that the sounds he heard outside were cougars or bears snooping around. On certain sleepless nights his imagination conjured a host of cougars and bears circling the tent, waiting for their moment. On several occasions, he'd thrown open the tent flap, certain he would see and need to confront a tooth-and-claw predator and been amazed to see nothing but his own empty boots stuffed with his socks, a benign breeze working the leaves and grass.

It was another thing entirely to have good reason to believe that two (or more) burly loggers were looking for you because you'd threatened to kill them.

He had moved his camp from the bunchgrass meadow to a soft knoll in front of a crook in a redcedar about fifty feet into the forest, thinking it would make him more difficult to find, but the new site didn't set him completely at ease. He'd already put the loggers on alert. The next time they met, all hell was likely to break loose, especially considering the loud retreat of the kid about his age and the size of the man with the mane of black hair and the grey-flecked beard who looked so much like himself.

The biggest problem, he decided, was the gun. If newfangled gear presented a problem in the wilderness experience, then a weapon like a gun presented a problem in the basic human experience. Though he couldn't see the pistol, it throbbed with a certainty of its own significance in the pocket of his day pack, which rested on the ground at the mouth of the tent. It was hard to take your mind off of a gun. Its power was too certain, its iconic potential for deadliness too emphatic. He'd imagined several times the scenario in which he heard voices approaching from the distance. The ever-mischievous forest had provided him with several of these anxious moments. Three or four times in the early dusk he was certain he heard the approach of a mob bent on revenge.

In spite of what he wanted to believe, the first step of action he took in every imagined fight scenario was to grab the pistol and ready it to bluff or blast his way out. He saw them coming to the tent door and saw himself unzipping it just enough to fire at them. He saw himself getting out of the tent before they arrived and hiding behind a tree opposite it and surprising them from behind with a volley of bullets when they stood before the tent to demand he come out.

How wrong was it to envision this extreme defense? How contrary to the pristine wilderness experience? Or, was it perfectly in keeping with the wilderness experience? Wouldn't a wild animal, if it could, invent, create, and take advantage of the edge a gun could give it? What animal wouldn't fight if it was cornered? Imagine trying to subdue a cougar bare-handed in a cell, backing it into a corner. You'd come into an experience of the cougar's tools, its teeth and claws. Was a gun, like any piece of gear, a human-animal tool, just like a spider's web or a cougar's claws? Yes, but the point was that humans could show restraint. What of his Makah ancestors in this debate? In his dual identities, Paul could shift from one lens to the next—white mainstream to Makah—just like that, like (was it really so easy? did he kid himself to tell himself this is how it worked?) slipping off one coat to put on another. They'd moved through the seasons using what was provided by the sea and land close to the coast—berries, halibut and salmon, mussels, clams, seals, whales. Paul felt the spear blade Uncle Jack had given him, wondering about its authenticity and sensing some disapproval from this distant ancestor, whom he imagined as a stern man of action, hardened by a hard life with slim margins, a warrior who'd use any advantage he could get. Paul sensed that this ancestor would feel he was wasting time with such a debate at all and that he might side with the logger's efficient use of resources over his own wish to preserve them. The earlier Makah had used what they had to their advantage against their enemies, including guns when they had them and could get them past the Indian agent. Their restraint seemed to come from lack of capability more than anything else, a contentment with where they were, freedom from the disease and blessing of fervent innovation. They hadn't thrown the balance out of whack because they weren't advanced enough, not because they wouldn't have if they could. Having the technological capacity and not using it was something else altogether.

Humans could build and use deadly tools against themselves and the Earth and its creatures, or they could choose not to build and use them. Ironically, in the choice not to build and use the deadly or irresponsible tools they could build, humans gained their true humanity. But what if you needed the deadly tool to keep the bad guys, who were sure to build and use the deadliest tools, from winning the day and carrying out their will? That's where the trouble started, there was the rub. How could you make that decision? How could you know you weren't, or wouldn't become, the bad guy? Paul decided he would make a choice.

In the morning, after a fitful sleep during which he heard, several more times, forest noises that sounded just like the voices of an angry timber-industry posse coming to string him up, he woke up to forest birdsong, a towhee wheezing its name nearby, and unzipped the tent to the same scene he'd zipped it up to the night before.

Once he was up and had heated water (3:05) and had his oatmeal, he unzipped the pocket of his day pack and pulled out the pistol and carried it through the forest, looking for a likely spot. He settled on a great blasted redcedar, like the one under which he'd camped and like the ones the Makah of his ancestry had cut and hollowed out for their canoes. This tree had cracked and fallen, leaving several large, moss-strewn, swordlike splinters, some of them eleven feet tall, above a cavity. He placed the gun inside this cavity, the splinters circling it as if the gun were some miscreant seed guarded by the jagged spears. He tied a grey bandana to one of the splinters and entered the GPS setting *Guntree*, telling himself he would come back to get it later, when this job was done—but only so that he could return the pistol to Dan.

Before leaving to meet Dan at the Sol Duc trailhead, he decided to go back once more to the Temple Grove to see if the loggers had left. He hoped to be able to report to Dan when they met that the mission had been successful, that the loggers had given up their initial incursion. He broke camp and packed everything away except his day pack and consulted his GPS to help him find his way back to the grove. It was encouraging not to hear their chainsaws, and as he moved over mossy logs and through sword fern and oxalis, he reminded himself how careful he needed to be this time.

About ten minutes later, he stopped when he heard the rustling of something big in the brush. Moments later, he saw the colors he'd glimpsed coalesce into a human form moving through the forest toward the place where he stood. He squatted behind the bough of a hemlock and peered over another rotting log. Paul could now see that it was the older logger from the day before. The man stopped and looked ahead, straight at Paul it seemed, and started moving right for him, coming up the ridge, carefully studying the terrain around him. After a few more steps, the man knelt down and examined a broken bit of fern, then looked up again, unmistakably this time, directly at Paul, making his way toward him through the forest without giving any sign whether or not he'd seen him.

Paul stood when the man, this bearish logger with the speckled beard and wild black hair, was only twenty-five yards or so away. The man stopped and they shared a silent gaze for a time, Paul wondering if the man had brought his own gun with him, Bill wondering if the boy, this militant tree hugger, would draw his gun again. For a moment, as they both held this gaze to the point where it felt like it would have to break, Bill questioned his decision to see if he could track the tree hugger back to his camp. Paul broke the gaze by turning and starting to move away, cracking limbs and rustling underbrush. Bill stood for a moment watching the boy as he scrambled away as quickly as the forest would allow and thought *now he'll go back to his camp for the gun.*

It wasn't difficult to keep the tree hugger in sight or within earshot, though at times the boy seemed to be putting a greater distance between them. Bill had some advantage in traction with his caulked boots on the nurse logs and in the damp rot of the forest floor, but Paul had the advantage of his youth.

Paul punched up *Guntree* on his GPS without breaking stride and made for it, thinking *just this once more to scare him, and to save myself, then never again.* When he arrived within sight of the cracked tree with its spearlike splinters, he stopped again to look back at the logger, who was doggedly climbing over and under blowdowns and branches, his hickory shirt and red suspenders flashing *still here, still coming* in the cracks between the undergrowth. It seemed as if the man was on a kind of autopilot, so steadily was he soldiering through the woods. With the exception of the first stares, when it had been clear the logger was looking at him with what appeared to be a kind of voiceless menace, the man seemed to concentrate only on the foliage he needed to avoid while determinedly and effortlessly following Paul's path.

Paul reached past the circle of jagged spears, felt the cold metal of the gun, and gripped it in his hand without pulling it from its nest in the splinters. "What do you want?" he called out.

There was no answer.

Paul tightened his grip, lifted the gun a few inches above the nest, and imagined the muscle motions that would carry it between two of the protective spears and what it would feel like to squeeze the trigger and hear the report rending the silence.

Bill heard the question and posed it to himself. What *did* he want? What *was* he doing? His father had begun training him in the pugilist arts early. On his twelfth birthday, he'd thrown Bill some old boxing gloves, put on some gloves himself, and beat the hell out of him. He'd taken his father's blows and kept coming till even a man as tough and dauntless as his father had to stop hitting him. Through the years that followed, though he had punished many men with whom he'd fought, including a few loggers who'd given him too much shit about being a virgin (before the picnic on the banks of the Elwha), and the Hells Angels that day eighteen years ago, and a man in a Ketchikan bar, and a fellow gillnetter who'd made the mistake of trying to pin an unflattering nickname on him, and a handful of other unremarkable scraps in bars, he had never killed anyone.

"Turn around," Paul said. "Don't cause any more trouble for yourself."

Again, there was no response.

"None of it's about you," Paul called out. "It's about the trees. And to protect myself."

Keeping his eyes on the tree hugger, who was leaning in a strange way against a blasted redcedar with tall spearlike shafts where it had rotted out and broken over in a blowdown, Bill sensed that this chase was different from any fight he'd been in, though his face had taken on the same expression of strange, unsettling relish witnesses had noticed in the other fights. Nothing like the possibility of death to remind you you're alive. Would this chase end with the tree hugger on the forest floor, broken and bloody but bound to recover in a few days, or would a chase like this need to end in something more than a sound beating?

An explosion rent the quiet followed by a whizzing and a rain of particles of foliage. An explosion of bark leapt into the air from the hemlock behind and above Bill. *There's the pistol*, he thought, calmly, though his heart was racing, from the instinctual crouch into which he'd fallen in the underbrush.

Paul lowered the gun, shaking as if the bullet had just missed *him*. He looked through the branches and undergrowth to the place where the logger crouched behind a huckleberry bush that failed to conceal him and thought *there he is, exposed, you could fire again and hit him*. But he dropped the pistol back into its nest below the spikes as if it were some diseased thing intent on crawling up his arm and into the core of his being and moved with greater purpose down the ridge and to the east.

Still crouching, Bill rested for a moment in contemplation of what had happened before the strange compulsion to follow the gun-toting tree hugger returned to fill the space temporarily occupied by the shock of having been fired upon, like water refilling a temporarily emptied basin of a spring. He stood and followed the sounds of twigs snapping, glimpses of the green rainjacket.

Paul heard branches breaking and underbrush rustling behind him and a fleeting backward look at a splash of black confirmed that the logger had taken up the chase, even after he'd been fired upon. Something in the logger's determination made it seem unlikely he would give up until a decisive reckoning had come to pass between them, something beyond the mere whiz of a bullet. Paul wondered if he would soon be the one dodging bullets. There had been plenty of time for the logger to go back for his own gun. Perhaps he was waiting for a good shot, which, when fired, would not be aimed high.

They kept moving down the ridge and to the east, occasionally sliding on conifer needles above moist unstable soil, clutching at roots, rocks, limbs, and moss. The sun beamed down through needles and branches in starry gleams and specks, its light animating the trees and moss in a profusion of greens. Some rays passed through unbroken to shine on slowly swaying strands of spider web. Swallowtails and Western Sulphurs dipped and rose with apparent unconcern for direction and soft breezes ruffled the leaves and needles. It was a beautiful day whose incongruity with the chase struck both of them as strange, and both of them in their own way thought about how even despite the chase they were glad to be in the woods on such a day.

They fell into a rhythm of stepping over and ducking under branches, which sometimes caught their pants, and using their hands in moss and limbs and dirt for stability, their own heavy breathing in their ears, an awareness of the other's presence an extra weight they carried, an infusion of energy to push them on.

Around three in the afternoon, Paul fought his way through a thick grove of alders to the clear gurgling water of the upper south fork of the Calawha. He stooped down and without running the water through the filter filled the Nalgene bottle he'd been drinking from as they'd made their way, willing away the contaminants that might give him giardiasis. He risked a quick glance behind him to redefine the margin between them at about fifty yards—the logger was just reaching the thick alders—though Paul was beginning to wonder if the man might disappear if he stopped turning around to see where he was, whether the logger might be an apparition, some trick of conscience, an older self he'd created to haunt and harry himself through the woods.

On the opposite side of the river, Paul faced another ridge of about 2,000 vertical feet, conifer tips on conifer tips all the way up to the jagged inclining crest, like the deep green fur of some colossal beast. He turned to look again when he had come to a rocky outcropping about a hundred yards up around which there was a small clearing affording him a view of the river below. The logger was stooping in the shallows to fill his aluminum canteen.

When it was filled and Bill was starting to wade the river again, he looked up and saw the arresting sight of the tree hugger's face and shoulders, his own face eighteen years ago, jutting out of the brush up the ridge.

"Give up now, and go back," Paul called down. "You'll never catch me."

For a moment Bill wondered if this doppelganger half his age could be right. He admired the confidence with which the tree hugger made this pronouncement as he had been admiring his fluid movement through the forest, though he expected he could and would catch the boy if that's what he wanted to do, if that's how this chase was meant to end. He asked himself for the hundredth time what he was doing in the chase now that it seemed to have nothing to do with defending the cut in the Temple Grove and what it stood for.

Bill waded the rest of the river with the same steady resolve he'd demonstrated throughout the day. When he was almost to the other side, Paul started to move again.

Several hours passed. Their muscles grew sore, blisters formed and burned on their feet, and their joints and bones, especially Bill's, started to ache. The forest darkened and a misty rain began to tap the needles and branches of the upper canopy, then drummed more loudly, trickling down to the undergrowth, nodding the leaves of huckleberry and oxalis, the tips of ferns, and running in rivulets down the ridge.

Without stopping, Paul raised the hood on his green heather rain jacket. Behind him, also without stopping, Bill took from his pack and donned again his worn black rainjacket. He had gained some ground on the tree hugger and could see signs of his passage in broken foliage and the places where he'd slipped and turned up a dark portion of loamy soil. In some places in this forest, even on a day when it wasn't raining, you could pick up a handful of rotting bark and wring a cupful of murky water from it. Most of the time the tree hugger registered as a blur of color, red and black for his day pack, a pale green for the color of his rain jacket.

By evening, the logger showed no signs of quitting. He'd even gained a little ground as they'd come up the ridge. The light was dimming and Paul was slipping more often in the wet soil. He wondered at the persistence of this logger and considered what he ought to do. Counterattack? Speed up and hide? A complete change of course? What were the rules for this kind of thing? Should he have kept the gun? What would Dan advise? He decided to pick up his pace during the last hours of light to try to gain a safe margin.

When the sun disappeared behind a ridge and the only light was in the gloaming, Bill couldn't hear or see the tree hugger for a time, which troubled him because the boy's disappearance seemed so sudden. The last time he'd glanced up he'd seen nothing but inscrutable forest, the trees in their silence unwilling to offer any sign they'd ever seen any human form in all their years. He remembered a story he'd heard in Alaska about a wolverine pursued by a man on a snowmobile over a series of ridges. Every time the wolverine got to the top of the next ridge, it turned to look back at the man on the snowmobile, which was gaining on the wolverine with each ridge. When the man crested the next ridge, the wolverine, who'd been concealed just over the crest, pounced on him, hitting him in the chest, knocking the breath out of him, and tumbling him from his snowmobile. The wolverine ran away in the direction from which they had come. For a time, hand on knife handle, Bill looked in vain for signs of the tree hugger's passing, thinking that, like the wolverine, he might double back for an attack. He listened for any sound of him moving through the forest, expecting him to pop out from behind one of the firs or from behind a stump or a slick snaky root at any moment, gun drawn. There was no shortage of places from which an ambush might occur in this forest. But, chance after chance, no such ambush came. Did he want the tree hugger to jump him so they could settle things?

As the darkness accumulated weight, Paul's headlamp cast only a dim orange light and occasionally no light at all until he jarred it back to brief life with a smack. Branches loomed as if they might attack before he could get a fix on them. After a time he decided it was senseless to try to carry on, tired as he was from picking up the pace. He turned and shined the headlamp on the darkening forest through which he'd passed and saw no sign of the logger.

Somewhat miraculously, through the crosshatching of thousands of branches and hundreds of boughs, all of them slowly losing their distinctness in the increasing darkness, Bill saw a small flash of orange light up the ridge and knew he was still on the right trail and not in danger of imminent attack.

Paul made his way a hundred yards or so farther into the forest, up the ridge whose crest he could tell he was nearing by the greater frequency of star-glimmer through breaks in the canopy. Sweating under his rainjacket despite the coolness of the night and the jacket's vaunted breathability, so exhausted and sore he thought he might surrender to the logger's will if the man were to come upon him right then (unless a fresh injection of adrenaline found him in the moment), he collapsed at what he took to be the top of the ridge and resisted the temptation to look back again for fear his headlamp would give him away. He drank some water and ate half of one of his two remaining energy bars and, as quietly as he could, half of one of two apples (with what felt like thunderous chomps) and one of his last handfuls of trail mix, thinking of the high-calorie, freeze-dried meals miles away in his big pack at the broken camp. He took off his boots and tended to some blisters and tried to stay awake where he sat on the forest floor with his back against a silver fir, a stout branch in his hand, and a few large rocks within reach to fend off cougar, bear, or logger.

A short time later he woke up to the smell of smoke and cooking food and saw, on a higher portion of the ridge and no more than fifty yards to the west of the place where he sat, the flicker of firelight on the boughs, ascending sparks. He crept from his tree, clutching the stick, and crawled up the ridge. From a safe distance outside the circle of firelight, he looked down into a declivity where the logger was sitting beside a small fire and eating a sausage he'd stabbed on the end of a big hunting knife.

Bill sat on a rotting log that had fallen in such a way as to make a good bench—soft with moss, if a little damp. He did not know how far the tree hugger had made it but judged it wasn't very far unless he'd found more batteries for his headlamp, which had looked to be dying the last time he'd seen it. He doubted anyone had the fierce inhuman gumption to push through this forest in complete darkness when cougars and bears did their hunting. This is the strangest, maybe not the most difficult, game I've ever tracked, he thought, remembering the bears and moose and wolves he'd helped his clients track and kill and which he'd skinned for them. He chuckled forlornly and asked himself again what he was doing and added a few more answers to the list. A guy could make it to thirty-eight—an age at which you thought when you were still a boy you'd have everything figured out and the world on a string—and still feel like you didn't know a god-damned thing. All ages must be like this once you reached them—dim husks in comparison to the glowing prospect for wisdom and certainty they'd presented when you were young. You've blown a gasket, he'd been telling himself all day, thinking of the whirring in his chest over the Makah girl that seemed connected to this chase in some strange way he sensed but couldn't confirm. Gone and sold the whole farm . . . chasing your lost youth, he thought. Trying to discern any differences between the tree hugger and himself, anything that would help him dismiss the similarities, he pored over each brief recollection: the boy as he'd seen him the first time in the Temple Grove; and earlier that day just before he'd been shot at; and later, at the place up on the ridge above the Calawah. He shook his head and chuckled. They'll sure as hell never find you out here anyway. He bit into the hot spicy sausage at the end of the knife and thought of the note he'd left for the Maxey boy, or whoever else came back to their camp: *Went looking for him. –Bill.* He imagined them finding it and wondered what they would do when they saw he wasn't there. He hoped they had enough sense not to send any sort of search party after him or anything asinine like that and suspected they wouldn't. He didn't think it was likely he would go back to that grove. He was done with that. For some reason, he was in this hunt to the finish and everything after it was as blank as his bank account.

But why was that? What are you doing, Billy? he asked himself. Say you do catch him, what then? A dark image came in answer: he would slit the tree hugger's throat with the knife on a high cold peak with the wind whistling in the rocks and snow. He thought of the Binding of Isaac and heard the Bible's words with the rhythm and inflection of Pastor Smallet from the New Way Peak Oil Commune, where he'd lived and worked maintenance for his last year in Alaska. Some of the commune's members had saved his life when they found him nearly frozen to death beside his broken-down snowmobile on the icy surface of a lake where for the last hour before he passed out he'd watched a pack of wolves cavort and dance in the moonlight: *Take your son, your only son Isaac, whom you love and go to the land of Moriah, and offer him there as a burnt offering on one of the mountains that I shall show you.*

Was that what he would do? Or would God, or one of His emissaries, come forth to tell him otherwise? If that dark image had been some sort of vision, and that vision was true, then no. No voice would speak to stay him except his own, or the tree hugger's.

Or, would this tree hugger, who looked so much like him, kill *him*? Why hadn't he already? He saw himself falling, gutshot and left to die in a nondescript portion of this forest, like all the miles of underbrush they'd been through that day and probably would continue to plough through tomorrow and the next day, defining their lives in the absurd constancy of the chase. In this scenario, shot down and left for dead, he saw himself looking up into the glow of the green light toward the blue sky above the uppermost reaches of the conifer boles, the great trees, who gave of themselves for the betterment of man, standing over him and offering as a last rite their silence, the whisper of the wind through their branches and needles.

He realized that any anger at having his life threatened with the gun or his livelihood jeopardized by the spikes was spent, as was the frustration of having to respond to another bleeding-heart, out-of-touch, muddle-headed environmentalist (as his dear, departed mother would also have tabbed this particular tree hugger), even as the drive to continue the chase remained. And why was that? He thought of the girl he'd seen in the Albertsons and how it had set his heart to whirring and how the few days he'd spent in the woods with the Maxey boy, the prospect and challenge of good honest work, had begun to slow it down before it had commenced again the moment he saw this tree hugger lying exposed in the brush. Whatever its source, he was not going to turn back until the end, and he was faithful something would come to let him know the end for what it was.

He heard a faint rustling, clutched his knife handle, and looked in the direction from which the sound had come, but he saw no sign of anything—animal or human—within the circle of firelight.

Paul crawled away, back to the place beside the tree, then moved about a hundred slow yards farther to the east in the dark, formulating a plan to wake at first light and move quickly and silently down the other side of the ridge as soon as he could see anything at all. The Bogachiel was the next river valley over, and a good trail ran alongside it that would take him either to the Hoh River Valley across the high divide or past Deer Lake and down Canyon Creek to Sol Duc Falls, where he was scheduled to meet Dan tomorrow.

He sat awake for a time and thought of his mother back down in Port Angeles and the story he had to tell her that would prove he hadn't left because he was upset about the story she'd told him and the way she'd told it, about his biological father. He thought of the summer he'd helped Uncle Jack gillnetting salmon, and he saw the thickset man smiling, gold fillings glinting, as he tossed a salmon into the hold and said, "Them 'buchlids' think where we live is the end of the earth, end of the frontier. They come out all shaken up on the highway and ask us how we like living way out here at the end of creation. For us," his sweeping gesture indicated Vancouver Island, points north, "this is where the world *begins!*" He'd roared the last word so that it was seared in Paul's memory. He thought of Stephanie Barefoot standing in front of the trophy case to welcome him back to school, and about the llama lady and the free way Dan said she lived, wandering the mountains with her llamas. He wondered if Dan had sent out the communiqué that would save the trees in the grove. Just before he fell asleep from pure exhaustion, he imagined what the next day would bring. He saw himself jumping the logger. In the ensuing fight, which spanned the border between waking thought and dream, first one then the other took the upper hand as they tumbled down an endless meadow of lupine and hellebore.

15

The phone rang, startling Trace out of her contemplation of a story Tom had told her in an hour-long phone conversation the night before about a run-in he'd had with Greenpeace protesters at the Alang beach. She'd been thinking about the story as she stared out at late afternoon sunlight glinting in gold and silver stars on the Strait. Tom had seemed to need to tell the story, and she'd listened without interrupting him, occasionally wondering if she would have a chance, or if should make the chance, to tell him about Paul's absence.

On the fourth day of waiting for a signal from the beach master who would give coordinates for beaching the *Melinda Rae* in its final harbor, a Greenpeace group with a film crew had come alongside Tom's ship in a Zodiac raft with a little mosquito-whine motor. The crew had thrown a ladder with a grappling hook over the gunwale and boarded the ship like pirates. The group's leader, a bearded, bespectacled Finnish man named Leif, rattled off the history of the ship—a history Leif knew much better than Tom.

Three of Leif's cohorts, including someone whose video camera lights glared a harsh, interrogatory blaze into Tom's face, looked on to see what the ship's latest and last keepers would have to say about the process by which the *Melinda Rae* had come to be anchored off Alang. Their expressions suggested they were awaiting, with a strange sort of hope, Tom's turn as the blustery antagonist.

"I have to ask you to leave the ship," Tom told them. "At any moment the transfer of funds will be completed and we'll receive clearance and coordinates for beaching her. And we will carry out that end. We don't plan to be dissuaded from it."

"Now it's the *Melinda Rae*. Before that she was named the *Navee III*; before that, *Flipper*," Leif continued for the camera. "Before that, the *Melody Mae*. So many identities for one ship. Are there toxins on board this vessel, Captain? Is the ship stabilized by ballast water that will dump toxic oil into the sea? Do you know, Captain, that Alang was once a beautiful beach that is now ruined for everybody?"

Tom held up a document they'd been given before they left port, according to the instructions he'd been given if he encountered this kind of trouble. "This ship is in compliance with regulations and has been given clearance, as this document will attest," he said. "This is strictly legal."

"You are wrong, Captain. Because the name of this ship is not the *Melinda Rae* but the *Melody Mae*. You do not know your own ship, Captain, because you have come to it late in its life. There is asbestos in this ship and oil in its bilge water. We cannot let you take it to Alang. It is not safe for the shipbreakers. Even if they do not die, they are contaminated by toxins from these ships. This ship must go back to the place where it came from. To take apart this ship requires many men in suits like space suits to keep them safe from contamination. The U.S. and many other countries are too cheap to pay for the proper deconstruction of this ship, yes? So, they take the money from someone to have it disposed of this way. They use the rest of the world for their toilet?"

Did they really mean for him to answer these questions?

Tom had never known any of their outfits to be so aggressive. Typically, though he'd never experienced this, what resulted was a game of chicken in which the driver of the raft, coming eventually to the conclusion that he was not going to be a martyr to the cause, steered out of the way, letting the slogans on his banner do his work for him. Whoever was in charge of the bullhorn would shout out damnation to all concerned for bringing their toxins into this port, but the ship would come in for its grounding nonetheless. Sometimes the event would fetch some press coverage, most times not. After the initial beaching, the shipbreakers would come down from their shanty town to pull ships no one else in the world would take (because of the exorbitant cost of the safe disposal) further up onto the beach. They would break the ships apart and, with their bosses, reap the spoils from the sale of the scrap metal. In this way, the multimillion-dollar industry that kept these workers and their families from abject poverty would continue.

Tom stood silently through Leif's accusations, looking glum and keeping his temper in check by answering Leif only in his head: *This is my job. I have a mortgage on an expensive house in Port Angeles with a view of the harbor and a wife and a stepson who is like a son to me. The owners of the* Melinda Rae *needed a service and I am providing that service, just as they need the services of the shipbreakers here and the shipbreakers are going to provide that service because they have an interest in shelter and nourishment to survive, and clothing and shoes and maybe a few baubles to make their lives seem less bleak.* This, he told himself, as Leif continued to talk for the camera about contaminated bilge water, toxins, asbestos and PCBs in ships built in the 70s, the shell game that was shipping ownership, ecological catastrophe, the beautiful beaches this industry had ruined.

It seemed to Tom that they could have filmed this without him, that Leif's indignation could as easily have fueled his tirade in a Helsinki studio. Just fifteen or so minutes after they'd boarded, a lookout in a Jacques Cousteau cap came to the doorway and flashed Leif a signal. Leif signaled the rest of them, and all of them ran from the bridge and scaled the ladder down to their raft.

Not long after their Zodiac had left the ship, gunshots sounded over the whine of their outboard. Tom moved quickly out onto the deck to see a boat, presumably from the harbor, racing into a fog after the diminishing sound of the Zodiac's motor. Orange sparks flickered in the fog a moment before the sound of further shots reached them.

"Jesus!" said the first mate. "Who's in the boat, do you think?"

"I don't know," Tom said, "but they seem to be playing for keeps."

Fifteen minutes after the two boats had disappeared into the night, the telex beeped and the go signal came in on the radio: *Bangor Bangor Bangor. OK to beach. Call NYO Soonest*. The first mate told the second mate to heave anchor. Tom dictated helm commands to the first mate, managed his last files, and crashed the ship's computer. When the anchor was aweigh, the ship made its speed loop, shaking as it did so. They took a range on the beach and sped for a space between a navy frigate and a half-demolished freighter. The ship hit almost softly at first, then it began to shake violently as it pushed about fifty yards up onto the beach with the engines laboring and the RPMs going up to 110. The shaking reached a crescendo, and it seemed for a few minutes as if the *Melinda Rae* might come apart and make the breakers' jobs all the easier. Tom commanded the second mate to drop the anchors and the first mate to cut off the engines.

All on board grabbed their gear and headed for the lifeboats. The swell against the side of the ship was formidable. It rolled in and slapped Tom's lifeboat, submerging the bow and swamping it with 100 gallons of water. Once they were in the lifeboat, its motor refused to engage. And even when the motor did finally start, they discovered that the tiller had been smashed and would only turn to the port side. The boat shot forward, rammed the side of the ship, rebounded, then started turning in circles. A few moments later, the motor cut out altogether so that they were tossed in waves as if the force that controlled them was angry. Each swell pushed the lifeboat closer to the jagged edges of an abandoned hulk jutting out of the brown water, some forgotten piece of a former ship. The ferocity with which these waves crashed and boiled against the hulk's twisting steel made it seem unlikely they would pass the breakwater alive.

As he told it all to Trace, the fear was still in Tom's voice, a thinly buried tremolo.

The pumpman said he could see the second lifeboat, the one the first mate and the chief engineer were going to take, descending from the ship. When it was in the water, Tom called out to the first mate, and, once they understood what was going on, they arrived at the first boat just when it looked as if one or two more swells would crash it against the steel remains, which appeared and disappeared in the frenzy of swells.

They were able to throw a line to the second boat and commenced a tow. Now the problem would be to get past the surf to the beach. In one seemingly slow-motion moment that had the freeze-frame quality of a strobe light, Tom felt a big swell beneath the boat hurtling them violently toward the other lifeboat. They crashed into it with such wet savagery that it seemed miraculous no one was lost. The first mate put the motor full ahead and they charged through the surging breakers till they'd reached the shore, where suddenly hundreds of thin, hollow-cheeked shipbreakers appeared on the beach, pulling them and their gear out of the boats with great solicitude and many helping hands. When Tom looked back, he saw that both of the fiberglass lifeboats were cracked and thrashing in the surf. He went and hugged the first mate. Before they got into the cab, he looked back again and saw the ship-breakers in bright dhoti's and thin sandals braced against a rope as wide as a pylon attached to the *Melinda Rae*, pulling her to a Hindi cadence.

So many different worlds, thought Trace, in this one world.

Staring out over the changeable waters of the Strait, before letting herself muse further on Tom's story, Trace had also been entertaining a string of memories. She'd been thinking of her unsuccessful campaign, in her fifteenth summer, to be a princess at Makah Days. (Kicking a tribal commissioner's son in the shins for trying to kiss her hadn't helped her cause.) She'd also been remembering the bonfires on Sooes Beach with the elders singing some of the old songs over the drums, and a potlatch on Vancouver Island with fresh faces and lots of running around with other girls. She remembered also the long grasses that her grandmother dyed and wove into baskets that tourists could buy at Washburns, the grasses hanging on clotheslines to dry, blowing in the nearly constant wind. She remembered playing with her neighbors, the brother and sister, Tim and Jeanie, in a little sandbox in the front yard beside rusting hulks of cars and trucks too expensive to have removed once they'd died. She remembered the way people let their dogs run free, how they said hello in their cars by swerving toward one another, and how the men (and sometimes even the women) greeted one another with a hand gesture meant to jovially suggest the other person's dick was bigger, to acknowledge their gumption, their verve. Images played, too, of the crowded gym when one of the small town off-rez rivals (especially Clallam Bay or Lummi Island) came to town to play the Red Devils, the warrior tradition kept alive on the court. She remembered some of the parties out on the logging roads where she'd gone to drink and talk and dance before she got pregnant (and once or twice in the early days after Paul's birth, when her mom watched Paul and she wanted to pretend she was still free). The word would go around and they'd gather out on 200 Line or A, B, or C Line between timber harvests with a case of Olympia or Rainier, and someone sporting a red-and-black Chicago Bulls jacket would leave a car door open and let the bass and beat of a hip-hop song thump out inconsequentially against the trees and the dirt and the damp.

The line between her childhood and adulthood could be pinpointed to a specific day and time. Tom, with his love of precise machinery, could appreciate that.

As she sat and thought, she struggled with an impulse that had asserted itself as a low hum ever since, years ago, she'd strapped Paul into the old blue Dodge and left Neah Bay—a whisper that said *Go back to stay*. She'd fought this impulse, off and on, the entire time she'd lived in Port Angeles, and she fought it now with the answer that to go back would erase or diminish the good things she thought she'd built with Tom and Paul and the Center. Now, the whispering voice could ask, *Where is what you've built? What has it come to? Go back.*

The ringing phone pulled her from the depths of these reveries to the surface of her immediate situation. "Mrs. Granger. It's Stephanie. You might want to turn your TV to Channel 6. Okay? Channel 6. Talk to you later."

The television came back from commercial and the anchor introduced the story:

"The FBI two days ago apprehended Olympic National Park ranger Dan Kelsoe on suspicion that over a period of ten years he has been engaging in domestic terrorism. Authorities say Kelsoe, a twenty-year veteran of the Park Service, has been arrested on several charges, including destruction of federal property. Authorities say they have detained him for questioning in connection with several incidents over a ten-year period."

The local chief of police appeared on the screen speaking into a clutch of press conference microphones: "The FBI arrested Kelsoe on a Department of Natural Resources logging road early on the morning of July twelfth. He is currently being questioned in connection with a number of activities in which they believe he has participated over a number of years. These activities are thought to be eco-terrorist type activities on federal land, animal management sites, and organizing bombings at laboratories and car dealerships. Uh . . . disrupting logging operations, conspiracy to blow up dams, conspiracy to put wolves from Alaska into Olympic National Park without following due process, burning shelters, and other things of this nature."

That night, the story appeared on the national news. Trace remembered hearing about the bombings at Seattle and Portland car dealerships. Thank god, thought Trace, they didn't mention Paul in either one.

Where was he? Later that night, she climbed up the old madrone and sat on the roof looking up at the silhouettes of the mountains, which appeared closer than usual in the gloaming. The mountains, she thought, threw off a distracted energy tonight. They seemed less interested in sending signals than before, as if they had more important things to worry about than the fate of one mortal human.

When she went inside the house, the phone was ringing again. Trace sighed but rushed to answer it.

"Mrs. Granger? It's Stephanie. Did you see?"

"Yes."

"My father wants to talk to you. Here he is, okay?"

"Hi, Mrs. Granger. I'm getting ready to go down to the police station to help a friend in need of some legal services. That friend is the person just mentioned in the news story. Understand? I wanted to let you know that I might ask him a few questions that might be of interest to you. I'll be back in touch if this is the case. It looks like they're going to release him, and I would suggest that you talk to him yourself, but I suspect he's being released as a sort of pretense so they can watch him very closely to see what he does while he's free. I'm going to advise him to lay very low during this time because I think this is in his best interest. I'll bring you anything of interest. Okay?"

"Okay," she said, "I'll wait to hear from you." She hung up and looked out the big windows at the very last of the pink light on the waves of the Strait.

A few hours later Stephanie's father appeared at her door. "We're not alone," he said quietly. "I'm fairly certain I was followed." He handed her a folded piece of legal paper. "I'd better be off. I've got more work to do for my friend. Be careful who you call and what you say." Then he surprised her by giving her a hug. "No word from Paul?"

She shook her head.

Brent Sawtelle watched through the windows of his black SUV parked two blocks down the street as the computer man, Spears Barefoot, who was giving Dan Kelsoe legal advice, drove away from Trace's house.

When she was inside the house and had locked the door, Trace unfolded the page, which included a handwritten exchange:

> *Was P. G. with you?*
> Yes.
> *If yes, where and when were you going to meet?*
> Sol Duc Falls trailhead, one day from now.
> Hoh River trailhead, three days from now.

What did you do in such a situation? How could she help Paul? She wished the foe was better defined so she could fling herself at it with a fury born of pure faith in her son. But there seemed to be no clear path, no well-defined enemy to go after, unless it was Dan Kelsoe himself. But to go after him (he was already in the hands of the most powerful human force on earth) would be to show a lack of faith in Paul and his judgment in choosing to go along with Dan's plan, whatever it had been. *Dan asks?* had been followed by Paul's answer. The other enemies—the shadowy bureaucratic force of the FBI; the primeval force of the wild Olympics themselves; the quiet menace of Bill Newton, regardless of his kneeling in the Albertsons aisle; the ideological divide between loggers and environmentalists; Tom's presence in absence and the job he was doing, the very fact of those shoeless shipbreakers, the Greenpeace men, that hellish beach—these were difficult and diverse enemies, pervasive presences, real and psychic, to immediately oppose with the raw fury of maternal and spousal protectiveness.

She slept very little that night. It was as if she'd been transformed by everything that was going on into a ball of nervous energy whose purpose was to produce thoughts of Paul and Tom in trouble. In her dreams and when she woke, she saw and felt Paul in grave danger. He was set upon by a group of snarling loggers bent upon tearing him apart. He was bloody, broken-boned, and gasping for breath on jagged, mist-enshrouded rocks beneath a high cliff. He was being led from a black car to a courthouse by steel-jawed men in dark suits and sunglasses. When the light poured into the bedroom, she stopped trying to sleep and got up, filled with the certainty that she needed to find Paul so she could talk to him herself. How could she protect him if he wasn't by her side?

She thought of what Makah queens were said to do to help the *haw'iih*, the whaling chiefs, find success in the sea when they went out after whales in cedar canoes. The queens would accompany their husbands on the *oo-simch* ceremonies, the ritual bathing the men performed in fresh or tidewater. The men would attach themselves to their women with a line and swim out into the cold water, mimicking whales by blowing water into the air. They did this to purify themselves in preparation for the whale hunt. Afterward, while the men were hunting, their women were supposed to stay very still, so as to still the spirit of the whale. If they did it well, they could become the whale. Their stillness was meant to help their husbands both in the initial harpooning of a whale whose strange docility in the face of capture was brought about by the wives' own calm back in the village, and to becalm a thrashing harpooned whale who might otherwise destroy their husbands' canoe. Trace had always liked hearing these stories, but she'd never believed in them and had even scoffed at them a time or two. It didn't take much of a leap to see the double entendre, to think of the Makah men saying to their women, "stay still and let me harpoon you, and once harpooned, don't thrash." But now she found herself wondering, in the interest of doing whatever she could, whether what Paul needed from her in his current trial was that she might remain as still as possible, so as to still his would-be adversaries. For a time and with great effort, given the tumult she felt, she sat cross-legged and unmoving on the white carpet. She closed her eyes and breathed, focusing her thoughts on Paul, imagining a line tied from her to him, so that his troubles might also be compliant and still, accepting of what Paul wanted of them.

It was difficult to tell how much time had passed in this way, but she came out of the stillness with the contrary urge as strong as ever to do something for him, to move, to act. She went downstairs to Paul's room. The FBI men had taken all the Temple Grove articles Paul had clipped and hung, but, curiously, they hadn't taken the annotated map of the Olympics. She'd seen and heard them taking photos with a little James Bond gadget camera and they'd left the room a mess, but for some reason they hadn't taken the map itself. Untacking it from the wall, Trace noticed the place where he'd circled an area on the map below Rugged Ridge and labeled it *T. Grove*. She'd seen this before, but now she also noticed that written below this were four dates with no specified year—*July 12–15*. It was July 13. He had not written any notes. Trace was certain they'd taken a photo of those dates and imagined a judge's voice in a courtroom asking Paul about them.

She called a volunteer, arranged for her to come in and take over at the Marine Life Center for a few days, and began packing. She was stuffing a sleeping bag into its sack when the doorbell rang. She peeked through the hole to see Stephanie Barefoot on the doorstep, wearing a maroon fleece jacket, black fleece pants, and hiking boots. Trace opened the door.

"I think we need to try to find him before anyone else does," Stephanie said.

Trace stared out at her.

"I know, I shouldn't be . . . you probably think I'm nuts to be so involved, but I feel like he might need our help. I have a feeling he needs *someone's* help."

Trace looked at the girl in the doorway, wondering what fed this devotion beyond a high-school crush. Did she know something she wasn't saying? Trace glanced at the backpack leaning against the brick entry wall framing the front door.

"Are we on the same wavelength?" Stephanie said, glancing at the sleeping bag in Trace's hand.

"Yes, we are," said Trace, trying to release her skepticism. "But I don't want you getting into any trouble. He's my son. That's why I'm going to find him. . . . I really don't have a choice. But you . . ."

"I know. But I can help. My dad thinks Paul's in real trouble. Either from the loggers or from getting caught by the FBI. He told me not to get involved. He was worried when I was protesting in the Temple Grove, too, a few summers ago, but I'm glad I did that. Dad's back home in bed now, and I just slipped out. I'm going to try to help Paul, whether I go with you or not. I think he needs someone."

"I'm planning to be gone for a while," Trace said, "as long as I need to be, so if you need to come back, I won't be able to take you." She'd been wondering if this was a good time to listen to the voices telling her to go back to Neah Bay, maybe for good, but she hadn't yet been able to make the decision. She wondered if she couldn't decide because of the guilt she would feel for abandoning Tom (or would Tom come with her?) or because of a real abiding love for Tom or . . . something else. Things were stirred up and she didn't know where they would settle.

"That's okay," Stephanie said.

"What about your father? How will he know you're all right?"

"I left him a note."

Oh great, thought Trace, it's contagious.

16

A troop of boy scouts on horseback stood to the side of the trail as Paul approached. Their leader, perched atop a muscular bay cayuse, smiled and said, "Manpower instead of horsepower. Admirable. Where you coming from?"

"Up the Bogachiel," Paul said and continued quickly past.

Many of the boys astride their horses nodded or waved as Paul went by, all of them nearly his age or a few years younger, though they seemed almost of a different species, most of them still with some sleep in their eyes, lips stained red with bug juice, hair mussed from their recent wake-up at the camp called Twenty-One Mile. Paul glanced behind him, saw Bill about forty yards down the trail, and picked up his pace.

The scout leader smiled as Bill approached. "They're tough to keep up with, aren't they? We're not as young as we once were."

Bill nodded at the man but did not smile or take up the unspoken offer to banter as he kept moving down the line of mounted scouts, wondering why the boy hadn't taken this opportunity to stop and get help, then remembering that what he'd done in the Temple Grove required secrecy as much as what Bill had been doing, maybe more. As he gained some distance from the pack train, he heard the scout leader say, "All right boys, let's move out."

That morning at first light they'd seamlessly resumed their roles as if it had been a choreographed routine, both of them moving as soon as they could see, Paul starting a little ahead of Bill, Bill hearing him as soon as he was ready to move. They descended the ridge 2,000 feet, bushwhacking through thick forest, sliding at times, into the Bogachiel valley. They pushed through a copse of alders and bigleaf and vine maple and crossed the river and took the trail on the other side, moving much faster now that they didn't have to clamber under and over fallen limbs and trees, roots and rocks, bush and bramble, moss and rotted log.

For seven miles they moved over the trail in this manner as if they were front-running contestants in a race with defined parameters and an audience tuned in to watch them and broadcasters providing play-by-play and analysis, instead of makeshift devotees to a free-booting chase with no finish line or time constraints. From time to time Paul fought against the impulse to turn and face the logger and welcome whatever would come. He wanted to rid himself of the pressure of the chase, and he couldn't imagine meeting Dan near Sol Duc Falls with the logger on his heels, who would need to be explained and who would represent a failure in the mission, a messy snarl. He told himself he would turn and face the logger at the next fork in the trail and kept telling himself that he had to do it and better sooner than later. Adrenaline coursed through him, making his fingers and toes tingle in a bristling anticipation that increased the closer he came to the crossroads so that by the time he saw the place where the two trails diverged, he was so jumpy a Douglas squirrel in the underbrush made him start and turn with a fierce grunt as if the moment of reckoning had arrived. One branch of the trail continued past Deer Lake to Sol Duc Falls, where Paul was supposed to meet Dan Kelsoe later that day. The other ran along the low divide past the Seven Lakes Basin and down into the Hoh River valley, where he was supposed to meet Dan in two days if something happened and he wasn't able to make the first rendezvous.

Paul stopped at this crossroads and turned and stood facing in the direction from which the logger would come, his feet at shoulder width and his heart immense in its pounding. He told himself he welcomed this, that this is what needed to happen since he'd been so careless. This is what he had to do to clean things up. If necessary, he would let his body become a mess so the mission could stay clean. He was glad not to have the gun because he didn't trust himself not to use it. He took deep breaths to ready himself for a hand-to-hand encounter and stared at the logger as he came around the bend.

Bill stopped twenty paces away. They stood staring at one another for a few moments, nearly twins but for the difference in age, each waiting for the other to make the move that would force the chase into something else. When the boy did not draw the gun or move or speak, Bill continued forward as if this was something he did not relish but had to do. He realized that he'd been lulled by the steadiness of the chase, the miles they'd covered the day before and that morning, into a forgetfulness of thoughts about how it might end.

Paul stood his ground, thinking in a part of his mind, even as he prepared for the fight, that when it was over he would turn up the trail and leave the defeated man on the ground, or he would pick himself up off the ground and nurse his wounds as he continued down Canyon Creek to tell his story to Dan Kelsoe at Sol Duc Falls. Maybe one or the other of them would die on the trail. In the thrilling and dreamlike anticipation of the moment, it seemed that anything could happen. Blood propelled by his outsized heart pounded in his ears.

As he stepped toward the boy, Bill imagined his hand going for the knife, and he saw himself bringing it up in a single decisive thrust through the boy's rib cage followed by a twist into the heart after God failed to speak from the no-place where He hides to tell him to stop. He saw the boy falling into him, both of them covered in the boy's blood, and wondered at the source of such an image.

Paul remembered his dream of them tumbling down a meadow of lupine and hellebore.

When Bill came within a few steps of the boy and saw his own eyes in the boy's face, filled with the resolve to stand strong and hide his fear, Bill felt the desire to fight drain out of his body like a long exhalation of breath. He dropped his hand from the knife handle.

"At least you're not back there cutting down those trees," Paul said, his voice quavery with fear and expectation. "So, I'm happy about that," he said and smiled his quick flash of a smile, taking up again the role of unflappable environmental crusader so that it was as if he was hovering over himself, separate from himself and watching what he'd said.

The man said nothing in response, his lack of speech more unsettling to Paul than anything he might have said. They each looked into eyes so much like their own. Then the man raised his right hand very slowly, placed it on Paul's right shoulder and chest and held it there for a moment, as if this might be the first strange salvo in the fight to come, before pushing gently so that Paul understood that the man meant for him to turn in the manner of an opening door to let him continue up the trail. Paul turned in the expected manner, not wondering as he would later at why he didn't flinch at this touch or push the hand away. The man passed him, heading toward the high divide.

When he was about ten yards away, Paul called out, "I wasn't trying to kill you. I aimed high."

The man said nothing in response. Paul watched him walking until he'd disappeared around a bend. He glanced up the trail that would take him past Deer Lake to Sol Duc Falls, then he looked again down the trail the man had taken, which would lead past Hoh Lake and down into the Hoh River valley. He looked at both options twice more and stood a few minutes in contemplation. Then, disbelieving he was doing it even as he took the first steps, he followed the trail the man had taken deeper into the backcountry, thrilling at the choice, even as his tired hungry body complained against it with every step. He wondered the same way Bill had wondered when he was the chaser, at the compulsion to continue with this chase that had become something else, something unlike anything he'd ever thought he would see in his life. He explained his choice to follow the logger by telling himself he was worried about him—that a vacancy in the man's eyes seemed to promise a rare backcountry calamity or . . . something else he couldn't name. He still felt the man's touch on his right shoulder and chest where the big hand had gently urged him to open like a door.

Bill expected the boy was now moving up the fork in the trail at which he had stopped and that he would never see his younger self again. He expected the strangeness of the chase and the moment they'd experienced on the trail would disappear with time until finally he would forget it. His decision not to fight and perhaps kill the boy had made him feel as if he were floating along above the trail, the whirring in his chest blooming into a feeling of lightness, as if, after being emptied of the aggression he'd felt as he strode toward the boy, he was now being filled with something light as a sigh lifting him up to a new and grander vista. He had the sense that what he'd done at the fork in the trail had been the best decision he'd ever made, but he didn't understand why he felt this way. When he saw at a switchback in the trail that the boy was now following him, he sensed that he wanted to say something to him, but he didn't know what this might be. He asked himself how he felt about the boy's presence on the trail behind him as compared to his loss to the other fork, and, after some consideration, he admitted he was glad of the boy's presence in his wake. It was strange to admit this to himself, but the closest he could come to defining the feeling he'd detected in himself when he understood that the boy had decided to follow him instead of heading off into the ether from which he'd come, was hope, a sort of pleasant anticipation . . . for something, he had no idea what.

A woman leading a pack of five llamas was making her way along the ridge, which was still relatively bare except for some patches of subalpine fir and hemlock. Bill and Paul had gained a thousand feet of altitude to come near the top of Bogachiel Peak, then dropped down to Hoh Lake in its basin. They had now come to the place where gusts of wind had pushed flames up toward Hoh Lake, scorching the ridge clean in 1978. The transpiration from the brush that had grown in to replace the trees came up the ridge to pass over them in humid waves, as if the vegetation were sending them signals.

The woman said hello to Bill as he trudged by. She had pulled her llamas to the side of the trail to better let him pass, and they watched him with wide and wary thick-lashed eyes and a nervous shuffling of hooves. He gave her a solemn nod as he kept on, surprising her with his lack of interest. She'd grown accustomed to questions from most hikers she encountered in the backcountry. She turned to watch him for a moment with sharp eyes, as if she'd sensed something strange or unsettling in him. He certainly looked strange in his stagged-off jeans, flannel shirt, and suspenders—not your typical backcountry hiker. Some of the llamas danced restlessly in their harnesses and packs and rolled their big eyes as if they, too, had sensed something strange in the man.

When Paul came to the place where the woman was standing beside the trail, he stopped to admire the animals, careful not to let her know that he knew who she was.

"They're in training," she told Paul. "Let's see, there's Tiger, Scree, Buster, Tiffany, and Edelweiss." She was also careful not to let him know she knew who he was.

This was the woman Dan had told him about, and whom he'd once glimpsed from a distance, moving with easy grace in a valley below a trail they were clearing. He had seen hikers taking advantage of some of her trainees. She sometimes got into trouble for taking her llamas to higher altitude than the Park rules allowed. She lived on a farm off the road leading to the Hoh ranger station on land bordering the Park. Some compared her to Minnie Cooper, who had guided tourists in the Park during the twenties and thirties. Dan had said that environmental activists who'd gone to fight their battles in Washington, DC, and who were buried under mountains of paperwork, burned out from protracted wars with development and extraction interests, and sickly from too much time under fluorescent lights, came out to take trips with the llama lady to repair their frazzled wills. One day someone would tap them on the shoulder in a corridor of power, far from the land they were trying to save, and say, "It's time to see the llama lady," and they would know what this meant. She was said to be an expert on the effects of new technologies on the environment and was possessed of a vast knowledge of the chemicals (her husband had been a chemist before he died in a fall in the backcountry) out of which manmade things were composed and the bi-products of the petroleum and chemical and timber industries and their unintended harmful long-term effects on humans and the earth.

Paul stopped and ran his hand through the fur of the lead llama, Tiger, enjoying its coarse warmth for a moment.

The llama lady once again turned her icy-green eyes in the direction Bill had gone. "Are you with him?" she asked.

Paul returned from his llama-petting reverie to gaze down the ridge where the logger was disappearing into the shadow of a copse of subalpine firs, where small snowdrifts echoed one another on the up- and downhill sides of the trail. He wondered how to answer such a question, how much this woman knew or sensed. There was a moment during which he felt the whole story gathering momentum to come tumbling out. He stopped it with a simple nod—yes, he was with the man who'd passed—though the play in his dirt-smudged features, a hint of indecision preceding the nod, made the woman narrow her eyes in suspicion.

"Where you headed?

He almost shrugged but didn't want to seem unprepared, this deep in the backcountry. "Down the Hoh and out," he said and thought of Dan waiting in his truck or hiking up the trail to find him.

"Father-son outing, is it?" Her hair was long and grey and braided.

Again, he paused for too long and began to smile. "Yes . . . sort of like that, I guess."

Again, she pursed her eyes as if to say *wouldn't you know such a thing.* "I suppose your father has the heavy stuff?" she said and nodded at his day pack.

Paul blushed, glanced back at his small pack, and brought himself to smile. "We're taking turns," he said. "Not everyone needs llamas to make it back here." Somewhere in the phrase his jauntiness faded, putting the woman more firmly on the scent of something not quite right. He tried to end the encounter with a casual goodbye, but as he moved away, she grabbed his right forearm, looked directly into his eyes, and said, "You be careful," in a way that seemed to invite a deeper admission, or that was connected to the memory of lost loved ones of her own.

Below the area the burn had scorched they could see the glittering turquoise water of the upper Hoh running in braids through the changeable gravel channels, broken by log jams and islands filled with alder thickets. In the distance, beyond the valley and the next ridge, Bill first, then Paul as he gained the ground he'd lost while he talked to the llama lady, saw the peaks of the Olympus massif for the first time—Mount Mathias, the east and west peaks of Olympus, Mount Tom—their sandstone, black slate, and shale bodies covered in a tattered blanket of snow and ice.

Seeing the imposing breadth of the massif rising beyond the initial ridges above the south side of the Hoh River valley, Bill was struck by the notion that he wanted to climb one of the peaks whether trails led him there or not. People had told him since he was a small boy that his great grandfather whimsically climbed peaks in the Olympics with little gear or preparation. He would continue on his own to the top of one of those peaks. He told himself that the boy, who had no food and no sleeping bag and little of anything he would need in the small day pack, would give up and go home, while Bill pressed up into the thin air of the peaks to see what the view from the top of the tallest one might tell him about what lay ahead, or reveal something he had inside himself to help him face the rest of his life.

As Paul continued down into the Hoh River valley, he felt the imprint of the llama lady's fingers on his forearm and asked himself why, when he'd been given the choice, he'd opted to affirm a connection to the logger whose hickory shirt and black backpack and curly hair he could see below him on the switchbacks. He also thought of his mother. Something in the llama lady's no-nonsense bearing and in her skepticism had reminded him of Trace. He imagined her behind the counter in the Marine Life Center tending to the creatures in the cases, and he saw the octopus that was her favorite rippling in its aquarium. He saw her walking with a cup of coffee across the plush white carpet in front of the great windows in the house overlooking the Strait where she could sit lost in thought for hours. Then he thought of Tom and a time when he and Tom had hiked the Klahanie Ridge trail near Hurricane Ridge and Tom had shown him a watchfob made from the upper canine tooth of an elk. He told him it had been his great grandfather's when he was a member of the Benevolent and Protective Order of Elks, an organization that had hunted the Peninsula's elk to near-complete extinction to make watchfobs like the one he held out for Paul to touch. This was before Teddy Roosevelt established the 610,000-acre Mount Olympus National Monument in 1909 to try to save the remaining elk, which now bear his name.

On another hike they took to celebrate Paul's thirteenth birthday,

Tom asked Paul if he knew the name of a certain valley below Mount Angeles. When Paul admitted he didn't, Tom said the valley was called Beargut because a 1912 hunting party had brought a cannon with them and used it to shoot a bear that went tumbling down a ridge, spilling internal organs.

Not much of an outdoorsman himself, Tom was a font of dates, statistics, and strange bits of information about the human history of the Park, its white explorers, bureaucratic champions, namers, and names. Tom's grandfather had been part of a contingent of 3,000 children from towns all over the Peninsula, who gathered to greet Franklin Delano Roosevelt on his September 1937 visit to decide whether to commit to establishing a national park in the area. The children met the president in the rain in front of the Clallam County Courthouse in Port Angeles holding a banner that read: "Please, Mr. President, we need your help. Give us our Olympic National Park." The president told the crowd of children and 10,000 adults that they could count on his help. He later surprised the National Forest Service staff, who tried to hide evidence of their responsibility for a charred clearcut, by telling representatives of both the Park and Forest services that he was disgusted by the clearcuts he'd seen on his tour and determined to save as much large timber as he could. Of one of the clearcuts he'd seen on their trip, he reportedly said, "I hope the man responsible for this is rotting in hell!" He signed a bill protecting 638,280 acres on June 29, 1938. This was expanded over time to nearly one million acres. Some thought the Park was a triumph; others thought it was a despotic land grab by the most powerful entity in the world.

These remembrances gave over to thoughts of fathers and grandfathers and of the fact that Tom was not his biological father, which led, as Paul descended the switchbacking trail, to a fantasy conforming to the earlier lie he'd told the llama lady, in which he imagined he was now following his real father. In this dream, the two of them were on an extended camping trip in the Olympics with plenty of good food and the entire summer to explore and while away their time, traipsing through the Bailey Range, letting their thoughts go glimmering with the crystalline water of the Quinault in the Enchanted Valley.

Other times, as he wondered about the logger and why he was following him, Paul's mind moved unpredictably over the memories it held: snippets of insidiously catchy phrases from pop songs he didn't even like and advertising jingles he didn't know he knew till they were jangling in his mind. He thought again of the girl Stephanie Barefoot waiting to greet him beside the trophy cases with a triumphant smile on the morning he returned to school. He thought of the boys in the Elk Antler complex who'd asked him, with an odd formality, to be their bodyguard after he'd dropped Brink Forger. He remembered the Portland girl who'd struck up a conversation and stayed behind to eat her lunch with him as he repaired cedar planks on the trail to Cape Alava, and who'd invited him to the beach where she and her friends were camping, and the sea lions barking on Ozette island as the girl took off all her clothes and showed him things he'd been wondering about. He thought of sitting with Dan atop The Incisor and listening as Dan asked for his help with the Temple Grove action (while hinting that there were other activities, more deeply buried, covert and illicit, with which he could use Paul's help) as thunder rumbled over the Gray Wolf Range and he thought about what he would tell Dan about the adventure he was having and wondered if after it was all over he would still begin at Oregon State in the fall. And he thought of the mountain lion he'd seen on the trail down from Happy Lake, who'd stared at him for a few seconds and taken two steps toward him before leaping ten feet to vanish more completely than anything he'd ever seen.

As Bill led them down into the Hoh valley, thoughts of his Alaska days ran through his mind alongside the new strange hopefulness associated with the tree hugger who was now following him for some reason, and memories of the Makah girl in the frozen-food aisle, and the immediate concerns of placing the next solid step in continuance of the chase that was no longer a chase. He thought of a time when the pipeline broke near a fork of the Koyukuk River. He and the crew to which he'd been assigned went in to reseal the hole through which black oil gushed onto the spongy tundra. He thought of another sealing job near Livengood after a drunk, recently fired member of the crew took out his frustrations by blasting the pipeline with a shotgun. He remembered a time when he'd shot a brown bear charging and huffing through thick elderberry after a client's gun jammed. He thought of 2,000 pounds of salmon, glistening silver in the hold of the gillnetter *Intrepid Lucinda*. He pondered images, tinged with a pleasurable regret, of the three women who'd passed through his life like floating mist; and the scrimshaw art he'd taken to carving in whalebone, moose antler, and walrus tusk; and the scrubby wet slope of a Ketchikan clearcut at dawn; and the endless chopping of winter wood in the September rain at the Peak Oil Commune and Pastor Smallet saying, "God, we have sacrificed to be here to honor you and to ask that you forgive us and our even more wayward brethren, who are out there sinning yet, for being a scourge upon this earth for so long and for our terrible profligacy with the resources you've given us."

When he arrived at the Hoh River trail, Paul was prepared to turn west, to continue down the valley to the trailhead in the rain forest where he was to meet Dan, if he hadn't been able to meet him at Sol Duc Falls the day before. He looked to his right and left up and down the trail, just as he had studied the trail that would have taken him past Deer Lake. He didn't know which way the logger had decided to go, but he headed to the left and east for a time, just to make sure he hadn't headed that way, deeper into the backcountry.

After he'd gone about a hundred yards, he caught a glimpse of the logger's hickory shirt, red suspenders, and black backpack beside the moss-strewn trees—heading upriver. Paul stopped to consider his options just as he had at the last fork. His hunger and fatigue, the prospect of meeting Dan for a long debriefing over a burger, fries, and milkshake at the Hard Rain Café, pulled against the inexplicable urge to see what the man was doing.

After some time, he shook his head and continued up the Hoh River trail after the man, disbelieving his own choice, especially because it went against his hungry, aching body. He saw the man again in the opening of Lewis Meadow where a herd of twelve elk stood grazing, lifting their heads to chew and turning to watch the men with dim curiosity as they passed. The peaks of the Bailey Range were visible here for a time to the east—Mount Carrie and Cat Peak above a wisp of cloud.

Paul followed the logger up the increasingly steep trail in the narrower and narrower valley of the Hoh and down onto a bridge he'd helped repair under Dan's guidance during his first summer in the Olympics. The bridge's smooth boards creaked and groaned hundreds of feet above the river's narrow torrent.

Once they were across the river, still narrow but accepting the tribute that would help it grow into wide bends near the Pacific, they followed Glacier Creek up a series of switchbacks that gained them 1,000 vertical feet. When Bill was halfway across one of the switchbacks, he glanced down out of the corners of his eyes and smiled faintly, nearly imperceptibly, when he saw the boy making his way up the switchback below. "Tree hugger!" he called out. "I see you're still going my way. Don't feel obliged. I don't need an escort. Not planning on cuttin' down any trees . . . trampling any wildflowers up here."

Paul was surprised to hear him speak. He waited another switchback before he asked, "What *are* you planning?"

Bill smiled but didn't answer, feeling the pulse of his desire to arrive at the peaks they'd seen from the ridge over Hoh Lake. He was sure something in that cold, stark zone would unlock things in him he couldn't guess at now but would know when he felt their release.

Late that afternoon Bill stopped in the lengthening shadows of a grove of old alpine hemlocks near Elk Lake to drink water and have something to eat. Waterlilies floated on the surface above their own reflections, yellow flowers in bloom above green leaves beside the wavering reflections of the towering black-and-white peaks of the Olympus massif. Paul stood in the lengthening shadows of the grove, sunlight burning greenly on the tops of the boles and gleaming between the needles. He drank some water, ate the last bite of his last apple, and jealously watched from the shadows of the grove as the logger ate something that seemed more substantial.

As Bill chewed a stick of jerky, he wondered if the boy would come forward to force another reckoning.

"You realize you're heading up toward Olympus?" the boy asked after a time.

"Yes," the man answered. "And I guess you realize you're following me the same way." Their voices carried clearly across the lake. Then, after a time: "You ever see what a spike in a tree does to a saw blade? Or to the guy working the blade, if he's not in one of these new outfits with the shielded chamber. It's a bloody mess, pieces of blade flying around like shrapnel, looking for flesh."

"All the more reason they shouldn't cut down those trees and turn them into lumber," Paul said. "All the more reason to stick to second growth. Plus," he said, echoing something he'd heard Dan say, "when the blades break up and hurt people in mills, it's usually because the company was too cheap to keep things safe."

They sat in silence for a time before Paul said, "I guess you aren't chasing me anymore."

"I might've thought the last twenty or so miles would've settled that for you."

"Where're you going?"

Bill shook his head and stared down at the reflection of the great wall of snow-covered peaks rising above timbered ridges rippling in a small breeze.

Paul looked across the reflection at the man. "Why were you cutting down trees in a national park?"

"It's close to criminal how much good timber's locked up in groves like that in this Park," the man said. "And from what I understand, what we were doing was strictly legal." Bill looked up from the reflection at the boy in the shadows of the grove. "What's your name?" he asked with a sudden directness.

"Why do you want to know?"

The man shrugged. "My name's Bill," he said. He remembered the feeling he'd identified as hope after the boy had let him pass on the trail.

"Paul," Paul allowed.

"How'd you get mixed up in what you were doing back there?"

"I didn't get mixed up in it. I chose to do it because I love this place and I don't want to see it destroyed by people like you. People seem to destroy every good thing in the world. It's like the earth is infested and infected with us, and if we can't control ourselves and stop ourselves from devouring every last good thing, no one will. We're on the wrong path now and we need to get things right. How'd *you* get mixed up in cutting down trees that take a thousand years to grow?"

Bill shook his head: "To make money so I can live a good life. And to be able to spend time in the woods, in rugged country like this. And to provide timber goods for the world's use. You'd kill someone to save trees?"

"I told you, I aimed high on purpose. That was the first time I ever fired a gun."

"Where're you from?"

"Port Angeles. And Neah Bay, where my grandmother lives and my mother's from."

Bill considered this information for a time, the whirring in his chest resuming soft and low. "Your parents or anyone else—some organization—know you're out here?"

"No. I didn't know I'd be here. My mother doesn't know, and my fa—stepfather's out at sea, running an old ship up on a beach in India."

Bill knitted his brow for a time over this phrase as a stronger breeze rippled the lake, blurring all of the lake's reflections, men and flowers, and mountains. "What's your mother's name?"

"Why?"

Bill shook his head—no matter, feeling the pace of the whir increase.

"Trace."

Again, Bill turned his eyes from a contemplation of the reflection to look at the boy's face, which was now bathed in sunlight because he'd leaned out of the shadows. His own, minus the effects of a number of years. "How old are you?"

"Eighteen this past May."

Bill looked back into Paul's reflection and, though he sat in the same attitude as before, he felt as if some energy or extra animation had taken possession of him. He appeared burdened with the knowledge and at the same time it seemed as if he might levitate above the ground because of it.

"What's your last name?" Paul asked across the lake.

Bill sat as if made of stone.

"Tell me," Paul said.

Bill remained silent, staring into the reflection, readying himself to go. Now the boy would pull the gun again, and this time, Bill thought, he would not aim high. He would pitch forward into the lake and sink into its cool, comforting mud and silt. Is that what he wanted?

"I think I know," Paul said, standing.

"What would you say?" Bill whispered.

"Newton," Paul said.

Bill stood up slowly and left the lake, with Paul following him through the hemlocks and into a forest of silver fir and Alaska cedar, then gaining altitude, as they moved across the mud, loose slate, and shale of avalanche fields spotted with subalpine fir and hellebore.

Below them, the diminishing lake was dotted with intermittent concentric rings from the rises of brook trout feeding on mayfly spinners and mosquitoes as the lake fell into shadow. Paul gained some ground as they picked up elevation. Occasionally, views of a wide buttress of Mount Olympus, concealing the tallest peaks, came into view, its massive bulk glowing pink and gold in the setting sun.

17

"Got all your gear there, Linky? Good. Let's hump it out of here quick," said the gyppo Smitty to his nephew. He was carrying one chainsaw and the Maxey kid was carrying two more, a case in each hand. They'd found one of the cases in a creekbed on the other side of the saddle.

After they'd made their way some distance across the ridge out of the trees of the Temple Grove to the place where they would join the Park trail, they heard voices then saw a strange group of ten or more people in various hues of synthetic rainjacket—pink mist, grey heather, gecko green, ionic blue, purple ash—faces hidden behind video cameras, making their clumsy way down the trail toward the loggers.

Smitty and the Maxey kid both stopped their progress to watch, as if seeing a creature they'd never seen before in these woods. "Oh, Jesus," Smitty said under his breath. "It's a bloody boogin' circus. We need to get the hell out of here quick! Don't say nothing to no one on the way out. Walk right by. I mean it. Do they all every one of them have cameras?"

The group stood spread out in the forest under a light rain, looking like paparazzi awaiting celebrities beside a red carpet. As the two approached, the people in the group filmed one another and filmed the two men and the forest around them. "Wave to the camera, gentlemen," a tall man in an olive-night Helly Hanson jacket called out. "You're being featured today by ONPWO—the Olympic National Park Watchdog Organization. Good to see you today, Oliver Smith. And young Mr. Lincoln Maxey, I see you've got a couple of chainsaws there. Can you tell us what you were doing with chainsaws on National Park land? I think we passed the National Forest boundary a while back coming in here to find you. Ah, don't want to answer us? After you leave, we're going to go on down where you've just come from and take a walk through the Temple Grove and see if we can see just what happened there. Anything to confess?"

The group trailed them up the ridge and back down the other side to the place where Bill's and the Maxey kid's camp still stood—the tent, the cots, the fire pit, and the cooler minus what Bill had taken from it when he was preparing to follow Paul.

Two Subarus and two hybrid SUVs were parked on the old road beside Smitty's Ram truck next to a black Ford.

"How the hell did they unlock the gate?" Smitty mumbled to himself.

Trace and Stephanie had found the camp near the place where Stephanie said the earlier Temple Grove protests had been carried out, and Trace was looking down at a half-burned note written on a scrap of cardboard propped on rocks in the fire pit: *Don't come back!,* it said in what looked like it could have been Paul's handwriting. The note pinned to a log beside it read *Went looking for him –Bill* in blue ink that was smudged and beginning to streak down the paper. Once she'd seen these words in her rush to find any clues that would help her find Paul, she kept going back and forth from one scrap of text to the next, disbelieving the possibility they'd opened in her mind, yet unable to think of anything else they could mean until it began to seem as if these words were rotating blades that would lift her off the ground—*Don't come back, went looking for him, Don't come back, went looking for him*—over and over, faster and faster.

"What's wrong?" Stephanie asked. "What did you see?"

Trace shook her head—too difficult to explain, this sensation of lifting off the ground because of these two phrases, these half notes, that name.

When the two men, one young, one older, came into the camp and started dismantling it as fast as they could, accompanied by the group of people in fancy outdoor gear with video cameras, Trace went up to the men and asked, "Are you Bill? Who's Bill?"

The Maxey kid, the stocky younger man, looked at her for a second, shook his head, and continued past her to throw a sheathed hatchet into the cab of the truck.

"None of us is Bill," the older man said. "There is no Bill. Come on Linky . . ."

She saw that she'd gotten the boy's attention. Something about the name had pitched a spark in his eyes. The older man's denial was too quick and adamant. The younger man stopped to look at her for a second on his way back to the campsite from the truck. Perhaps he would be the one at whom she would direct the growing undercurrent of rage.

"Did you see a boy, a . . . young man out there in the woods? I'm looking for my son, Paul," she said.

The kid glared at her. "If he was the one putting spikes in those trees and stealing our food and gear, and pulling a gun on us, then, yes, I believe we did see your son up there," he said.

"Lincoln!" the older man said in a tone of command, and the boy went to help lift and heave a cooler into the back of the truck.

Trace stood processing this information, disbelieving what she'd heard about the gun and spikes. Was that something Paul would do? She had never known him to hold or see, much less use, a gun. Her mind turned back to Dan Kelsoe, sitting in FBI custody somewhere in Port Angeles. What had Dan taught Paul?

"Are you all right?" Stephanie asked.

Trace shook her head, no. Spikes and guns had lent fuel to the lifting sensation.

The tall narrator of the mobile film crew in the Helly Hanson rainjacket followed Smitty and the Maxey kid as they moved as quickly as they could from the camp to the truck, asking them as they went, "What kind of camp is this you're breaking up here that looks like it's been here at least three days? Maybe more."

A few members of the group were filming the license plates of the trucks. Others followed the Maxey kid.

"Who are you working for, gyppo?" the tall narrator asked. "Are you just a small agent for big timber? Timberforus, perhaps?"

Smitty stopped and stood in front of the camera, holding a folded-up cot at his side. He addressed the lens and its red light as if he was speaking to a news reporter at a press conference. "You can shut off all these cameras," Smitty said. "This boy was working on his own, and I just came up here to stop him. He was mistaken about a salvage job. That's all. What's happened is the guy he was working with, who has absconded from the scene out of embarrassment, I'm guessing, told this boy this was the right spot for a cut when it isn't. There has been nothing cut yet."

Someone absconded from the scene, thought Trace—*Bill* absconded from the scene.

A black SUV that had followed Trace and Stephanie with no pretense of secrecy pulled up slowly and parked behind the growing line of cars on the dead-end road. The FBI agent behind the wheel got out, walked around the front of his truck, and looked on at Smitty and the Maxey kid breaking camp and at the film crew buzzing around them. Trace recognized the agent as one of those who'd asked her questions in her living room.

"Bloody boogin' circus," muttered Smitty.

Trace stood watching the men load the truck, feeling as if she was lifting from the ground with this new information. "Where is my son, now?" Trace asked the Maxey kid as he carried the hastily collapsed tent to the truck and threw it in the bed. "When did you see him last?" she asked.

He seemed not to hear or to be deliberately ignoring her.

"Where is he now, and when did you see him last?" she repeated more loudly, coming up behind him. She tried to grab his shirt, but he slapped her hand and jumped away saying, "Get off me, lady!"

The older man had climbed into the driver's seat and started the engine. "Let's go, Linky. Please get out of the way, m'am. We got to go."

They had broken down the little camp, leaving only some ashes in the fire pit. The two notes and everything else had been loaded into the truck. Trace stood between the kid and the passenger-side door.

"If that is your son out there, who you're asking about, his ass is fixed," the Maxey kid said. "Bill Newton'll see to that. If your boy doesn't shoot him first. I'm guessing they're working it out up there as we speak." He nodded toward the thickly treed ridge, then climbed in the truck and shut the door.

Newton. As the truck pulled away, Trace felt like she was flying over this saddle between ridges, as if on the back of a Thunderbird, up to a vantage that would let her see all the ranges of the Olympics and Paul and Bill somewhere out there in them "working it out."

She watched the truck drive past the FBI agent leaning against the hood of his black SUV, his face expressionless, as if he was striving to give the impression he'd just come upon the scene by happenstance.

If your boy doesn't shoot him first? Just when she thought she knew Paul, again and again, he rippled out of focus. Did this mean she was wrong to have had faith him, or that he needed her faith now more than ever, misguided as it seemed he was? Once the gyppo's truck was gone, the tall man with the camera focused his attention on her, and the other members of the strange film crew gathered around to film her as well. "What is your involvement in this?" he asked.

"I'm looking for my son," she said.

"Leave her alone," said Stephanie.

"It's Paul Granger's mother," one of them said.

Trace looked at the woman who'd said it, a middle-aged lady in a pink mist rainjacket, whom she'd never seen in her life. How did the woman know who she was.

The man turned off his camera and let it fall to his side on a strap around his shoulder. "Was your son with Dan Kelsoe?"

"We think so," Trace whispered, with a glance back at the FBI agent.

"Spiking trees is not the answer," the man said. "Dan Kelsoe is a throwback to a less effective era of environmental protest. We're in a new era, now," he said, holding up his camera. "Within hours the images we've captured here will be on the Internet for all to see. If your son turns up, give him my card. We could use him, if he's willing to adopt new ways." He handed her a business card, and, after filming his exchange with Trace, the rest of them also let their cameras fall. Apparently finished with Trace, the man said to the group, "Let's take a short break, have some water, rest up, then get ready to hike down into the Temple Grove to see what damage they've done. There's no need to film our way in there. Make sure you have plenty of juice to get lots of footage of the grove itself, including any trees they've cut down."

When the group was ready, Trace and Stephanie watched them go a distance up the ridge before following them.

"I'm sorry he may be in trouble, Mrs. Granger," Stephanie said. "I hope he's going to be all right. Do you think he really has a gun?"

Trace shook her head. "I'm not sure what I know or think about anything anymore." The sensation of flying had subsided, but she could feel her heart beating in her chest. Where was he? What had he done?

"And who's Bill Newton, do you think?" Stephanie asked. "That guy said Bill Newton would . . . what did he say? 'fix Paul,' or something. That doesn't sound good."

Trace shook her head no to make Stephanie stop, because it would take too long to explain everything and because it didn't sound good, none of it, not at all. She remembered the bear of a man she'd seen in the frozen-food aisle and felt a tingling at her neck as if the coarse hairs of his beard were there now. She thought of the impulse she'd had in the Albertsons to interrupt his departure, to tell him he had a son, and thought now that that might have made a difference.

When the two women had gone a distance up the ridge, the FBI agent grudgingly left his SUV to follow them on foot between the great trees, leaving his partner, Brent Sawtelle, in sunglasses and a hat, behind the tinted windows, feeling claustrophobic in what he was coming to think of as a plush, moveable cell and wanting nothing so much as to get out and hike down into that grove of trees.

18

Firelight flickered across Bill's face and was absorbed into the snarl of his beard, his thick tufts of black hair. He was rapt, in a close contemplation of the ancient shifting shapes of the flames and hoping something in their consumptive flickering might help him discover answers to questions that had eluded him over the course of his thirty-eight years, no questions more perplexing than the ones that had found him on the shore of Elk Lake a few hours ago. Occasionally he stirred something in a pot out of which tendrils of steam rose into the air with the smoke.

Paul stepped out of the subalpine forest into the firelight and stood staring down at Bill for a few moments before sitting down on a rock across the fire from him. They sat in silence for a time with no sound but the click of the spoon as Bill tended to the pot.

"Did you know," Paul said, after a time, "that it's illegal to have fires up this high?"

Bill seemed not to have heard him. He stirred the pot and after several minutes of silence poured some chili from it into a small bowl and some into a bigger bowl and stood, reached across the fire, and gave the bigger bowl and a spoon to Paul.

Paul hesitated a moment before accepting the spoon and the bowl. After he had sat down again, he stared into the bowl for a time. There were no other campers at Glacier Meadows to give him food. He mumbled his thanks, and they both sat eating in silence but for the tap and scrape of their spoons on the tin bowls—Paul taking pains to eat slowly so Bill wouldn't see how hungry he was, Bill assimilating his own uncomfortable gladness, the hopeful feeling that had begun when he'd made the decision to push past the boy and when he'd seen that Paul was following but not knowing what to say.

When both of them had eaten and Bill had refilled both of their bowls and they'd both eaten some more, Bill said, "I've always found heat improves chili."

Paul looked into his empty bowl and nodded agreement, at least about hot chili but not about fires which could destroy the delicate plants that grew so torturously at altitude. "I have a backpacking stove at the campsite back on Rugged Ridge that can boil water in about three minutes," he said.

"Hmm," said Bill, "Pretty fast."

After that, they sat for a long time in silence, both of them staring into the flames, their shadows billowing on the rocks and on the needled branches of the subalpine firs and hemlocks. The stars above glimmered brightly through wisps of cloud, as if to acknowledge a promised appointment.

"My mother told me about you," Paul said. "I know what happened that day by the Elwha."

Bill nodded. "I saw your mother in the store before we came up into the woods. I told her I was sorry for what happened. I didn't know about you."

"She's a good mother," said Paul. "And she thinks what's bad in me might have come from you."

"That's fair. Probably true."

"Don't you think it's strange what's happening?"

Bill nodded. "We ought to stick together to get ourselves out of any trouble that might come from what happened back in the grove."

"So you're not going back?"

Bill shook his head. "I'm going on up the peak, to the very top. And I don't know if I'm ever going down."

"But you're not prepared. You don't have the right gear. I've climbed it. You need rope and an ice axe and crampons."

"My great grandfather . . ."—it struck Bill that he was telling Paul about his own ancestor—"used to do well enough without any of that stuff. Climbed up during the day and still had energy for dancing at night." His face animated for a moment with the telling in a way that let him know by feel the kinds of things he wanted to say to Paul, but the momentary satisfaction was checked by a recognition of all that stood between them and the time they'd lost, the value and trials of which time was beyond both of their reckoning.

"I can show you how to go," said Paul.

Bill shook his head. "I don't want you to get in trouble. We've been on a long jag here." Bill paused and considered telling him it seemed he'd been raised well, despite his work in the Temple Grove, that it seemed like Trace had done a good job based on his drive and his ability in the woods, but he stopped himself. "You'd better turn around and go down in the morning. We can exchange information . . . if you want."

Paul didn't answer. He sat for a time, then stood and walked out of the firelight and disappeared into the cold subalpine night. He left Bill feeling regretful of the beginning he'd tried, torn between making a clean break and ignoring for the rest of his life what he hadn't known till earlier that day, or kindling a connection with his . . . still difficult to say even to himself . . . son.

Paul settled into a small cirque behind some boulders. Ever since he'd seen the man down the felled Douglas fir back on Rugged Ridge, he'd carried an inchoate suspicion about Bill's identity. He had not summoned the realization into the light for a better view because you couldn't summon what you didn't fully recognize was there, and because it was too strange to face directly. Some things remained indistinct until events knocked them into the light, till new developments forced you to see more clearly what you'd been carrying the whole time. Within sight of the glow of Bill's fire over the crest of the small cirque, Paul sat against a rock that had been left in the basin by the slow retreat of the Blue Glacier as human industry and addiction to convenience made the world warmer. He thought about the story his mother had told him of his conception, and he thought about the shadow father he'd carried for as long as he'd understood the concept of fatherhood, since long before his suspicion that the logger in the Temple Grove might be his father. He thought about the way he'd seen his mother struggle to support them—waiting tables at Bushwhackers—how one night, after one of the deadbeats of the parade of them she'd dated before Tom—either the burned-out deadhead or maybe it was the sometime millworker who claimed to be a disowned scion from a wealthy family—after one of these guys had broken her heart, he'd heard her crying in the bathroom. He remembered another time hearing her talking to her mother about how hard it was to make it, though she always turned down offers to return to the benefits that would come to her on the reservation, always made the decision to struggle and fight on her own. He remembered what he could of these deadbeats, many of them charming at first but who later, one and all, revealed their indifference or outright resentment of his existence, in the days before Tom. He thought about the way his mom sometimes seemed disconnected and numb even in the days since Tom. He turned over the story his mother had blurted out about this man, Bill Newton, and what had happened that day on the banks of the Elwha, and he remembered how she'd paused in telling the story, even though she was angry at him for breaking Brink Forger's nose, before she'd said that word, as if she was searching for the proper euphemism, like looking for a good way off a steep ridge and seeing no better way than to take the plunge.

An oblong rock about the size but triple the weight of a human head lay within reach of his right hand. It had been sloughed by some former terminal moraine of the Blue Glacier. He placed his hand on the rock and felt the irregularities of its surface and saw himself hefting it over his head with both hands and bringing it crashing down.

Bill awoke to the first illumination of the basin and its meadow to see the boy, Paul, who was his son—that fact ricocheted uncomfortably, starkly in his mind before he'd had a chance to wake up—standing at twelve paces with a large rock cradled at his chest. He was like a figure seen through cascading water. Confirmation of Paul's existence in this attitude required vigilant study. It needed to be checked and rechecked to be believed.

Paul raised the rock above his head, stepped forward . . .

Bill was aware of feeling sympathy for the boy at odds with his own preservation, good will toward a human being who seemed to mean him ill. At the same time, he was aware of the novelty of this strange confluence and of the power he seemed to have gained when he'd put a hand on Paul's chest and pushed gently past Paul back at the crossroads. He thought *here it is* as the whirring in his chest produced a high-pitched whine he thought someone might actually be able to hear. Realization of the act was pitched in this high whining key not because of the expectation of the confrontation—that, he understood—but because all of the events that had led to this moment seemed part of something bigger, something beyond his understanding, something that might lift him into the air and carry him away. He had sensed the moment of violence since he'd seen the boy stand up in the sword ferns of the Temple Grove, or maybe even since he'd heard the distant clanging coming over Rugged Ridge, or maybe even since he'd seen evidence of Paul's existence in Trace's eyes in the Albertsons aisle. Or maybe he knew it before then and during all his time in Alaska. The feeling that it would come to something like this had been building in him all this time.

He was ready to feel the rock. But he was less ready to look into the causes of the whirring precipitated by everything that had led to this moment: the fight with the Hells Angels; and the rappel down to the beach with Shoot Morley; and meeting the girl on the beach that night and getting a ride with her back to Forks; and the date with Trace and the impulse, fed by the wild gusts of wind down the valley, to erase his (and her) virginity that day on the Elwha; and all the causes behind his desire for her; and all the years he hadn't known about the boy (his mother and Troy must have known and not told him) even as, somehow, he did know about him; and the brief moments, up to and including, the thirty-second cosmic joke that had led to the existence of this eighteen-year-old human being, his son, who was not a joke at all and almost his size and who looked like Bill himself in the moment when the thirty-second act had passed; and the myriad forces that had brought them together in this basin of the Blue Glacier; and the strange fact of their meeting in the grove followed by the chase that was not a chase which had led them to the realization of their relationship and on to this moment. All of this played in the key to which the whirring had elevated as, seated and as if a powerless spectator to what was fated to unfold, Bill faced the hoisted rock in silence and with open eyes.

The rock landed with a crushing force in the center of the fire pit, displacing charred particles of wood and raising a cloud of ash. Just before he released the rock, Paul thought: *If Bill Newton hadn't . . .?* And after he'd let it go he was glad, because of what it said without his having to speak and because actual violence in this moment would not have been in keeping with his sense of himself, even as it might have confirmed his mother's sense of Bill Newton in him.

19

Trace and Stephanie hiked through the trees of the Temple Grove, to the place where the great fallen Douglas fir lay up the slope like the sole slain combatant in a showdown between giants. Fresh sawdust lay scattered around its wide stump. It had taken the ONPWO camera crew some time to find it. Now they swarmed over the fallen tree, filming it to document the fact it had recently been cut down. For a time they had fanned out to look for others but found only a small number of lesser trees and snags that had been removed in the area near where the single tree was laid out.

As Trace walked quietly through the great Douglas firs, she tried to attune herself to Paul and to the trees themselves. Now that she was closer to him (if the boy back at the road was to be believed), hotter on his trail, she thought she might be able to sense something from, or send something to, Paul through the trees, this network of living beings who might whisper a message each to each until it reached him wherever he was in these woods. She looked for physical signs of his passing in the underbrush, and, when she saw none, listened for a signal such as those she felt she'd received from the mountains when she was back in Port Angeles. Nothing definitive came, though she sensed Paul had passed through the grove and that the trees knew this and knew she was Paul's mother and bore no grudge against her because of it.

One of the ONPWO crew focused his camera on Stephanie for a moment as she placed a hand on the furrowed bark of the grounded bough of the only old-growth tree Bill and the Maxey boy had felled. Her hand rested on the bough not far from the place where Paul had placed his hand before he drove in a timber spike. Even on its side the tree was a few inches taller than she was. She contemplated for a time the fact that it had taken over ten human lifetimes for the tree to reach this size and imagined what it could become now that it was down—a fleet of wooden rowing shells, how many guitars or cellos—a thousand?; houses in which lived people who appreciated the feel and grain of rare wood; a warehouse full of paper on which might be written great novels, books of poetry, blueprints for a better world. She thought of other things the tree could become: sawdust, reams of paper for a law office, resins, glues, even tooth paste. How could you weigh the worth of any or all of these uses against what the tree had meant while it grew here on this ridge?

"Yes, here look, some of these trees have been spiked!" the tall narrator called out to the others. "Come and see," he said. "There's just the smallest indentation, and whoever did it colored it over with a brown marker."

Many of them gathered around to look at the small indentation where the spike had been driven into a standing tree and colored brown.

"Here's another one!" someone else said. "Here too," a third camera person called out.

"Looks like your son did quite a lot of damage in here. Did you come to admire his handiwork?" the tall man said as he passed by Trace to look at another tree alleged to have been spiked. The FBI man also had a little camera out and was snapping shots of the spikes in the trees as he and the ONPWO members found them.

Trace said, loud enough for all of them, and especially the FBI agent, to hear, "My son had nothing to do with this!" though she wasn't sure she believed it herself.

Trace and Stephanie hiked over the ridge back to Tom's truck, trailed at a distance by the FBI agent. Trace drove down the logging road to 101, down 101 to Sol Duc Road, and down to the end of Sol Duc Road to the Sol Duc Falls trailhead. The agent's SUV followed them the entire way, its driver making no pretense of being covert, and parked at the other end of the parking area while the afternoon wore on.

“I hope Paul doesn’t come out now,” Trace said, eyeing the SUV’s black bulk and impenetrable windows. “What would they do? Take him away before I even got to talk to him?” She looked over at the truck, covering her mouth when it occurred to her the agent might have some kind of listening device trained on them.

“I guess they would,” Stephanie said. “I don’t know what we could do to stop them. But we’d be here to make sure they couldn’t hurt him. And to find out where they were taking him.”

Twice they walked up the trail in the early evening, through the mossy old-growth groves whose silence might have seemed malevolent if Trace hadn’t felt very strongly that the landscape around them was on Paul’s side, even as she understood the landscape was on no one’s side. The same, somewhat reticent agent followed them up the trail both times, walking not too far behind them, as if he too just happened to have chosen that moment for a stroll.

On the first walk, the agent let them pass him on their way back to the truck, smiling rather formally and nodding as they went by, his sunglasses as dark as the tinted windows of the SUV. When she was close enough to him to smell his cologne and see that he was a young man in his late twenties, Trace felt the rage rise from her belly into her throat—maybe he was the one who would feel this tumult growing inside her—but she told herself to be careful, not to vent her fury at this man who was just a cog in an enormous, complicated bureaucratic machine.

On their second trip up the trail, after they had turned around to go back the other way and were passing the man, Trace turned to face him. “Why are you here?” she asked as calmly as she could, though her voice shook as she said it. Stephanie steadied Trace’s arm as if to suggest she should rethink this direct communication, or to make sure Trace didn’t say too much.

The agent paused for a time, apparently too surprised by the direct address to know what to do. “I think you know the answer to that,” he said, “given what we saw earlier this afternoon. Why are *you* here?” In the SUV, unseen behind the tinted glass, Brent Sawtelle could hear their conversation through a microphone on his partner. He liked something about the woman. Perhaps what he liked was her fierce interest in saving her son. His wife's love for their daughter back in Bethesda had given him something else to love in his wife. He'd also always been fascinated by Native Americans (though all his farmer relatives along the Klamath bad-mouthed them in their wars with them over water). He had twice traveled east from Eugene to the Pendleton Round-Up, a rodeo where the teepees and the fancy-dancing were his favorites. He wondered how the pieces of the puzzle would fit together, if the boy Paul would emerge here in the hope of meeting Dan Kelsoe. Did the boy know that Kelsoe was likely a major planner of three bombings, in addition to numerous other activities? This boy with his whole life before him, set to go to Brent's own alma mater in the fall, might be just the informant they needed. They thought he would be willing to regain his future in exchange for information that would help them build their case. He braced himself for an intervention, should one become necessary, but he didn't want to compromise his undercover status unless it became completely necessary.

Trace started to answer. She and Stephanie were twinned in the dark lenses of the man's sunglasses. She read his silence as smugness and took a deep breath, something appropriately withering about to fly from her mouth, something so familiar in this stand-off, Indians vs. the U.S. government. She stopped herself and turned to walk away. To say anything to the man might get Paul in deeper trouble, especially considering what she'd heard about spikes and guns. She left him behind her, this young agent of the powerful republic.

Later in the evening, as the shadows lengthened, and the last of the golden light pooled greenly on certain corners of the forest, Trace and Stephanie ate some sandwiches Trace had made. They joked about offering sandwiches to the agents—"Here. If we feed you, will you promise to leave Paul alone?"—and watched the trailhead and wondered if Paul might have come to the trailhead, seen the SUV, and headed back into the woods without anyone ever knowing it. They talked about the fact that Stephanie would leave for college in a few months. Trace picked up a book Stephanie had been reading off and on as they kept their vigil. *The Odyssey*, she said, and opened it to the first page of Fagles's translation.

"I'm reading it for one of my classes in the fall, to get a head start."

Trace read, "Sing to me of the man, Muse, the man of twists and turns driven time and again off course, once he had plundered the hallowed heights of Troy." She hefted the book in her hand: "Hmmph," she said, approvingly.

"It's good so far," said Stephanie. "It's full of spells, gods and goddesses, and adventures in strange lands with weird creatures. Odysseus is good at getting out of trouble, but he needs a lot of help because he angered Poseidon. All he wants is to get back home. There are also a lot of boats skimming over the water in it. Reminds me of the Makah."

Trace thought, *what do you know about the Makah?* but decided not to argue with the comment, which sounded true enough. She nodded and looked out at the darkness increasing all around the big hemlocks, cedars, vine maple, spruce, and sword ferns, the golden pools all gone now. It seemed as if this darkening shade was something the vegetation exhaled each night to cloak itself. This place felt far from the sea. She thought of Tom making his way back home. She was scheduled to pick him up in two days.

As they sat waiting, Trace surprised herself by telling Stephanie about Tom's job wrecking the last-leg ships at Alang and the dangerous work of the shipbreakers who met him there. She did not tell her that lately she wasn't sure whether she would stay with Tom, or how an inner voice saying go back to the reservation at Neah Bay seemed to be getting stronger. Was it because she was closer tonight, physically closer, to the rez? She told Stephanie about Claire Wittington, the woman who'd taught the class Trace took at the community college and who'd given her a job at the Marine Life Center before she moved to Seattle. Trace also told Stephanie that, strange to admit, she missed Pishpish. She could tell, whenever she got back to the Center after being gone for a long time, that Pishpish had noticed her absence and showed signs—a gleam in the eye, a readiness to press against the glass to get closer to Trace—of having missed her. She told Stephanie that tomorrow they would go to Neah Bay, where she would introduce Stephanie to Paul's grandmother and to Uncle Jack, the fisherman and machinist who, despite his struggle with alcohol, had been a kind of father to

Paul during some times before Tom when he'd needed a father. If Paul didn't come out of the woods tonight, and it looked as if he wouldn't, Trace said they would talk to her Neah Bay family about what to do. She didn't tell Stephanie that she had not yet told anyone at Neah Bay about her current difficulties out of pride and because certain factions on the reservation expected and wanted to see her fail.

Stephanie said she looked forward to meeting Trace's family. She'd been to Cape Flattery once with her mother and father, after stopping in to see the museum celebrating the ancient Makah village at Ozette and driving through the town of Neah Bay. They'd hiked the trail and looked out at the ocean from the northwesternmost point in the continental United States. They hadn't stayed long, but she remembered her father saying into the wet wind blowing up off the Pacific, as if to himself: "The place where westward expansion died and we had to turn back and look inward."

"Well," said Trace, "that's one way to look at it, but that's not how people in Neah Bay see it. For us, the Cape is where the world begins. We all grew up with that idea."

Stephanie was silent for a few moments before she said, "That's really cool."

As the darkness increased to blackness, Trace told Stephanie about a time, not long after she'd married Tom, when Tom and Paul and she had driven the ten miles from Port Angeles to Sequim to visit the Olympic Game Farm. They had driven the same Chevy, the truck they were now sitting in, through the "safari" area. A large brown bison had licked the oats they held out in their hands, its big blue tongue slobbering down the window as they squealed and laughed, all three of them crowded together in the cab.

Later, they watched a mountain lion pace behind the bars of its cage. The look in its eyes suggested it had long ago decided the best way to deal with its plight was to fantasize about making meals of the children who came to see it. Paul noticed that its pacing, perhaps the pacing of its predecessors, had worn a dark path in the concrete below the bars, and he stared at the sorry old lion till Trace told him to come and see the bear.

They gathered with a group of people in front of a high fence behind which rubber tires and other chewed up "toys" were strewn about. After a time a strong-looking woman came out of a shed leading an immense waddling brown bear on a chain. The crowd gasped at the bear's size. Its claws, looking like portions of extended bone and filed to dullness, jutted seven inches from its massive paws.

The trainer was dressed in a red flannel shirt and worn jeans, wore sunglasses, and had a husky voice. She said, "This bear is a 1,000-pound Alaskan brown bear. This bear is also a movie star. His credits include the role of Gentle Ben on the television show *Grizzly Adams*. Wave to the folks, Ben," the woman said and gave a hand signal. The bear stuck out its tongue, pantomimed an erratic wave, looked at the woman holding its chain, and snapped its jaws to catch a treat. Some people in the crowd clicked photos and clapped; three or four of them trained video cameras on the show. After the waving, the trainer had the bear roll over, cover its face at a suggested point of shame, and stand up and turn around on its hind legs. When the show was over, the woman said, "Wave goodbye to the folks, Ben," and gave it another hand signal. The bear stood up to its full height of ten feet and pantomimed a wave. The woman tossed it another treat.

When they were heading back to Port Angeles at the end of the afternoon, ten-year-old Paul said, "I'm coming back here someday soon to set that bear free."

"That bear'd eat you up and say 'yum, now what's for dinner,' " said Trace.

"I'm going to set all those animals free. Even the buffalo and that old goat. And then I'm going to climb on that big bear's back and ride him way up into the mountains. Far away from everything and everybody. And that's where I'll stay for the rest of my life."

"You'd be just like Grizzly Adams," said Tom.

"I'd be just like *me*," said Paul.

"Well," said Trace, and chuckled. "Will you at least invite your mama to come along with you?"

"Nope," said Paul.

Trace was surprised that this small disavowal carried a sting. She hadn't expected it and was silent for a time in its aftermath. They crossed a bridge spanning Morse Creek. Paul knelt on the seat and looked back at white rapids playing over rocks to see if anyone was fishing. When they had passed over it, he sat again and stared down the road. A mile farther, when they were within the commercial strip of Port Angeles, he said, "You can visit sometimes," and Trace smiled.

"I know the game farm," Stephanie said. "Those buffaloes can get pretty aggressive, going after that game-farm bread with their long blue tongues. Wild-animals-behind-bars-sadness is a distinctive, classifiable variety of sadness, one of the saddest there is." Stephanie sighed. "The bears there don't look right—fat and probably suffering from the bear equivalent to diabetes from all that bread." They sat quietly for a while. "I wonder if he's gotten his wish now," she said, then regretted having said it. "I mean, living up in the mountains." Then she reconsidered and said, "I'm sorry. I'm sure he'll come out soon. And we'll make sure they don't hurt him when he does."

It was still strange to hear Stephanie counting herself as Paul's protector. "It's okay," Trace said. "It's pretty hard not to know what's going on out there. The dreams I have about him. That night we heard him rustling around in his room and when we went in, he had his backpack packed and a flashlight and some pruning shears. We caught him opening the front door. He was really going to go and try to let those animals go."

Trace smiled to remember it, and she looked out the front window just as a young elk with velvet antlers emerged from the trailhead they'd been watching so intently. The elk walked deliberately, in a somewhat stately manner, right between their truck and the dark-windowed SUV.

They were silent for a few moments as they watched the elk, almost without breathing, both of them imagining the agents in the truck also taking in the strange march.

"Wow!" said Stephanie said, "That was weird."

Trace managed to nod. She felt river spray, saw sun glinting on her two-month-old son.

A short time later, Stephanie looked suddenly thoughtful, pulled a notebook from her pack, and scribbled something into it.

Trace looked down to read

In case they're listening in . . . Do you think they've got the car bugged?

Trace took the pad and wrote a question mark.
Stephanie took up the pad again and wrote:

They're going to follow you, but not me. Right? So maybe I can go wait for him at the Hoh trailhead, while you throw them off our trail?

Trace read the note and nodded her approval as Stephanie took the pad again and started writing the details of what she had in mind.

20

As Bill prepared to continue up the path, passages from Pastor Smallet's reading of the Binding of Isaac echoed in his head more loudly and persistently than they had before, even though he tried to push them out as he walked away from Paul, heading up the trail without his backpack: *He bound his son Isaac, and laid him on top of the altar, on top of the wood. Then Abraham reached out his hand and took the knife to kill his son. But the angel of the Lord called to him from heaven, and said, "Abraham, Abraham!" And he said, "Here I am." He said, "Do not lay your hand on the boy or do anything to him; for now I know that you fear God, since you have not withheld your only son, from me.*

This seemed as likely a place as any to hear a divine voice. Would some god or gods speak to him here, bestow the appropriate words, given what they'd learned about each other at Elk Lake?

After Paul flung the rock into the ashes, he retreated a few hundred yards down the trail with the intention of continuing all the way down and out as the sun rose, but he didn't get far before the urge to turn back and continue up the mountain after Bill Newton, who was his . . . father, returned. When he'd gotten back to the camp, Bill Newton was gone, his backpack resting beside the fire pit.

In the slight dreams he'd snatched in a short fitful sleep between cold awakenings, Paul was Thunderbird sailing down from his bone-littered aerie on Olympus to hunt for whales. In the dream, the rusting hulks of cars also rested in the cave with him. This made Paul wonder what it took to change the lore, which seemed to need the dusty shroud of the ages to be considered authentic. Paul flew along as Thunderbird, soaring over the braided channel of the Hoh to its mouth in the ocean and throwing lightning serpents into the breaching back of a whale before diving down to grab it up in great talons. The dream ended with a stab of pain, which he realized within the dream was the feeling of his own Thunderbird talons digging into his own whale flesh.

The strange feeling of the dream stayed with Paul as he continued to climb. He stopped when he could once again see Bill Newton working his way steadily up the trail that would soon cease to be a trail as it gave way to the rocks of the terminal moraine, a land of ice, snow, firn, talus, and scree.

When Bill had ascended about a quarter-mile through meadows made lush by glacial run-off—wind-blown bunchgrass ringed with red paintbrush, arctic lupine, valerian, and bistort—he became aware of a presence behind him. When he turned to look, he saw Paul following at a distance of about fifty yards, moving in the same dogged way he had the day before and in the same way Bill had moved when he was following Paul before that.

Bill stood a moment watching Paul make his way up the trail. He couldn't bring himself to think of Paul as his son, though an awareness of this fact now rang a constant rebuke, tempered and haloed by the feeling of hopefulness he'd first felt after passing the boy like an opened door on the trail up from Hoh Lake. He turned to continue up the mountain, concentrating on the simple task of placing one foot in front of the other toward whatever would come, toward what voice, if any, would speak to him at the top of the peak named for the dwelling place of the Greek gods. He felt he ought to say something—the perfect thing—to his son, whose presence, he was deciding, was like a gift, but he didn't know what someone could say that had the power to recover the kind of ground they had lost. He realized that he didn't even know what he'd lost in not knowing about his son for all this time. He felt in his shirt and jacket pockets for the scrimshaw bear in the hope that touching this talisman might give him what he needed, but he found all of his pockets empty. He would stop and turn and say something, once the perfect thing had better formed in his mind or had come to him from the thin-aired regions to which he was aspiring. Perhaps through the aspiration he would discover the right thing to say.

Marmots whistled warnings to one another and their fat brown forms skittered into the shadows between rocks as the men moved through the spoils the glacier had left in its retreat: rocks covered in algae slowly being reclaimed by subalpine forest. One marmot, perched on a rock with its head tilted up in a way that suggested it expected to receive or impart important information, remained unmoving beside the trail instead of whistling and skittering beneath the boulders like its burrow mates. As the men passed, first Bill and then Paul, the marmot watched them closely. Its boldness raised an identical chuckle from both, a sideways glance and a quick expulsion of breath, though Paul also thought of Uncle Jack and his admonition to watch out for strange behavior when he was up in the woods.

To both men the miraculous coincidence of having found each other in the way they had constituted a colossal door—the small door of Bill's push past Paul on the trail become this great door—that had opened into a vast room beyond speech and willed action, where to carry out premeditated action or say willed things might freeze or evaporate, shift or impede the great current that seemed to have lifted them up and was carrying them along from moment to moment.

Bill moved through the scattered rocks of the terminal moraine of the Blue Glacier below a blue sky overspread with wispy clouds scattering as if they were being chased. He came to the glacier's thick, silty snout and tested his caulks on the ice at the base and began to climb, slowly at first, then, as he got higher, more and more in the manner of an inspired ecstatic offering his life to the moment following the one he was in. The knowledge that Paul was watching from below buoyed him in some strange way, pushed him up toward the words that could recover the ground they'd lost. Or was Paul's presence satisfying because he was punishing himself, putting himself in danger for Paul to see? Coexistent with the buoyancy was the knowledge like a weight around his neck, a rock in his gut, that Paul was watching. He made himself concentrate on each careful kick into the ice, each stab, because he sensed that to dwell too much on the new fact of his fatherhood or on the Makah girl way down below them, Trace, who'd carried and delivered and raised this boy, was to risk a deadly vertigo when answers and clarity, he hoped, might be found farther up.

Paul might have called out to Bill about the foolishness of what he was attempting and advised him on the sort of gear—crampons, an ice axe, ski poles, good strong rope—he needed in order to help him do what he seemed intent on doing, but the silent space into which they had entered through the immense door of the new knowledge seemed to forbid it. He stood and watched Bill make his defiant, nearly miraculous way up the glacier's snout using the caulked boots, the hunting knife, and the force of a will like none Paul had ever seen. He thought of what Bill had said about their ancestor who'd climbed peaks during the day and danced in Forks at night.

Paul split off and backtracked to a place where the trail had forked to the left, which led him up the trail-less rocks and scree of the glacier's terminal moraine to a place with a vantage of the entire Blue Glacier—the relatively flat lower basin, the massive icefalls above the basin sweeping farther up to the great bulbous snowdome, and the rocky peaks above that.

For a time Paul watched the lower basin in the place where it met the glacier's snout, the place where Bill would emerge if he was successful. When he didn't see Bill Newton anywhere on the glacier, he assumed Bill hadn't succeeded in climbing the snout. He half-expected to see Bill come up the rocks he'd just climbed, assuming Bill must have come to his senses and given up the first attempt, or fallen, in which case he would need help below.

After several minutes, just when he was about to turn and go down, Paul saw movement at the place where the snout met the lower part of the basin. A human form as speck wriggled out onto the wide top of the glacier, stood up, and began making its way up the long face. Paul exhaled through o'd lips and, keeping his eyes on Bill, descended the great pile of rocks and jumped the moat at the edge to move across the surface of the basin in a path that would lead him to intercept Bill Newton on the face of the Blue Glacier.

As he moved, Paul imagined telling Bill Newton some of the things he'd learned about the glacier from Dan and in his own climbs—things he might have told someone he was guiding to the summit of Mount Olympus: This was the lowest elevation glacier in the lower 48 states and owed its existence at this low elevation to a yearly average of twenty feet of snow blown in from the Pacific. The glacier had surged forward 500 feet between 1960 and 1980, followed by a steady retreat (a mass wasting of as much as fifty feet a year) since 1986. If this trend continued, the glacier would eventually waste away, possibly within his lifetime. What looked like snow on the glacier's face was not really snow but a reconstituted combination of snow and ice called "firn" which had been blown together by the fierce winds that sometimes swept down the face of the glacier. He imagined telling Bill that the glacier was moving down the side of the mountain very slowly, like a river, about five inches a day, an amount almost perfectly offset by what melted each day. The glacier was moving up to five times more quickly in the icefall between the high rocky peaks and the flat lower section into which the glacier curved. He imagined telling Bill that the coast tribes, including the Makah, believed the Thunderbird had an aerie in a cave on Olympus and that this legendary whale hunter would throw ice and snow down on anyone who approached the summit with a lack of respect. He would tell Bill that these peaks had been on the bottom of an ocean millions of years ago.

An icy katabatic wind, generated by the glacier itself, blew down the slick face to rustle Paul's hair, and a new surge of adrenaline coursed through him due to the danger of being on the glacier without ropes and an ice axe.

Bill sensed Paul's absence once he was halfway up the glacier's snout and was amazed and strangely grateful to see Paul's silhouetted form following him across the face of the long curving basin, which felt like the perfect stark setting for the strange drama in which they found themselves. When Paul was within shouting distance, Bill felt a sudden inspiration and turned to yell, "I didn't know about you. I tried to tell your mother in the store. Begged her to forgive me for . . . what happened." The place did strange things to his words, bent them, muted and spun them. "I left. I lived . . . in Alaska . . . since then, and . . . ," he trailed off, frustrated by the difficulty of explaining the loneliness and wonder of his fugitive life in Alaska, his hard breaths emanating in white puffs.

Paul heard but didn't know how to respond, couldn't yet leave the silent zone where he always imagined the *tumanuwos* listening to him, for fear of violating something preordained.

In the deep crevasses, and in the valleys where water had melted the ice, and even in the moats where the warmer rocks that had gathered a measure of sunlight met and melted gaps in the ice, and in the small basins, some as big as bathtubs, where rocks fallen onto the ice accelerated the melt, the glacier gave off an otherworldly electric-blue tint because the ice broke up the colors in sunlight and absorbed all but the blue light, which reflected back to the eye. The color gave the impression that the glacier was alive, a colossal sensate entity whose lifeblood and force rested in the color it gave to the Hoh—the river a great thrumming artery connecting it to the ocean as if to a heart.

Behind father and son moving slowly up the glacier's face, way down the valley at the mouth of the Hoh, a Pacific storm had gathered and was pushing up the valley. Paul felt the first wind at his back, the cold stabs of the first drops of moisture, and he turned to see black clouds towering to outdo the peaks. The sight drew an expulsion of breath and made his guts churn.

Aware the entire way of the presence of the boy behind him, Bill fell into a steady rhythm. As he trudged up the face, he waited for something else to say, thinking that if he tried too hard he was certain to say the wrong thing. It was best to concentrate on the steps he was taking or he might founder under the weight of the new awareness. It occurred to him that perhaps he had already died, that the bullet had hit him when the boy fired the gun way back in the forested ridge above the Calawah, and he was now trudging through or toward his afterlife. He shook this off as a dangerous delusion and told himself he needed the thinner air, the guidance of a god or a good pattern of thoughts that would find him at the summit of Mount Olympus. It was possible, though he didn't know for sure, that he was making an offering of himself to the divine beings who inhabited the grandly ascetic zone in which he and Paul found themselves. The air felt purer than any he'd ever inhaled. The bulk of the snowdome below the west peak of Olympus suddenly caught the sun. As if offering a sign, the surrounding walls of rock were momentarily fringed with gold, before the light disappeared into shadow, and Bill also turned to see the towers of cloud speeding to overtake them. This was another world, he thought hopefully despite the clouds, with different rules from the world below, different possibilities. From the summit of one of the peaks presiding over the wide basin, someone might see the fresh path they could take when they returned to the snarled confusion of their off-mountain lives.

For a time he stopped and stood at the edge of a crevasse, which was thicker than any he'd already encountered, running north-south across the glacier below the long icefall. He stared down into its maw—cool blue running to black in the deepest reaches, snowflakes now spiraling down into it. He remembered hearing about his great grandfather leaping over crevasses with reckless abandon, other climbers in his party going as fast as they could and still failing to keep up. Bill leaped the seven-foot expanse as he'd leaped other crevasses on the way and continued up the face of the glacier toward the icefall connecting the lower glacier to the rocks and the snowdome above, thinking of his ancestors and trying not to think too much of the boy following him but thinking of the boy all the more for not thinking of him.

"You can't go up that way!" Paul called from below. "You're headed for the icefall and you can't climb it!"

It was snowing now with an alarming intensity. The basin was all blacks and greys through a shifting prism of white.

Bill heard him but kept on. He was undertaking something he couldn't stop. He leaped another crevasse at the foot of the icefall and moved up the silt-strewn, four foot wide bridge separating the sliver of solid ice from another crevasse and leaped over this one to cling to the ice on the other side and made his way up a series of edgy bumps, like treacherous stairs, the snow swirling around him. He continued up a steep face, steadily kicking his caulks into the ice, jabbing in his knife when he needed it.

Paul stood in front of the first big crevasses below the icefall and called out again into the hushing snow, "It's not climbable! If you'll come down, I'll show you how to go!"

Bill heard him but kept on. He moved to avoid a deep wide crevasse and climbed up to a place where the gap wasn't as wide and leaped onto the narrow bridge stretching across the glacier just before the next crevasse. He punched his toes into the inclining ice and started up, one kick at a time, sending small particles of ice and firn down below him, avoiding the toothiest, slickest-looking ridges, the jagged lips of the crevasses.

"Come down! I'll show you!" Paul called again, silencing himself when he remembered that even the vibrations of a shouting voice could set the icefall into turmoil, so ready was it to fall down the mountain faster than the pace to which it was confined. He was amazed at how far Bill Newton had made it up the uneven snarl of ice, so far by now that he could better hear than see the boots kicking into the ice, the unorthodox way he stabbed the knife. It seemed possible that without an ice axe or rope or crampons or a helmet or any of the gear he should have had and without the techniques vital to success in the endeavor, Bill Newton would defy everything Paul had ever heard about the impossibility of climbing the icefall and make it to the top.

Bill stopped for a moment, clutching ice that was numbing both his hands through the logging gloves. He had reached the steepest incline he'd encountered so far. From this perch, he tried to look down in the direction from which Paul's voice had come. All he saw was swirling snow. Over his heavy breaths—had he ever felt so alive!—an internal voice asked *how will this end?* and advised steady clinging to the ice and careful choices in the steps to come until he'd reached the vantage from which all would be clear. This same voice willed him up the icefall at any cost because it was the route he had felt called to and to which he was now committed. Perhaps he could climb above the storm and look down onto the clouds and out above them at the places where he'd tried to live his life and would continue to in a new way with the wisdom he was sure to find. Another voice asked if he should accept Paul's offer. Even though he couldn't see him, he sensed him waiting on the slope below and hoped he might call out again.

Bill kept still for a time, weighing the voices with a strange sense of calm, given the place where he stood. If he followed the voice telling him to climb with Paul's help, he needed to be sure the decision was based on something other than a fear of the difficult terrain above him. If he decided to continue up the face of the icefall on his own, he needed to be sure the decision was based on something other than a fear of accepting Paul's help. All at once, both of these choices were thrust aside by a surge of feeling so strong that he acted on it at once. He would push up at all costs, will himself up as Great Grandfather Jimmy Newton would have done. The boy below him would see what their kind could do. He tested his footholds and pulled out the knife and thrust himself up and stabbed the knife into the hard ice, his face red, his neck muscles and veins bulging with the effort, his breath roaring in his ears.

Paul didn't know which way was up, which down. The snow danced in chaotic flux all around him. He thought of the still marmot's expectant face and interpreted it as a warning, a sign. The concern he'd had for Bill Newton climbing the icefall now shifted to himself. He felt stupid for being so ill-prepared. He turned very carefully 180 degrees and started walking in the direction he hoped would lead him down the glacier, watching for the deep crevasses they'd passed on the way up, casting a last glance up the icefall Bill Newton was climbing.

Five times, Bill pulled out and stabbed the knife into the ice face, crawling incrementally up, his grunts muffled by falling snow. He thrust his body up with a push from his tenuous footholds and stabbed in the knife, his body a current of defiance. On the sixth attempt, though the knife penetrated the ice, his caulks failed to find purchase in a place where he tried to kick them in and his right foot slid out and his left foot failed to find a hold. His hands held him up for a moment on the knife handle, but he slipped and fell away leaving the knife stuck in the face of the icefall as he went sliding down. He slammed into and cracked a pillar that had been precariously supporting several tons of ice in the form of seracs, some as big as pianos. He slid at great velocity into a steep slick section of ice he'd avoided by pure chance on the way up and fell scrambling into a crevasse with the seracs above him unsettled and whistling down through the snow after, then all around, then past him.

He felt pain in his back and legs and head where he had hit the pillar and wondered if this was what he'd been seeking, and he felt a strong, strange sense of relief as warm wishes flew from him down to Paul on the glacier below. He felt an unaccountable comfort in the knowledge that he was falling toward his son, and worry that he might be bringing all of this down on his son's head, before the pain of impact stopped him and everything darkened, flickered, white and impossibly blue.

A separated piece of one of the biggest seracs, unsettled by the tumult and fragmented against the surface of the icefall above, slammed into Paul's right shoulder and chest (he'd turned when he heard the crashing ice), spinning him around and flattening him against the surface of the glacier. It took him a moment to come back to himself. He slowly stood into the immense silence, something in its vast layers of nothing reminding him of the presence of the *tumanuwos*, their potential malevolence if mishandled. His heart pounded. He worked his shoulder to be sure it was okay and was pleased to feel it rotate in its socket even though it throbbed and stung. He thought of Bill Newton and wondered what might have befallen him and he brought his head in close to the GPS, which he'd earlier forgotten he had, to reorient himself. Then he continued in the direction he'd been walking, one careful step at a time, into the swirling white.

21

Paul thought he'd never been so glad in his life as when he realized he'd finally reached the terminal moraine, which realization occurred only when his boot scraped some snow from a rock. He went back to Bill's camp, stoked a fire in the fire pit beside the rock he'd thrown into its center, and sat warming himself and eating some jerky he found in the pack Bill had left as he looked up in the direction of Mount Olympus. Later that night, he stopped by the closed and locked ranger station at which the ranger on duty had left a note—*Repairing trails at Sol Duc Park. Back on Thursday*. He wrote a note with the brown felt-tip, *Saw a man going up the icefall of the blue glacier during the storm. Heard an avalanche.* For some time before he left it, he debated whether it made sense to leave it and whether or not to sign it. In the end he left the note unsigned.

A team of five climbers from Seattle, two lawyers, one prominent surgeon, and two technocrats on their way to Mount Olympus, arrived at Glacier Meadows a few hours after Paul had left the note. Paul heard them arrive and warily approached their camp when they'd settled in. The men were in their fifties, and they were sitting on a log, cooking on lightweight cookstoves, talking about how much Seattle had changed in the last thirty years—the traffic, the sprawl, the big-city problems it was beginning to face. They also talked about how their sons and daughters had no interest in a trip like this when they would have killed to go mountaineering when they were their kids' age. They were discussing the city's current problems in a way that suggested the problems were in some way theirs to solve, the city's emerald reputation theirs to uphold. As he walked into the mens' appraising gaze, Paul noted that their gear was state of the art, top of the line, and he wondered distantly if they knew Stephanie Barefoot's father.

Paul spoke to them through his exhaustion. He told them he thought he'd seen a climber go up the iceflow in the storm and asked if he could join them when they went up the next morning, no farther than the icefall. They were surprised and did not immediately consent to his request. They asked Paul who this man was to him, and he told them he didn't know the man, thinking as he said it *my father, my father*. One of the men offered to call for help on his satellite phone. This froze Paul for a moment. He hadn't anticipated this possibility. He told the man not to call, feeling a churning in his heart and gut as he did so. "I might be wrong," he said. "It was hard to see."

For a time after that they asked him questions to see what manner of fool he might be: "You up here alone?" "Going for the summit?" "When'd you get started?"

Paul answered the tribunal to their satisfaction and left them to thoughts of their children, scattered and grown and immersed in their own lives, who rarely wanted or had time any longer to come with them on trips into the woods. He left them to wonder in silence how many more years their own lives would give them to enjoy the challenges and hardwon beauty of this kind of trip into Seattle's vast backcountry playground.

Paul went to sleep that night imagining his rendezvous with Dan Kelsoe the next day, if he could make it down in time, and all the things he'd have to tell him, though he didn't think he would mention anything about his relationship to Bill Newton. The next morning he awakened in Bill Newton's old flannel sleeping bag, which smelled of smoke and grease, thinking that there was no question that Bill Newton could have used the bag more than he. He'd had a dream about Bill Newton beside a glimmering river, standing taller than the tall conifers on both banks. The dream reminded Paul of the stories Tom made up about a giant, like Seatco, who roamed the Olympics. In the dream, as Paul approached the river on a trail, Bill Newton laughed a booming laugh and called him "son." In another dream, the spear blade in his pocket sprouted the rest of the spear tip, the shaft, then the skeletal structure, muscles, organs, skin, and hair of Paul's ancestor, who then threw the harpoon through Bill Newton's chest, after which Bill Newton fell to the ground like a cut tree.

Paul broke camp at sunrise as soon as he heard sounds of departure from the climbing party. He shook the dusting of snow from the sleeping bag and joined the party as they prepared to set out, embarrassed by his lack of gear and wondering if they might lend him some of theirs. His right shoulder and chest were sore in the place where the ice had hit it the day before, and he rubbed it as he approached the group, who met him with a renewed solemn appraisal. The lawyers seemed to calculate liability, the doctor, Paul's physical health. The technocrats scanned Paul's gear, horrified at its paucity. They loaned him some of theirs and let him rope up with them for the climb.

Bill regained consciousness with ice inches from his eyes and slowly came to the realization that the glacier had caught him, somehow, without killing him, at the bottom of a crevasse enclosed in a space made by the seracs that had tumbled down with him. That he was alive at all was some sort of miracle and not immediately credible. If he was alive, he'd been reborn into pain and numbness. It took him some time to assimilate the view he saw when he turned his head: dark shadows at the edges of the great pieces of ice, what little light reached them bringing out an aching blue. Accompanying the images, once he'd processed them, was an urge to brace against the bottom of the crevasse and push up against the ice, out of the place where he was trapped, and the knowledge that this was an impossibility, that it would require a colossal strength. This was followed by the realization that it was likely he would die a slow cold death where he lay, which made him think of the fix he'd been in on the frozen lake in Alaska, when the New Wayers saved him and he woke up in a warm cabin surrounded by their voices.

For a long time he lay still, wondering on a few occasions if the blue he saw might be the rare shade of some afterlife. He'd felt his ribs move with the ache of breathing for an hour or more before he fully credited the idea that he was still alive. The realization brought a painful chuckle. He lay there for what seemed like hours longer not daring to move, a puddle of ache on ice, as the light making its way down the walls of the crevasse gradually decreased. A small black bird flitted down into the crevasse through the snow, landed beside his head, chirped amiably, flew away.

When he finally attempted to move, a stabbing pain shot up out of the more general ache in sharp tendrils up and down his back, but he found he could move. He shimmied until his face, neck, and shoulders were out from under the serac that had landed above him, which he realized must have come inches from crushing him and was probably shielding him from other large sections of ice above. When the time came, he would be able, perhaps, if his body still worked, to shimmy all the way out of the tight spot and try the wall of the crevasse, maybe brace against both walls and climb all the way out. For the time being he decided to wait in the shelter the ice provided.

He shimmied back out of the snow and lay listening to the wind on the glacier and watched snow accumulate on the floor below him, which he saw was run through with a crack leading deeper still. Every now and then he extended his arm to clear the snow. Twice he wriggled forward and looked up at the swirling flakes finding their way down between the walls, greyish white against white and blue, just to remind himself he wasn't stuck. After a time, he felt he could hear between his own breaths, the snow stacking up flake by flake and decided this must be what it felt like to be a bear in a cave shutting its system down for the winter. He saw the light decrease until everything was dark and he felt the night's coldness feeding all his other aches. Throughout the night, he kept clearing away the snow, from time to time pulling some into his mouth. He wondered if he would freeze in the night and resigned himself to this fate as he had once before on the lake with the cavorting wolves.

He slept, and when his eyes opened in the morning the brief panic he felt at not knowing where he was brought him into a sharp awareness of the abiding strength of his will to live. He dug away the snow that had fallen in to cover the outlet and wiggled his upper body out into the opening and rested, breathing heavily from the exertion, facing blue sky between the long walls of the crevasse.

While he slept he'd dreamed about Paul resting behind one of the glass doors of the freezers in the frozen-food aisle of a supermarket. The woman at the check-out told him he needed more money to pay for what he wanted to purchase. In the dream, he rifled his pockets but never came up with enough.

He rested in this manner, feeling oddly content with his view up the walls of the crevasse at the blue sky (the storm had long since passed) and not yet settled on what he would do, if anything, to try to get out, when he heard voices coming from the face of the glacier above. A voice, distant but familiar, was calling his name and asking him questions for which he couldn't find the voice to answer. It was too strange to be found like this. He heard a disturbance on the glacier's face, some drips and firn landed on his face and chest. The silhouette of a hooded form haloed in sunlight was peering over the edge and asking him if he was all right. Other hooded silhouettes also peered over the edge. Then a glowing form was descending between the walls above him on a rope, dangling between patches of white and the otherwordly blue speckled with silt. A short time later, he saw his own face, but younger, hovering between the walls and looking down at him with what looked to be genuine concern.

When they had roped Bill Newton up to the surface, they were all amazed, Bill Newton more than anyone else, that he could stand and walk. The lawyers, the doctor, and the technocrats stood around marveling, without saying anything aloud, at his logging outfit. Paul asked Bill, somewhat conspiratorially, if he was all right to go down, and Bill said he was, so Paul told the climbing team that he would see the saved man the rest of the way down and thanked them and convinced them after a time that they should resume their climb while the weather held. For a long time, the members of the team watched the two strangers who looked so much alike moving down the glacier. Later, in the years when day hikes on flat trails were all the men could manage, they would tell the story of the odd rescue to one another, to their grown children and grandchildren, and to dinner party guests, never omitting the detail of how strangely dressed both men were—one like a lost logger, the other like a lost day-hiker. In these later discussions and tellings, they would maintain their assumption that the two were father and son, though at the time each had puzzled on the strange resemblance without mentioning it (there was the mountain to climb).

Paul and Bill covered seventeen miles in silence, Bill a sleepwalking ache shot through with pain, Paul bone-tired. They descended into a steady misting rain, stopping to rest and drink water every three or so miles. Neither knew or much considered what would happen next, how they would part once they were out, knowing what they knew.

Given the lateness of the hour, Paul was more surprised with every mile he covered not to see Dan Kelsoe coming up the trail to meet him. He wondered what Dan would make of the fact that he was traveling with the enemy and how he was going to tell Dan everything he wanted to tell him without talking about his relationship to Bill Newton. As they neared the Hoh River trailhead, the hikers they passed changed from hardcore backpackers ready for the backcountry to rainforest tourists in jeans and cotton t-shirts, many of them holding umbrellas, seeing what it was like to walk a small portion of the mossy realm where it rained an average of 150 inches a year. Paul approached each new person on the trail with the expectation that it might be Dan. He almost walked past a particular not-Dan figure who had gained his notice more than many of the others because she was a girl roughly his age, when he saw her stop and he heard his name.

When he looked more closely, he saw that the girl was Stephanie Barefoot from school.

"Paul!" she gasped. "Thank God, you're all right!"

He started to nod. For some reason, for a portion of a second, it seemed plausible that she knew everything that had happened over the last few days. "Yes . . . ," he said and trailed off in a mumble. "Wait," he said.

She looked down the trail behind her and then up the trail in front of her. Behind Paul, she saw Bill Newton shambling ghostlike over the trail. She stared at Bill for a moment, her eyes wide, struck that they were together as much as by their resemblance to each other.

Paul followed her gaze both ways. He looked at Bill Newton and back at her but couldn't decide what to say about Bill to this girl. The normal range of introductions seemed unequal to the occasion, so he remained silent.

Stephanie remembered . . . *working it out up there* and wondered if this was Bill Newton, the man whose name had so troubled Trace, and what exactly he and Paul might have worked out. The man looked like the ghost of a long-dead logger standing in a kind of unreal hover on the trail five yards away, his presence, even in and perhaps enhanced by this state, immense and electric.

"I don't think I was followed," she whispered to Paul, casting glances at Bill, who might have heard and might not have. "I'm here to pick you up and take you to your mother. I rode in with Uncle Jack, who's waiting at the trailhead. If you want, I can tell you about it as we walk," she said, then stepped forward and hugged him. "I'm so glad to see you. We were worried. Your mother, especially."

He returned her hug gently and nodded, taking in the strangeness of Stephanie Barefoot talking to his mother about him.

Stephanie reached up and kissed him on the cheek, just to the left of his mouth.

They started to walk the last mile of the trail together—Stephanie behind Paul, Bill behind both of them—past brooding bigleaf maples shaped over many hundreds of years into twisted forms covered entirely in moss. The Hoh, their growing companion for the last seventeen miles, rushed within its wide gravel channels toward the Pacific, where settlers in the 1930s and again in the '70s had planned to drill for and refine oil.

"That's Bill Newton?" Stephanie whispered.

Paul paused a while as he felt the box open on the secret he'd planned to store for a long time, then half-turned and nodded.

"Are you okay?"

Again, Paul half-turned and nodded, seeing the form of Bill Newton five yards behind Stephanie.

"Is *he* okay?" she asked, thinking of Paul's right arm quick-rocking and Brink Forger writhing on the ground, holding his nose as blood splattered the cafeteria floor.

Paul was silent for ten feet of trail before answering, "Yes. How do you know so much?"

"We saw some of the loggers who were working with him in the Temple Grove. And one of them told us," she whispered. "Plus, your mom saw him, too, in a grocery store in Port Angeles. The FBI . . . ," she began and went silent as a group of hikers of the daytime-tourist variety—a mother and father with a young boy—passed in the opposite direction. "The FBI," she continued in a quiet voice, "is looking for you. They've been following your mother and they got Dan Kelsoe. My father is giving him legal counsel. Your mother is waiting with your grandmother at Neah Bay while your uncle and I came here because we thought they wouldn't be as likely to follow us."

Paul stared at the dirt, roots, rocks, needles, and cones in front of him as he moved past the turquoise of the constantly roaring river, glimpsed through rare gaps in the underbrush. He was tired beyond tired from the exertions of the last few days and hungry for a big meal and a milkshake at the Hard Rain Café. His shoulder hurt from the place where the piece of the serac had hit it; he wanted to rest and wondered how much longer he'd be able to keep running. He'd looked forward to talking to Dan about everything that had happened, though he wasn't sure how much he would've told Dan about Bill Newton. He was also eager to get home and tell his mother everything. It troubled him that she had found out about what he was doing and that she was out looking for him, that his troubles seemed to have found her, the last thing he wanted. He stopped and half turned toward Stephanie again.

She raised her eyebrows to say *what is it?* with somewhat hopeful anticipation.

Again, Bill, the bearded wraith dragging along behind them, stopped and stood still.

"I shouldn't go home," Paul said. "I should stay out here."

"Aren't you tired? Don't you need to rest? No one followed us to the trailhead—I'm pretty sure. They're following your mother. Your mom and grandmother and Jack think you'll be safe if you can get back to Neah Bay."

He stood thinking for a moment, looking at Bill, then in the direction of the river. His thoughts were interrupted by a faint sound growing louder by the second. All of them came to a gradual awareness of the *thup-thup-thup-thup* of a helicopter blade coming up the valley over the river, moments before they saw a black helicopter pushing the turquoise water into frenetic lines and creases. The pilot and copilot were looking out of the cockpit directly at them. Two more men who didn't look like hikers or tourists were coming toward them down the trail speaking into their wrists. Stephanie recognized the agent who'd waited beside the Sol Duc. Behind them, Uncle Jack, who claimed to be uncomfortable in the woods because it always made him ache for the sea, was out of breath and signaling madly—either for Paul to make a break for it or give himself up, Paul couldn't tell.

Paul dropped his backpack, crashed through the alders, vine maples, huckleberry, and Oregon grape, jumped off the bank into the river, and started wading then swimming across, the water taking his breath away, icy hands insisting him downstream, filling him with a panic that his already-tired muscles might fail him.

Bill stood stunned at this development for a moment, then followed Paul, the cold of the river briefly numbing his aches.

The helicopter hovered and its two pilots focused on Stephanie while Paul and Bill swam the river, swept down fifty yards in the Hoh's powerful sweep, both gasping against the steely hands of ice. The helicopter adjusted its route to hover over the rocky former river channel of the opposite bank. Paul stood out of the water, and, menaced by the wind from the blade, his long black hair wet and wild, waded onto shore, then moved across the stretch of sand and stones and twisted driftwood, his numb legs wobbly on the rocks. Bill followed him, bothered even more by the helicopter, which had lowered as if to land on him.

For several minutes the helicopter hovered above the place where first Paul then Bill had disappeared into an alder thicket, the blades pushing the trees into a riotous dance. They both felt the wind at their backs as they scrambled to make themselves disappear in a log jam in an old river channel.

"Paul Granger," a loudspeaker from the helicopter intoned over the thupping blades. "You are under arrest by the United States Federal Bureau of Investigation. Come out and peaceably turn yourself in to the agents across the river."

Stephanie couldn't recall ever feeling so helpless. This seemed like it might possibly be the most important moment of her life and she felt inadequate to meet it. Should she throw rocks? One of the men approaching on the trail snapped a photo of her, then turned to take a photo of Jack.

"Hey," she said. "I didn't say you could do that!"

"There is a second, unidentified fugitive with the first. Do we pursue them across the river?" the first agent asked into his wrist. "Roger," he said and nodded to the agent beside him.

"Ain't we got fun," the other said. He put the camera into a pouch at his waist.

The first one turned to Stephanie and said, "We'll speak to you later, Stephanie Barefoot," and with a nod called back, "Jack Parks," before wading into the river himself, followed by his partner.

"Leave him alone!" Stephanie yelled as the men gave up wading and swam the rest of the river.

Paul had begun to shiver in the cool air in a hollowed-out space under a western hemlock whose three-foot-wide roots made it look as if the tree had sprouted legs for the purpose of walking away. He sat in this crook of the tree, looking through the branches bordering the gravel bar of the Hoh to see if the men would come after him and waiting for the infernal noise of the helicopter to go away. Bill leaned against one of the hemlock's low-hanging roots and looked through the diamond-stitching of the underbrush at the men in pursuit.

"You go on. I'll stay," he said, and gave Paul a sad, imploring look.

Paul heard him but didn't say anything for a time. "You come with me, too," he finally answered.

Bill shook his head and looked out at the men on the far shore moving across the river.

The helicopter hovered interminably over the log jam and the alder and maple grove in the old channel, pushing the branches into a frenzy of movement, till it was clear to the pilots that Paul was not going to give himself up. Finally, it turned and moved away down the valley.

Just as its concussive noise receded, Bill first, then Paul, saw, without much surprise but with a sense of dread, two wet men coming up onto the bank and making their way across the gravel bar. They exchanged a glance full of resignation to their fate as chased men and which communicated a tacit pledge to be chased together. Paul stood out of the protective nook of the leglike roots and moved through the vine maple, huckleberry, oxalis, and crackling fern fronds across the old river bottom and began moving up the ridge on the other side as fast as he could go.

He assumed Bill was trailing behind him, but when he glanced back, he saw Bill walking across the gravel bar toward the two approaching men. Paul paused to take in the sight of his father before continuing on into deeper forest, wondering how much he would be able to count on his beleaguered body.

Bill wobbled across the gravel bar, pledging himself to his son, thinking of the form in silhouette descending from the sky to pull him from the glacier. Both of the agents stopped and drew pistols from shoulder holsters and ordered Bill to lie down on the gravel with his hands behind his head. He complied, and heard their boots scraping in the sand and gravel as they came up to him. One of them secured handcuffs around his wrists as the other stepped forward to gaze off in the direction in which Paul had gone. "I'm going in pursuit," he said, and as soon as he heard it, Bill braced, swung his feet, and took out the man's legs after which both men kicked him and hit him and tightened the handcuffs as Stephanie Barefoot on the opposite shore jumped up and down and shouted for them to stop.

As he moved, Paul told himself not to look back until he was certain he'd taken advantage of the time Bill Newton had bought him, an image of Bill Newton wobbling over the gravel and rocks beside the river toward the men vivid in his mind, as it would be for a long time to come. As he moved up the ridge, Paul wondered if this was how the rest of his life would be. Always another ridge. So many times, hiking in the Olympics, he'd struggled to get to the crest of a ridge that, from his limited vantage below had appeared to be the highest point for miles around, only to discover, once he'd reached the top of *that* ridge, another rising beyond the first, which, once crested, gave him his first view of yet another ridge, higher still, on and on. Even atop Mount Olympus, the clear blue sky, the moon, the sun, and more distant stars would beckon higher.

22

Trace stepped out onto the shaky footbridge spanning the Elwha. Some of the boards creaked, and the cables supporting the bridge stretched taut. The roar of the river filled her mind. Summer had hung on for the first three weeks and three days of September, then two days ago the first extended rain of fall had blown in off the Pacific to cover the Peninsula in a slow symphony of drips that pocked parking-lot puddles, filled ruts in the roads, nodded millions of needles and leaves, swelled the rivers and covered the highest peaks in snow.

She'd just come up the Elwha River trail for the fourth time in her life, thinking, as she hiked, how a place you never knew you'd ever see could come to mean so much. She counted the trips as she made her way past Elk Overlook and Rica Canyon, and Krause Bottom, names she knew because of Tom. The first time was the trip with Bill Newton for "the picnic." The second was the dark-purposed trip with Paul, when the river that should have been so impassive and deadly seemed to save him. The third was a trip she'd made with Tom and Paul some seven years ago, in 2000, when they'd hiked as far as Krause Bottom, about a half-mile away from the meadow where Paul had been conceived. They'd gone that time because Paul had heard a fellow student at school talk about the hike up the river, and he'd wanted to go so badly they finally couldn't refuse. Tom told her she didn't have to go, that he could take Paul himself, but she said she thought it might be good for her to go again with Paul.

As they'd hiked in that time, Tom had kept up a steady stream of facts about the human history, the white history, not the subsumed native history, of the places they were seeing. She realized now that he had done this for her benefit, to try to distract her from her personal connection to the place. When he'd exhausted what he knew of the white history and the place names they were seeing, he talked about the places in the Park named for Greek mythology—Mount Olympus and the peaks named Panic, Aries, Athena, Icarus, Apollo, and Aphrodite. There were also the Valhallas, a seldom-climbed range three-and-a-half miles southwest of Mount Olympus, named for the resting place in Norse mythology where warriors who'd fought bravely in battle were carried by the beautiful maidens, the valkyries, when they died, and Vidar, a peak in the Valhallas named for the son of Odin who tore apart the jaws of the wolf that had swallowed his father, and other peaks named for Vili, the Norse god who gave people the ability to feel and understand, and Bragi, god of poetry and husband to the fertility goddess, Frigga, who also had a peak in the range named for her, and Baldur, god of spring, sunlight, and joy, and Mimir, god of wisdom.

On and on he went so that she might forget as she thought about Makah and Quileute and Klallam and Quinault names for these places, most of them lost to the deliberate cultural erasure carried out by the United States government, or perhaps some never named in any way except the most essential, necessary, fleeting. She thought of their contentment not to name every peak and felt proud of this restraint, a pride she kept quietly to herself as they walked and Tom talked and talked. Now, as she hiked through the forest of silver fir, feeling a faint but unmistakable promise of the coming winter in the air, Trace smiled fondly to remember how steadily, if awkwardly, Tom had kept the information coming to try to distract her from her own memory of the place, how he cast sidelong glances to see how she was doing, and she felt a deep affection for him and knew she was right to support him in his current difficulties.

Occasionally she consulted her watch to make sure she wouldn't be late for her appointment.

When she came to the place where she had the choice of descending into the valley at Hume's Ranch, she paused a moment before deciding she had time, that she wanted to go there. She continued down the narrow trail to the place on the little bluff above the alders where the flannel sleeping bag had been spread and she had been rushed into and unmade as Paul was made. She stood in the very spot, as nondescript and pristine-seeming as all the others in this wild place, and waited in the silence, the roar of the river in an altered course from the one it had taken that day, new log jams, the river's older courses claimed by alder thickets, to see what would find her. She felt nothing but a stillness that made her think any malevolent power the place might once have had over her was gone. She breathed for a time in this new quiet, looking at the water glimmering between logs, sticks, branches, and leaves. If they stayed true to the current plan (she'd believe it when she saw it), the dams downstream would be torn down and the steelhead and salmon would return.

A week ago, she'd received an anonymous note. She was sitting behind the cash register with all of her morning work done, all the creatures fed, the tanks and filters cleaned, and was watching Pishpish in the tank across from the desk. It soothed her to watch the undulating of Pishpish's arms and the ripples passing through her body. It seemed that Pishpish was also watching from behind Trace's faint reflection in the glass. This morning Pishpish was lavender and burnt-orange to brown at the edges of her body where it met her arms, a relaxed color for her, calm but somewhat pensive, perhaps, bordering on mournful, as if she understood, sensed, or was reflecting Trace's mood. A carrier dropped the Center's mail on Trace's desk and she was casually sifting through it when she came upon the typewritten envelope with no return address and a cryptic note inside.

> Trace,
> Elwha River trail. Bridge leading to Dodger Point. 9/27
> 3:00. Come alone.

She looked up from the note at Pishpish, who had turned a bright mottled red, so that it looked as if she was covered in a blush or a rash, which blush rippled into a deeper red, then another, deeper still—all these reds rippling like fireworks in waves over Pishpish's amorphous body. Trace stood to make sure Pishpish was all right, and took some steps toward her aquarium only to see Pishpish settle back into a calmer light blue, a gleam as if of understanding in her eye.

During the following week Trace went over every possible person who could have written the note—Bill Newton; Dan Kelsoe; the young FBI agent she'd seen on the trail; the gyppo logger, Oliver Smith, who was responsible for contracting the cut in the Temple Grove; the young logger with the hot temper; an Indian-hating prankster who'd read about Paul or seen him on the news and wanted to mess with her; the tall man who was the head of the ONPWO; the couple from Seattle who'd come upon her and Bill Newton that day years ago and had seen her on the bridge; Stephanie, with some revelation she'd never told Trace before; or Paul himself, or someone who knew something about what had happened to him. She didn't let herself believe that Paul had written the note, because she thought to hope this too much would make it less likely to be true.

Paul was considered dead. She refused to credit it, but this was the common belief, even though he was officially listed as only missing. Over the course of the whole ordeal, even when others seemed certain he was dead, her mind and heart presented her with the possibility that he was still alive, again and again, with an endless supply of hope she hadn't guessed she had. She was nearly certain that Paul had written the note, that no one but Paul would meet her there, even though another more cautious region of herself advised against lingering on this possibility and sent her back to cycling and recycling the list of names. She thought about the note and the meeting almost constantly for the entire week. Even when it wasn't foremost in her mind, as she worked at the Marine Life Center and tried to help Tom in his crisis, as she heard about the efforts her mother and Uncle Jack were organizing to keep looking for Paul, she thought about the moment when she'd stand waiting on the bridge. She didn't tell anyone about the note and planned to keep the appointment alone.

Now the moment had almost arrived. It was 2:55 and she was standing in the middle of the bridge, in a place she hadn't visited in eighteen years, above the steady roar of the rain-swollen Elwha, in the very place where she had stood when Paul had slipped from her grasp. Even now it made her shudder—made her fingers and toes tingle, her heart leap to her throat, and a wave of sadness and regret sweep over her—to remember his little body no longer in her hands and falling.

Tom had been home from India for a month. As they'd driven back from the airport, she had told him the story of all that happened while he was gone. He absorbed it in silence during the telling and was silent for a long time after. Later, shaking and nearly weeping in the living room with the great windows onto the spectacular view and the soft white carpet that his job afforded them, he'd told her the rest of his own tale.

The direct flight from Bhavnagar to Bombay the day after the beaching of the ship was cancelled because of monsoon-force rains in Bombay, and the van that was supposed to take them the four hours to Ahmedabad for a flight from there to Bombay had foundered when the fan belt broke two hours into the trip. The driver flagged down a public bus in which they would continue the rest of the way to Ahmedabad for the plane to Bombay, where they would catch another flight back to New York. From there Tom would fly to Seattle, where Trace would pick him up. The narrow distance between the Ahmedabad bus and the cars and other busses heading in the opposite direction, made it difficult to sleep—a game of chicken every time they passed a car, truck, or bus going the other way. Occasionally, charred former cars, trucks, and busses appeared at the side of the road in front of fields of what he guessed was rice. Phrases from Leif's tirade ran through Tom's mind—*asbestos . . . lead paint . . . PCBs . . . oil in the bilge water . . . released into the environment and into the workers' bodies*—accompanied by images of Trace and Paul back in Port Angeles. What would they do if he changed his job? Would Trace talk it out with him when he got home? Could he ever get on as a pilot for the Strait or in the Sound given what had happened in Prince William Sound three years before he'd met Trace? If he left his job, how would they pay for Paul to go to college, if that's what Paul wanted? What else could he do? How could you live well and live with yourself?

He went to sleep to these questions and was awakened by a loud, metallic crash. When he opened his eyes, chicken feathers fell around him like snow. Someone was moaning. Someone else shrieked over the sound of a mechanical hiss. It smelled of diesel fumes, exhaust, and burning rubber. He felt moisture on his face and when he put his hand to it saw on his fingers the glimmer of a liquid that could have been his or someone else's blood shining in the orange light of the flames. He was on his side on the side of the road. It occurred to him that this was par for the course. Beginning with the spill, from time to time afterwards, it seemed to him that he had become a punching bag for a variety of life's blows, not the least of which was the realization and acceptance of the fact that he and Trace could not have children together. He stood up and started walking past the wreckage of the bus they'd struck, saying Trace's name as if she was the most valuable thing he might lose as a consequence of what he had just survived and as if her name was a mantra to protect him from what might still come.

Home at last in Port Angeles, in the living room with Trace, his head on her lap, he told her how much he needed her and missed her in that moment when he thought his time was up, and about the things the Greenpeace raiders had said and how he didn't know if he could do it anymore. She listened to him, stroking the thinning hair on his heavy head in her lap as she looked out at the moonlight on the Strait. She knew what it would mean if he quit his job and couldn't find another one. The house would have to go when they couldn't meet the mortgage payments, and who knew what work he would find? Would he go with her, back to the rez? Would she want him to?

The unofficial consensus among all the interested parties was that Paul had met his end in the Olympics not long after the FBI agents in the helicopter and on the Hoh's northern shore reported seeing him swimming the river and disappearing into the forest. Immediately following his escape, the authorities initiated an APB to track him down. A host of different parties and organizations with all their resources—their bloodhounds, helicopters, and experts with ski poles, "the whole king's horses and king's men of them," Uncle Jack said—searched the Park as thoroughly as they could over the next few days—a strange combination of rescue mission and federal criminal manhunt—without finding him, though they did find his camp near the Temple Grove. With every day after the first week, the search cooled till it was almost completely dead.

Bill Newton wasn't saying anything to anyone. He began his silence with the FBI agents who captured him on the gravel bar. It took them an hour to wrestle his immobile hulk to the edge of the river. They felt they couldn't get too rough with him while the girl and the Indian watched from the opposite bank. Their prisoner, who felt he had found within the crevasse the purpose he'd been seeking on the mountain, finally stood up and let them lead him across the river, both of them at times clutching Bill to steady themselves. Bill himself needed both agents' help to make it down the last of the trail to the parking lot. He stumbled several times and fell down once, his face and beard mashed into dirt, against a root. He experienced a vague desire to sit down and think about the events of the last four days for a long time, but even if he had the freedom to do this, he knew he didn't yet have the capacity to assimilate any of it. A strange warmth, an unaccountable satisfaction seemed to be carrying him down the trail. His thoughts intermingled with a woozy feeling and the pain and the tiredness and what turned out to be cracked ribs and badly damaged vertebrae that might have been translated: I was born in the glacier, ushered into life by my son, raised by the Feds. By the end he was dimly aware of their hands on his.

Brent Sawtelle, who'd waited in the SUV at the Hoh River trailhead to maintain his cover, had heard what happened during Paul Granger's attempted arrest. He'd been surprised to hear that a new player had entered the game and was even more surprised when he saw his fellow agents hauling a giant of a man with wild hair and beard, in full-on logging gear, across the parking lot past gawking tourists.

"He won't tell us who he is. But he was with the kid."

"I heard," said Brent, looking in the rear-view mirror at their prisoner while the other two were positioning him in the back seat. He noticed, in a way that the other two agents did not, and immediately, that this man looked just like the photographs they had on file of Paul

Granger. He remembered the circumstances of Paul's birth as told in the dossier, the fact of the rape and the missing father. He nearly said this to the others, but something in the set of the man's eyes, his stillness, the sense that the man knew what he was thinking, stopped him.

Bill's silence, his stillness, continued with Spears Barefoot, who, at his daughter's suggestion, became the mysterious misfit's pro-bono lawyer. Spears also hoped to find out more about Paul so he could convey the information to Trace. Smitty and Lincoln Maxey and Timberforus had coordinated their stories to make Bill sound like the one who had initiated the cut in the Temple Grove. In addition to this charge, there was the further complication that the Port Angeles police and the reservation at Neah Bay had contacted Trace about the warrant out for Bill Newton for her alleged rape, a charge that Trace explained to Spears, and Spears to Stephanie, who considered in a new light seeing Paul and Bill together on the rainforest trail and what the Maxey boy might have meant when he said, "They're working it out up there . . ."

Repeatedly, authorities from multiple organizations asked Bill Newton questions about Paul's possible whereabouts, what the two of them had said to each other before he gave himself up, why they had been together at all, and why they had both run away. None of the men and women who asked ever got anything from him beyond a doorlike stare and a strong sense of solid conviction in the comfortable way he held himself and something peaceful in his eyes that suggested that's all they were ever going to get, even if they tortured him half to death, which occurred to some of them. After more than a month of this, Spears got permission for Trace to meet with Dan Kelsoe and Bill Newton in the government building in Seattle where he was being held. The ten-year statute of limitations for the rape was up, but Trace's mother and some others on the reservation wanted to test the laws that made it difficult to try someone off the reservation for a rape of a tribe member. The FBI wanted to keep the rape on Bill Newton's record in case it might prove useful in their case against him and Paul and Dan Kelsoe, whose relationships with one another took some time to come into focus.

She drove alone, took the Bainbridge Island ferry across the Sound to Seattle, then drove to a soulless building in Ballard. Spears met her in the building's parking lot. He was dressed now in a black suit, the garb of his trade, in which she imagined him breezing unhindered through the corridors of power. His manner was solicitous and casual, and she felt like she could feel a hint of self-consciousness in his performance. It seemed he was acting as calmly as possible to try to calm her, his professionalism a shell, something he'd formed to help him survive and thrive like one of the creatures in the Marine Life aquarium. Both men were being questioned in the same building. Spears had earlier told Trace that he'd once seen the two men passing one another in the hallway. Spears said that during this encounter Dan Kelsoe had frozen where he stood and turned beside his escort to watch Bill Newton pass, struck by the resemblance and staring after this older Paul figure as if he'd seen a bear or wolf. He didn't turn and move till he was urged forward. Spears later told Dan who Bill Newton was, and the coincidence made Dan ponder the difficulty of ever coming to any certainty on any action when the world could fling something like this into your plans.

First, Spears took Trace past a screening line busy with no-nonsense security guards and through two locked checkpoints, up an elevator, and down a hallway into an interrogation room to see Dan Kelsoe. This is a place, thought Trace, where they apply pressure to get to the real story, but with its airless, brightly lit rooms, it felt more like a place where stories go to die.

Dan gushed about Paul and apologized again and again without saying anything, his performance (everyone seemed ready to perform for her) calling up in her again the anger and sadness that had gradually subsided as she'd begun to make peace with Paul's disappearance. On a few occasions Trace wondered whose side Spears was on, so often, in response to one of her questions of Dan, did Spears give his head a little shake as Dan looked imploringly at his legal counsel to see what he would be well-advised to say. At one point in the conversation, Trace turned to Spears and said, "Are you going to let him talk?" sensing the strong agreement (yes, let him talk!) of the FBI who were surely watching them.

In a paternal tone, Spears began, "Trace—"

"No. No," she said. "You're not letting him say anything, and you," she said, turning to Dan Kelsoe, who looked miserable, the pink scars down his face flushed, his eyes pleading with her to understand his reticence. "You didn't have to involve him. He's a good boy, and now his future is smudged. He didn't need you pushing him."

Dan closed his eyes and nodded in a rhythmic way till the nod spread to his body. He began to rock in a way that it was easy to imagine he might rock to soothe himself in his cell at night. He was in agony because he'd meant to be Paul's perfect mentor, had thought he was teaching him to save the good things in the world and it had come to this. He said, "I know, I know," but nothing more.

Trace released a long sigh into the silence, and they stood without saying goodbye. Spears ushered her out of the room and toward the next visit. He tried to place a hand on her elbow, saying, "I know it's frustrating, but you have to understand—" but stopped speaking when Trace shook off his hand. Between security checkpoints in the halls smelling of disinfectant, she said, "This is too much for one day."

Bill was wearing an orange jumpsuit and plastic handcuffs and sitting in a bare room, at a bare table with chairs on either side. He had lost a lot of weight, and Spears noticed hopefully and recounted later, thinking he might finally speak, that the prisoner seemed more agitated to see Trace Granger than any of his previous interrogators. For a time he seemed not to know what to do with himself. It looked as if he wanted to fly out of the room. The impression was of a wild animal faced with the thing it most feared. Trace was as shocked by his resemblance to Paul as she had been in the frozen-foods aisle. The resemblance was strengthened now by the gauntness of Bill Newton's face, the greater prominence of his brown eyes. His hair and beard were longer and more flecked with grey.

The two of them sat across from each other in silence for a long time, Bill making sporadic eye contact, Trace trying to still a rage that felt like it needed to crash onto someone. "He's your son. Did you know that?" she began with some fire.

Bill Newton nodded, more than he'd granted any of the men and women who had tried to get him to talk.

"Do you know where he is?"

He shook his head, thinking of Paul in the mossed-over roots of the great western hemlock in the former log jam of that old channel of the Hoh, his face pale, eyes pleading for rest.

"He saved me," Bill Newton said. "Came down out of the sky," he said, "when I was stuck down in the ice." He almost smiled thinking of the rock Paul threw hitting ash, the silhouetted form between the walls of the glacier against blue sky, a sense of Paul alive in the world.

Behind the one-way mirror, agents were suddenly alert to record what he said.

"Do you think he's still alive?" Trace asked. It was as if Bill Newton had become the wildness into which Paul had disappeared; she needed to know how to search him for what he knew as one might search a forest, and she knew her anger at him wouldn't help her in this task.

Bill Newton shook his head. "I hope he is," he said, and he felt the impulse that had driven him to his knees in the store. "I'm glad I met him. I wish I would've known him sooner."

"Why were you two together coming down the trail? You said he saved you?" she said.

Bill Newton looked at Spears and looked at the door and shook his head and didn't say anything more, though Trace saw something in his eyes that she came to interpret as a great store of reparative wishes.

"What," she asked, "did you try to say to me in the store that day?"

He'd been trying to tell her he thought often about what happened that day on the Elwha and how things might have been different and how he carried her with him from that day on and that he was sorry. But he only managed to say the last of these and that he thought Paul seemed like a good kid who'd been raised well.

They ended the interview in more silence after Bill again refused to say why they'd been together on the trail, beyond saying that Paul had pulled him from the deep crevasse. Once she was back home, assimilating the new Bill Newton she'd seen that day, Trace maintained her habit of climbing the old madrone and sitting on the roof of the house on the bluff to look up and ask the great dark forms of the mountains for signs. She still occasionally practiced being still for a time as a way to help Paul in his trials. Whatever might help, she was willing to try. Now the mountains seemed to guard what they knew. They no longer appeared to glow with some knowledge, with assurances that he would be all right. Even though she thought that if he was still out there he'd be deep in the backcountry, she took to regularly hiking into the Park herself after work and on the weekends, going to places Paul had noted on his map. During these hikes, she was sometimes haunted by visions in which a piece of his clothing winked at her from between branches. When she went to take a closer look into these visions, she saw that the stitch indexed Paul's perfectly preserved body splayed out on amber rocks under ten feet of clear water. His eyes were wide open, his long black hair rising and falling in the current.

Tom didn't go with her on these hikes. He seemed to be in a state of shock at Paul's absence, his near death experiences in India, his job dilemma. At first he spent most of his time in the basement cruising the Internet, watching television, burying his toes in the luxurious white carpet, waiting for his next assignment to a doomed ship bound for breakdown in the third world and trying to decide how he would respond when the call came. After a few weeks of this, he took to building model planes and ships the way he had as a child, carefully gluing the tiny delicate parts together and painting them, applying the decals. It was something he had tried to get Paul to like but in which Paul had had very little interest. More recently, Tom had given up his model airplane and ship building to paint watercolors of natural scenes from the Peninsula—misty beaches, snow-capped peaks, foggy marinas, wide trunks, the green vale of his native Chimacum valley. Once he'd had some practice, he started on a splotchy map of the Peninsula—indistinct, so that it seemed as if what it represented might wash away at any moment—covered at its edges with wavery representations of what you'd find in that part of the Peninsula—surf and sea stacks with shore pines near the ocean beaches; a few river scenes beside the rivers; a cougar, half hidden in a swirl of green brush and brown boughs. It amazed Trace how good he was at this. She nearly gasped when she first discovered this talent in her pensive mariner. She sometimes went down to the basement to watch him work and to tell him he should show this one to Paul, which made Tom pause in his work for a moment and look at her as if to try to see if she meant it (that Paul was alive, that it was worthy of showing?), before nodding and resuming the scratching of brush against paper.

Before she left for her freshman year at Whitman College in Walla Walla, over the Cascade Mountains down in the southeastern part of the state, Stephanie accompanied Trace on a few of her hikes into the Olympics. Stephanie's mind was full of speculations she sometimes shared about what might have happened to Paul, all of which involved his safe escape and some of which involved Paul living off the land where no one could find him, deep in the mountains he loved. Stephanie felt partially responsible for his flight that day. She worried that she'd led the FBI to him, and imagined the things she might have said to make him stay and try to seek refuge on the reservation, though she knew that had he stayed, the agents would have arrested him and he would be embroiled in the trial with Dan Kelsoe. That was better than being dead, of course, if he was dead, which she couldn't bring herself to believe or even imagine.

The FBI had interrogated Stephanie shortly after Paul had run away. Two agents had questioned her in the dining room of the house on Mount Angeles Road while her father paced the kitchen floor and tried to listen in. The experience made her so angry that she gave in at one point to an outburst, accusing her interrogators of wasting everyone's time, not to mention the country's resources, by refusing to go after real criminals. She'd written a number of e-mails and letters to Trace from school, asking about any progress on the search and vowing her support till the end: "I'll come back right away. Say the word, if you need me."

Trace did not know that Stephanie sometimes awakened in her dorm room with the awareness of a fleeting memory of a dream about Paul, on a few mornings an image of him obscured by the verdant growth of the temperate rainforest, his sad face glancing back across the wide blue expanse of the Hoh one last time before resuming the burden of the hunted. On one morning she dreamed he was standing in the doorway of her dorm room. The dream was so real it took a few waking hours for the vividness of the impression to fade. In her freshman Core class they were reading *The Odyssey*, and as Stephanie read about Homer's characters going to sea in black boats, she thought about the Makah, contemporaries of the Greeks, skating across the water in their redcedar canoes. She thought about Paul and imagined him alive somewhere in the Olympics and, because she had conflated Odysseus's story with Paul's, she discussed, with more passion and urgency than her fellow classmates, the gods making decrees atop the original Mount Olympus, young Telemachus's struggles with the suitors, the resourcefulness of Odysseus in his long journey home, the clever faithfulness of Penelope.

Stephanie's father was defending Dan Kelsoe in the federal case against him. Since the visit to the federal building in Ballard, Dan had written Trace a letter apologizing if he'd led Paul astray and for his reticence at their meeting, saying he thought of Paul as his own son (and thinking but not writing, "more than my own son") and, for that reason, doubly regretted anything he had done to contribute to Paul's loss. He said he held out hope that Paul would come home soon—he certainly knew the Olympics well enough to survive in them—and assured her he would continue to deny Paul's involvement in any kind of illegal activity, which would be easy to do, as he was innocent. He also wrote about Paul's rare affinity with the spirit of the Park and how that was something Paul and she should be proud of. In closing, he asked her to burn, shred, or otherwise destroy the letter.

It seemed to Trace that the FBI had stopped following her a few weeks after Paul's disappearance, but could you ever know such a thing, especially if they were doing a good job? Presumably, they'd grown tired of sitting outside the Marine Life Center hearing her as the school year began in September telling fifth-grade classes about Pishpish's eating habits (crabs, squid, abalone), intelligence (like that of a housecat), and life span (about four years, two more for Pishpish) or listening in at night at the house as Trace attended to Tom while he modeled and painted and tried to right himself.

The gyppo Smitty and the Maxey kid had let Bill serve as the scapegoat for the trees they had cut down, and Timberforus had announced from its Atlanta headquarters that they were officially (for the second time) backing down from the sale and demanding the return of their investment to the Forest Service. The CEO of Timberforus was rumored to have secretly arranged to have the single giant Douglas fir felled in the Temple Grove hauled out and made into a floor, a deck, and a hot tub for a vacation home in Breckenridge, Colorado. The bridge-timber spike, removed from the tree and re-driven into a beam, became a conversation piece and a place to hang towels.

Trace stood on the bridge at the appointed time, sifting the facts she knew and wondering at other possibilities, leaning her arms against the railing and staring downstream at the Elwha—milky white in the rapids over mossed-over rocks, turquoise in the pools, clearer in the shallows—wondering at the constancy of a strong river like this one and how miraculous it was, if you thought about it, that rivers never went dry and how kindness from people who did not have to be kind, but from whom kindness nevertheless sprung, was no less miraculous—when she felt the footbridge shake. At first she thought it was the wind, till the whole bridge moved again and kept shaking.

A figure approached from the other side, a tall, gaunt, clean-shaven man with close-cropped hair and wearing a thick, bushy sweater that looked to have been made from some unconventional sort of wool under a green rainjacket.

On a certain level she knew immediately that it was Paul, on another, and because of her self-imposed skepticism, it took her a few moments of the figure's steady approach, the tipping and swaying of the bridge above the river, for her to credit this knowledge, with a surge of joy. He was alive—an older, darker, taller, thinner, cleaner-shaven, shorter- haired version of himself. He stopped and stood five feet away from her, wearing a stern expression for a moment so that it seemed as if he hadn't recognized her or might be upset with her for some reason. Now that he was closer, she could also see something around his neck—a leather strap run through a small, crude bear carved out of bone or tusk resting against his chest, alongside a piece of something else she couldn't identify that also looked like bone. His grave expression broke, and he smiled for a second the mischievous smile he flashed when he knew she would understand something others wouldn't. "I guess I went and did it now, didn't I?" he said.

She held back a moment to play along. "You sure did," she said. "Am I seeing a ghost?"

"You could say that," he said, trailing off, thinking that soon he would tell her about the chase with Bill Newton and the big seracs he heard but couldn't see tumbling down Blue Glacier and the small one that hit him; and the chase with the FBI men who'd given up sooner than he expected; and the kindness of the llama lady who'd taken him in when he showed up, shivering, at the sliding-glass door reflecting the llamas in a field, the forest in back of her farmhouse, and how she'd gotten him warm, fed him, helped him return to himself after the near-death battering the woods had given him.

He appreciated the fact that Trace had come into the Olympics to meet him in this place. Of all the places he'd considered for this meeting, this one had kept asserting itself. He knew it was close to the place of his conception, a place that must still haunt her. Or did his existence erase the haunting? The bridge was also just beyond where most day-hikers stopped and far from the surveillance cameras likely to find them in any "civilized" setting. There was another pull he'd felt from this place that he couldn't explain. The river below their feet rushed and roared to a pool where it eddied against rocks.

He smiled again, a flash of white teeth that quickly gave way to a more grave expression. His face was tanned and hollow below his cheekbones. His eyes had gained a great deal of gravity and what looked like the weight of a specific sadness to underlie what she had taken (most of the time) for simple goodness and wonder—what must have been, that day eighteen years ago, only a few hundred feet below where they stood, a promise of forgiveness, even if in some deeply buried strata of himself—or was it closer to the surface?—he still remembered falling from her hands into the river.

It occurred to her with a sharp pang how little was settled for him—her son, this wanted man—and she wondered how long they would have now before something came to interrupt the present visit, what their next move should be, if there was anything she would be able to do for him at all in what was to come. She let break the cool façade she was holding and moved to embrace him as if she expected a wind from Thunderbird's wings or the cycling blade of a black helicopter to come ripping down the valley and blow them both away.

After a time, she felt his muscles tense and he gently pushed out of the embrace. "I have a lot to tell you," he said, just above the river's constant roar, "and I shouldn't stay long."

She dried tears from her face with her hands and remembered other tears she'd shed down near the river as they walked from the bridge, and as they walked to and sat looking out over the oblivious meadow (or did it know on some level) with the Elwha trickling beyond the alders, she thought it seemed possible to erase everything except the fact of his birth and his presence beside her in this moment.

He told her everything he'd been thinking—about his part in the Temple Grove mission with Dan Kelsoe, and everything that had happened in the woods with Bill Newton—the chase that had ceased to be a chase and the descent into the Blue Glacier crevasse, and the black helicopter coming up the Hoh, and Bill Newton whipsawing his legs to take down the agent on the gravel bar. He told her how he'd begun to lose his mind in the woods, though no one seemed to be chasing him, and how it was most frightening when he felt euphoric when the hypothermia set in. He told her how he made his way, blindly, knowing it was his last chance, and showed up shivering and half-dead at the llama lady's door, and how she brought him back to life. She had him do chores on the ranch after she'd helped him regain his strength with tea and thick stews, and she'd helped him devise a plan to return to his life—everything up to the moment yesterday morning when he'd hiked from her house into the forest and made his way to meet Trace in this place.

Trace held back her jealousy of this woman who'd rescued Paul. She told him again how happy she was that he was still alive and that she knew he was alive all along, and she told him everything she'd done to try to find him, and how worried she'd been, and about the terrifying dreams she'd had when she didn't know where he was and about the good wishes she sent him every day when she first woke up and when she climbed the old madrone to sit on the roof, and about her hikes into the Olympics, and how she had gone ahead and paid the deposit at Oregon State so he could still enroll, and about the painting Tom was doing of the Peninsula.

She hit him playfully on the shoulder once they'd finished their stories. "I can't believe you're sitting here," she said. "Why didn't you write or call once you were out? Send me a message some way?"

"We knew they were watching and listening to you," he said. "They may be still, and I didn't want to get you in trouble."

She didn't like that "we" and the way it seemed to exclude her. The river winked through gaps in the alder leaves and through interstices in a log jam. "They said something about Dan Kelsoe's bombing car dealerships." She could tell that that caught him off guard. "What if you turned yourself in?" she asked, thinking of the agents in the house, the young agent at the Sol Duc trailhead. "If you cooperate, it could only be a misdemeanor for the spikes in the trees."

Paul shook his head in a grave new way that suggested that not only was turning himself in not an option but also that he might decide to mistrust her for suggesting it. The reaction sent a thrill through her, a different channel of fear, and she realized it would have been one or the other—fear of losing him to them, or losing him to what he would need to do to keep away from them.

She saw a cloud pass over his face and a few moments later he told her he had to go. He would hike back across the Park to the llama lady's place. She was, even as they spoke, contacting Spears and another man, someone who knew how to forge new foolproof identities with computers, who could help them generate a new identity for him.

"So you'll . . . ?" she asked.

"Become someone else," he said and smiled in a strange way that suggested he believed this had already happened. After he got back to the llama lady's cabin, he was planning to hike from Rialto Beach up to the reservation at Neah Bay, skirting headlands and walking along the beach where he could. He wanted to take one last hike in the Park before he had to go away. He said he wanted to see the beach she'd taken him to when he was three, the first day he could remember, and he told her he wanted her to be at the reservation, if she could make it, with the others, in a week to see him off into his new life.

If she could make it . . . as if she would do anything else. "Can't you just come home with me?" she asked.

"It's too risky, for both of us," he said.

She watched him cross the bridge from which he had fallen from her hands and wondered what the meeting he'd spoken of could mean. Even though she was sad to have lost him again, she hiked light-footed all the way back to the trailhead, thinking the identity of the person she'd been called to meet could not have been better, even if it was now in flux, and reminding herself to stay her own doubts about whether or not the meeting had actually taken place, remembering the first and second times she'd walked this same trail—the first in the stunned aftermath of what had happened by the Elwha, the second gripping Paul to her breast and making him promises. Now she fought the suggestion that the last meeting and its reverberations with the others and the lingering sense of his presence, strong and lean and competent against powerful foes, was something she'd willed into a vivid daydream.

But to rely on a new identity, to erase himself? She didn't like the sound of that.

23

One week later Trace was relieved to see Paul seated with his back to her on a chair in a room that was empty except for a bare wooden table surrounded by chairs. He was silhouetted by bright light, the first the area had seen in two months, pouring in through a large window open onto the Strait, whose water glittered gold and silver-starred between boats docked at the marina.

She stood in the doorway and looked at him for a time. Two men from reservation security whom she vaguely knew had greeted her and Tom amiably at the door and nodded them into the room.

Tom joined Trace in staring at Paul from the doorway and touched her shoulder as if to steady himself, her last-leg ship. "Is it really you?" Tom asked, and Paul turned to face them, though they couldn't see his face for the bright sunlight pouring into the room. "I was afraid we'd lost you," he said.

Paul stood and walked out of the light, his face becoming clear as he crossed the room. He nodded and smiled at both of them—a flash of white teeth that quickly gave way to a more grave expression, and Tom and Trace, in turn, gathered him into fierce embraces.

Within the next five minutes the door opened and closed three more times as Spears arrived, followed by Uncle Jack and Trace's mother, who had told Trace when she'd stopped in at the house behind Washburns that Paul had shown up smiling at her door the night before, fresh from his hike all the way up the twenty miles from Rialto to Shi Shi and that she thought for sure it was one of the *tumanuwos*. "I wanted to call you,

Tracie," she said, "but they told me they thought you were still too hot."

"It's okay," Trace said. "I saw him before that, about a week ago. All this cloak and daggers stuff," she said, "just about seeing Paul," and she shook her head.

The last to arrive was a tribal council member, who was skeptical about the meeting because the Makah had only a month ago had a run-in with the feds over a successful rogue whale hunt carried out by some of the same hunters who'd captured the whale in 1999. These hunters had been frustrated that it was taking so long to get permission for a new hunt and had gone on their own hunt in a spirit of civil disobedience. The Coast Guard had cut the whale loose and its carcass had fallen to the floor of the Strait for the bottom feeders to devour. The men who'd done it were being charged with federal misdemeanors, and the tribe had condemned what they'd done. Now, it seemed, the reservation was also being asked to be seen as a last bastion for paper Indians in trouble with the feds for breaking the law to save trees. With all of this playing in his head, the council member sat down with a sigh, his skepticism and the weight of due process visible on his face.

The llama lady had delivered Paul to the trailhead at Rialto Beach at the end of his sanctuary on her ranch near the Hoh. In her ranch house, Ansel Adams prints hung on the walls and books by Carson, Leopold, Stegner, Lopez, Albee, Dillard, Ehrlich, Williams, Saner, and Bass rested on the shelves. It was the place Paul had expected it might be. She'd kissed his forehead and sent him off with a wave, watching as he started down the beach and thinking about Dan Kelsoe's endorsement of this young man, Dan's thinking that the country needed more young people like Paul, who were similarly invested in protecting its best places, its best idea. She saw what he meant but shook her head about the uphill battle the boy would face. This hike seemed like a last hurrah, and one she would not begrudge him—she was rooting for him, working for him—before he'd be caught and tried. Before they got their teeth into him and fixed his red wagon the way they almost always did.

Paul had planned his trip carefully so as to work with the tides that could trap you with crashing surf against rock and logs if you didn't think ahead. The first day he had hiked from Rialto past the sea stack with a wave-carved arch called The Hole in the Wall to a campsite near a memorial for Chilean sailors lost in the October 1893 and November 1920 storms on that coast. On the second day he hiked past a monument for seventeen Norwegian sailors lost in the wreck of the *Prince Arthur*. Their captain saw a light and thought it was from the lighthouse on Tatoosh Island and turned the ship onto rocks that snapped the vessel in two. Paul continued past a long sandy beach, Sandpoint, and visited the petroglyphs at Wedding Rocks, evidence of some of his ancestors' long habitation in this place. As he hiked the beach he gathered into garbage bags and tethered with rope into a great heap as many "unnatural" things as he could—Styrofoam, bits of plastic, fishing floats—and towed this human beach detritus behind him till he moved slowly and conspicuously, the dragged mass making an indentation in the sand and snagging on logs and rocks. Smaller bits of plastic that could never be removed, no matter how painstakingly one went about it, comingled with the sand and stone at the high-tide mark, making him wonder once again if it was possible that the things humans made could be seen as no less natural than the things made by animals or natural processes. Some of the hikers he passed congratulated him on his work, which to many of them must have seemed hopeless given the number of human-made objects on the beach. Others seemed to assume he was an employee of the Park, someone hired or a volunteer serving time. Still others steered clear of him, so that it seemed as if they were chagrined by his work or troubled by the way it reminded them of how much saving the world needed when they'd come to savor these remote beaches guilt-free. As he gathered up the plastic floats, he remembered seeing the glass floats from Japanese fishing boats his grandmother had found on the beach, one of which they kept in the bathroom in their house in Port Angeles and three of which his grandmother kept in the kitchen of her house in Neah Bay. Three times, when the bulkiness of what he was carrying made it impossible to go any farther, he stopped to stash the trash he'd found out of sight of hikers on the beach, hoping to notify rangers and vowing to go back and haul it out somehow in three separate trips.

On the first day, as he made his way along the coast, walking along the wet sand and over slippery rocks and driftwood logs, sometimes needing to climb above the beaches into the forested headlands to avoid crashing waves, and while his batteries held out, he listened to the MP3 player (set on continuous replay) of the whaling song Uncle Jack had given him, the high plaint of Jack's voice telling of the place where the abovewater and underwater worlds met, and of the visions the singer had gained into the mysteries of the deep. On the second day, he began to sing the song quietly to himself. One night, under a wide wash of stars, he sat on a stump before his tent under a tree hikers had completely covered with rope and bright fishing floats, and sang the song full-throated out over the beach and against the roar and hiss of the surf till he noticed three newly arrived hikers—two men and a woman—standing rapt on the beach below and listening as if to the call of a wild animal.

At Cape Alava, where he spent the third night, he looked out at the slight indentation, a subtle dip at the center of the arced beach, where Makah from the ancient village at Ozette would have left and returned to the beach in their dugout canoes. Not far from his campsite, the Makah had erected a memorial to the village at Ozette, the place at which tidal erosion following a 1970 storm revealed longhouses filled with artifacts 500 to 1,000 years old attesting to the Makah's brilliance at living in that place. There were spearpoints made from mussel shell, and antler barbs, such as the one on his necklace, whale saddles with otter-tooth inlay, spruce-knot halibut hooks, nets made from nettle, woven cedar mats and hats, dugout canoes made from the boughs of redcedar—all resting there as if the people had only recently left the rooms. His grandmother told stories about coming out to Ozette in the seventies to see what they were finding, something new every day. She hiked out with his mother strapped to her back and listened to some of the elders remembering the uses and names of the things that emerged. A few years before Trace was born, some hippies (his absconded grandfather among them) living out by Shi Shi Beach called the tribe to say a landslide had revealed what looked like an old village. They said if something wasn't done, it would be lost to the waves. So the tribe called in an archaeologist from Washington State University and started to unearth the artifacts. The memorial at the site noted that the artifacts had given the Makah new strength and had revealed their rich culture and proud heritage.

Paul was in a space to think of leave-takings, and he peered into the void of his own future through the small channel where canoes must have passed all those years ago. This was the westernmost point in the continental United States and it seemed a good place to think of what might come next, of ends and beginnings. It was also the place where he'd spent the night in the tent of the girl he knew only as Portland girl, waking to the sound of Steller sea lions barking on Ozette Island off the coast. His future seemed not to include going to Oregon State any time soon. In two days he'd find out what they'd planned for him, the group of strangers who'd taken an interest in his life, and he wondered if he'd like the escape route and the new identity they invented for him. If he could have full say in what he would do, and ultimate freedom, he thought he might suggest a life spent roaming the Olympic National Park, helping to preserve it. Or, to earn a livelihood working to restore the Elwha River when they removed the dams. He wondered if this was something he could do in secret, if it was possible to have a job and secure a meaningful life off the grid, living as someone else.

He fell asleep to the roar and hush of the waves, which morphed in his early dreams into the breathing of a whale that he speared. The dream began in the seconds after he'd thrown the spear, and he felt the spray of the water and heard the whistle of the line as it raced out, followed by the slap and glug of sealskin floats as they hit the water, and felt the surge of the canoe as it raced forward after the whale. Somehow, at the same time, he was riding on the back of the whale holding onto its tall dorsal fin. In the dream, the whale was simultaneously a live whale and the whale saddle, found in the old village at this beach, with otter-tooth inlay he'd seen at the Makah Cultural and Research Center.

The next morning and six miles farther up the beach, after a thigh-deep crossing of the Ozette River where he saw three bald eagles on shore pines looking for salmon, he made a wild dash to avoid the tidal surf at Point of Arches. In the stories his grandmother and Uncle Jack told, the small and large rocks sticking up here were the children of

Tatoosh Island and Destruction Island, who'd lived together at the mouth of the Hoh River for many years. Finally, the two separated after a bad quarrel. As Tatoosh canoed with her children up the coast, she grew angrier and angrier at her former husband and abandoned their children at the Point of Arches because she suspected they would probably grow up to be just like their father. Paul stopped at a certain little brown alkaline creek trickling into the ocean near Shi Shi Beach. He looked around to see if he could recover anything specific from the time his mother had taken him to this beach when he was three, a time he'd come to think of as his first clear memory. An image of her looking troubled, tracing something with a stick beside the creek, the rocks and the surf in the distance behind her. The memory of her lifting him into the sky to nuzzle his chest and belly. He was almost back to Neah Bay now. He lifted a smooth piece of driftwood and threw it into the place where the little creek met the incoming waves and imagined he was both the thrower of the harpoon and the whale feeling its sting.

In the Makah stories the whale gave itself up willingly to its hunters. He wondered how they squared that with the all-day and overnight rides harpooned whales sometimes gave their would-be captors and thought he remembered that the whale's willingness had something to do with the preparations the hunters made, the empathetic stillness of their wives. He thought of the whale they'd pulled up on the beach that day, how its eye had looked kind and nearly mirthful, full of beneficent resignation, as if it was sending him good wishes despite what his people (he wasn't sure he wanted to call them his people in that moment) had done. Or, maybe that was a sign that the whale had given itself up to help the Makah recover what they'd lost for so long.

He spent the final night beside the creek at Shi Shi Beach and hiked out and along the road to Neah Bay the following morning to show up at the door of his grandmother's house and see her eyes go wide and feel her arms welcome him into a great embrace.

The men closed the doors, and they all sat at the table facing the window onto the marina and the glittering water of the Strait. The room crackled with conspiratorial energy.

After an awkward silence, when it was unclear who should speak, Spears gave in to his tendency to preside. "I'm here at some risk," he said, "but I wouldn't be here at all if I didn't think it was worth it. My first question to all of you is: Are we agreed we're not sitting here with Paul Granger? That the person here and *alive* before us is someone else? Are we all ready to swear to one another and to anyone who asks that Paul Granger is dead? And that we will help create his replacement, a new person who will come to life after a brief . . . gestation in Alaska?"

The Makah in the room listened to the computer man with bemusement and a remoteness from concerns over official mainstream identity, but with a readiness to accommodate calamity. They looked around at one another and at Paul. The council member's frown deepened. Trace was amazed, stunned, at the question. She'd spent the last three months insisting Paul was alive—not someone else, but the Paul she knew, the Paul she'd raised.

"I don't feel dead," Paul said, and many of them chuckled.

"Reports of your death are greatly exaggerated," said Uncle Jack.

"And yet, Paul Granger, who is not you, did die up in the Olympics."

Spears assured all of them he would do all he could in the computer realm, with the help of a very powerful and capable person he knew, to secure a valid Social Security number and other documents that would forge Paul a new identity so that he would be free to return after a time and live his life. He said he thought this was what the case required and he was happy to do it. "We've decided, and Paul agrees, that it's best for him to lie low for a while until his new identity has been secured. An unnamed party has provided some contacts and given Paul directions and a deed to a remote cabin in Alaska where he can stay in the interim."

The tribal council member drummed his fingers on the table and suppressed a series of questions and objections with a sigh he hoped wasn't too loud. He would let this one go. There were only so many things to which he could devote his attention.

Trace frowned at the notion that things had been decided and she found Uncle Jack's eyes. He nodded, hiding a smile. Trace had talked to him and to her mother, and they had talked to others about another, alternate path for Paul that they didn't want to reveal until the time was right. She thought of Bill Newton and looked to see how Paul—or not-Paul, what should she call him?—was reacting to this news. She saw that he was looking at her to see what she would think of it. He wore a look of such strong resolve, such a plea for understanding, that she made herself be quiet. When the time came, he would have a choice that she had helped provide. She felt good about that and secure enough to wait and see what he would do.

After they finished discussing the details of this new person's departure and heard how Spears thought they should proceed in helping him to be born, they all agreed to give the immediate family some time alone.

Not-Paul? . . . the boy/man formerly known as Paul, what did they want her to call him? sat on one side of the table, Trace and Tom on the other.

"So, you're ready to go again, so soon?" she said. "You're sure, Paul, that this is best?"

"I have to be ready," he said. "There's no choice."

"You could still turn yourself in," Tom said. "Cooperate with the authorities. Have you given enough consideration to that option?"

Paul shook his head in that way she'd seen in the meadow near the Elwha that seemed to say *don't make me lose my trust in you.*

Trace kept silent. He needed her faith in him. She couldn't imagine Paul in one of those rooms where they had Dan and Bill, that was to be avoided, but to pursue this path, or the path about which he would soon learn, was to risk a lifetime of such rooms and worse. He had been back for such a short time and already he was on his way out again. Is that how it had to be? She supposed so, if he wasn't going to turn himself in. She reached out, clasped Paul's hands in her own, and nodded her support.

The witnesses to the reinvention reassembled at an unmarked trailhead that only residents of Neah Bay knew about. It led out to the true northwesternmost point in the continental United States. They walked along the trail, brushing against lush vegetation still wet from the months of rain, to a place where the path gave way to cliffs overlooking the endless churn and yaw of the Pacific—boiling water, seabirds on the endless wind, shore pines clinging to sea stacks.

He's falling away from me always and forever, Trace thought, as she watched Paul walking the trail in front of her. Spears was saying something about getting documents to him and awaiting news of his new name and how much Stephanie would have liked to be there to see him off.

Below the cliffs, riding the swells, Uncle Jack was idling in his old gillnetter.

Paul secured a rope around the bough of a shore pine and rappelled down the cliff, remembering in his muscles and bones as he approached the deck of the idling boat, his descent into the crevasse to rescue Bill Newton. As soon as Paul's feet hit the deck, Uncle Jack gunned the motor to get it out of its precarious position against the rocks. The boat took off with a puff of diesel smoke and Paul stumbled to regain his balance.

"Showoffs," said Trace's mother.

Once the boat was a safe distance from the cliffs, Uncle Jack idled the boat in the swells rolling in to break against the rocks.

Another boat was anchored 300 yards out at the edge of a kelp bed, one of the twenty-footers they rented at the marina.

Paul looked up and waved to the group on the cliff assembled to watch him go.

"Don't get eaten by one of those big old bears they got up there," Trace's mother called down, hugging Trace into her chubby side as she said it.

Paul looked up at all of them in his grave new way as the boat headed out, putting water between them. His heart was beating fast and his guts were churning with excitement and worry and a fear he'd never felt about the wildness of the place to which he was heading. He carried in his backpack the rolled up watercolor map Tom had painted of the Peninsula, with Paul wavery and indistinct in its center, as if his painted image might pour off the paper if it was tilted the wrong way, smiling enigmatically and resting jaunty arms on snow-capped peaks. He also carried instructions and a crude deed to Bill Newton's cabin, as well as some money Spears had gathered to get him started and a collection of gear Jim at the outdoor store had donated for his use, and a Krugerrand Tom had pressed into his hand.

As the old boat vibrated along, pounded by the waves, Paul thought of the vast wildness toward which they were heading and how different it would be from the wildness of the Olympics, and he thought about the two jailed men in his wake—Dan Kelsoe and Bill Newton and how there were powerful forces that wanted to see him join them. He sat in a seat in the back of the boat, looking at peaks of the Olympics, visible now that they were far enough from shore. Over a space of five minutes (or could it have been longer?) he so lost himself in thought about where he was going that he forgot about the mountains, and when he looked up from the boat's wake to recover them one last time, they were lost in a bank of clouds.

In that moment, Bill Newton was in the government building in Ballard, sitting on a hard cot, looking out at a strip of permanently grey sky, and imagining Paul finding the cabin exactly as he'd left it when he'd gone up the river in his snowmobile that cold February day on which he would have died if not for the members of the New Way Commune. He hoped things would go well for Paul up there, much better than they had for himself. The whirring in his chest was gone. In its place, a deep hush. He was calm in his own skin like he'd never been before, and the future was like a wall of light he approached without fear and without hope. He believed he had access to the calm and to the light because he'd chosen to push open that door at the crossroads in the Olympics. At night before he slept he composed and recomposed in his head a long letter to Paul filled with advice about survival in Alaska and in the world at large and suggestions of things Paul should be sure to avoid doing. The agents and officers who saw Bill Newton noted with what quiet serenity he carried himself through his days under dim lights. They could not have known about the wall of light, or that a part of him was always up in the woods cruising and felling timber or just walking between great boughs. Everyone who saw him noted with what peacefulness he moved through the corridors and rooms to which he was confined and many of them wondered how he had come to find such calm.

Dan Kelsoe was stroking with his right hand the clawmarks on the left side of his face and wondering how many years they would give him. On a certain level he didn't care that he'd been caught, but he bitterly regretted, every day, getting Paul involved in the action, successful as it had been. Now he prayed with some intensity to all the beautiful gods of the forest that Paul was alive somewhere out there.

Stephanie Barefoot was racing through the Route-112 curves along the coast, carrying out, in a cross-state drive, exactly what her father had told her not to do, though she would be twenty minutes too late to see the goodbye her father had whispered would happen at the Flattery Rocks. Over the course of the entire drive she'd been imagining telling Trace, "We knew it! No one else believed!" She'd also been seeing herself waving to Paul, whose long black hair blew in the wind as he cast off in a redcedar canoe and paddled over what she thought of as the wine-dark sea, and she asked him over the sounds of the ocean to promise to write from his exile, whoever he turned out to be.

In this same moment, the same two FBI agents who had visited Trace were knocking on the llama lady's door to ask questions about Paul Granger, which questions the llama lady met with polite answers that sounded full of the asked-for information but which dispersed mistlike in the air before her interlocutors. The agents were sniffing at the trail that would lead them to Cape Flattery in time, even as one of their number, who could have saved them some time, was already there.

Brent Sawtelle had been living undercover near the reservation for three weeks, stewing in the near-constant rain, which had only broken earlier that day as if blessing the escape of their quarry, who he had seen with his own eyes and with a camera was very much alive. During this whole time, Brent had been pretending to be an avid sport fisherman and acting the part by fishing for salmon, rockfish, and halibut (something he loved to do anyway) while also watching Uncle Jack and Trace's mother's house. While Uncle Jack's boat idled for goodbyes, agent Sawtelle watched it (and the people gathered on the cliff) through binoculars from the fishing boat he'd rented from the marina and had anchored off a kelp bed. In the hand not holding the binoculars, he held a phone he would use, as soon as he found the gumption, to summon the Coast Guard. He was surprised at his own lack of resolve and tried to pinpoint its source. He had come close to deciding that his inability to act had something to do with what he'd learned about Paul Granger and his mother, Trace, especially when he'd listened in as Trace talked to the girl, Stephanie Barefoot, about Paul when he was young—something about a bear and wanting to live up in the woods. Or perhaps it had more to do with the slow breath of the waves, the sun glinting on the kelp heads, and the rain that fell and fell until it loosened any resolve you'd formed about yourself and what was right and wrong back in the fluorescent-lit corridors of the East.

One day earlier that October, Brent had walked out of the cabin where he was staying on Hobuck Beach to feel the full force of a Pacific storm. Sixty-mile-an-hour gusts howled in his ears and stung his face with ocean spray. He'd come to think that the wind was erasing who he used to be, loosening all the ties to his old life—all his work in Quantico, his investment in the case, even, and most disturbingly, his ties to his wife and daughter whom he hadn't seen in a month. It disturbed him how much the storm's irrational force spoke to him. Later, he tried to explain to his wife the exhilaration he felt as the storm broke. Judging from the silence on the other end of the line, his explanation had failed, which made him feel that she was another thing the wind had loosened (or proven was already loose) in his life, that the force connecting him to her was unequal to that wind and rain and spray.

Twice, he'd put the binoculars down and dialed all but the last number that would bring the Coast Guard down on the boat within the hour, and twice he'd stopped and had sat deliberating over spikes in trees that would never see a sawblade, and his own forced absentee fatherhood, and his mom and stepfather back in Eugene, and how a big success on this case could boost his advancement in the Bureau, and about the reckless destruction and loss of property due to the bombings of the car dealerships, and Paul Granger, who'd once talked about setting animals at a game farm free, cuffed and sitting in a cell, and the power of the phone call he could make or not make any second now.

The Coast Guard had only one month ago stopped an illegal Makah whaling operation and apprehended an outfit whose members were frustrated with how long it was taking to get clearance for a legal hunt. They had managed to kill a gray whale on their rogue outing that the Coast Guard made them cut loose so that the body of the whale sank to the bottom of the Strait. Since he was already on the reservation to see if Paul, or anything about Paul, turned up there, Brent had been called in to help with the case against these men. He'd ridden in a helicopter and snapped photos of the whale where it remained in the water looking alive but for its great stillness, floats trailing from the places where it had been harpooned. Brent was puzzled by the degree to which he identified with the slow sinking of that whale.

As Uncle Jack's boat began to grumble over the waves, Trace felt too much to say anything. Was this the best solution? Was this her last chance to reverse the direction of things, to call him back to shore, into her protective sphere? What would a good mother do in this situation? Paul, not-Paul, formerly-Paul, seemed to be looking back at only her for his last few visible waves. Or did she imagine that? She let herself believe his eyes were on her and convinced herself he would miss her, that he was sad to be leaving her, that he was always hers and that he forgave her for everything, even what he didn't know, as she forgave him for always falling away.

The moment of his departure, his sad smile as he stood and waved from the deck of Uncle Jack's old gillnetter, never blurred in her memory over the next year despite all that followed: the absurdity of Bill Newton, months later in court, driving his defense and the prosecution crazy by swearing under oath, from what seemed a place of quiet calm, that he'd been up in the Temple Grove both trying to cut down and drive spikes into the trees; the absurdity—or was this finally the truth?—of her testimony that Bill Newton had never raped her, that she had been mistaken all those years ago about her complicity in what had happened on the banks of the Elwha and talked into pressing charges by an understandably upset and concerned mother and a community ready to vilify a Forks logger, and she wished to drop all charges and clear Bill Newton's record. What he had done was wrong, but Paul wasn't wrong and what Bill Newton had done to help Paul wasn't wrong. There were complexities in these situations that defied easy sides, simple notions of right and wrong.

In the agonizing night before the day when she was supposed to testify in the trial, she'd come in the early morning to the firm resolution that she would forgive Bill Newton. There was a kind of justice, she thought, that didn't live in civic buildings or the decisions of judges with fancy degrees or in the deliberations of a jury, but that resided in an individual's own reckoning, deep in one's own conscience. All present were impressed by her composure on the stand as the prosecuting attorney tried to malign Bill Newton's character, and she steadfastly erased the attempt. She could see that in her stand she was disappointing various constituencies—the federal government who wanted to use the rape (despite the expired statute of limitations) to besmirch Bill's character, and the tribe who wanted to use this case as leverage to gain more power in prosecuting rapes committed by non-tribe members against tribe members, and even a few on the Port Angeles police force who had long thought of Bill Newton as one who'd gotten away and shouldn't have. When Trace left the stand, many noticed and later told one another about a look that passed between Bill and Trace in which was written a story of the sort you didn't expect to hear in a courtroom. There was a suggestion of our depraved capabilities, gratitude, guilt, resignation, possibly even lost love, an uplifting sense of hope, in that gaze. There was, too, in that gaze, nearly, *nearly* the possibility of a return to the moment just before the ripping of the fabric of the afternoon that day on the banks of the Elwha. As she walked from the stand, Trace thought to herself: *It was the right thing to do, even if it was a lie; I hope you're worth it.* She knew that to know it and believe it were the first steps in making it true. And that was not lost on him. The guilt he felt for what he'd done and his knowledge of its wrongness were compounded with the faith she'd shown in him.

There was also the strangeness of her visit to the llama lady to learn more about the time Paul had spent recuperating at her ranch, and to thank her for saving Paul. During this visit, before Trace knew what was happening, the story she'd never told anyone loosened from the place where she'd held it so long and came tumbling out into the air to the silent percussion of the llama lady's reassuring nods as Trace wondered if she'd ever be able to bring herself to tell Paul.

Trace watched till Jack's boat had passed Tatoosh (the island that was the woman who'd escaped Destruction Island and abandoned her children on the way) her eyes occasionally shifting to the smaller, closer boat bobbing at the edge of a kelp bed—something strange about that boat being there with its one passenger. She kept watching both boats after the others, including Tom, had headed back up the trail. She was the only one still watching the sea's rise and fall—its swell up the rocks and its long stretch out to the horizon—when the distant dot of the boat carrying Paul away from her strained against oblivion, seemed to blink a few times, then shifted, in some indefinable fraction of a second, to nothing. He was gone again, for the third time, in the way that really hurt. He was gone, for however long he would need to be gone—forever, or until he returned as someone completely new. She stood watching the nothing where he had been and smiled to think of her part in giving Paul a choice he would soon have to make. She took a long deep breath that happened to coincide with a swell rolling in from a long way out to wash over the cliff face, then she turned away from the sea to see that her own mother was standing a short distance up the trail watching her.

"Change of plan," Uncle Jack said suddenly, turning his gold-toothed grin to Paul as he turned the wheel so the boat was running a course toward, instead of perpendicular to Vancouver Island. This coast was sometimes known as the graveyard of the Pacific because so many ships and boats had foundered there over the years. "Something the techies back there don't know nothin' about. Your mother's idea. And your grandmother's," he said, and laughed at the expression of surprise and disbelief on Paul's face.

An island covered in fir and shore pine approached, sheer black rocks and surging surf against it. An eagle lifted from a shore pine and some ravens harried it over the water. They went no-wake speed as they came up to the island, whose rock walls were similar to some places at Neah Bay. Jack steered the boat around a wall of charcoal rock and into a deep cove where the water was calm and dark and occasionally troubled by big swells. Deep water swirled and boiled close to the rocks. When the anchor was dropped, they climbed into the small dinghy and Uncle Jack rowed them to the pebbled shore, where they beached the dinghy beside a long cedar canoe of the old style resting there, with no sign of a paddler.

"You go alone from here," said Uncle Jack once they were standing on the shore. "Take this," he said, indicating the canoe. "Go around the rocks and steer for the lights of fires you see on the beach on the other side," he said. "It's your choice. Your mother and grandmother told me to make sure you know that. I'm happy to run you all the way on up the coast if that's what you want."

Paul gazed back in the direction of Neah Bay. "My mother?" he said and smiled.

Jack nodded and smiled, some gold catching the late afternoon sun, wrinkles alive on his face. "Indian women, boy, always got a plan, even when you think they don't. *Especially* when you think they don't."

"I'll do it," Paul said after a few moments of silence. "I'll take the canoe."

"Ha-ha!" Jack said and clapped, "Ha-ha! Now, watch the rip doesn't get you when you head around. We'll wait a bit for the tide to change. Meantime, watch this," he said, and taking off his jacket to reveal a T-shirt that said, "No Toxins in These Moccasins" he started to sing the song he'd given Paul and to dance the dance. "Do it with me," he said, and Paul danced with him till he began to know the steps. Jack said, "You've been practicing!"

After they'd danced for a time on the empty shore, they sat on driftwood logs and watched the small waves lap the beach. "When I was drunk and had been for a long time and almost a goner," Jack said, "my mother brought me over here, to the coast on the other side. We found a clean cold stream running into the water and she helped me do the *oo-simch*. We prayed and cleansed till I was . . . I wouldn't say better, but in a place where I could think about getting better. Some good people over here, too, helped me out. You tell 'em I said 'hey.' "

Paul watched Uncle Jack row back out in the dinghy and they waved to each other as the old gillnetter chugged back out of the cove. Paul placed his pack in the canoe and pushed it out into small waves. He jumped in and sat down as it glided out. He readied and pulled with the sharp cedar paddle. As Jack had predicted, the tide was ripping fiercely around the point of the island. It tried to pull the canoe away from the calmer water on the other side out into the Strait. If this was a favorable tide, Paul thought, he didn't ever want to see a dangerous one. He struggled against it, surprised at its force, the way it seemed to want to pull him back out into the Strait. He pulled as hard and rapidly as he could until he began to inch forward, gradually rounding the corner out of the current's grip, thrilling the place in him that loved exertion in the face of danger even as it was strange and unsettling to experience this feeling above water instead of on land. It was dusk and orange bonfires whose reflections carried a long way out over the ripples burned on the shore against tangled driftwood. He paddled for the shore against a faint wind, much as Stephanie had imagined he might, the water rippling, marbled murrelets diving for baitfish that the waning sun made glimmer in their beaks before they swallowed them and dived for more.

As he drew closer to shore, silhouetted forms came away from the fires toward the beach, blotting out the firelight, the steady ponderous forms of adults, the light and darting forms of children. Twenty or so canoes lined the beach. The rocks crackled under their feet as he paddled faster to gather speed for the beaching in a gap between canoes. His canoe skritched across the rocks onto shore.

"Welcome, traveler!" someone said. "We were expecting you!"

"We understand you're in some trouble and need a little help," someone else said.

Some children, a boy about four, and a girl of perhaps six or seven, came in for a closer look. Two men took hold of the gunwales. Paul stepped out onto the rocks, lifted up his pack, and stood among the greeters.

"Come and eat something. You must be hungry from your trip," said a woman standing up the beach. She reminded him of his grandmother in the way she carried herself and in the way she talked. She had a proprietary air about the fire, which he could now see was surrounded by roasting salmon fillets on sticks stuck into the ground.

Someone else said, "This'll be a good place for you to be for a while."

He walked up the beach, too stunned by his new surroundings and these people who seemed to have been expecting him, to say very much. He didn't know the precise name of the place where he was, but his surroundings felt familiar in a way that seemed to stretch beyond a mere affinity of these people and this place to his Makah relatives across the Strait. He turned to see if he could see the coast he'd left behind but it was blocked by the small island he'd canoed around, whose name he also realized he didn't know.

A young woman offered him a cedar plank of steaming roasted salmon, and some older men asked about his crossing. Someone mentioned "Old Jack" with a chuckle that implied knowledge of stories about him. There was conversation around the fire of a canoe trip up the coast, the next day's paddle, whether the weather would continue unseasonably favorable. Some people about his age stood on the beach on the outskirts of the firelight wearing fleece and nylon, and he wondered if these might be members of the new tribe he'd imagined. After Paul had eaten, a man with laugh-lines like ripples and kind, sad eyes said, "So. Do you have a song?"

The question stopped all conversations, and Paul didn't feel he could say no to the expectant faces around the fire. Uncle Jack must've set him up. Someone struck up a drum that Paul had noticed without noticing, and someone else joined the first, another, and Paul set down his cedar plank and stood from the log and began, haltingly, to dance as Uncle Jack had taught him, burning with self-consciousness and feeling like a fraud. After three rounds of the beat he heard himself singing the song which was uncomfortable and faint in his throat. Those who heard him were aware at first of his wish to be elsewhere, but as he continued they were also aware of a sadness and a loneliness and a wonderment in and under his voice that let them sense the story he had to tell of his meeting with his father, whom he did not know was his father, in the Olympics, and also some sense of what the Olympics meant to him, the circumstances of his conception, his love for the trees of the Temple Grove and how that love had been complicated, his exile from his former country, a status some knew about and most sensed. His voice narrowly escaped its early wavering to rise, plaintive and high and mounting in confidence, as his feet step-step-shuffle-turned in the soft sand and clicking rocks, the small whisper of his nylon jacket sleeve brushing his side, till he was free of the awareness of hearing himself singing the words and simply singing the song he'd been given about going down into the depths at the meeting place between worlds.

A NOTE ON SOURCES AND ACKNOWLEDGMENTS

Identifying the various sources for a novel is a bit like trying to identify and isolate what water in the main channel of a river has come from which of its various tributaries. A lifetime of sense perceptions, direct and textual observations, oral accounts, and imaginative flights come together and intermix in the channel of language and story that is a novel. How might one isolate the sense impressions granted by a place that contribute to a novel in which place plays a big role? What glimmer on the water? What gust off the Strait? What whiff of low tide in the estuary, breeze off the lupine? What gull cry? What sink of the feet into sand or river gravel? What snippets of conversation from cafes and bars? What family stories? What conifer silhouettes through fog?

One could say this novel had its beginning when in 1934 my grandfather Ray S. Christ accepted an opening and moved from Seattle to become Port Townsend's new doctor. He proposed to a nurse with Eastern Washington roots he'd literally run into one day at Seattle Providence Hospital named Josephine Elizabeth Reasor. He proposed to her on a bluff overlooking the Strait of Juan de Fuca and they rented a house on Calhoun Street in Port Townsend. This meant that my mother was born on the Olympic Peninsula and grew up riding horses with her sisters and brother on the beaches in and around Port Townsend and in the foothills of the Olympics. And because my mother wanted my two brothers and me to know our grandmother (Ray died before I was born) and her brother's and her sisters' families, my brothers and I were introduced to and also fell in love with this place.

The novel has tributaries in many experiences of the Peninsula in times before my memory, and in the times when my family lived in Seattle and Port Angeles, and, after we moved away from the Peninsula, in the visits to relatives for a few months every summer. We could count as a source for this novel my classmates at Franklin and Fairview elementary schools in Port Angeles in 1980 and '81, many of whose fathers worked at the paper mill then owned by Crown Zellerbach. They used steel ball bearings, "steelies," instead of marbles in our playground games and proudly told mythical tales of loggers beating up Hells Angels. Many early hikes in the Olympic National Park contributed to this novel—hikes to PJ Lake and Lake Angeles, Mildred Lakes, trips to swim in the deep turquoise of Lake Sutherland and Lake Crescent, hikes up the Elwha River from Whiskey Bend to Krause's Bottom and Hume's Ranch, hikes to Cape Alava and Shi Shi Beach. On one of these hikes to Lake Angeles, when I'd just graduated from college, I met a boy about thirteen or fourteen seemingly unattached to any adults, who made a habit of hiking alone in the Park and talking to the people he met. This meeting, years before I knew it, was the font of the character Paul.

Once the novel was under way, I fed its growing currents with more pointed trips out to the Peninsula. In the summer of 2003 my then girlfriend (now wife), Jenna, dropped me off at the Whiskey Bend trailhead, and I hiked up the Elwha, over the low divide, and down the Quinault River to Lake Quinault, where Jenna found a different version of me—thinner, famished, dirtier, more at-peace. In 2006 I lived for a time in a double-wide trailer on the Sol Duc and took day trips to the Park boundary near Rugged Ridge and to Ruby Beach, Cape Alava, Neah Bay, the Forks Timber Museum, the Makah Cultural and Research Center, and the Port Angeles Marine Life Center. More recently, I've made a number of trips out to the Peninsula from my home in Eastern Washington to stay and talk to folks at Neah Bay, to return to Shi Shi Beach, and to flyfish for steelhead on the Hoh, Sol Duc, Calawah, and Bogachiel Rivers—the best kind of research.

Many texts served as tributaries to the main channel of this novel.

The spirit of the poems of Richard Hugo haunted me during the writing. Those poems in *Making Certain It Goes On* about the Peninsula were especially influential, most notably "A Map of the Peninsula" in which Hugo writes "the rivers have good names . . ." and offers the would-be mapmaker (or poet) attempting to write about the Peninsula the following warning/prophecy: "Soak the map / In rain and when this cheap dye runs / Only glacier and river names remain." Also, directly influential beyond the general haunting of all of his work was Hugo's poem "Cape Alava," which considers the westernmost point in the Continental United States and the long-ago location of an ancient Makah village.

For the natural and cultural history of the Olympic National Park, I am indebted to Tim McNulty's *Olympic Natural Park: A Natural History* and a welter of other maps and field guides about the mountains and the flora and fauna of the region. For the specific human interactions with the region, Robert L. Wood's *The Land That Slept Late*, Ruby El Hult's *The Untamed Olympics* and *An Olympic Enchantment*, Murray Morgan's *The Last Wilderness*, and Francis E. Caldwell's *Beyond the Trails* were all valuable. For information and stories behind the place names in the Park, Smitty Parratt's *Gods and Goblins* is a quirky treasure trove of information.

Many contemporary works of prose set in the Pacific Northwest and specifically on the Olympic Peninsula helped me consider how to approach writing about this place and its people. Some texts in this category include Ivan Doig's *Winter Brothers*; Michael Byers's *The Coast of Good Intentions*; some of the stories in Charles D'Ambrosio's *The Dead Fish Museum*; David Guterson's novels set on the Peninsula (*Our Lady of the Forest* and *The Other*); the fiction and nonfiction of David James Duncan; the fiction, nonfiction, and poetry of Sherman Alexie; James Lynch's *The Highest Tide;* Susan Vreeland's *The Forest Lover.* Though it was published a few years after I'd already finished this manuscript, Jonathan Evison's *West of Here* is similarly invested in a fictional version of this place. All of these books helped me think about how to best go about writing my own contemporary fictional version of this region.

For fiction set largely in the outdoors, the novels of Cormac McCarthy, some of the fiction of Thomas McGuane, Molly Gloss's *The Jump-*

Off Creek, and the work of Rick Bass were all particularly instructive.

For the cultural battles over timber and the spotted owl controversy and information about logging William Dietrich's *The Final Forest* and James Lemond's *Deadfall* were very helpful.

The novel owes a debt to a tradition of novel-writing in and outside of the region and to novels and books about ecological concerns. An incomplete list of these might include Ken Kesey's *Sometimes a Great Notion*, Edward Abby's *The Monkey Wrench Gang*, T. C. Boyle's *Drop City* and *A Friend of the Earth*, Dave Foreman and Bill Haywood's *Ecodefense: A Field Guide to Monkeywrenching*, Craig Rosenbraugh's *Burning Rage of a Dying Planet*, Susan Zakin's work on Earth First! and the environmental movement in *Coyotes and Town Dogs*.

For the cultural history and present of the Makah and other Nuu-chah-nulth cultures and about Neah Bay, the book owes a debt to Charlotte Coté's *Spirits of Our Whaling Ancestors*, Patricia Pearce Eriksons's *Voices of a Thousand People*, Jacilee Wray's *Native Peoples of the Olympic Peninsula*, Linda J. Goodman and Helen Swann's *Singing the Songs of My Ancestors*, Ella E. Clark's *Indian Legends of the Pacific Northwest*, Elizabeth Colson's *The Makah Indians*, James Swann's writing about the Makah and Neah Bay in *At the Entrance to the Strait of Fuca, Washington Territory (1870)*, James G. McCurdy's *Indian Days at Cape Flattery*, and Andrew Sullivan's *A Whale Hunt*.

In addition to conversations and time spent with my relatives in Port Townsend, Sequim, and Port Angeles over many years, some conversations and notes pointedly devoted to research contributed to the novel. For information about contemporary and traditional life at Neah Bay, Aaron and Stephanie Parker, Maria Pascua, and Eva Arsaga were generous with their time and forthcoming with details. I'm hopeful that the book does justice to the complexities of Trace and Paul's Makah heritage without suggesting that this is the totality of who they are. I'm grateful to Luke Betts for permission to republish the poem "The Sins of the Logger," an apt expression of the timber community's frustrations and worldview.

My seafaring cousin Bill Rich, an oil tanker captain who bears no resemblance at all to the character Tom, was extremely generous in providing information and detailed notes about his own experiences with ship-breaking.

While the Temple Grove itself is based on old-growth Douglas fir groves I've experienced in the Olympic National Park and elsewhere, this one is fictitious and as much about the space between a human's temples as about an actual grove. If the sources for a novel are a river, then the novelist's mind is like a pool in the river where the sources for the novel, factual and invented, tumble and swirl and out of which flows the new channel of words that becomes the novel. Storms of revision might change the course of the river below the pool, and a reader might experience this new river as a long winding expanse with general trends even as it offers small, individuated moments—swirling eddies, soft riffles, raging rapids. A novel is about all the moments in that novel. I am grateful to have been alive to experience this amazing territory and to have had the opportunity to shape this river.

Further, I'm grateful to a number of people who supported this book in a variety of ways. I'd like to thank all of my relatives on the Peninsula for their warmth and hospitality over many years, which warmth and hospitality runs under the place in ways not fully represented in this book. They are Bev and Phil Rich, Bob and Jan Crist, Connie and Bruce Thomas, Rich and Susan Cox, and their families. I'd like to thank my parents, Robert and Elizabeth, who gave me an introduction to the wonders of the place and to the world, and my brothers Greg and Andrew and their families, with whom I've had many happy hours exploring the Peninsula. I'd like to thank my colleagues in the English department and on the faculty of Whitman College. I'd like to thank Whitman for the gift of sabbatical leaves, financial support for research, and for fostering a supportive environment for artistic production. I'd like to thank all of my wonderful Whitman students who've taught me a great deal about writing and life in the Pacific Northwest. My students Christine Texiera and Miriam Cook both offered helpful perspectives on an early version of the novel. I'd like to thank Gaurav Majumdar and Chetna Chopra for their friendship during the writing of the book and Gaurav for his good listening about challenges in the writing and revising. Thanks to Michael Hoffman and Linda Kolko and to

David Hoffman, Betty Hoffman, and Kara Silverstein for their support and encouragement. Alice Tasman has been constant in her enthusiasm for this project. I'm very appreciative of Marianne Keddington-Lang for taking a chance and for her steady support of this novel at UW Press and for her expert guidance in shepherding it through the process of review. Thanks to Betty Hoffman for her keen eye in the late proofreading. Thanks to Gretchen Van Meter, Marilyn Trueblood, Thomas Eykemans, Alice Herbig, Rachael Levay, and others at the Press for their help, some of it still to come, in shaping this river of words into its best channel.

I'm especially grateful to my wife, Jenna, who scribbled notes about place names on a rainy day in Forks way back in 2001 when this book was far from well begun and who has since helped shape the book in many ways, and to our sons, August and Harper, little beams of wonderful light and life who I hope will experience and come to love many of the places mentioned in this book.

Walla Walla, 2012